Barbara Taylor Bradford was born in Leeds, and was a reporter for the *Yorkshire Evening Post* at sixteen: at eighteen she became woman's page editor. By the age of twenty she had graduated to Fleet Street as both editor and columnist. In 1979 she wrote her first novel, *A Woman of Substance,* and that enduring bestseller was followed by thirteen others: *Voice of the Heart, Hold the Dream, Act of Will, To Be the Best, The Women in His Life, Remember, Angel, Everything to Gain, Dangerous to Know, Love in Another Town, Her Own Rules, A Secret Affair* and *Power of a Woman.* Nine have been made into television mini-series and three more are currently in production. Her novels have sold more than 58 million copies worldwide in more than 88 countries and 38 languages. Mrs Bradford lives in New York City and Connecticut with her husband, film producer Robert Bradford.

*By the same author*

A WOMAN OF SUBSTANCE
VOICE OF THE HEART
HOLD THE DREAM
ACT OF WILL
TO BE THE BEST
THE WOMEN IN HIS LIFE
REMEMBER
ANGEL
EVERYTHING TO GAIN
LOVE IN ANOTHER TOWN
A SECRET AFFAIR
POWER OF A WOMAN

BARBARA TAYLOR BRADFORD

# DANGEROUS TO KNOW

# HER OWN RULES

HarperCollins*Publishers*

This omnibus edition published in 1999 by
HarperCollins*Publishers*

HarperCollins*Publishers*
77-85 Fulham Palace Road,
Hammersmith, London W6 8JB



ISBN 0 261 67263 0

Printed and bound in Great Britain by
Creative Print and Design (Wales), Ebbw Vale

*For Bob, with all my love*

**'Mad, bad, and dangerous to know.'**

***Lady Caroline Lamb,***
***speaking of her lover,***
***the poet Lord Byron***

# The Narrators

# *Part One*

# VIVIENNE

## Loyalty

# One

The first time I met Sebastian Locke I fell in love with him. He was thirty-two years old. I was twelve. I had no idea at the time that he was my mother's lover. Nor did I know then that ten years later I would marry him.

Now he was dead.

He had died in mysterious, even suspicious, circumstances. It was not yet known whether he had died of natural causes, committed suicide or been murdered.

We were divorced. I had not seen him for almost a year, until last Monday, when we had lunched together at his request. Obviously the police hoped I might be able to throw some light on the matter of his death, but I could not. I was as perplexed as everyone else. However, they had just arrived to see me, and I told my secretary Belinda that she could show them into the library.

A split second later I was shaking hands with Detectives Joe Kennelly and Aaron Miles from the Major Crime Division of the Connecticut State Police.

'We're baffled, Mrs Trent,' Detective Kennelly said as we all sat down. 'Until we get the autopsy report we're working in the dark. As you already know, the circumstances are suspicious, so we can't rule out foul play. But who would want to kill Sebastian Locke? Surely such a good man didn't have enemies, did he?'

They both focused their eyes on me, intently.

Silently I stared back at them. I did not say a word. I could think of several enemies, any one of whom might easily have murdered him. However, I was not about to mention this to the police. That was a family matter, and, oddly enough, even though we had been divorced for eight years, I still thought of myself as being a member of the Locke clan, and was treated as such by the family – what was left of it.

Clearing my throat, I said finally, 'Naturally, a man like Sebastian met a lot of people on his travels around the world, and from all walks of life. I suppose he *might* have made an enemy or two, unintentionally, of course. Powerful men often do inspire hatred in some, for no reason other than the power they possess.'

Without shifting my steady gaze, I pursed my lips, shrugged helplessly and finished, 'But I'm afraid I can't point a finger at anyone in particular, Detective Kennelly.'

His partner said, 'Was Mr Locke in the habit of coming up to Connecticut alone?'

Genuinely puzzled, I frowned. 'He was no longer married to Betsy Bethune, his last wife,' I responded. 'I suppose he might have come to the farm alone. Unless he brought a friend or colleague along, or invited special guests to join him for the weekend.'

'I meant was he in the habit of coming up to the

farm when the servants were off?' Detective Miles clarified.

'No, he wouldn't do that . . . well, I shouldn't say that. Actually, I don't really know what he was in the habit of doing any more. We had been divorced for a number of years, and I saw him infrequently of late.'

'However, you did see him a week ago, Mrs Trent, and only a few days before his death,' Detective Miles reminded me.

'That's true. We had lunch together, as you most obviously know. From his appointment book, I've no doubt.'

Detective Miles nodded. 'Yes, we did see your name in his book, along with the other appointments he had that day.'

'We spent a couple of hours lunching at Le Refuge on Eighty-Second Street on the East Side, just a few blocks away from my apartment,' I volunteered. I had nothing to hide.

Detective Kennelly's tone was brisk when he asked, 'How *was* Mr Locke? What kind of mood was he in that day? Did he seem despondent? Troubled in any way? Worried perhaps?' The detective raised an eyebrow quizzically.

I shook my head. 'None of those things. In fact, just the opposite. He was very Sebastian Locke, very much himself . . . calm, cool, collected. That's the way I always think of him –' I broke off. I felt the tears bringing a lump to my throat. *Sebastian was dead*. It didn't seem possible. I still hadn't taken it in; I found it hard to conceive that he was no longer alive.

Taking a deep breath to steady myself, I cleared my throat, and went on slowly, 'That's the way he always was. Very much in control of himself and the situation. And his demeanour was perfectly normal at lunch.'

As the words came tumbling out of my mouth, I realized this wasn't the truth. Not quite. Last Monday Sebastian had not been himself at all. He had been ebullient, excited and certainly not as low-key as he usually was. That sombre streak of his had not been even remotely in evidence. In fact, he had actually seemed cheerful, a most unnatural state of affairs for him. But I did not confide this to the two detectives. What was the point? I was absolutely certain Sebastian had dropped dead of a sudden heart attack. He was no more the kind of person to commit suicide than I was. Nor was he a candidate for murder, for that matter. He did have enemies, political enemies, at least so *I* believed, but, looking at it rationally, I seriously doubted that anyone would go so far as to kill him.

'Yes, Sebastian was absolutely *normal*, Detective Kennelly,' I reiterated, and with a degree of firmness. 'There was nothing at all untoward in his behaviour, and he spoke very positively about his plans for the rest of the year.'

'And what were those plans?' Kennelly asked.

'He was going back to Africa again, to oversee a particular distribution of aid to the poor and the sick, and then he was going on to India. To Calcutta, to be exact. He said he wanted to pay a visit to Mother Teresa. He'd always been a big supporter of her clinic, had given her a lot of financial support in the past. He told me he would be coming back to the States in December, because he intended to spend Christmas here in Connecticut.'

'And you didn't see him again that week?' Detective Miles leaned forward.

'No, I didn't, Detective Miles.'

'What about up here in Connecticut this weekend?' he asked.

'I had a deadline to meet, and I was locked up finishing my story, first in the city and then here. In this very room, in fact, and I hardly left it for the entire weekend.'

'I see.' Detective Miles inclined his head in a small show of courtesy, and slowly stood up. His partner Kennelly also rose.

I said, 'When actually *did* Sebastian die?'

'Time of death hasn't been determined yet, but probably some time on Saturday evening,' Miles answered me.

It was Kennelly who said, 'Thank you for your time, Mrs Trent.'

'I haven't been much help, I'm afraid,' I answered.

'At least you've established Mr Locke's mood for us, his frame of mind, and corroborated what everyone else has said so far, namely that he was acting like himself right up to the time of his death,' Kennelly said.

'I'm sure he died of natural causes. Jack and Luciana agree with me.'

'We know that, Mrs Trent. We've talked to them at length,' Detective Miles volunteered.

I was fully aware of this, but I made no further comment as I walked the two policemen to the door of the library. 'When will you have the results of the autopsy?' I enquired quietly.

'Not for a while,' Detective Kennelly replied, pausing on the threshold, turning to look at me. 'Mr Locke's body hasn't been moved from the farm yet. But later, probably tomorrow, it will go to the Chief Medical Examiner's Office in Farmington. The autopsy will be performed immediately. However the final results are not necessarily quick to come in.' He gave me a faint smile that seemed somehow apologetic.

'We'll be in touch, Mrs Trent,' Detective Miles added.

Sitting down at the desk a moment later, I picked up my pen but merely stared blankly at the pages spread out in front of me. Earlier, I had attempted to edit the piece I had finished on Sunday night, but without much success. Receiving the news of Sebastian's death this morning, and the arrival of the police ten minutes ago, had broken my concentration. I was finding it virtually impossible to get back to work. Not surprising, I suppose, under these terrible circumstances.

My thoughts were entirely on Sebastian; I had thought of little else but him since Jack phoned me with the shocking news of his death.

Gazing blindly into the empty room, a myriad of thoughts jostling for prominence in my mind, I put the pen down and leaned back in my chair.

Sebastian had been a part of my life for as long as I could remember, and perhaps more than anyone he had been the greatest influence on me. Even though we had had our noisy quarrels, heated differences of opinion and stormy, emotional episodes that left both of us very shaken and upset, we had managed always to patch things up, to stick together, to remain close, no matter what. Knowing him all my life though I had, it was after our divorce that we had come to understand each other; and it was only then that our relationship acquired a certain degree of peace and serenity.

Our marriage had been tempestuous at times and short-lived; through the passing of time I had come to realize why it had been so volatile, and brief. Put simply, the forty-two-year-old experienced man of the world had not known how to cope with the twenty-two-year-old child who was his new bride. Me.

An image of Sebastian on our wedding day flashed before me, and once again my throat closed with a sudden rush of emotion. Tears pricked behind my lids; I blinked them away. On and off, for the last few hours, I had been shedding tears . . . tears for Sebastian, dead at fifty-six, and with so much more of life to live . . . tears for myself . . . tears for Jack and Luciana . . . tears for the world.

Difficult, haunted and troubled man though he had been, he had nevertheless been a great man. A good man. No matter what he was in his personal life, his shoulders had been strong enough to carry so many of the world's burdens, and his heart had been filled with compassion for those who were suffering and in need.

A French journalist had once written about him that he was a beacon light in these darkly turbulent and troubled times we lived in. Certainly *I* deemed this to be the truth. The world would be a lesser place now that he was no longer in it.

Oh Sebastian, you were too young to die, I thought, and I put my head down and closed my eyes, reliving Jack's phone call of this morning. I had been checking the facts in my story when Belinda had told me that Jack Locke was on the line . . .

'Jack! Hello!' I exclaimed. 'How are you? And more importantly, *where* are you?'

'Here. In Connecticut. At the farm, Vivienne.'

'That's great. When did you get in from France?'

'Two days ago, but Vivienne, I –'

'Come on over for supper tonight! I've just finished this long piece for the London *Sunday Times* Magazine, and it'll do me good to cook, to relax with –'

Cutting me off in a peremptory way, he said swiftly, 'Vivienne, there's something I must tell you.'

I detected an odd note in his voice, and it made the hackles rise on the back of my neck. Stiffening, I clutched the phone tighter in my hand. 'What is it? What's wrong, Jack?'

'It's Sebastian . . . Vivienne . . . I'm not sure how to tell you this, how to break it gently, so I'm gonna come right out with it. He's dead. Sebastian's dead.'

'Oh my God! No! It can't be! What happened?

When did he die?' I demanded shrilly, and then I heard myself wailing, 'It can't be true. He can't be dead. No, not Sebastian.' My stomach lurched, and then as agitation fully took hold of me, my heart began to pound against my ribcage.

'It *is* true,' Jack insisted. 'I got a call this morning. Around nine-thirty. From Harry Blakely. The tree man. The arborist who looks after the trees at the farm. You know him don't you?'

'Yes.'

'Harry called me to tell me he'd found Sebastian's body out back. Near the lake. Harry had gone to the farm as he usually does Mondays. He was heading down to cut off the tops of some dead willows. He stumbled over the body. Sebastian was sprawled face down, near those rocks at the far end of the lake. He had a gash on his forehead. Harry said he looked as if he'd been outside all night. Maybe longer. Once he'd established that Sebastian was dead, Harry went up to the house to call the State Police in North Canaan. He told them about finding the body. They instructed him not to move it. Not to touch a single thing. Then he called me at the house in Manhattan. I grabbed Luciana, who's in from London. We took Sebastian's helicopter out here. Harry was also disturbed about the mess in Sebastian's library. The room was in total disarray. A lamp was overturned. A chair was on its side. Papers were strewn everywhere. And the french doors were ajar. The glass was broken in one of the panes. Harry thought it looked as if it could have been smashed on purpose. By an intruder.'

'Are you saying that Sebastian may have been *killed?*'

'It's possible. Very possible,' Jack said. 'The circumstances are somewhat suspicious, wouldn't you say?'

'From what you're telling me, it does look strange, yes. On the other hand, Sebastian might have had some sort of attack, a stroke perhaps. He could have staggered around the room, then gone outside to get air . . .' My voice petered out. It was foolish to speculate. But a second later I did just that again.

'Do you think he fell and hit his head, Jack? Or are you suggesting he was chased out of the house, and then struck by someone? The intruder? If there was one.'

'I don't know, Vivienne. I wonder if we'll ever know.'

'Oh, Jack, this is just horrendous! I can't believe he's dead. I just can't.' I found myself weeping once more.

'Don't cry. Please don't. It won't bring him back.'

'I know it won't but I can't help it. I've loved him for as long as I can remember, since I was a child. And I still cared deeply for him, despite the divorce.'

'I know,' he muttered.

There was a silence between us.

'How's Luciana?' I asked at last, trying to ignore Jack's coldness, this seeming lack of feeling I was detecting.

'She's fine. Holding up. She'll be okay.'

'Would you like me to drive over to Cornwall? I can be there in half an hour, in three-quarters of an hour at the most.'

'No, you don't have to come. But thanks for offering. Anyway, this place is crawling with police. That's another reason I called. To alert you. They'll be over to see you. Some time today. You're in Sebastian's appointment book. They asked me who you were. I told them you were his ex-wife. *One* of his ex-wives. You were with him very recently. I guess that's why they want to talk to you.'

'I understand, Jack, but I really can't tell them anything. Sebastian was in the best of spirits. And health, as far as I could tell last Monday. Oh God, it's a week ago exactly that we lunched. I can't believe this, I just can't,' I sobbed.

Fumbling for my handkerchief, I blew my nose and tried to get a grip on myself and my emotions.

'It's the shock,' I mumbled into the phone after a second or two, 'the unexpectedness of it. How can Sebastian be dead? He was larger than life, and he seemed so invulnerable. *Invincible*. To me, anyway. I thought nothing would ever happen to him, that he would live for ever. Well, at least that he'd live to be an old man. Actually, I always thought of him as being immortal, if the truth be known.'

'He was only too mortal,' Jack said in a low, tense voice. 'Listen, I gotta go. I can see two detectives heading this way. Walking up the back lawn. Looking as grim as hell,' he snapped.

'Jack, please call me later!'

'Sure.'

'*Please*.'

'Okay! Okay!'

He sounded more impatient than usual.

'And please tell Luciana how sorry I am. Perhaps I ought to speak with her now.'

'She's out. Taking a walk. We'll all meet up later.'

He was gone without another word, without even saying goodbye. I sat there holding the phone in my hand, as if turned to stone, listening to the interminable dialling tone. Finally, I replaced the receiver.

Ever since that call this morning, I have been numb from shock, full of grief, disbelieving. Now I felt drained. A vast emptiness settled within me. It was as if I were quite hollow, just a fragile shell.

I have never experienced such feelings before. No, that's not true. I have. When my mother died with this same kind of suddenness, this awful abruptness that always leaves others reeling and lost. And when my second husband Michael Trent suffered an unexpected heart attack, a fatal heart attack, I was devastated, floundering, cast adrift then, just as I am today.

Life is hell; no, death is hell, I muttered to myself, and then wondered why those I loved had been taken from me with such breathtaking unexpectedness.

Pushing myself up out of my chair, I left the library. In the corridor, I poked my head around the door of Belinda's cubby-hole of an office, told her I was going for a walk and pulled an old wool cape out of the coat closet.

I stood on the back step and took several deep breaths. On this Monday afternoon at the beginning of October the weather was positively glorious, and mild, like spring. I glanced up. The arc of the sky was vivid blue and clear, and everything appeared to shimmer in the bright, golden sunlight. The trees had already started to turn, the leaves changing colour from verdant green to yellow, russet and scarlet; some were a deep, plummy purple, others a mellow gold tinged at the edges with the palest of pinks. It was fall, that special time of year when tourists from all over the world come to Connecticut to see the magnificent foliage, which is so breathtaking.

Moving quickly along the stone-flagged path, I headed across the lawn towards a small gazebo which stood at the edge of a copse of trees. I loved this remote corner of the garden where everything was bosky, still and silent.

My grandmother had built this gazebo many, many years ago, long before I was born. It had been created for my mother when she was a child. She had grown up in this old colonial stone house which stood in the hills above New Preston, a picturesque little town in the north-western highlands of Connecticut.

Climbing the three wooden steps, I went inside and sat down on the bench, pulling the cape around me, shivering slightly. Yet it wasn't cold today. The sun was a huge bright orb, and we were enjoying an extraordinary Indian summer, the likes of which had not been seen around these parts for a long while. I had shivered a moment before only because I felt the presence of ghosts here in this rustic little structure, saw them all . . . all of them. I found myself falling backward in time to be with them.

*

Gran Rosalie, with her pretty pink complexion and snow-white hair piled high on top of her head, sitting there so proudly, with such dignity, on the bench in front of the round table.

She was pouring tea from her old brown china pot with the chip on the lid, which she would not throw away because she said it made the best tea. Gran was telling me stories about this lovely old house, Ridgehill, which had been in her family for generations. Built in 1799, it had been passed down from mother to daughter, and had always been owned by a woman, never a man. That was the stipulation in the will of Henrietta Bailey, my great-great-great-great-grandmother. It was she who had built the house with her own money, and she who had been one of the most powerful matriarchs of the Baileys. My gran was a Bailey, descended directly from her; Bailey was part of my name.

My grandmother had the most beautiful of voices, cultured, lilting, full of music. She was reminding me that one day the house would be mine. Carefully, she explained about Henrietta and her will, told me how my amazing ancestor had wanted the women of the Bailey family always to be protected. So the house must pass from mother to daughter, even if there were sons. If there were no daughters then the house passed to the wife of the eldest son. I loved to hear the history of my family. I cherished Gran's marvellous tales . . .

My mother was here now . . . all golden-light and brightness, a shimmering kind of woman with her abundance of red-gold hair, perfect, milky skin and startling green eyes. His emerald eyes, my father called them.

Now he was with us too . . . the Irishman. Black Irish, Liam Delaney was, my gran told me that. Black Irish and something of a charmer, a twinkling rogue of a man, a man whom women fell for at the drop of a hat, at least so my gran said to me time and again when I was growing up.

He was tall and dark, with rosy cheeks, sparkling brown eyes and a brogue as rich as thick, clotted cream. The Black Irishman, the twinkling rogue, had been a writer. I suppose I have inherited his penchant for words, his flair for stringing them together so that they make some sort of sense. His had been a powerful gift; I'm not so sure that mine is of quite the same magnitude. Gran always said that if it wasn't, then it was only because I hadn't kissed the Blarney Stone in County Cork, as my father had claimed to have done. Gran used to say it was surely the truth, for no one else she knew had such wondrous powers of persuasion as he.

He left us, though, my father did, one day many summers ago, telling us he would be back within three months. But he never did return, and I have no idea to this day whether he is dead or alive. I was ten years old when he went off on that journalistic forage for new material, travelling into the far, far blue horizons of the world. Twenty-six years ago. Perhaps he *was* dead by now.

My mother had seemed sad at first; she had cheered up only when his letters began to arrive at regular intervals. She read parts of them to me as they came in one by one; but only small portions, skipping the intimate bits, I suspect. I've been brought up to believe that my father was quite a man with the fancy words, especially when it came to wooing women.

First he was in Australia, then he went to New Zealand, and finally he left the Antipodes and travelled to Tahiti. Fiji was another port of call as he wandered around the Pacific, God knows in search of what. Other women? More exotic women? Not long after my mother received a letter from him postmarked Tonga communications had abruptly ceased. We never heard from him again.

When I was small I used to think that my mother was suffering from a broken heart, that she was endlessly yearning for my father. I had not known then that eighteen months after Liam Delaney had set sail for those exotic isles of Micronesia, she was already falling in love with Sebastian Locke.

In my mind's eye I saw him quite clearly, walking across the lawn towards me, just the way he had done all those years ago.

Sebastian Locke, heading in my direction, long-limbed, slender, the embodiment of nonchalant grace, walking towards *me*.

That summer's afternoon, the first time I ever set eyes on him, I thought he was the most beautiful man I had ever seen. He was far more handsome than my father, which was saying a lot indeed. Sebastian was tall and dark-haired like my father, but whereas Liam's eyes were velvet-brown and deep, Sebastian's were a clear, vivid blue, the brightest of blues. Like bits of sky, I recall thinking that day, with a piercing quality to them. It was as if they could see right through you, as if they could see into your mind and heart. I really believed he knew exactly what I was thinking; even last Monday I had thought the same thing over lunch.

Sebastian was wearing white gabardine trousers and a pale blue shirt on that stifling July day in 1970. The shirt was made of voile, almost flimsy in weight. I've liked voile shirts on men ever since. The shirt was open at the neck, with the sleeves rolled up, and his face and arms were tanned. His body was tanned as well. I could see it through the voile. He was a lithe man, very fit, athletic.

He had leaned against the posts of the gazebo and smiled at me. His teeth were very white and even in his sun-bronzed face, his mouth sensitive, and the vivid eyes were set wide apart in that arresting face.

Those eyes regarded me unblinkingly, and with great interest for a few seconds. It was when he said, 'Hello, young lady, you must be the famous Vivienne,' that I had felt myself becoming hot around my face and neck. Then he had stretched out his hand to me. As I took it he nodded slightly, as though acknowledging me yet again. He held on to my hand much longer than I expected, and as I looked up into that open, clean-cut face, my own very serious in its expression, my heart had skipped several beats.

And of course I had fallen hopelessly in love with him. I was all of twelve years old at the time, but I felt much older on that particular day. Very grown up. After all, it was the first time a man had actually made me blush.

Sebastian was thirty-two but looked much younger, extremely boyish and carefree. Vaguely, I somehow knew that he was the kind of man women automatically gravitate to; somehow I understood that he had charisma, sex appeal, that *je ne sais quoi* the French forever talk about.

In any case I was all agog over him. I never did get him to admit it to me, but I was certain he felt something special for me that day.

On the other hand, he might have liked me simply because I was the daughter of my mother, the beauteous Antoinette Delaney, with whom he was having a grand love affair at the time.

That afternoon, when he sauntered up the steps of the gazebo and seated himself next to me, I knew he was going to play a huge part in my life, in my future. Don't ask me how the young girl that I was then sensed this. She just did.

We talked about horses, which he knew scared me to death. He asked me if I would like to come to Laurel Creek Farm in Cornwall to learn to ride.

'I have a son, Jack, who's six, and a daughter, Luciana, who's four. They're already astride their ponies and doing well. Say you'll come and ride with us, Vivienne, say you'll come and stay at the horse farm. Your mother's a fine equestrienne, as you well know. She wants you to ride as proficiently as she does. You mustn't be afraid of horses. I will teach you how to ride. You'll be safe with me.' He was correct in that, I did feel safe with him, and he did teach me to ride well, showing much more patience and understanding than my mother. And I loved him all the more for that.

A long time later, many years later, I realized he had been trying to make us into a family, that he had wanted my mother for himself. For always. But how could she have been his for ever? She was married to Liam Delaney, and *he* had gone missing far across the ocean. Until she got a divorce she could never remarry. Not Sebastian. Not anyone.

Still, Sebastian *had* tried to blend us into a tight-knit little circle, and in certain ways he succeeded.

That afternoon, staring up at him, I had only been able to nod mutely as he talked about horses, tried to reassure me about learning to ride. I was rendered speechless by this man, totally mesmerized by him.

I was under his spell.

And I was for ever after, for that matter.

It was Belinda who broke into my memories and my golden dreams, who scattered my beloved ghosts to the far corners of Gran Rosalie's garden.

'Vivienne, Vivienne!' she called as she hurried down the path, waving frantically. 'It's *The New York Times*. They're on the phone.'

I leaped to my feet on hearing this and raced towards her. We met in the middle of the lawn. '*The New York Times*?' I repeated, searching her face, my heart sinking.

'Yes, they've got wind of it . . . wind of Sebastian's death. They seem to know that the police were called in, that the circumstances are suspicious. Etcetera,

etcetera. Anyway, the reporter wants to have a word with you.'

The mere thought of tomorrow's headlines around the world sent a chill surging through me. And of course there *would* be headlines. A famous man had died, a man of conscience and compassion . . . the world's greatest philanthropist. And he might have been murdered. I shrivelled inside at the mere thought of those headlines. The press would turn his life upside down and inside out. No one, nothing, would be sacrosanct.

'The reporter wants to talk to you, Vivienne,' Belinda said more urgently, taking hold of my arm. 'He's waiting.'

'Oh God,' I groaned. 'Why me?'

# Two

'Why me?' I repeated later that evening, staring up at Jack. 'Why did you choose me to be the spokesperson for this family?'

He had just arrived for supper a few minutes ago, and we were in my small den at the rear of the house, a room he preferred; it was intimate, warm, with its red-brocaded walls and old Persian carpet. He hovered in front of me, his back to the fire, his hands in his pockets.

Returning my stare, seemingly at a loss, he did not answer. Then shaking his head in a thoughtful way, he started to speak, stopped, frowned, and pursed his lips.

'Well, Vivienne,' he said at last, 'I'm not sure why.' He shook his head again. '*Liar*,' he said emphatically. 'I'm a liar. And a coward. That's why I sicked the *Times* on you. I didn't want to talk to them myself.'

'But you're the head of the family now. I'm not,' I protested.

'And you're a journalist. A *respected* journalist. You know better how to deal with the dreaded press than I do.'

'Luciana could have spoken to them. She's Sebastian's daughter.'

'You're his ex-wife,' he shot back.

'Oh, Jack, *please*.'

'Okay, okay. Look, she's been out of it all day, ever since we got here. She can barely speak to *me*, never mind *The New York Times*. You know how fragile she is. The least little thing upsets her.'

'It always has. I never expected her for supper tonight, even though she accepted. I knew she wouldn't come,' I retorted. When we were children growing up together, Luciana had usually been the one to hang back, to drop out, to claim tiredness, even sickness, when she didn't wish to do something, or if she was faced with a difficult situation. But fragile she wasn't. I knew that for a fact. She was strong. And tough. Not that Luciana ever let anyone know this. Dissembling came to her readily; she was a facile liar, an expert spinner of tall tales. Her father once told me she was the cleverest liar he had ever known.

'How about a drink?' Jack said, cutting into my thoughts about his half-sister.

'Of course!' I exclaimed, jumping up. 'How rude of me. What would you like? Your usual scotch? Or a glass of wine?'

'Scotch, please, Viv.'

I went to the table near the door and fixed his scotch, a vodka on the rocks for myself, and carried them back to the fireplace. Handing him his glass, I sat down.

He muttered his thanks, took a great gulp of the amber-coloured alcohol, and stood nursing it in both hands, ruminating.

'It's been a terrible day,' I said. 'The worst day in a long time. I still can't quite accept the fact that Sebastian's dead. I keep expecting him to walk in any minute.'

Jack made no comment, merely sipped his drink and rocked back and forth on his heels.

I regarded him over the rim of my glass, thinking how unsympathetic and without emotion he was. I experienced a little spurt of anger. Jack could be so cold, cold as an iceberg. At this moment I hated him, as I had sometimes hated him as a child. His father had been found dead this morning, in the most peculiar circumstances. Yet he was behaving as if nothing had happened. And he certainly wasn't showing any signs of grief. It struck me as being most unnatural, even though father and son had never really been close. I had been distressed for the entire day, fighting tears, engulfed by sadness. I mourned Sebastian, and I would go on mourning him for a long time.

Suddenly, without preamble, Jack said, 'They took the body.'

Startled by this announcement, I gaped at him. 'You mean the police took the body away?'

'Yep,' he answered laconically.

'To Farmington? For the autopsy?'

'You got it.'

'I really can't stand you when you're like this!' I exclaimed, and I was surprised at the harshness of my voice.

'Like what, sugar?'

'For God's sake, come off it, you know what I mean. So cold and hard and detached. Half of it's pretence anyway. You can't fool me. I've known you for the best part of your life and mine.'

He shrugged indifferently, drained his glass, went and poured himself another drink. Walking back to the fireside, he continued, 'That detective, Kennelly, told me we'll get the body back tomorrow.'

'So quickly?'

He nodded. 'Apparently the Chief Medical Examiner will do the autopsy first thing tomorrow morning. He'll take out tissue and organs, plus blood and urine samples, and –'

Shuddering, I shouted, 'Stop it! You're talking about Sebastian! *Your father*. Don't you have any respect for him? Any respect for the dead?'

He gave me an odd look but made no comment.

I said, 'If *you* have no feelings for him, so be it. But just remember this: *I do*. I will not permit you to speak of him in such a heartless, cold-blooded way.'

Ignoring my remarks, Jack said, 'We can have the funeral later this week.'

'In Cornwall,' I murmured, trying to adopt a softer tone. 'He once told me he wanted to be buried in Cornwall.'

'What about a memorial service, Viv? Should we have one? If so, where? More importantly, when?' He grimaced. 'As soon as possible. I have to get back to France.'

Though he was infuriating me again, I held myself still. Exercising great control, I responded calmly, 'In New York. I think that would be the best place, certainly the most appropriate.'

'Where?'

'At the Church of St John the Divine,' I suggested. 'What do you think?'

'Whatever you say.' Jack flopped down in the chair near the fireplace and regarded me for the longest moment, a speculative look entering his eyes.

'Oh, no,' I said, catching on at once. 'Oh no, no, Jack! You're not going to talk me into arranging the funeral and the memorial. That's for you to do. You and Luciana.'

'You'll help, though. Won't you?'

I nodded. 'But you're not going to shrug off your responsibilities, as you have so many times in the past,' I warned. 'I won't let you do that. *You* are the head of the Locke family, now that Sebastian's dead, and the sooner you understand this the better. There's the Locke Foundation to run, for one thing, and you'll have to pick up the torch he dropped when he died.'

'What do you mean?' he asked sharply, his eyes on mine. 'What torch?'

'The charity work, Jack. You'll have to carry on where he left off. You'll have to tend to the sick and the poor of the world, those who are suffering, just as he did. Thousands are depending on you.'

'Oh, no! No *way*, sugar. If you think *I'm* going to hand out money like a drunken sailor, then you're crazy. As crazy and as foolish as he was.'

'This family's got so much money it doesn't know what to do with it!' I cried, furious with him.

'I'm not going to follow in Sebastian's footsteps, trailing halfway round the world and back, dispensing largesse to the great unwashed. So forget it, Viv, and don't bring it up again.'

'You'll have to run the Locke Foundation,' I reminded him. 'As the only son and heir that's not only your inheritance but your responsibility.'

'Okay, okay, so I'll run it. Long distance. From France. But I ain't no saviour, out to cure the world of its ills. And illnesses. Just remember that. My father was a madman.'

'Sebastian did a great deal of good, and don't *you* ever forget *that*.'

Slowly, he shook his head. 'It's odd. It really is.'

'What is?'

'The way you adore him still after all these years. And after all the things he did to you.'

'I don't know what you mean by that. He treated me very well. Always.'

'Better than the other wives, I've got to admit. He liked you.'

'Liked me! He *loved* me. Sebastian loved me from the very first day we met, when I was twelve –'

'Dirty old man.'

'Shut up! Furthermore, he continued to love me after we split up.'

'He never loved anyone,' Jack announced swiftly, scathingly, giving me a pitying look. 'Not me. Not my mother. Not Luciana. Not her mother. Not your mother. Not his other two wives. Not even you, sugar.'

'Stop calling me sugar. It's disgusting. And he *did* love me.'

'I told you, he wasn't capable of loving. He couldn't

love anyone if his life depended on it. It wasn't in him. Sebastian Locke was a monster.'

'He was not! And I know he loved me, do you understand that? I know he did,' I answered heatedly, swallowing my anger, clinging to my composure.

'If you say so,' he muttered, giving in to me, which he frequently did. Averting his head, he stared into the fire, a morose look settling on his face.

As I sat watching him, thinking how sad it was that he was so wrong about his father, thinking how little Jack had known about him, it occurred to me that he bore a strong resemblance to Sebastian tonight. Their profiles were the same; Jack had inherited his father's strong jawline and aquiline nose, as well as his fine head of dark hair. But his eyes were a faded, watery blue, not the bright cornflower hue his father's had been. As for their characters and personalities, they were as dissimilar as any two men could be.

The moroseness stayed with Jack throughout supper. He ate sparingly, drank a lot, and said little.

At one moment I reached out and touched his hand, and remarked softly, in my most conciliatory voice, 'I'm sorry I shrieked at you.'

He did not answer.

'Honestly, I am. Don't be like this, Jack.'

'Like what?'

'Mute. Unresponsive. So infuriatingly mule-headed.'

He stared at me, then he smiled.

When Jack smiled his face lit up, and he was engaging, almost irresistible to me. That was the way it had always been. I smiled back, my affection for him once more intact. 'It's just that I can't bear it when you're nasty about Sebastian.'

'We see him differently, you and I,' he mumbled, swigging more of my best red wine, the Mouton Rothschild which Sebastian had sent me last year.

He continued, 'You've always been . . . agog about him . . . so . . . so adoring and worshipping. Look, I don't wear the same kind of rose-tinted glasses, Viv.'

'You adored him too, when you were little.'

'That's what *you* think. But it's not true.'

'Oh Jack, don't lie to me. This is Vivienne you're talking to . . . good old Viv, your best friend.'

He threw back his head and laughed. 'Jesus, don't you ever let up? When it comes to persistence, you're like a dog with a bone.'

'Only when we're discussing Sebastian Locke,' I countered.

'Well, one thing is certain, your loyalty is commendable, sugar.'

'Thanks. And stop calling me *sugar* in that awful tone of voice. You know I hate it. You do it just to get my goat.'

He grinned, reached out and squeezed my hand. 'Truce?'

'Truce,' I agreed, as quickly as I had when we were children.

We spoke about other matters for a short while after this. About France, Provence to be exact, and our respective homes there, houses which Sebastian had given us at different times. Although I did not dare remind him of this. It was obvious to me that he was as unrelenting about his father in death as he had been during his lifetime. Jack had never given Sebastian the benefit of the doubt, nor apparently did he intend to do so now. It was too late, anyway.

It was when we returned to the den to have coffee that Jack suddenly started to talk about the circumstances of Sebastian's death once again.

Settled in an armchair, with his coffee and cognac on a small side table next to him, he said, 'The police had me check through his things. In the library. The rest of the house. No valuables were taken. As far as I could tell.'

'Does that mean they've now ruled out the possibility of an intruder?'

'They didn't say.'

'It's perplexing.' I sat back in my chair, my mind turning over the few facts we had. 'When I lunched with Sebastian he mentioned that Mrs Crane was away on vacation . . .' I stopped and looked at him.

'What are you getting at, Viv?'

'I guess I think it's a bit odd that Sebastian came up to the farm when there was no one there to look after him. When she was away. Even the police think that, Jack.'

'He told me on Thursday that he had some work to finish. He gave me the impression he was looking forward to being alone up here, from his tone and his attitude.'

'Maybe he wasn't alone, though.'

Jack threw me a swift look and his brows puckered. 'That's a possibility. Somebody could have been with him. Yes, of course they could.'

'And that somebody might have ended up doing him bodily harm,' I pointed out.

'Only too true.'

'By the way, why did you and Luciana suddenly come to the States? Was there a special reason for this visit?'

'We didn't come to kill Sebastian,' he said, and gave me a smirk that was oddly ghoulish.

'For God's sake, I wasn't implying any such thing. And do stop it. You know your facetious talk only infuriates me. Grow up, act your age, Jack. This is very serious . . .'

'Sorry, Viv. Luciana and I came in for the annual meeting of Locke Industries,' Jack explained in a quiet, more subdued tone, sounding suddenly and effectively chastened at last. 'It was supposed to be held tomorrow. Naturally, it's been cancelled.'

'I should hope so! Anyway, I must go back to my original reaction of earlier today, when you first told me Sebastian was dead. I was certain he'd had a heart attack, or possibly a stroke. And to tell you the truth, I still believe, deep down, that that's what happened.'

When Jack made no response, I gave him a penetrating look, asked, 'Well, don't you?'

He brought his hand up to his face, rubbed his mouth and his chin, suddenly reflective. 'I don't know,' he answered. 'This afternoon I would have agreed with you, but now I'm vacillating. Not sure of anything.'

'Do you honestly think he was attacked? By an intruder?' I pressed.

'Maybe. He could have gone into the farmhouse and surprised a burglar.'

'Before the burglar had an opportunity to steal anything? Is that what you think? After all, you said there's nothing missing.'

'Well, the paintings and the major art objects are in place. On the other hand, Sebastian could have had something else there worth stealing, something to tempt a thief.'

'Such as what?' I frowned, shaking my head. 'I don't get it, Jack.'

'Cash, Vivienne. You know Sebastian always carried a lot on him. I was often warning him about that. Or maybe there were some documents around.'

'*Documents*,' I said sharply, staring at him. 'But if someone stole documents that smacks of premeditation, doesn't it? Listen, a thief breaking in at random, looking for loot, is one thing. A thief breaking in and stealing documents is a different thing altogether. It suggests prior knowledge to me.'

Jack nodded. 'You're right there.'

'What made you think of documents? Are there any missing? And what kind of documents did you have in mind?'

'I don't know, and to be honest I don't know why I thought of them. Except that Sebastian said he was going to the farm to work. Whatever else he was, he wasn't a liar. If he said he had to go over papers, then he was telling the truth. But there weren't any, at least none that he'd been working on –'

'What about all those scattered around the library?' I cut in.

'The letters on the floor and spread over the desk were just the usual things. Correspondence, bills, personal notes from people. The way he spoke on Thursday he sounded as if he had real work to do on important documents. Come to think of it, he did actually say *documents*, I guess that's why I just thought of them now.' He lifted his shoulders in a shrug. 'Look, I haven't been at Laurel Creek Farm in a coon's age, Viv, so how would I know if there's anything missing? Mrs Crane's the best person to ascertain that, but then only as far as the art is concerned. Not even she would know if any papers have disappeared.'

'No, she wouldn't.' I let out a long sigh. 'It looks as if we're back to square one.'

'Yep . . .' Jack shook his head, his puzzlement surfacing again. Then he said suddenly, in a torrent of words, 'Look, Viv, I disagree with you. I don't think he died of natural causes, as you do. I think he was killed. Most probably by an intruder. Sebastian surprised him. The intruder ran out. Sebastian chased him. They struggled. And Sebastian got himself killed. Sort of inadvertently.'

'Or he was murdered by someone who was with him at the farm, for reasons we don't know,' I remarked.

Jack pondered for a moment. Then slowly, and more thoughtfully than usual, he said, 'We're speculating. We'd better stop. It'll lead nowhere.' Pinning me with his eyes, he added, 'Let's admit it, Vivienne, we won't know exactly how he died until the police get that autopsy report from the Chief Medical Examiner in Farmington.'

I could only nod. I agreed with him, at least as far as his last comment was concerned.

# Three

Long after Jack had left, I prowled around the house, stacking the dishwasher, clearing up, making the den and the dining room neat and tidy.

At one moment I even had another stab at my story, hoping to do the final edit, but I was not very successful. I would try again tomorrow, and if my concentration still eluded me I would have to let it go out as it was.

The hall clock was striking midnight by the time I climbed the stairs of Ridgehill and went to my room, feeling weary and worn down.

Like all of my female forebears, I occupied the master bedroom that stretched almost the entire length of the house. Situated at the back, rather than the front, it was a charming room with rafters, many windows and an imposing stone fireplace. French windows on either side of the fireplace opened out on to a wide balcony suspended over the garden. This was the most marvellous spot in the world for breakfast on spring and summer mornings, especially when the lilacs were in bloom.

Ridgehill stood at the top of Tinker Hill Road. Set amidst a copse of trees, it looked out over Lake Waramaug. When my illustrious ancestor Henrietta

Bailey built this house she had thought things out most prudently, had chosen well when situating the master bedroom within the overall architectural plan. The views were spectacular from the many windows, were panoramic in their vistas.

I went and stood at one of the windows, moving the curtain slightly, staring out across the tops of the trees towards the large body of water far below. The lake was as flat and as unmoving as black glass, and above it the sky was littered with tiny bright stars. There was a harvest moon tonight, silvery and perfectly spherical, riding the black clouds. It cast a sheen across the murky waters of the lake, touched the tops of the trees with brilliance.

What a beautiful night, I thought, as I let the curtain drop and turned away. After undressing, I slipped into a nightgown and climbed into the grand old fourposter. Turning out the bedside lamp, I pulled the covers up over me and settled down for the night, hoping to fall asleep quickly. It had been such an exhausting day emotionally. A day of shock. A day of sorrow.

Moonlight filled the room. The silence was a balm. I lay there drifting with my thoughts; Sebastian was foremost in them. We had shared so much in this room. So much pleasure. So much heartbreak. I am convinced that I conceived my child in this room, his child, the child I lost in miscarriage. And, once again, I found myself wondering if Sebastian and I would have remained together if that child had been born. Perhaps.

Cradled in his arms, I had lain in this bed, weeping

on his shoulder, and he had comforted me about the loss of our baby. How could Jack believe he was a monster? Nothing was further from the truth. Sebastian had always comforted and nurtured me. And everyone else, for that matter. Jack was so terribly wrong about him; his judgement about Sebastian was flawed, just as it was flawed about most things in his personal life. He had made a mess of it and he loved to blame others, especially his father. I loved Jack like a brother, but I saw him with clear eyes.

Sebastian had always been there for me, for as long as I could remember, since my childhood. I recall so well the afternoon he had come to me, after my mother had been found dead at the bottom of the cellar steps at his farm. I had just arrived from Manhattan; Jess, my mother's housekeeper, had phoned him the instant I had walked through the front door and he had rushed over to Ridgehill immediately, full of concern for me.

It had been such a warm June day, unnaturally hot for that time of year, and I had been sitting on the balcony of this room, distraught, sobbing, my heart breaking, when he had come looking for me.

Eighteen years ago.

I had been eighteen when my mother died. So long ago now. Half my life ago. Yet it might have been yesterday, so vividly did I recall it.

I found myself focusing on the past yet again, and I walked back into that June afternoon of 1976.

*

'Vivienne . . . darling . . . I'm here! I'm here for you,' Sebastian said, coming through the bedroom and out on to the balcony like a whirlwind.

I lifted my head and blinked, staring at him, my eyes blinded by my tears and the bright sunlight streaming out behind him.

He was by my side in an instant, sitting down next to me on the long bench. Anxiously he looked into my face and his own was bleak, strained. A muscle pulsed in his temple, and his startlingly blue eyes were dulled by sadness.

Wiping away the tears on my cheeks with his fingertips, he enveloped me in his arms, held me close, soothed me as though soothing a wounded child.

'It's such a terrible tragedy,' he murmured against my hair. 'I cared for her too, Vivienne, so I know what you're suffering. I'm suffering myself.' As he spoke his arms tightened around me.

I clutched him. 'It's not fair,' I sobbed. 'She was so young. Only forty-two. I don't understand how it happened. *How did it happen?* How did my mother fall down the basement steps, Sebastian? Do you think she got dizzy and lost her balance? And why was she going into the basement, anyway?'

'I don't know. No one knows. It was an accident,' he replied, then drew slightly away and looked down into my face. 'You're aware that she'd come to stay with me, whilst some of the rooms at Ridgehill were being painted, but I wasn't in Connecticut last night. I was in the city for a Locke Foundation dinner. I got up at the crack of dawn and drove out to the farm, wanting to have breakfast with her. And also hoping to go riding with her later. When I arrived, the whole place was in an uproar. Aldred had found her body earlier and had called the police. Then he'd spoken to Jess, told her to get in touch with you. By the time I got hold of her, you were already on your way to New Preston.'

I nodded, and before I could say anything my grief overcame me once more, and fresh tears flowed. Sebastian continued to comfort me; he was so kind.

At last, I managed to say to him, 'Jess believes my mother died instantly. Do you think she did? I couldn't bear it if I thought she'd suffered.'

'I'm sure Jess is right. When someone tumbles down a steep flight of stairs I think it must go very fast . . . in a terrible rush. There's no question in my mind that she did die immediately. She couldn't have suffered, rest assured of that.'

Conjuring up the image of my mother falling to meet her doom, I suddenly cried out in my anguish. He held me closer, calming me as best he could. 'I know, I know,' he said softly against my hair.

'You're going to miss her, Sebastian,' I eventually muttered. 'You loved her too.'

'Yes.'

I buried my face against his chest and held on to him as if he were the only thing I had left in the world. In a way, he was; he was my safe haven.

Sebastian stroked my hair, smoothed his hand down my arm, continuing to murmur gentle words. I pressed myself even closer, and I felt as though I were somehow drawing strength from him.

We sat together like this on the balcony for a long time, and eventually a kind of peacefulness drifted over me and my tears finally ceased altogether. But he made no move to get up, and neither did I; and so we continued to sit on the old bench.

And then I held my breath, hardly daring to move. Something quite strange was happening to me. My heart was pumping rapidly; my throat had gone dry and was suddenly constricted.

The blood rushed up into my face; I understood exactly what was happening, understood myself only too well. I wanted him to stop kissing my hair and kiss me instead. I wanted his mouth on mine. I wanted his hand stroking my breast, not my arm. I wanted him to make love to me. Without knowing it, he was arousing me sexually, and I discovered I didn't want him to stop. When I realized how damp I was between my legs my face flamed. I was mortified.

I did not dare to stir in his arms. I did not dare to look at him. He could read my mind; he'd always known what I was thinking ever since I was a little girl.

And so I continued to sit there, waiting for these extraordinary feelings to subside, to go away. I was confused and embarrassed. How could I be experiencing such feelings, today of all days? My mother was lying dead in the morgue at Farmington.

I shuddered. Sebastian had been her lover for over six years. And now I wanted him for myself. I shuddered again, hating myself for my dreadful thoughts about him, hating my body, which was so betraying me at this moment.

Thankfully, at last, Sebastian's arms slackened and

he let go of me. Tilting my face to his, he kissed me lightly on the forehead. He attempted a smile, looked as if he were about to speak, but remained silent.

Eventually, he said in a low, concerned voice, 'I realize you must be feeling very much alone, but you do have me, Vivienne dear. And you mustn't worry about a thing. I will look after you. I know it's impossible for me to take your mother's place, but I am your friend, and I'm here for you whenever you need me.'

'Ever since that day you found me in the gazebo, that first day we met, I've felt protected by you,' I replied, and I meant every word.

Again he tried to smile, but without much success. After a brief moment, he said, 'You must always come to me, whatever the problem. I won't let you down, I promise.' A small sigh escaped him, and he said, almost to himself, 'You were such a lovely child. You touched my heart.'

And now he was dead, no longer there to protect me, and my life would be that much poorer without him. I pushed my face into the pillow and it was a long time before I could stem the tears.

I must have eventually fallen asleep, for when I awoke with a start sunlight was streaming in through the many windows. Last night I had forgotten to draw the curtains and a new day had dawned. I could hear the chirping of the birds outside, and far away, in the distance, the *cawk cawk* of the Canada geese circling the lake.

I eyed the clock on the bedside table, saw that it was almost seven and slid down into the bed, luxuriating for a few moments longer in the comfort and warmth. And then reality thrust itself into my consciousness, and with a rush of sudden intense pain I remembered the events of yesterday.

*Sebastian was dead. I would never see him again.*

I held myself still, breathing deeply, thinking about him, recalling so much about him, so many little things. We had been divorced for eight years, and I hadn't seen all that much of him in the last three. But before then he had been such an important and integral part of my life, and for over twenty-one years. *Twenty-one*. An auspicious number to me. I had been twenty-one years old when Sebastian had first made love to me.

His image was so very clear in my mind at this moment. I saw him exactly as he was that year. *1979*. I was twenty-one. He was twenty years older than I, but he never seemed it, not ever.

Closing my eyes, I pictured him walking into the library downstairs. It was the night of my twenty-first birthday. Sebastian had thrown a fantastic party for me at Laurel Creek Farm, held in two flower-decked marquees in the garden. The food had been delicious, the wine superb, the band the best, transported for the occasion from Manhattan. It had been a glorious evening. Until Luciana had ruined it. She had been so nasty to me towards the end of the evening that I had been taken by surprise, thrown off balance, and horrified by the mean and hateful things she had said to me. Stunned and hurt, I had fled. I had come home to Ridgehill . . .

•

Tyres screeched, slewed to a stop on the gravel. A car door banged ferociously.

A split second later Sebastian stormed into the library, his body taut, his face white.

Forlornly, I stood by the french windows leading out to the garden. My handkerchief was screwed into a damp ball in my hand; tears were still close to the surface.

I had never seen him looking so furious before, and as I stared at him I realized he was terribly upset.

He stared back at me, and his eyes were chips of blue ice in his drawn face. 'Why did you run away like that? Like a frightened colt?' he demanded in a stern voice. Then he crossed the room in a few long strides and drew to a standstill in front of me, stood looking down at me.

I was silent.

'*Why?*' he demanded again.

'I can't tell you.'

'You can tell *me* anything, and you know it! You've been confiding in me since you were a little girl,' he said, his anger still apparent but under tight control.

'I just can't. Not about this.'

'*Why not?*'

I continued to gape at him stupidly. Then I shook my head emphatically. 'I can't.'

'Come along,' he exclaimed in a warmer, more cajoling tone. 'We've always been such good friends, you and I. Real pals. Vivienne, please tell me what happened, what made you bolt.'

When I said nothing, he went on swiftly, 'It was Luciana, wasn't it? She upset you.'

I nodded, but still I did not open my mouth.

'She hurt you . . . she said something . . . *contemptible*. Didn't she?'

'How do you know?'

'I know my daughter only too well,' he snapped. 'Tell me what she said.'

'Sebastian, I can't. I'm not a sneak.'

He scrutinized me a little more intently, and nodded to himself. 'Integrity's bred in the bone, especially in your bones. Do you know, Vivienne, you're the most honourable person I've ever met, and whilst I understand your reluctance to tell tales out of school, I do think you ought to confide in me. After all, the party was very special . . . to us both. Certainly giving it for you meant a great deal to me, and I was startled when you ran off the way you did, looking so upset. In all fairness, I think you should tell me exactly what happened.'

He was right, of course he was. Taking a deep breath, I plunged: 'She said I was a problem to you. A nuisance. That you wanted to be rid of me. She said you resented me, resented having to look after me . . . She said I was a charity case, a nobody, just the brat of one of your –' I stopped short, unable to continue, and swallowed hard.

'Go on,' he commanded in a clipped, rather brusque tone.

'Luciana . . . She said I was just the brat of . . . of one of your whores,' I whispered.

His mouth tightened in anger, and I waited for him to explode. But he did not. He merely shook his head looking dismayed, and muttered in a tight voice,

'She's a liar, my daughter. There are times, Vivienne, when I believe she's the cleverest liar I've ever known. A better liar than Cyrus, and that's saying something. But she's very often foolhardy, stupid in the lies she tells. As she has been tonight. Yes, Luciana is a little fool.'

'I'm not a nuisance to you, am I?' I whispered.

'Of course not! Surely you must know that by now. Haven't I proved to you that I care about you, care about your wellbeing? And what about your party? I wanted to give it for you, and I enjoyed doing so.'

I nodded. I could not say a word. It wasn't that I was tongue-tied. Rather, I was mortified and angry with myself. I realized how ridiculous I must look to him, how untrusting of him I must appear. He had never let me down, and I knew him to be a scrupulous man, a man of his word. Naturally he didn't resent me. Nor did it matter to him what my school fees cost, or my clothes and my upkeep. Money had never mattered to him. He had so much of it, he was almost contemptuous of it. Or so it seemed to me. Certainly he gave a great deal of it away. I had been an idiot, listening to Luciana. She had driven me away because she was jealous of me and my relationship with her father. All of a sudden I thought of her jealousy when we were children. She had manipulated me tonight; worst of all, I had allowed that manipulation.

He put his hand under my chin and lifted my face to his. 'Tears, Vivienne? Oh dear, what a sad ending to such a beautiful evening.'

'I'm sorry, Sebastian,' I answered, sounding choked. 'I'm so very sorry.'

Wiping my damp cheeks with his hand, he murmured, 'Hush, darling, hush, there's nothing to be sorry about.'

'I shouldn't have listened to her.'

'No, you shouldn't,' he agreed. 'And remember, don't pay attention to a thing she says in the future. Or anything Jack says, for that matter. He's not quite as bad as she is, and he's not a liar, but he can be devious.'

'I won't listen to either of them,' I promised. I took a step forward, looked up into those bright blue eyes which were so carefully regarding me. My own expression was intense. 'Please say it's all right between us.'

His sudden wide smile made his eyes crinkle at the corners. 'Nothing will ever come between *us*, Vivienne. We're far too close, and we always have been. We're friends for life, you and I. There's a very special bond there. Well, there is, isn't there?'

I nodded. I couldn't speak. I was overwhelmed by him, by the potency of his looks, his sexuality; and I was engulfed by my own erupting emotions. I wanted him to belong to me, I wanted to belong to him in the truest sense. I tried to say something but no words would come.

Looking momentarily puzzled, he gave me a questioning glance, his eyes narrowing as he said, 'You've got the oddest expression on your face. What are you thinking?'

I took another step nearer, leaned into him and

kissed him on the cheek. Finally finding my voice, I said, 'I was thinking how wonderful you are, and how wonderful you've always been to me. And I want to thank you for my birthday party. My very special party.'

'You're very welcome,' he said.

Holding my head on one side, I gazed up into his face. 'I'm twenty-one. I'm grown up.'

'You are indeed,' he said with a faintly amused smile.

'Sebastian?'

'Yes?'

'I'm a woman now.'

There must have been something unusual in my expression, or perhaps it was the inflection in my voice. But whatever it was, he stared back at me in the oddest way and for the longest moment, that puzzled look more pronounced. Unexpectedly, he took a step towards me, then he stopped abruptly.

We exchanged a long look, one so deep, so knowing, so full of longing, I felt my breath catch in my throat. Before I could stop myself, and almost against my own volition, I began to move forward, drawing closer to him.

It seemed to me that he watched every step I took, and then without uttering a word, Sebastian reached out for me. He pulled me into his arms with such fierceness, I was startled. And he held me so tightly I could scarcely breathe.

And everything changed. I changed. Sebastian changed. Our lives changed irrevocably. The past was demolished. Only the present remained. The present and the future. Our future together. We were meant to be, he and I. At least, so I believed. It had always been so. Our course had long been set. Somehow I knew this. Moving his head slightly, Sebastian bent down and kissed me. When he moved his tongue lightly against my lips, I parted them quite naturally. Our tongues touched. My legs felt weak and I held on to him tighter than ever for support, as he continued to kiss me in this most intimate manner. Without warning, he stopped, held me away from him almost roughly and looked down into my face.

I knew he wanted me as much as I wanted him. He had already told me so without uttering a word. And yet I detected hesitation in him.

I took hold of his hand and led him upstairs. Once inside the room, he let go of my hand and moved away from me, hovered in the centre of the floor. I felt, rather than observed, his uncertainty. After a moment, he said in a strangled voice, 'I came to take you back to your birthday party . . .' His voice trailed off.

'No! I don't want to go back. I want to be here. *To be with you*. That's all I've ever wanted, Sebastian.'

'Vivienne . . .'

We moved at the same time.

We were in each other's arms, holding on to each other. Eventually we drew apart. He struggled out of his dinner jacket, threw it on a chair, undid his bow tie as he walked to the bedroom door. With one hand he locked it; with the other he began to remove the sapphire studs from his evening shirt, and his eyes never left my face as he walked back to me.

I opened my arms to him. He came into them swiftly, held me close to him. He undid my zip and suddenly my evening dress was a pile of white lace at my feet. Drawing me towards the bed without a word, he pushed me down on it, lay next to me, took me in his arms once more. His mouth found mine. He caressed every part of me, his hands moving over me with such expertise I was soon fully aroused, spiralling into ecstasy. When he entered me a moment later, I gasped, cried out and he stopped, staring down at me. I assured him I was all right, urged him on, wrapping my arms around him. My hands were firm and strong on his broad back and I found his rhythm, moved with him, inflamed by his passion and my own urgent desire. And so we soared upward together, and as we reached the peak I cried out again, as did he.

We lay together silently. Sebastian's breathing was laboured and his body was damp. I went to the bathroom, found a towel, came back and rubbed him dry. He half smiled at me, pulled me to him, wrapped his long legs around my body and rested against me, still without speaking. But there was no awkwardness in our silence, only eloquence, ease.

I let my fingers slide into his thick black hair; I ran my hands over his shoulders and his back. I kissed him as I wanted to kiss him. It was not long before we made love again and we did so without constraint.

Satiated, we eventually lay still. After a while, Sebastian raised himself on one elbow, looked down at me. Moving a strand of hair, he said quietly, 'If I'd known you were a virgin, I wouldn't . . .'

I pressed my fingers against his lips. 'Don't say it.'

He shook his head. 'It never occurred to me, Vivi, not in this day and age . . .' His sentence trickled away and he shook his head, a little helplessly, I thought.

I said, 'I was saving myself.'

A dark eyebrow lifted above those piercing blue eyes.

'For you,' I explained with a smug smile. 'I saved myself for you, Sebastian. I've wanted you to make love to me for as long as I can remember.'

'Oh Vivi, and I never even guessed.'

I reached out, touched his face. 'I love you, Sebastian Locke. I've always loved you. And I always will . . . all the days of my life.'

He bent down and kissed me softly on the lips, and then he put his arms around me, holding me close to him, keeping me safe.

The phone was screaming in my ear.

I roused myself from my half-dozing state and my memories instantly retreated. Reaching out, I lifted the receiver, mumbled, 'Hello?'

'It's me,' Jack said. 'I'm coming over. With the newspapers.'

'Oh God, don't tell me,' I groaned. 'Lousy headlines, I've no doubt. And obituaries.'

'You got it, kid.'

'You're going to be besieged by the press,' I muttered. 'Perhaps you *are* better off coming here. Maybe you should bring Luciana with you, Jack.'

'She ain't here, Viv. She's skipped it, gone back to Manhattan.'

'I see,' I said and sat bolt upright. 'Well, that's not surprising.' Sliding my legs out of bed, I continued, 'I'll put coffee on. See you in about half an hour.'

'Make that twenty minutes,' he answered brusquely and hung up.

# Four

It was quite obvious that Jack was in one of his peculiar moods. His face proclaimed it to me before he had walked even halfway across the kitchen.

'Good morning,' I said, carrying the coffee pot over to the table and putting it down. When I received merely a curious, grunt-like mumble from him, I added sharply, 'So, we're maungy this morning, are we?'

The use of this word caught his attention at once, and he glanced at me rapidly. '*Maungy*. What does that mean?'

'You've heard it before so don't pretend you haven't. It was a favourite of Gran's. She often used to call you maungy when you were a snot-nosed little boy in short pants.'

Ignoring my acerbity, he said evenly, 'I don't remember,' and flopped into the nearest chair. 'And I don't know its meaning.'

'Then I'll tell you,' I answered, leaning over the table, peering into his face. 'It means peevish, bad-tempered, or sulky, and it's a Yorkshire word from the West Riding where my great-grandfather came from.' I paused, said in a lighter voice, 'Surely you haven't forgotten Gran's marvellous stories about her father? She never failed to make us laugh.'

'George Spence. That was his name,' Jack said, and then grimaced. 'I need a life-saving transfusion. Strong coffee. Immediately, sugar.' He reached for the pot, poured cups of coffee for both of us, and took a gulp of his.

'Jack, don't start the day by calling me sugar. Please. And so that's *it*, is it? You have a hang-over.'

'A beaut. Hung one on. Last night. When I got back to the farm.'

His occasional bouts of drinking were nothing new and had worried me off and on, but I had stopped trying to reform him, nor did I chastise him any more, since it was a futile waste of time. And so I refrained from commenting now. I simply sat down opposite him, eyeing the newspapers as I did. 'How bad are *they*?'

'Not as bad as we expected. Quite laudatory, in fact. Not much muck-raking. You're mentioned. As one of his five wives. Front-page stories. Obituaries inside.'

I pulled the newspapers towards me. Jack had brought the *New York Post*, *The New York Times* and the *Daily News*, and as I spread them out in front of me I saw that they were more or less saying the same thing in their different ways. A great and good man had been found dead, circumstances suspicious. All three papers deplored his death, sang his praises, mourned his passing. They carried photographs of Sebastian, all fairly recent ones, taken in the last couple of years. He looked wonderful – distinguished, handsome and loaded with glamour, dangerously so. But that had ceased to matter.

Skipping the *Post* and the *News* for the moment, I concentrated on the *Times*. The front-page story by the reporter who had spoken to me on the phone yesterday was well written, careful in its details, cautious in its tone and scrupulous in its accuracy. Furthermore, I was quoted verbatim, without one word I'd said being altered. So much for that. And certainly there was nothing sensationalized here.

I turned to the obituary section of *The New York Times*. The whole of one page was devoted to Sebastian Lyon Locke, scion of a great American dynasty, billionaire tycoon, head of Locke Industries, chairman of the Locke Foundation, and the world's greatest philanthropist. There was a simplified version of his life story; every one of his good deeds was listed along with the charities he supported in America, and there was a fund of information about the charity work he did abroad, especially in Third World countries. It had obviously been written some years earlier, as most obituaries of famous people were, with the intro and the last paragraph left open, to be added after the death of the particular individual had occurred.

Glancing at the end of the story, I was surprised to see only four names. I was mentioned as his former ward and his ex-wife – as if the others had not existed – along with Jack and Luciana, his children, and Cyrus Lyon Locke, his father, whom I'd completely forgotten about until now.

'Oh my God! Cyrus!' I cried, lowering the paper, looking over the top of it at Jack. 'Have you been in touch with your grandfather?'

'That old coot! He's more dead than alive. Rotting in Bar Harbor. In that mausoleum of a place. It ought –'

'But have you *talked* to him?' I cut in. 'Does he *know* about Sebastian's death?'

'I spoke to Madeleine. Yesterday. Told her everything. The old coot was sleeping.'

'Did you tell her to bring him here for the funeral?'

'Certainly not. He's too old.'

'How old is he?' I asked, frowning. Cyrus's age escaped me for the moment, but he had to be in his eighties.

'He was born in 1904. So he must be ninety. He's too old to travel.'

'I don't know about that . . . look, he should come, Jack. After all, Sebastian was his only son.'

'His last surviving son,' Jack corrected me.

'So what did Madeleine say?'

'Not much. As usual. Gave me her condolences. Talked about Cyrus being frail. But not senile. I can't stand her. She's the voice of doom. Even when she's wishing you well.'

'I know, impending disaster does seem to echo in her voice. And I'm sure what she said about Cyrus is true, that he's not senile. Cyrus Locke has always been a remarkable man. Quite remarkable. A genius, really.'

The phone rang, interrupting our conversation. I went to answer it.

Picking up the receiver, I said, 'Hello?' and then glanced over at Jack. Covering the mouthpiece with my hand, I murmured, 'Talk of the devil. It's for you, Jack.'

'Who is it?'

'The voice of doom with an Irish accent.'

'Hello, Madeleine,' Jack said into the phone a split second later. 'We were just talking about you. And Cyrus. Vivienne wants to invite you to the funeral, Madeleine.'

I glared at him.

Ignoring me, he listened to Madeleine for a few minutes, said goodbye and hung up. He lolled against the door jamb with a thoughtful expression on his face. 'I left this number at the farm. With Carrie. Mrs Crane's niece. She came in to help. Until her aunt gets back. Tonight.'

'Thanks a lot,' I said, and sighed, threw him a reproving glance. 'Tell me, Jack, why is it you have the need to put the burdens of this family on me most of the time? This funeral is your responsibility. Yours and Luciana's.'

'Forget Luce. All she wants to do is run. Back to London. To that twerp of a British husband of hers.'

'Isn't he coming for the funeral?'

'Who?'

'The husband. Gerald Kamper.'

'Who knows? But *he* wants to come. Grandfather.' Jack made a face. 'To the funeral of a son who loathed him. Can you beat that?'

'I knew he'd wish to be present.'

'*Merde,*' Jack muttered half to himself.

'It'll be all right, we'll manage well enough,' I reassured him. 'And it *is* only natural he wants to attend his son's burial.'

'*Only natural!* Don't be so *stupid*! There's nothing natural about Cyrus Locke. Just as there wasn't anything natural about Sebastian. *He* had no feelings. Neither does Cyrus. Faulty genes, I suspect. And the old coot's a monster like his son was. Better he remain in Bar Harbor. With his secretary-housekeeper-mistress-jailer. Or whatever the hell she is. I –' Jack stopped and grinned in that awful, ghoulish way of his, and added, 'We won't be able to keep him away. Cyrus wants to be sure.'

'Sure of what?'

'That Sebastian's really dead. That he's six feet under. Kicking up daisies.'

'Oh, Jack.'

'Don't *oh Jack* me in that pathetic way. Not this morning. You did it yesterday. All day. No tears either. I've had enough. You're just a sentimentalist, kid.'

'And you're the most unpleasant person it's ever been my great misfortune to know. You disgust me, Jack Locke. Sebastian's dead and you act as if it's of no consequence, as if you don't care.'

'I don't.'

'Talk about Cyrus being unnatural. *You* certainly are.'

'Chip off the old block, eh?' he laughed hollowly.

'You make me sick. Sebastian was a wonderful father to you.'

'Go and tell that to the marines! You should know better. He was never a father to me. Never cared about me.'

'He did.'

'I've told you before. I'm repeating myself. *He couldn't love anyone.*'

'He loved me,' I announced and sat back, glaring at him.

Jack laughed harshly, and there was a disdainful expression on his face when he exclaimed, 'Here we go again! He was crazy to get you into the sack. That I'll readily concede. He had the hots for you. Even when you were just a kid. He couldn't wait to get into your panties.'

'That's not true.'

'Sure it is. We used to call it the Gradual Seduction of Vivienne. You know, like the title of a play.'

'Who?'

'Luciana and I.'

'What do you mean? Why?'

'Because for years *we* watched *him* watching *you*. Fascinating. The fat cat waiting to pounce. On the little mouse. Waiting for you to get a bit older. Smarming all over you. Catering to your every whim. Flattering you. Showering you with gifts. Softening you up. Getting you ready for him. He couldn't wait to seduce you, Viv. We knew that. Luce and I. He did it as soon as he dared. As soon as it was safe. When you were finally twenty-one. The night of your twenty-first birthday party. Jesus, he couldn't even wait until the next day. The big seduction scene had to be that night.'

'Jack, listen to me, it wasn't like that, honestly it wasn't. Sebastian did not seduce me.'

Jack threw back his head and guffawed. 'Trust you to always defend him. No matter what.'

'But it's the truth,' I protested.

Shaking inside, filled with a fulminating rage, I vacated the kitchen. I left Jack sitting at the table drinking his third cup of coffee and smoking a cigarette. Seemingly he had started that bad habit again.

I went into the library and, seating myself at the desk, I began to read my piece for the London *Sunday Times* Magazine Section, trying to calm myself as I did.

And then automatically I picked up a pencil and began to edit, doing the kind of fine tuning that was important to me in my work as a journalist. I was so furious with Jack my adrenalin was pumping overtime. But my anger gave me the extra steam I needed, enabled me to push my sadness to one side, at least for the time being. Within two hours I had finished the editing job. I sat back relieved, not to mention pleased with myself.

When Belinda pushed open the door a few minutes later I was taken by surprise. She was not due for another hour and I gave her a puzzled look as I greeted her.

'I'm early because I thought you might need me for something,' she explained, walking over to my desk, sitting down in the chair next to it. 'I brought all the newspapers, but I guess you've seen them already.'

I nodded. 'Jack arrived with them three hours ago. By the way, is he still occupying my kitchen?'

'No, he's set up camp in my office, where he's talking on the phone, making the arrangements for the funeral and the memorial service.'

'I'm glad to hear it. I had the dreadful feeling he was going to start acting like the flake he can be at times. That he'd goof off, leave everything to me.'

'He's speaking with the pastor of the church in Cornwall right now,' Belinda explained. 'Talking about Friday for the funeral.'

'We agreed on that last night. And he wants to have the memorial next week. On Wednesday, to be exact.'

Belinda looked at me askance. 'I wonder if that gives us enough time? I mean, to inform everybody.'

'Honestly, Belinda!' I shook my head, smiling faintly. 'The days of the carrier pigeon and the tribal drum are long gone. They're extinct. All we have to do is give the announcement to the television networks and newspapers. Or rather, have the Locke Foundation do it, and the whole world will know within twenty minutes, I can guarantee it.'

She had the good grace to laugh. 'You're right. I sound like an imbecile, don't I?'

Paying no attention to this remark, I went on quickly, 'There is one thing you can do for me, Belinda, and that's field any calls from newspapers for me today. I really don't feel like speaking to the press. I need a little quiet time by myself.' I glanced at my watch. 'Lila's supposed to come to clean today, isn't she?'

'Yes, she is. But not until one. She had a dental appointment at eleven. She called me yesterday to say she might be a bit later than usual.'

'No problem.'

'About the press, Vivienne, don't worry, I'll deal with them. If they insist on talking to you though, at some point, shall I have them call back tomorrow?'

'Yes. No, wait a minute, I have a much better idea! If Jack's still here, pass the press over to him. And if he's gone back to Laurel Creek Farm, give them the phone number there. He's as capable of dealing with them as I am.'

With these words I escaped.

# Five

Upstairs in my bedroom it was calm, tranquil, with sunlight filtering in through the many windows.

Opening the french windows I went outside on to the wide balcony, marvelling at the mildness of the morning, wondering if this extraordinary Indian summer was nature's gift to us before we were beset by the violent winter weather typical of these parts. The Litchfield hills can be harsh, storm-swept and snow-laden from December through into the spring; in fact there was frequently snow on the ground as late as April.

But I would not be here in winter. I would be in France at my property in Provence. For a long time now I had lived in an old mill which Sebastian and I remodelled some years before, and it was there that I wrote my books, mostly biographies and other works of non-fiction.

Sebastian and I found the property the first year we were married, and because I fell madly in love with it he bought it for me as a wedding present.

The day we stumbled on it there was a piece of jagged wood nailed to the dilapidated old gate on which someone had scrawled, in black paint, *Vieux Moulin* – old mill – and we kept that name. A second primitive wooden board announced that the land and the mill were for sale, and it was those neglected acres of land that eventually became my beautiful gardens.

We enjoyed working on the mill together, Sebastian and I, and much of its restoration and renovation was inspired by his ideas as well as mine. Vieux Moulin and Ridgehill were my two real homes, one because it had been in my family for hundreds of years, the other because it was truly of my own creation. It didn't take much prompting for me to become quite lyrical about them both, since they were truly special to me. I divided my time between these two old houses; the one-room studio in New York was just a pied-à-terre, a convenient place to hang my hat and put my typewriter whenever I needed to be in the city for work.

When I had arrived in Connecticut in August, on my annual visit, I intended to return to Provence at the end of October. I still planned to do so. However, there was the matter of the autopsy report; I felt I couldn't leave without knowing the facts. On the other hand, the police would be dealing with Jack and Luciana, Sebastian's next of kin, and not with me. There was no real reason for me to hang around, other than my own anxiousness, my desire to know the truth about his death.

I wondered what the autopsy would turn up, what the Chief Medical Examiner's verdict would be. An involuntary shiver ran through me despite the warmth of the day, and determinedly I tried to cling to the belief that Sebastian had died of natural causes.

Pushing my troubling thoughts aside, I went and

leaned against the wooden railings and glanced around. The trees in the gardens below, and sweeping down the hillsides to the waters of Lake Waramaug, seemed more brilliant than ever, fiery-bright plumage silhouetted against a clear cerulean sky. Some leaves had already started to fall earlier than usual, I noticed, and I knew that by the middle of the month the branches would begin to look bare and bereft.

*Bereft*. That was exactly how I felt.

I wondered dismally if I were the only person mourning Sebastian. Certainly his children weren't grieving, and who could really know what an old man like Cyrus felt? He was, after all, ninety years old, with one foot in the grave himself. He had survived three of his progeny; now the last one was dead. How terrible it must be to outlive your own children, to have to bury them.

For a long time Sebastian had been the only remaining offspring of Cyrus Locke. As far as we knew, he was the only one living. There was a sister who had disappeared years ago, and what had happened to her was a genuine mystery, baffling to us all. She might be dead or alive.

Sebastian was the eldest child of Cyrus by his first wife, who had not survived the birth. There had been three other children by his second wife, Hildegarde Orbach Locke, two girls and another boy.

Glenda, Sebastian's half-sister and the closest in age to him, had committed suicide years before. His half-brother Malcolm had drowned in a boating accident on Lake Como in Italy, in questionable circumstances. And Fiona, the youngest sibling, was the one who had vanished into thin air seven years ago, lost somewhere in that nether world of drugs peopled by the addicted, the depraved, the pitiful and the homeless. The walking dead, Sebastian had called them.

Ever since her disappearance, Sebastian had been searching for Fiona and, as far as I knew, detectives in the employ of Locke Industries continued to look for the vanished woman.

The ancient patriarch Cyrus Locke aside, there were only Jack and Luciana left. And neither of them had children. How tragic it was that the Locke dynasty had so badly disintegrated into such a sorry state over the years; this great American family was almost finished, defunct. Malcolm Lyon Locke, the founding father, would turn in his grave if he knew. I couldn't help wondering what he would think of his descendants if he were alive. That canny Scotsman from Arbroath, who had set sail for America from Dundee in 1830 and had been a millionaire by the time he was twenty-eight, would most likely be disappointed. And I, for one, wouldn't blame him.

If Luciana continued to hate the idea of children and would not permit herself to conceive, and if Jack did not remarry and beget a child, then the Lockes truly would be extinct. Well, not quite. There were some cousins, grandchildren of Cyrus's brothers Trevor and James, but they were somewhat ineffectual, nonentities really, who kept in the background and lived off their unearned incomes.

There was a knock on my bedroom door and I

heard Jack's voice calling, 'Can I come in, Viv?'

'Yes,' I answered and as I went through into my bedroom the door opened and he rushed in, looking triumphant.

'I've done it!' he exclaimed. 'I talked to the pastor over in Cornwall. Funeral's set for eleven. Burial forty-five minutes later. At Cornwall Cemetery. Up the road from the church.'

'I know where it is,' I murmured. 'I was thinking, Jack, maybe we ought to ask a few people back to the farm for lunch –'

'*A wake?* Is that what you mean?' He looked at me curiously.

'No, of course not,' I replied, shaking my head swiftly. 'Not a wake. Just a simple lunch for a few close friends and family.'

He guffawed. 'That's a belly laugh! What family?'

'There's you and Luciana. And me. And your grandfather and Madeleine. You can't very well send *them* back to Maine without feeding them. Also, I'm sure some of your Locke cousins will want to come. And there will be a few of Sebastian's friends, people from Locke Industries and the Locke Foundation. His assistants, his secretaries, close colleagues.'

'I suppose you're right,' he admitted grudgingly, looking put out. 'We'd better make lists. Compare notes later.'

'What about the other wives that are still alive coming to the funeral? Betsy Bethune, for instance?'

'You can forget about Betsy,' he muttered. 'She's playing the piano in Sydney. She's apparently on some sort of world concert tour.'

'And what about Christabelle?'

'Good God, Christa! What made you think of *her*? I don't know where *she* is. Neither does Luciana. She's probably dying. Of cirrhosis of the liver. Somewhere. Don't invite her. Luciana'll have your guts for garters. She can't stand her mother.'

'What about the memorial service at St John the Divine?' I asked, changing the subject.

'Luce is responsible for that. She promised to handle it. Today.'

'Did she finally agree to have it there? You know how . . . how contrary she can be.'

'You call *me* a flake, *her* contrary. You're being pretty damn tough.'

'I am. It's about time somebody called it correctly.'

'Brutally honest today, kid. Is that it?'

'Yes. And you've been callous, cruel and cold-hearted about Sebastian. *Savage,* in fact. I find that hard to tolerate. You're impossible, Jack.'

'Okay, okay. Let's call it quits. Put our gloves away. Shall we?'

'My pleasure.'

He swung around and headed to the door, but paused on the threshold. 'Let's just get him buried. And memorialized. Then I can beat it. Go back to Paris.'

Instantly, a nasty retort sprang to my lips, but I bit my tongue, and I said in a cool, businesslike tone, 'You'd better have the public relations people at Locke Industries prepare the various announcements, and then we'll go over the material together.

Just to make sure they strike the right note. That is, if you wish me to help you.'

'I do. I've just spoken to Millicent Underwood. At the Foundation. She's already working.'

'*Amazing.*'

'What is?'

'Your sudden and inexplicable efficiency.'

'I want to get this out of the way. Over and done with,' he answered. Then he smiled at me.

I stared at him.

I took in that wide, genial smile, noted the complete lack of concern in his eyes, registered yet again the absence of sorrow, and I knew. He was glad. Jack was *glad* that Sebastian was dead.

This clarity of vision on my part, this sudden rush of knowledge stunned me. I could only incline my head before I turned away from him, walked across the floor to the small writing table in the seating area of the bedroom.

I stood with my back to him, composing myself. 'I'll start making my list,' I mumbled without turning around. I could not bear to look at him.

'See ya, Viv.' Jack slammed the door behind him and was gone.

I remained standing with my hands resting on the writing table, trembling, endeavouring to calm myself. And with growing horror I could not help wondering if Jack Locke had come back to America to commit a crime. Had he returned to murder his father? The mere thought of this sent a chill trickling through me.

*

And I felt chilled to the bone for the rest of the day as I went about my chores, trying to keep busy. I put my papers in order, filed my notes and labelled the tapes from my tape recorder. The moment I finished a story I categorized all the relevant research material and put it away for safety, and now I welcomed doing this. It kept my mind occupied.

At the end of the afternoon, not long after Belinda had gone home, I lit the fire in the den, made myself a large mug of tea and settled down in front of the blazing logs.

Not unnaturally, my mind was on Jack and that terrible thought I had had about him earlier in the day. I turned this over in my mind now. It was one thing not to care very much that your father was dead, but quite another be to actually *joyful* about it. Was Jack happy because he had detested Sebastian so much? Or was it because he was going to inherit all that money, all that power? I seriously doubted that power meant anything to him but certainly money did. And people did kill for money.

I sat staring into the flames, trying to squash my disturbing thoughts without much success. My mind kept turning on Sebastian's death and Jack's possible involvement in it. *Patricide*. There was nothing new about that. It was an old story, as old as time itself.

Suddenly I had the need to talk to someone about my worries; the problem was there really wasn't anyone I thought I could trust. Perhaps Christopher Tremain. Certainly he was the only person whom I felt absolutely sure about. Kit was kind and wise, and he had proved to be a good friend to me.

I was nothing if not decisive, and so I reached for the phone on a nearby table, lifted the receiver, began to punch in the numbers for France. Then I stopped, reflecting for a minute, and finally put the receiver back in the cradle. My natural caution had taken over.

There was no way I could call Kit. That would not be right, not fair to Jack, who had been my lifelong friend. We had grown up together and he was like a brother to me. And after all, it was only a suspicion on my part, nothing else. There was another consideration. Kit was not particularly kindly disposed towards the Lockes. He had taken an instant dislike to Jack the first time he had met him, and he frequently spoke of Sebastian in scathing tones.

I sighed, thinking of Kit. He was an American painter of some renown, and about two years earlier he had bought a property in the area where I lived in Provence. As we got to know each other better, we realized we had a lot in common and there was also a strong physical attraction between us. About a year ago we had become quite seriously involved with each other, and for some time now he had wanted me to marry him. I kept stalling. I loved Kit and we were compatible, but I wasn't sure I could make the kind of commitment to him he needed and wanted. I suppose I balked at marriage: I had had my share of wedded bliss. Of course he was disappointed, but this did not alter our relationship.

On several occasions, just before I had left for New York, Kit had made a couple of snide remarks about Sebastian, and he had even gone so far as to suggest that I was still in love with him. Foolish idea that was.

Now, on further reflection, I realized I could never talk to Kit about Jack. He was a good man, and very fair, and I was confident he would keep an open mind. But unburdening my worries to him was not a solution to my dilemma, and it would be a rank betrayal of Jack. Nor could I take anyone else into my confidence.

Better to keep my own counsel.

# Six

The night before the funeral I was restless. Sleep proved to be elusive. I tossed and turned for several hours before I finally got up in desperation and went downstairs.

Glancing at the hall clock, I saw that it was already three in the morning. Nine o'clock in France, and for a split second I thought of calling Kit. Not to confide my worries, since I had decided against doing that, but simply to hear a friendly voice.

In a way, I was a bit surprised he had not called me. He must have heard of Sebastian's death, and it struck me that the least he could have done was pick up the phone to say a few kind words to me. After all, Sebastian had not only been my husband for five years but my guardian as well, and surely it was obvious to my friends that his passing would have a distressing effect on me.

Marie-Laure de Roussillon, my closest girl friend in France, had phoned me yesterday to express her sympathy and ask if there was anything she could do, as had several other good friends in Paris and Provence.

On the other hand, to be fair and to give Kit the benefit of the doubt, perhaps he did not know.

Right now he was painting day and night in preparation for his next show, to be held in Paris in November. The last time we talked, about ten days ago, he had been hell bent on finishing a huge canvas which was the last of his works for the current exhibition.

When Kit painted in this single-minded and dedicated way, he did so in total isolation. The only people he saw were the French couple who looked after him and his house. He never read a newspaper, watched television or listened to the radio. He followed a simple but extremely disciplined routine: paint, eat, sleep; eat, paint, sleep, paint. Sometimes he painted eighteen hours a day, almost non-stop, and he continued like this for as long as it was necessary, until he had put the very last brushstroke on the canvas.

I suppose I could have phoned, given him the news myself, but I was reluctant to interrupt him. I was also conscious of his mild dislike of the Lockes. I didn't want to get a flea in my ear for intruding, disturbing his routine; nor did I wish to expose myself to some of his sarcastic remarks.

For a moment I toyed with the idea of calling Marie-Laure, just to chat for a while, and then decided against it. She ran the family château and vast estate near Ansouis, and early mornings were generally excessively busy for her.

Meandering through into the kitchen, I boiled a pan of milk, filled a mug with it, added a spoonful of sugar and went into the library.

Turning on a lamp, I sat down on the sofa and

slowly sipped the hot beverage. It had been Gran Rosalie's cure-all when I was growing up, and now I took great comfort from this childhood remedy. Perhaps it would help me fall asleep when I went back upstairs to bed.

I knew why I was restless, filled with such unprecedented unease. It was the thought of tomorrow. I was dreading the funeral; dealing with Jack and Luciana was not going to be easy, nor did I look forward to coping with Cyrus Locke and Madeleine Connors.

In my experience, families seemed to behave badly at large gatherings like funerals and weddings; I was absolutely certain Sebastian's funeral was not going to be an exception to this rule.

In an effort to relax I purposefully shifted my thoughts away from tomorrow, focused on my own immediate plans. And after only a few minutes I made a sudden decision. I was not going to hang around here any longer than was necessary. There was no real reason for me to do so. Once the memorial service had taken place in New York next Wednesday, I would leave. I would book myself a flight to Paris for that night.

I longed to be back in France, back at my quaint old olive mill situated between the ancient villages of Lourmarin and Ansouis in the Vaucluse. There, under the shadows of the Lubéron mountains, amidst my gardens, olive trees and endless fields of lavender, I knew peace and tranquillity. It was a world apart.

Certainly I am at my happiest there. It was the one

spot where I worked best over long periods of time, where I could truly concentrate on my writing. For some weeks I had wanted to get back to the biography of the Brontë sisters I was writing. Actually, it was vital that I did so; the manuscript was due at my publishers at the beginning of March, and I had only four months to finish it.

The thought of a long stretch of work over an unbroken period of time was suddenly rather appealing to me, and I found myself filling with that special kind of excitement which usually precedes a creative period for me.

As I settled back against the antique needlepoint cushions, feeling happier, thinking lovingly of my home in Provence, my eye caught the large photograph album on a bookshelf next to the fireplace. There were pictures of Vieux Moulin in it, and I had a sudden desire to look at them.

I rose and went to get it. Returning to the sofa, I opened the album, but instead of seeing the mill in Lourmarin, as I had expected, I found myself staring at photographs of my twenty-first birthday party in 1979.

I studied them for a brief moment.

How revealing it is to examine photographs after a long time has passed. How different we look, in reality, from the way we remember ourselves, years ago. Whenever I cast my mind back to that particular birthday party, I think of myself as being so grown up at twenty-one. But of course I wasn't. My image, captured here on celluloid, told me how innocent and young I was in my off-the-shoulder white lace dress and string of pearls. My dark brown hair was brushed back, fell around my face in a soft, unsophisticated pageboy style, and my high cheekbones were not as prominent as they are now. My wide mouth looked tender, vulnerable, and a very serious pair of green eyes looked out at me from the album, expectant and trusting.

I peered at my face more closely. Not a line, not a mark. I smiled to myself. Why would there be? I was very young, just a girl, inexperienced and untouched by life.

Sebastian was with me, smiling and debonair in his flawlessly tailored Savile Row dinner jacket, his gleaming white shirt punctuated down the front with those deep-blue sapphire studs which he had had such trouble removing later that night.

Here was Luciana, a bit plumpish in her pale pink taffeta, looking as if butter wouldn't melt in her mouth, her short curly hair a golden halo around her radiant face.

Even at thirteen there had been a certain lusciousness about her, despite the puppy fat. How much older she actually appeared to be in this particular shot, certainly much older than the little girl she really was at the time. And she had had the mouth of a thirty-year-old on her. I knew that only too well.

I regarded the picture of Jack for a long moment. I couldn't help thinking he looked like a little old man. His hair was untidy and his dinner jacket was rumpled; his whole appearance was decidedly unkempt. The expression on his face was surly, disgruntled, and with a start I realized he had not actually changed much. He was exactly the same as he had been at fifteen. Jack had never grown up, more's the pity.

Flipping the pages, I came to a series of photographs of Sebastian, which I had taken that summer, when we had been on vacation in Nantucket. My favourite was a shot of him standing nonchalantly on the deck of a sailing boat belonging to his friend Leonard Marsden. It was called *The Rascal*, and at the time we had joked about the name being so appropriate for Leonard, who was something of a playboy.

Sebastian's white open-necked shirt emphasized his deep tan, and he was so boyish, so carefree in his appearance that the snap took my breath away for a minute. His hair was tousled by the wind, his eyes very blue beneath the dark brows; he had been forty-one years old that year, but he certainly didn't look it. Not at all.

Nor had he looked fifty-six at lunch last week.

I had told him this at one point during the meal, and he had laughed delightedly, obviously pleased and flattered by my comment. And then he told me I didn't look my age either, going on to remark that I appeared to be ten years younger.

A bit of a mutual admiration society it had been that day. And I had reached out, squeezed his hand resting on top of the table, told him that we both seemed to be defying time.

My comment had amused him even more. 'You've always been my favourite, Vivi. I suddenly realized how much I've missed you. We've got to see each other more often, my darling girl. Life's too short not to spend some time with those one genuinely cares about.'

I reminded him that he was the one who was constantly travelling the world non-stop, whilst I was either sitting in New Preston or Lourmarin, and was therefore extremely easy to find. 'Don't worry, Vivi, I'll come and find you,' he had promised, smiling into my eyes. And I knew he meant it. But that could never be. Not now. It was too late.

Sighing sadly, I moved on, turning the pages, skipping over our winter holiday in Sun Valley, Idaho, that same year, ignoring the photographs of my graduation from Wellesley the following summer.

But I did pause for a second when I came to the section I had filled with our wedding photographs. Here I was in all my young glory, the sweet little bride in a short, white silk dress holding a posy of white roses, gazing up at her handsome groom through eyes that saw no one but him.

My adoration of Sebastian was so patently obvious, and so touching, I felt my throat tighten with the remembrance of our years together as husband and wife.

I leaned back, staring into space, thinking.

We were married in July 1980. The summer of my twenty-second year. That was just after I had graduated from Wellesley.

Once Sebastian and I had become lovers the previous year, I had not wanted to go back to college. Instead I had wished to stay with him, to travel with him, to be at his side all the time.

He would not hear of my dropping out. In no

uncertain terms, he had told me I must complete my education and graduate. That was when we had had our first really major row. Naturally, we had patched things up in no time, since neither of us ever harboured a grudge.

Still, I have no trouble recollecting the way we had locked horns about that particular issue, and with such ferocity we had both been shaken by my headstrong stubbornness and dogged determination to get my own way. He won. I lost. But Sebastian conceded that he had met his match. As for me, I was astounded at myself. I had not known I could be such a hellion.

Ever since our affair had started I had hoped he would ask me to marry him. Nonetheless, I was caught off guard and surprised when he did so. He had always gone on so alarmingly about the age difference of twenty years. This was something which had never bothered me in the slightest; he was young and boyish in so many different ways that I never thought of him as being older than I.

'Who are we going to get to give you away?' he had asked a few weeks before the wedding. 'By rights, I should do so, as your guardian, but since I'm marrying you I can't very well give you to myself, can I?'

We had laughed uproariously, and in the end we had decided that Jack should give me away. We had grown up together, he and I, and he was the next best thing I had to a brother.

The marriage took place at Laurel Creek Farm, in front of a local judge who was a long-standing acquaintance of Sebastian's. The ceremony was held in the beautiful walled rose-garden. It was simple and short, and once it was over there was a luncheon in the marquee on the lawn for the friends and family who had attended. Later that afternoon Sebastian and I had driven into New York City for dinner, glad to escape, to be alone, and married at last.

The following morning we set out for Africa, where we were to spend most of our honeymoon.

Our first stop was London, and Claridge's Hotel. Sebastian had booked a suite for us there, and we were staying for two weeks. He had certain business matters to attend to, and he had also wanted to get me rigged out properly for our impending African sojourn. 'You must have the right clothes, Vivi, you must be comfortable. We have to combat the heat, the sun, the constant travel, and the cold at night,' he had explained to me.

I had only been to London twice, both times with my mother and Gran Rosalie, and it was a special treat for me to be back there again with my husband.

I met many of Sebastian's friends; we went to smart luncheons and elegant dinners; we attended the opera at Covent Garden, and saw several plays in the West End. I relished every minute of it. I was madly in love, and so it seemed was he. We spent a lot of time in bed giving pleasure to each other. He made love to me most expertly, spoiled me outrageously, dressed me fashionably and showed me off proudly.

At one point, during the first week of our stay, Sebastian took me on our special shopping expedition for the appropriate clothing for East Africa, our next destination. He bought me light-weight cotton trousers, cotton safari jackets, short-sleeved cotton shirts, as well as four pairs of really good soft leather boots and several wide-brimmed felt bush hats for protection against the sun.

At the end of the two weeks in London we flew to Nairobi. This was to be our base for the three or four months Sebastian had planned for us to stay. And as long as I live I will never forget those months in Kenya. I was besotted with my husband, thrilled to be his wife, to share so many things with him, but I was also captivated by Africa the moment I set foot there. It was one of the most spectacularly beautiful places I had ever been to in my life, and I was awe-struck.

Sebastian knew Kenya extremely well, and it gave him a great deal of pleasure to show me his favourite spots, the areas he loved the most, and which had enticed him back time after time. And how truly magical they were.

Piloting a small plane owned by a friend in Nairobi, he flew me over the vast expanse of land that was the Great Rift Valley. This ran from the north to the south of the country, and was bounded by soaring escarpments so high and formidable they defied description. At times the Great Rift Valley, arid and desolate in parts, seemed to resemble a giant moonscape to me, and when I mentioned this to Sebastian he agreed and said he found it an apt description.

In contrast were the lush and verdant savannahs where we went on safari. It was here that we either drove or trekked, photographing the extraordinary wildlife – leopard, lion, elephant, buffalo, rhino, cheetah, gazelle, zebra, wildebeest and giraffes.

It was from the savannahs that Sebastian took me into the Maasai Mara Reserve, and once more I was stunned and overwhelmed by the beauty of the land and the big game animals roaming across their natural habitat. I felt transported back to the beginning of time, when the earth was young.

Moving on, we drove down to Lake Victoria at a leisurely pace, spent a week relaxing on its fertile shores. When we were rested and refreshed we struck out again, heading south toward the Tanzania border and Mount Kilimanjaro.

What an awesome sight that massive volcanic mountain was, and its elevation was so high that its twin peaks were lost in clouds and mists, only visible if one dared to venture upward, upward, and farther upward. Neither of us was a mountain climber, and so we hiked only a short distance up its easier, much lower, slopes.

We camped in the foothills of Kilimanjaro, and explored the surrounding area, and at night we made love under its giant shadow. The night skies were incredible. We would lie beneath a sky so clear, so smooth it looked like a high-flung canopy of perfect, untouched black velvet.

'A sheltering sky,' Sebastian would say to me time and again. One night, as we lay entwined in each other's arms, listening to the night sounds, staring up at the crystal-clear stars, he had explained: 'It was here in this land, under this same sky, that human life began eons and eons ago. This is the Cradle of Mankind, Vivi.' I listened attentively when he talked to me about Africa; I learned so much from him about that land, and about so many other things.

Following the sketchy, somewhat loose triangle Sebastian had mapped out, we moved slowly back up to Nairobi from Kilimanjaro, in order for him to show me the lakes and highlands of that particular area which he loved and knew intimately. Here too the land was extravagantly lush and spectacular, and I was more spellbound than ever. Oh, those green hills of Africa . . . how they captured my imagination and my heart. I was forever in their thrall.

Poring over the album, my eyes settled on some snaps that had been taken of us on safari. Here were Sebastian and I, standing with our arms around one another, underneath a vivid flame tree in Thika. I thought I looked rather smart in my safari jacket, trousers, and riding boots, my bush hat set at a jaunty angle.

Next to this I had placed an enlarged shot of the two of us flanking a Maasai herdsman. He was so proud and dignified, regal in his colourful, exotic tribal dress. The Maasai are tall and slender, a nomadic tribe who mostly herd cattle but are also renowned as fierce warriors.

And finally here we were, posing on the edge of Lake Nakura, one of the many soda lakes in Kenya, where the flamingos live. I stared hard at the pictures, marvelling once more, thinking how amazing that scene was. The flamingos were a moving, tidal wave of pink and flame, millions of wings spread across the vast dark waters of the lake. It was the most astonishing sight.

I have never forgotten those months in Africa with Sebastian . . . the memories are as fresh and vivid now as if I had been there only yesterday. In fact, it had been fourteen years earlier.

Flipping the pages rapidly, not particularly interested in our other trips to other places at different times, I came at last to the old mill in Provence.

For a moment, I was quite startled at the images of the dilapidated, tumbledown structure which I had captured so carefully on film. I had completely forgotten what a dreadful ruin it had been, truly an eyesore when we first came across it by accident.

After leaving Kenya, Sebastian and I had made our way to France. We had spent several months at the Château d'Cose in Aix-en-Provence, which he had owned for a number of years. We had all gone there for the summers in the years when I was growing up, when my mother was still alive, and they had been memorable holidays. It was Jack's favourite place; he felt at home there and because of his love for the château he had made a strenuous effort to learn French. And he had succeeded admirably.

During our travels around the Provençal countryside, Sebastian and I had stumbled upon the old mill. It was situated near an olive grove amidst rolling fields, just outside the centuries-old village of Lourmarin. It was secluded enough to be absolutely private, protected by plenty of acreage, yet it was not so isolated from village life as to make it boring.

Initially Sebastian purchased it for me as a wedding

gift, because I had fallen in love with it and the surrounding land, as well as with the picturesque village. However, once we started work on the reconstruction he began to recognize its great potential. He decided it would make a perfect home for the two of us in Europe, and he made the decision that we would live there for part of every year.

For some time Sebastian had been losing interest in château life and the winery, his charity work taking precedence. More and more, he left the running of the château and the land to an estate manager, and paid only short annual visits. Since he was as enamoured of the mill as I was, he gave the château, its land and winery to Jack that year as part of his inheritance. Jack had been thrilled, had spent every summer in Aix thereafter and had moved permanently to France once he graduated from Yale.

In these early photographs of mine, Vieux Moulin did resemble a heap of old grey stones, a formless relic that would defeat anyone, even the most stoical, who was hoping to resurrect it, to bring it back to life. As things turned out the project had gone well. Rebuilding and remodelling the original structure and adding two new wings had been one of the most satisfying endeavours I had ever undertaken. Sebastian had enjoyed it too, and we had spent some happy years there together until our divorce. And even afterwards he occasionally came back to stay with me when he wanted to escape the world.

Moving through the album quickly, I came at last to the photographs I'd wanted to see in the first place, the shots of Vieux Moulin finished.

How splendid it was, gleaming in the sunlight under a pale blue summer sky swept with white clouds. My favourite shot was of the house from a distance, viewed across the purple lavender fields at that hour in late afternoon when the sun is just about to set. It had an unearthly golden glow about it that was captivating. And next week, all being well, I would be going back there.

Holding this thought I closed the album and went upstairs to bed.

# Seven

Sebastian's funeral was a distressing ordeal for me in a variety of ways, and I was sorrowful and forlorn as I sat in the front pew of the little church in Cornwall.

Jack and Luciana were on one side of me, Cyrus Locke and Madeleine Connors on the other, and I felt wedged in amongst alien beings, even though they were the nearest thing to family I had.

It was not that any of them had said anything unpleasant to me, or behaved badly. Rather, it was their attitude which disturbed me. I detected a singular lack of grief in all of them, and this made me angry inside. But I bit down on that anger, kept a calm demeanour, presented an inscrutable face to the world.

I sat perfectly still in the pew, my hands folded in my lap, wishing this day had never come into being. We all had to die at some time or other, none of us was immortal, but Sebastian had died too young, too soon. And how had he died? That was the thing that worried me.

Surreptitiously, I stole a look at Jack, who was seated next to me. He was pale, had dark rings under his eyes, and his expression was as inscrutable as mine. Only his hands betrayed his nervousness.

I closed my eyes, tried to concentrate on the service; after a moment I realized I was only half listening to the current president of Locke Industries, who was giving one of the eulogies. My thoughts were on Sebastian's father, who was sitting on my other side.

I had expected Cyrus to resemble a cadaver, to be at death's door. After all, he was ninety years old, but he looked surprisingly fit to me. His white hair was sparse, thinly combed across his mottled bald pate, and the skin of his face was almost transparent, stretched so tightly over bones which were unusually prominent. Yet his eyes were bright, not a bit rheumy or vacant, and I'd noticed a spring in his step when he went up the path ahead of me earlier. A tall, thin man with a mind like a steel trap, that's how I remembered him, and he didn't seem much different to me today. Older yes, and frail, but not quite as frail as Madeleine had made out to Jack. When he had spoken to me outside the church a short while ago he had sounded lively and sharp. It wouldn't surprise me if Cyrus Locke lived to be a hundred.

It was Luciana who had startled me the most, when we had greeted each other as we alighted from our cars. I had not seen her for a couple of years and her appearance was appalling. She was so bone thin she looked ill, and yet I was certain she had no real ailments. Her extreme thinness came from excessive dieting, I was convinced of that.

If Luciana ever did get pregnant she would probably have a hard time carrying the child. But pregnancy was not a priority with her; she had constantly proclaimed to the world that she did not want children.

The sad thing was that she had lost her looks, lost the lusciousness which had sat so well on her when she was young, and which had made her so pretty and appealing. Her head appeared to be too big for her wasted body and her legs were spindly. It didn't seem possible she was only twenty-eight. She looked much older.

At least she was wearing black, thank God. She was so contrary, so determined to be different, to flout the rules, I had half expected her to show up in a bright red ensemble. One thing was certain: she had obviously not managed to persuade her husband to come to the funeral; or maybe she had not invited him. Gerald Kamper was noticeably absent.

Jack coughed behind his hand, and began to fidget; I roused myself from my thoughts and focused my attention on the person speaking. It was Allan Farrell, who had been Sebastian's assistant at the Locke Foundation. He spoke beautifully about Sebastian, and with enormous sincerity. I was touched by his eloquence about a man he had been devoted to, and with whom he had worked so closely for so many years.

About fifteen minutes later the service came to a close, and we all filed out of the church and headed for the cemetery at the top of the hill in Cornwall.

The impact of seeing Sebastian's coffin being lowered into the ground was overwhelming. I began to weep, finally understanding that this was the end. I would never see him again. He really was dead – and almost buried.

I heard a strangled sob, and swiftly I glanced at Cyrus standing to my left. He turned to me helplessly and I saw the tears trickling down his ancient cheeks, saw the pain on his face. I knew then that he was suffering as much as I was.

Taking hold of his arm I helped to support him, as Madeleine was doing on his right. He and I huddled together under the trees, shivering in the cold, but drawing a measure of comfort from each other in our mutual grief.

A sharp wind had blown up, scattering the leaves, whirling them around our feet as we walked away from the graveside and down the path to the cemetery gate.

I experienced an overwhelming feeling of sadness and a sense of finality as we left; a part of my life had come to an end. Nothing would ever be the same again.

At one moment I lifted my eyes, glanced up at the sky. It was clear and cloudless and a very bright blue, like his eyes had been.

Jack had heeded my advice and had invited everyone back to Laurel Creek Farm for lunch. Mrs Crane, on duty again in full force, had had the good sense to cater for lunch, and she had hired plenty of local help to assist her.

Madeleine led Cyrus into the drawing room and I followed closely behind. The three of us sat down near the fire, the old man reaching out eagerly to warm his hands in front of the blazing logs, once he was seated in a chair.

As a waiter approached with a tray of drinks, both Madeleine and I took a glass of sherry, and I turned to Cyrus and said, 'Why don't you have one too? It'll warm the cockles of your heart.'

He looked at me alertly, then nodded his acquiescence.

As I handed him my glass and took another one for myself, he murmured, 'My mother used to say that . . . when I was a boy growing up. It'll warm the cockles of your heart, Cyrus, she used to say.' He looked off into space, as if he saw something we could not see. Confronting ancient memories, perhaps, conjuring up long-dead faces, going back to his youth.

'To be sure and it's an Irish expression,' Madeleine volunteered, breaking the silence. 'It was one I grew up with myself. Back in Dublin.'

'I thought it was English,' I said. 'Gran Rosalie said it was, anyway.'

'Sylvia. That was her name,' Cyrus murmured. 'My mother's name was Sylvia.'

'Yes, I know,' I replied. 'I think I know every single name in the Locke dynasty. Sebastian told them to me, going all the way back to Malcolm from Arbroath.'

'*Dynasty*,' he repeated, and stared at me over the rim of his glass, his narrowed eyes flinty and sharp. 'Are you mad, Vivienne? There is no dynasty. It's kaput, gone, finished, extinct.' His glance sought out

Jack and Luciana mingling with the guests at the far end of the room, and he added acidly, 'And those two poor specimens are not likely to provide any future heirs in order to regenerate it.'

'You never know, Cyrus, you never know,' Madeleine soothed. 'Don't be so negative.'

'Who can help it?' he muttered, tossed back his drink, handed me the empty glass, and went on, 'Another sherry, please, Vivienne.'

'Do you think you should?' Madeleine fussed, and scowled at me. 'You'll get tiddly,' she warned, clucking to herself.

Giving her a scathing look, he said, 'Nonsense, woman. And even if I do, so what? I'm ninety years old. What can happen to me now that's not happened to me in the past? I've seen it all, done it all, lived several lifetimes already. Might as well get drunk. Nothing else to do.'

'Of course I'll get you another sherry, Cyrus,' I said, hurrying off with his empty glass.

When I returned with the refill, he thanked me, took a quick sip and said to Madeleine, 'I'm hungry. Can you fetch me something to eat, please?'

'To be sure and that's a grand idea!' she exclaimed, looking pleased as she stood up.

I watched her walking across the floor in the direction of the dining room, a plumpish, handsome woman in her late sixties, with a kind face and bright red hair that most obviously drew its colour from a bottle these days. I thought it curious that after fifty years of living in America she still had a pronounced brogue.

Once we were alone, Cyrus tugged at my sleeve, pulled me closer and, peering into my face, said, 'We loved him too much, you and I. Far too much. That was the trouble. He couldn't accept it. Frightened him.'

I gaped at the old man, startled by his words. 'Yes . . . yes,' I said slowly, 'maybe you're right.'

'You were the only one, Vivienne. You were the best. The best of 'em all. The only one who was any good. Except for what's her name . . . Jack's mother? She might've measured up one day.'

'Josephine,' I said. 'Jack's mother was called Josephine.'

'Breeding was there, but no stamina,' he muttered almost to himself, then drew himself up slightly and stared into my face again. 'You were the best,' he reiterated, nodding his head.

'Oh,' I said, and hesitated, at a sudden loss. 'Well, thank you for saying that. I'm not sure it's true, though. The –'

'Write a book,' he interrupted, tugging at my sleeve again. 'Write a book about him.'

'Oh Cyrus, I don't know about that –' I began, and paused, shaking my head. 'That's a hard one, a tough assignment for anyone. And he's certainly a tough subject to write about. There was always something so . . . so elusive about Sebastian, and I don't think I'm the right person anyway. I could never be objective.'

'Do it!' he snapped and his eyes fastened on mine.

'Do what?' Madeleine asked, returning to the fireside with a plate of food for him.

'None of your business,' he said, sounding irritated.

'Now, now, don't let's be cantankerous,' she murmured. 'Come along, let's eat, shall we?'

'Stop treating me like a child,' Cyrus muttered, glaring at her.

I rose quickly. 'I think I should go and talk to a couple of people . . . some of those I know from the Locke Foundation,' I said. 'Excuse me Madeleine, Cyrus, I'll be back in a few minutes.'

I made my escape, and headed towards Allan Farrell who stood talking to Jordan Nardish, a colleague from the foundation. I told Allan how moved I had been by his eulogy. Jordan agreed that it had been very touching, and the three of us stood talking about Sebastian for a few moments before I excused myself. Slowly I made my way around the room, acknowledging everyone I knew, talking to them for a moment or two, hoping to make them feel welcome. And we all shared our reminiscences of Sebastian, spoke sadly of his untimely passing.

I was on my way back to join Cyrus when suddenly Luciana was standing in front of me, blocking my way.

'You're something else,' she said, her dark-brown eyes hard, her expression frosty.

'I'm sorry, I don't understand what –'

'Don't give me that!' she exclaimed in a peremptory manner. 'You know very well what I mean. Waltzing around here, playing the grand hostess, acting as if you're the grieving widow. You've been divorced from him for over seven years, for God's sake, and married to someone else in between. Enjoying it though, aren't you? Being the centre of attention again.'

'*Enjoying it,*' I sputtered in astonishment. 'How can you say such a thing? Sebastian's *dead* and you think I'm *enjoying* this!'

'It's true, you are! I've been watching you. Sucking up to Cyrus, floating around, preening yourself,' she shot back, her thin face twisted with dislike. 'After all, it's not as if you cared anything about my father.'

I was furious. Drawing in my breath in anger, I stepped closer to her, gripped her arm tightly and stared hard at her. 'Now you listen to me and listen very, very *carefully,*' I said in a low, harsh voice. 'Don't think you can pick a fight with me, because you can't! I won't allow it! And I won't permit you to create a scene at Sebastian's funeral, which is what you're trying to do. As for caring about him, I've loved him all my life, and you know it. I will always love him, and my life's that much poorer without him in it, the world a lesser place now that he's gone. Furthermore, you'd better start behaving in an appropriate manner as befits his daughter. You're only making a fool of yourself, starting in on me. Try to show a bit of dignity, Luciana. And grow up!'

I let go of her arm abruptly and walked away quickly, leaving her standing alone.

Crossing the long hall, I went up the staircase. I was shaking inside and close to tears. I needed a few moments alone to compose myself.

# Eight

The door of Sebastian's upstairs study was ajar. I pushed it open and went in, glad to escape the crowd downstairs, and wanting to recover from my little skirmish with Luciana.

How hateful she was. She had not changed; when we were growing up she forever targeted me, tried to make my life miserable. Seemingly she still had that need.

Moving across the floor, I went to one of the windows, parted the lace curtains, stood looking out at the back gardens and the stables beyond. For a split second, in a flash of memory, I saw us out there in the stable yard – Jack, Luciana and me.

We were all astride our horses, waiting for Sebastian, who was mounting his gelding. Without warning, my horse Firebrand had bolted, almost throwing me, and would have done so if I had not managed to hang on tenaciously. Sebastian had galloped after me and had helped me to rein in the horse.

Only later that day did Jack tell me that Luciana, then eight years old, had been responsible. He had seen her giving Firebrand several hard prods with her riding crop, which had caused my horse to take off like lightning. I might easily have been killed.

Even though we were both shocked that she had done such a wicked and dangerous thing, and should be punished for it, we had not told Sebastian. We did not dare. He would have exploded, been harsh with her. It had been our secret, one of many we shared as children. Jack and I had been best friends, and he had never failed to stand up for me, or take my side. He too had suffered at Luciana's hands and, in consequence, he was forever wary of her.

Long ago I had come to understand that she had many problems when it came to her father, the chief ones being jealousy and extreme possessiveness. Even in death. That was quite apparent to me. Very simply, she had not wanted me to be present today. If the truth be known, she had probably not wanted Jack there either. Nor her husband.

Continuing to stare out of the window, I could not help thinking how sad and lifeless the stable yard looked. Once, it had been full of bustle, with horses, dogs, grooms, stable boys and children milling around. But for years now it had been deserted.

After my mother died in 1976, Sebastian's passion for horses had lessened. A year later he had started to sell them off, and he had given away quite a number. By the time we were married his bloodstock had dwindled down to almost nothing, and the few horses he kept were for us to ride when we went to the farm at weekends.

Also, around this time Sebastian's involvement with his charity work had increased to the point where it occupied him constantly. He had his hands full with Locke Industries and the foundation; we were travelling more and more, and doing good, helping others, had become his main passion.

Aldred, his manager of many years, died in 1981. After that everything changed at the farm. By the time we were divorced all the horses had finally gone. What was once a thriving stud farm of some repute had become just another charming old farmhouse sitting in the midst of hundreds of magnificent acres.

In the last few years, Mrs Crane had been in charge, acting as housekeeper when Sebastian was in residence, caretaker in his absence. By the time she took over, all the old outdoor staff had left, except for Harry Blakely, the arborist who looked after the trees. The gardens were tended by a team of part-time gardeners, who came from a local nursery to keep them properly maintained.

Turning away from the window, I thought: nothing ever remains the same, everything changes, but then as I stood regarding the study I had to amend this thought slightly.

The room was exactly the same as it had been the day I finished decorating it eleven years ago. Nothing had changed here. Crimson-glazed walls, dark-green plaid carpet, and English antiques which I had culled from different rooms in the farm still made the right statement, in my opinion. Sebastian must have thought the same thing, since he had left everything intact.

I walked through into the adjoining room, which had once been mine, and discovered that the little sitting room looked the way it had in my day. A melange of blues played against bright yellow walls, and the pieces of black-lacquered chinoiserie furniture remained where I had placed them so long ago.

Curiosity truly getting the better of me, I wandered into the master bedroom. I was not in the least bit surprised to see that this, too, was unchanged. Shades of *Rebecca*, I muttered to myself, thinking of the old movie, and wondered what Sebastian's last wife had had to say about my decorating skills.

But if I remembered correctly, Betsy Bethune had not spent much time at Laurel Creek Farm. She was a famous concert pianist and was usually performing on a stage in some foreign capital, while Sebastian had been thousands of miles away, giving aid to the poor and the sick in some Third World country. Which was why, in the end, they had divorced. They never saw each other, were never together, and Sebastian had told me at the time that it was pointless to continue the marriage.

I noticed a photograph of me in a silver frame, standing on an antique French chest of drawers between two windows. I went over, picked it up and looked at it.

It was an enlargement of a snap he had taken on our honeymoon in Africa. There I was, in my safari gear and wide-brimmed bush hat, smiling at the camera. Sebastian had written across the bottom: *My darling Vivi at the foot of Kilimanjaro*.

I continued to gaze at it for a moment, and then I placed it back on the chest, surprised but also touched that he had kept it there for all these years.

'You can have that. If you want,' Jack said, making me jump.

I swung round. 'My God, don't creep up like that! You gave me such a start,' I exclaimed.

He strolled into the bedroom, joined me in front of the chest. Lifting the photograph, he studied it for a moment, then handed it to me. 'Take it. It's yours.'

'Thank you. That's so nice of you, but are you sure?'

He nodded. 'I'd keep it myself. But I have better pictures of you. And Luciana won't want it.' As he spoke his mouth twitched, and he tried to suppress a laugh. He was unsuccessful and began to chuckle.

I laughed with him. 'She came at me like a spitfire a few minutes ago.'

'I noticed. What was it all about?'

'She accused me of playing the grieving widow.'

Jack shook his head slowly, looking bemused. 'She's off the wall. Pay no attention to her.'

'I don't. But she did make me terribly angry. I wanted to slap her. That's why I came upstairs, in order to get a hold of myself.'

'Thought as much. That's why I came after you.' He peered at me, looking concerned in the same way he had years ago. Clearing his throat, he added, 'Are you okay, kid?'

'I'm all right, really. It takes more than Luciana to do me in, as you well know. I suppose I am a bit vulnerable, though. And I was absolutely furious the way she tried to make a scene, today of all days. She's as maddening as she ever was.'

'You're right about that.' Jack opened the top drawer of the chest. 'There's another reason I followed you. Wanted to give you some of his stuff. It's in here. Choose anything.'

Taken by surprise, I said nothing. Returning the photograph to its place, I looked in the drawer with him.

'It's all mine. He left it to me.' Jack took out a small black velvet case, showed me a pair of ruby cufflinks. 'Would you like these?'

I shook my head. 'But thanks anyway. However, there is something I'd love to have . . .'

'Anything, Viv.'

'His sapphire evening studs . . . if you don't want them . . .' I looked at him swiftly. 'I'd understand if you didn't want to part with them.'

'I don't want them.' Jack began to open more of the small velvet boxes, finally found the studs, and handed them to me. 'They're yours. There's a pair of cufflinks. Somewhere. They match. Ah, here they are.'

'They're beautiful, thank you, Jack. It's so thoughtful of you.'

'I told you, take whatever you want. That goes for the farm too. It belongs to me now. Do you want his desk? Any furniture you had? When you were married.'

'No, no, and thanks again. It's lovely of you to offer, but the things you've given me are enough, and they really are so very meaningful to me.'

'Change your mind, let me know.'

We walked out of the bedroom through the main door, which led directly on to the upper landing. As we headed along the hall towards the staircase I paused, touched Jack's arm. 'I suppose you haven't heard anything from the police, have you? About the autopsy, I mean?'

'You'd be the first to know.'

'I don't understand it, Jack. Why is it taking so long to get the report?'

'The Chief Medical Examiner wants to make every possible test. To be absolutely sure. That's why he's taking his time. Nothing unusual. It's not even a week, Viv. Don't forget that.'

'Believe me, Jack, I haven't,' I said.

The following Wednesday morning, the memorial service for Sebastian was held at the church of St John the Divine in Manhattan. The whole world came – statesmen, senators, representatives of foreign governments and all those who had personally known and loved him, or had admired him from afar.

Luciana had done her work well. The church was filled with flowers; the eulogies were moving, touched me deeply. Beautiful things were said about the man who had done so much for the world. I sat with Jack, Luciana and her husband Gerald, who had flown in from London.

The moment the service was over, I took a cab to Kennedy Airport and caught the night plane to France.

# Nine

Whenever I returned to Provence I always felt a great sense of anticipation and excitement, and today was no exception. I could barely contain myself as I sat in the back of the chauffeur-driven car, watching the landscape slide by the windows.

We were travelling from Marseilles up through the Bouches-du-Rhône, heading for Lourmarin in the Vaucluse, and Vieux Moulin. I could hardly wait to get there.

I had arrived in Paris from New York this morning, and taken a flight to Marseilles, where the driver from the car company I used was waiting for me at the airport.

His name was Michel, and I had know him for several years. Michel was a pleasant, friendly and accommodating Provençal who was extremely well-informed about the whole area. He could be relied upon to supply accurate information about local towns, villages, ancient châteaux and churches, antique shops, stores and restaurants, although he only volunteered the information when asked. This was one of the reasons I liked him as a driver; he was never overly familiar or chatty, and therefore not in the least bit intrusive. I preferred to be quiet, to relax and think when I was being driven. I couldn't abide a constant stream of conversation.

I glanced out of the car window, thinking how extraordinary the landscape looked on this sunny and mild October afternoon. It seemed to be aglow in the legendary light of Provence that dazzles the year long, and which has captivated artists for centuries.

So many painters have come here to paint, attracted by this most spectacular light and the vibrant colours of the earth – terracotta running into burnt sienna and a mixture of browns, russets bleeding into gold, apricot and peach, bright marigolds, acid yellows and every shade of green. These were the hues that came startlingly alive under the purest of blue skies.

Vincent Van Gogh had splashed these brilliant colours across his canvases, thickly layered and richly textured. And in so doing he had created the first brightly coloured paintings of the nineteenth century and at the same time immortalized the landscape of Provence and himself.

Sebastian had been an avid collector of post-Impressionist art at one point in his life. He had loved Van Gogh's work, had owned a number of his paintings; I could not help wondering to whom he had left them in his will, and then decided it would surely be Jack who would inherit them.

Michel was heading further inland, and it was not long before we were skirting the town of Aix-en-Provence, which I knew well after years of spending vacations at the Château d'Cose. No doubt Jack would be arriving there next week; I suddenly realized I had no desire to see him. I had had enough of him for the time being.

The roads were virtually empty this afternoon and we were making good time. We were soon leaving the Bouches-du-Rhône behind and driving into the Vaucluse. This was the *département* of Provence I loved the most, and where I have lived, off and on, for the past fourteen years with both of my husbands.

One of the things which appealed to me about it was the diversity of its terrain. Fruit orchards, vineyards and olive groves gave way to flat fields, rolling hills and the mountain ranges of the Lubéron. Where I lived, just outside Lourmarin, the countryside was wonderfully colourful for the whole year. This was largely due to the enormous variety of trees, wild flowers and fruit which flourished and benefited from the longest growing season in France.

Of course it had other attractions as well. The village was charming and picturesque, and was known as the capital of the Lubéron. It was also considered to be a sort of cultural capital for the Vaucluse. Many painters, musicians and writers like myself lived in the village and the surrounding area, and it was once the home of the great French writer Albert Camus, who is buried there. Music festivals, concerts and art exhibitions were the norm the entire year.

As we drew closer to Lourmarin I opened the car window. The warm, sweet air wafted in, carrying with it the mingled scents of wild flowers, rosemary, fruit, lavender and pine, familiar smells I loved and which always heralded home for me.

We were moving through open, pastoral countryside now, land filled with bountiful orchards and vines, olive groves and my own lavender fields stretching almost all the way to the mill.

*'Voilà! Regardez, Madame Trent!'* Michel suddenly exclaimed, breaking the silence.

As he spoke he slowed the car and just ahead of us, silhouetted in a jagged line against the pale blue sky, was the little medieval village perched high on top of the hill.

'It's good to be home, Michel,' I said, my excitement increasing as he turned off the narrow dirt road we had been travelling, and headed up the long driveway leading to Vieux Moulin. Stately cypress trees, elongated, dark-green sentinels, flanked the drive on each side all the way to the paved courtyard which fronted the house.

The late afternoon sunlight was dappling the ancient stones of the sixteenth-century mill, and they looked as if they had been touched here and there with brushstrokes of gold. The many windows sparkled in the warm light, and the courtyard was filled with huge olive jars planted with vivid flowering plants that were cheerful and welcoming.

The big oak door stood wide open, and as we drew to a standstill in the courtyard Phyllis and Alain Debrulle, the couple who worked for me, came rushing out.

Phyl, a transplanted Englishwoman married to a Provençal, gave me a warm smile and a hug, and said, 'Welcome home, Mrs Trent.

'Hello Phyl, you can't possibly know how truly glad I am to be here.

'Oh, but I think I can,' she replied.

Alain shook my hand, smiled broadly, and told me I had been missed, then he turned to Michel, who was taking my luggage out of the trunk, and spoke to him in rapid French.

*'Ah oui, bien sûr,'* Michel said. *'Merci beaucoup.'* Looking at me, he added, 'Alain invite me to the kitchen for a coffee.'

'Yes, I know,' I said. 'Come and see me before you leave, Michel.'

*'Oui, Madame. Merci.'*

I hardly had a chance to catch my breath before the phone started ringing. It occurred to me that the whole of Lourmarin must know I had returned from New York. Clearly the village had its own kind of tribal drums.

When I picked up the receiver for the umpteenth time in the space of ten minutes and said *'Oui?'* rather sharply, I discovered it was my close friend Marie-Laure on the line.

'I'm just calling to say a quick hello, Vivienne,' she explained and then asked worriedly, 'but is there something wrong?'

'No, of course not. Why?'

'You sound . . . how shall I put it . . . a bit rattled.'

'I'm all right, really I am.'

'You had a good journey, I hope.'

'Yes, it was easy, Marie-Laure, after all these years I guess I've got it down pat. But can you believe it, the whole town seems to know I've arrived . . . I've already had a number of phone calls. I must be the big event of the day.'

I heard the laughter and warmth in her voice as she said, 'Yes, I think you are, *chérie*. It was Madame Creteau who told me, when I was at the boulangerie early this morning. She said Phyl had told her you were due around five o'clock this afternoon. I hope I am not calling at a bad time.'

'No, no, it's lovely to hear your voice. Still, I must admit the village tomtoms never fail to surprise me. They're the equivalent of bush telegraph in darkest Africa.'

'That's one way of describing it, yes,' she exclaimed, laughing. 'But you know how the locals love to gossip, to be into everybody's business, they just can't help it. They mean no harm. I'm glad you're back, I've really missed you.'

'I've missed you too, Marie-Laure. How's Alexandre? And the girls?'

'We are all well, Vivienne.' There was a moment's hesitation on her part, and then she said in a low, sympathetic tone, 'I want to tell you again how sorry I am about Sebastian. It is such a loss for you. I do hope you are not suffering too much.'

'I've been sad, of course, that's only natural. And in a way, I feel as if a door has been suddenly slammed on a period of my life that was very special to me,' I murmured, sitting down on a nearby chair, glad to talk to her. 'As you know, we didn't see that much of each other lately because he was travelling constantly, but we kept in touch by phone. Obviously his death has been a great shock to me. It was something I never expected, Marie-Laure.'

'How could you? He wasn't old, only in his fifties, and he always appeared to be so fit to me.'

'Yes, he was. I think I'll feel much better when I know *how* he died. Unfortunately, Jack hasn't had the autopsy report from the police yet.'

'*Really?* I thought you'd know everything by now,' she said, sounding surprised. Then she went on rapidly, 'There's been nothing more in the newspapers here. A few days ago they were filled with stories. The French press made his death sound most suspicious.'

'So did the New York papers. But what can you do . . . Anyway, to be honest the way he died *is* a bit of a mystery. I was glad to finally get away, it was all so upsetting. Of course, I had to stay for the memorial service, it was very important to me that I attend.'

'How did it go?'

'Very well. The church was packed. A lot of dignitaries were there from our government, and from foreign governments as well. And there were delegates from the UN, heads of charities, people from all over the world actually. The famous and the not-so-famous. It was very gratifying that so many people came to pay their last respects. But I crept away once it was over, picked up my luggage and went straight to Kennedy. I couldn't wait to get back to my normal life.'

'And I can't wait to see you. Can you come to dinner on Saturday night? It's just us, just the family. Perhaps you'd like to bring Kit?'

'Thanks, I'd love to come and I'll ask him later. I know he's been painting furiously, trying to finish the last big canvas for his show next month. I haven't called him yet, I just haven't had a chance,' I explained.

'You'll come by yourself if he's not available, but I'm certain he will be. Oh yes, I'm very sure of that,' Marie-Laure said knowingly, always the incurable romantic. 'I had better go, Vivienne. I'm in the middle of paperwork for the antique show next weekend.'

'And I must unpack. See you on Saturday, darling. Oh, about what time?'

'Around seven. *Ciao*.'

''Bye, Marie-Laure.'

We hung up and I went in search of Phyl.

Leaving my bedroom in one of the new wings, I walked along the hallway which linked this new part to the original structure. The latter was built entirely of large stones, ranging in colour from soft sand and golden tones to various pale pinks and deep greys, all exposed in the sixteenth-century manner.

Dating back to 1567 or thereabouts, the nucleus of the mill was a central area composed of four huge rooms which we had turned into the main living quarters. Virtually undamaged when Sebastian bought the mill for me, the interior rooms only needed repairs to their walls and ceilings. These were the rooms where the olives used to be pressed between gargantuan circular stones, and they were impressive. Immense vaults, several of which were thirty feet high, separated these massive spaces from each other and added to the grandeur.

A number of smaller rooms, forming the outer perimeter of the original structure, were in the worst tumbledown state when we took possession of the property. All needed to be rebuilt; this we did, turning them into a series of storage rooms, pantries and a laundry.

Throughout the mill we laid down new tile floors, put in many additional windows, doors and extra beams to reinforce the ceilings. Sebastian had insisted we use old wood and stones for our remodelling, either culled from the mill's rubble or bought from local builders; we also selected only those tiles and other materials which had an aged look to them. It was impossible to distinguish the new from the old, and the finished effect was awe-inspiring in so many different ways, but mostly because the infrastructure looked as if it had been there for ever.

The hallway led down three steps into the kitchen, which was the crux of the central area of the mill and part of an open floor-plan. The dining and living rooms flowed off it, as did the library. Although it was full of the most up-to-date appliances, it had great warmth and a rustic, country charm with its ceiling beams, exposed stone walls and terracotta floor. Adding to the cheerful Provençal mood were the many baskets, copper pots and pans, dried herbs, sausages and cheeses hanging from the beams.

An enormous stone fireplace was the focal point, its generous hearth holding a giant-sized basket of logs, polished brass fire tools and tall wrought-iron candlesticks, almost five feet high, topped with plump wax candles.

An old French farm table surrounded by wooden-backed chairs stood in front of the fireplace, and I went and sat down at it.

Phyl was standing near the stove and she glanced at me as I did so. 'A watched pot never boils,' she said, nodding at the kettle on the stove. 'I'm making you a cup of tea. I was going to bring it to you in the bedroom.'

'I'll have it here, thanks, Phyl. And then I'd like you to help me unpack, if you wouldn't mind.'

''Course not,' she answered, and glanced anxiously at the kettle again.

'By the way, Michel didn't leave, did he?' I asked. 'I haven't paid him yet.'

'No, he's still here, Mrs Trent. He drank a coffee, then went outside with Alain. To have a cigarette, I suppose.'

I nodded and said, 'Phyl, the house looks wonderful. You've kept it up beautifully. Thank you.'

She said nothing, but from the look on her face I knew she was pleased. Taking the kettle off the stove, she carried it to the nearby sink, poured some water out and returned it to the gas stove.

'A watched pot,' I reminded her, and reached for the telephone as it began to ring.

'Hello.'

'I can't believe you're home and you haven't called me,' Christopher Tremain said.

'Hi, Kit. Listen, I haven't called anyone yet. And you *are* at the top of my list. You just beat me to it by a few minutes.'

'That's good to know. How are you? Did you have a good trip?'

'I'm well. And the trip was quick, easy.'

'Then you're up to having dinner tonight? At least I hope you are.'

'I'd love to see you, I really would. But I need to unpack, get settled in, get my papers organized, the usual stuff. You know what it's like. And after all, I have been away for almost three months.'

'Don't I know it, darling. But all right, I'll let you off the hook tonight.'

'Marie-Laure's invited us to dinner on Saturday.'

'That's great, you've got a date. But what about tomorrow? Can we have supper?'

'Yes, that'll be nice. How's the painting going? Did you finish your last canvas?'

'I did. On Tuesday night, or rather, in the middle of Wednesday morning. I'm feeling a bit done in, but I'll be up and running by Saturday.'

'Are you sure about supper tomorrow? Maybe you're too exhausted.'

'I'm not going to cook it, just eat it. Listen, Vivienne . . .'

'Yes, Kit?'

'I just heard about Sebastian. His death. This morning on CNN. They had some coverage of his memorial service. I'm sorry. Are you holding up?'

'Yes, I'm fine, thanks.'

'You must think I'm thoughtless, not calling you,

but I didn't know. I've been leading an isolated existence.'

'You don't have to explain, I realized you were probably holed up in your studio, going at it around the clock.'

'Are you sure you're all right?'

'Yes, I'm positive. What time do you want to have supper tomorrow?'

'You call it, Viv.'

'About seven-thirty, is that okay with you?'

'Yes. I'll come and pick you up and you can give me a drink, before I take you out on the town.'

# Ten

'Mrs Trent, you have a phone call,' Phyl said, walking down the steps that led out from the library to the swimming pool.

'Not another one,' I groaned, pushing myself into a sitting position on the garden chaise. 'I never knew I was so popular with so many people in Lourmarin.'

'It's Mr Locke,' she said, coming to a stop next to me. 'He's calling from New York, he said.'

As she spoke I glanced at my watch. It was three-thirty on Friday afternoon and therefore nine-thirty in the States. Taking the cellular phone from her, I pressed line one. 'Hello, Jack, I thought you'd be in Paris by now.'

'Hi, Viv. I will be. Later today. I'm taking the French Concorde. At one-thirty. How is it there? Warm and sunny, yes?'

'Correct. I'm sitting near the pool relaxing.'

'Viv, I've heard from the police. Detective Kennelly called me. Ten minutes ago. I just hung up from him. The autopsy report's in.'

I sat bolt upright, swinging my legs off the chaise, gripping the phone that much tighter as I did. 'What does it say? What's the conclusion?' I asked urgently.

'Suicide. Sebastian committed suicide. He died of

barbiturate poisoning. Complicated by an excessive amount of booze.'

For a fraction of a second I was stunned. Then I gasped, 'I don't believe it! That can't be! Sebastian would never commit suicide. There must be some mistake.'

'Afraid not. That's the Chief Medical Examiner's verdict. That he killed himself.'

'But – but – couldn't it have been accidental?' I suggested, grasping at straws.

'No, Viv. It wasn't an accident. There was too much of everything in his system. The Medical Examiner did innumerable tests. They've ruled out everything else.'

'What about the gash on his forehead?'

'That didn't kill him. I just told you. Barbiturates and alcohol did him in. That's what Kennelly said.'

'How can the Medical Examiner be so sure it wasn't an accident?' I demanded, my voice rising in my anxiety.

'*I just told you*. There was far too much of everything in his bloodstream, brain, tissue and organs. The stuff had to have been taken on purpose. You can't argue with a toxicology report. Facts are facts, they don't lie.'

'But he'd never kill himself. Not Sebastian,' I protested, truly convinced of this and therefore still disbelieving.

'How can you say that!' Jack snapped impatiently. 'You've not been married to him for years, Vivienne. Nor spent much time with him lately. How could you know what was in his mind!'

'He was happy,' I blurted out. 'Very happy that day –'

I stopped short, suddenly realizing I did not wish to say any more than this.

'Sebastian happy!' Jack spluttered. 'Come off it! He was never happy. Not in his entire life. He was always morose, sombre. On the edge. He was a killjoy and a spoilsport. I ought to know. I lived through enough of his moods.'

I felt a rush of cold anger sweep through me and I wanted to berate him, tell him he was wrong, tell him that he was being cruel, judgemental and unfair. But I held myself in control, and said steadily, in a contained voice, 'He seemed happy the day we had lunch at Le Refuge, that's all I'm trying to say, Jack.'

'That was on Monday. By Saturday he'd taken his life.'

'So that's when the Medical Examiner set the time of death?'

'Yes. Saturday night. And why Sebastian did it we'll never know. All *I* know for *sure* is that Chief Medical Examiners don't make mistakes.'

'I just can't believe it,' I repeated.

Jack said, 'Believe it. That's what happened. It was suicide.'

'And so bang goes your theory about an intruder,' I remarked.

'And yours about a heart attack or a stroke,' he shot back.

'Jack, how do the police explain the mess in the library? The overturned lamp and chair, the scattered papers?'

'They don't. Because they can't. They weren't there.'

'But they must have some sort of theory, surely? They're used to this kind of investigation.'

'They don't speculate. They only deal in facts, Vivienne.'

'He must have staggered around,' I said, thinking out loud. 'Before he went outside. I wonder why Sebastian went outside, went to the lake, Jack?'

'I've no idea. These are imponderables. We'll never know more than we know now. Listen, I gotta go. I gotta call Luciana. Fill her in. Get to the airport. See ya, kid.'

He was gone, as usual, before I could even say goodbye. I clicked off the cellular phone, lay back on the chaise and closed my eyes. My mind was racing.

I was furious with Jack. His attitude about his father appalled me. Since Sebastian's death he had not been able to speak about him without sounding critical or churlish. I found this disrespectful, insulting to Sebastian's memory, but there was no point in taking Jack to task about it. My words would be falling on deaf ears.

Only a few minutes ago he had spoken to me about Sebastian's death as if referring to a stranger, without emotion or feeling. Or concern for my feelings, either. He was cold and heartless, and this troubled me.

Back in Connecticut, just before the funeral, I had wondered if Jack had killed his father. But I had dismissed that idea. Now I wondered again if Jack *had* done it, after all. Had he given his father doctored drinks, alcohol laced with barbiturates? A deadly mix, we all knew that. Did doctored drinks add up to the perfect murder?

I sat up with a jolt, impatient with myself, and squashed this horrendous thought. I doubted Jack had killed his father. He was difficult, even hateful at times, but he was not wicked.

I also doubted that Sebastian had committed suicide. He had no reason to do so; he had everything to live for. I knew this for a fact. I knew it because Sebastian had told me that himself, he had told me he had never been happier, that he was about to start a new life, begin his life all over again.

Lying back on the chaise, closing my eyes, I reconstructed our lunch together at Le Refuge, relived the last time I had seen Sebastian Locke alive.

I was early. It was only twenty minutes past twelve. Nevertheless I increased my pace as I hurried up Lexington Avenue, heading for Le Refuge on Eighty-Second Street. I was due to meet Sebastian at twelve-thirty and I wanted to get there before he did.

I succeeded, but only by a few minutes.

I just had time to sit down at the table and catch my breath before he walked in, as punctual as he always was.

A few heads turned to look at him discreetly as he headed towards me. And even if the other patrons didn't know who he was, they could not help but notice him. He was tall and distinguished and he had the most glamorous aura about him.

At fifty-six Sebastian was as slender and athletic-looking as he'd always been, and I thought he was more handsome now than ever, with his deep tan and the wings of white in his dark hair. He wore a grey pinstripe suit, his white shirt set off by a pale-grey silk tie, and as always he was immaculate from the top of his well-groomed head to the tips of his well-polished shoes.

His face was serious, but his bright blue eyes were smiling as he arrived at the table. Bending over me, he squeezed my shoulder and kissed me on both cheeks before sitting down.

'Vivi, my darling girl, I'm so glad to see you.'

'I am too,' I said, smiling across the table at him.

Then we both started to talk at once, and stopped instantly, laughing at ourselves.

'It's been months, Vivi, I feel I have so much to tell you,' he said, reaching out, grasping my hand, holding it tightly in his.

'Almost a year,' I remarked.

'Is it that long?' A dark brow shot up in surprise. 'Too long then, darling. We must rectify that at once, not let it happen in future. But, thank God for the telephone.'

'Yes, thank God for it, but you don't use it as often as you used to, or should,' I murmured, and added swiftly, 'however, that's not a reproach.'

'I know it isn't. And you're right. You'll consider this is a poor excuse, but I have been in some out-of-the-way places. Not to mention trouble spots, and phoning can be difficult at times. As you well know, having been there with me on many occasions.'

'You've been doing wonderful work, Sebastian, cutting through all that red tape in so many countries, getting so much done. You've worked miracles lately,' I praised.

'I've had a lot of good help. And we've been able to bring aid to people directly, which has been a breakthrough. Getting food, medicine and medical supplies to those who are truly in need is gratifying. We've also managed to move in qualified doctors and nurses. Mind you, I'm afraid I've been creating more ripples than usual, if not indeed waves, wherever I go. I've antagonized a lot of people, Vivi, by refusing to deal with disintegrating governments and bureaucratic nincompoops who are quite frequently corrupt.'

'Nothing's changed,' I said, shaking my head. 'You're still a rebel at heart.'

'Am I?' He threw me a swift glance then laughed lightly. 'I like to think of myself as being merely practical and efficient, a good businessman, Vivi, even when doing my charity work. I want to get things done the easiest way, the fastest way, but then you know that.'

The waiter came and Sebastian ordered a bottle of Veuve Clicquot, which is what he usually drank, and then he went on, 'But enough of me. What's been happening with you since you came back? The last time we spoke was in July, when you were still at Vieux Moulin.'

'Not much really. Work mostly. I've just completed a story on the shift to the right in American politics, for the London *Sunday Times*, and I've almost finished my book on the Brontë sisters. I was in Yorkshire in early August, visiting Haworth, and then I made my way here, as I always do in summer. To escape the –'

'"Tourists in Provence, and to reacquaint myself with my roots",' he finished for me, his eyes crinkling at the corners with hidden laughter.

'You do know me well,' I murmured, thinking how accurately he had quoted me. But then how often had I said those words to him?

'Don't I just, darling. Your patterns don't change much, Vivienne.'

'Neither do yours.'

'I suppose not.'

The champagne was brought to the table, the bottle shown to him, opened and poured.

We clinked our glasses and Sebastian said, 'Where are you going to be spending Christmas?'

'Provence, I think.'

'Oh, that's a pity.'

'Why?'

'It would have been nice to see you over the holidays. I'm planning to be at the farm in Connecticut.'

'That's a change, you're usually travelling the world, doing good somewhere, not celebrating,' I exclaimed, taken by surprise at his announcement.

'I felt like an old-fashioned Christmas,' he said, smiling at me. 'The kind we used to have years ago, when you and Jack and Luciana were still children.' He shrugged his shoulders lightly, and went on, 'Don't ask me why.'

'Nostalgia, perhaps,' I suggested, eyeing him thoughtfully. 'We all suffer from that at different times.'

'True. Let's order, shall we? Before we forget to do so. As we so often have in the past.'

I laughed, remembering the times we had been so busy talking we had forgotten all about eating. After looking at the menus we both decided to have grilled sole, and once the food had been ordered Sebastian started to talk to me about India at great length. I had been there with him many years ago to visit Mother Teresa, but we had only stayed in Calcutta briefly.

As I listened to him, as usual intrigued by everything he had to say, I realized there was something different about him today. It came to me after a moment or two. *He was lighthearted*. In the past few years, since our divorce, he had always seemed morose and gloomy whenever we met. It had often struck me that he was burdened down with worry – about the state of the world, his charity work, the Locke Foundation, Locke Industries, his problematical children. *Heavy-hearted*. Today he was exactly the opposite.

Without thinking twice and before I could stop myself, I blurted out, 'You're happy! That's what it is, Sebastian. You're happier than I've seen you for years and years.'

He sat back in the chair and gave me an appraising look. 'You always were the most perceptive, Vivienne. And yes, I *am* happy. Very happy. Like I've never been –'

He broke off, and glanced away.

'What's the reason?' I asked.

He was silent for a few seconds and then he slowly

turned his head and gave me the most penetrating of looks.

It was then he told me.

Slowly, he said, 'I think I can explain without hurting you, or upsetting you, Vivi. I just said you are perceptive, but you're also an intelligent, understanding and compassionate woman. Yes . . . I know I can tell you this without causing you pain.'

'We've always been able to tell each other anything and everything,' I reminded him. 'How often you used to say that to me when I was growing up. And afterwards.'

'You know, Vivi, when you were a child you touched my heart. And when you were twenty-one you captivated me . . . I was entranced by you. That's why I married you.'

'I thought you married me because you loved me,' I said so quietly my voice was hardly audible.

'I did love you, I do love you, Vivi, and I always will. You are the most special person to me. But when we married I think I was simply entranced by that child who had touched my heart and who had grown up to be the most lovely young woman. And who so adored *me*. Perhaps that's one of the reasons our marriage was always so explosive . . . you were too young really, far too inexperienced, and so very vulnerable. I was too old for you. But I wanted it to work, God knows I did.'

'So did I. And although our marriage *was* fraught, it was very passionate, you can't deny that, can you?' I challenged.

'I don't! My God, of course I don't, you should know better than that.'

'What are you trying to tell me, Sebastian? That you've fallen in love again?'

He leaned across the table and his face was suddenly so glowing, so alive, so youthful even, that I was momentarily thrown off balance.

He said, 'Yes, I've fallen in love, Vivi. With someone who totally amazes me, astounds me. And I love her in a way I've never loved any other woman, or *anyone*, for that matter.' There was a slight hesitation, and he added gently, 'I loved you in a different way. The love I feel for this woman is something . . . something of another world, something that I can't explain. It's the most extraordinary experience of my life. I've never felt quite like this ever before and I know I won't feel this way ever again.'

'She overwhelms you sexually,' I murmured, believing this might well be the truth. He was a very sensual man.

'She does. Very much so. But it's more than that. Much more. I feel absolutely complete and whole when I'm with her. It's as if part of me was missing until she came into my life. She seems to balance me in so many ways.' He paused and gazed at me, reached for my hand. 'I'm sorry, Vivi, I don't mean to hurt you.'

'You're not,' I reassured him and I meant what I said. 'I know you loved me, well, love me, in a *certain way*, I understand that. You love her *differently*, that's all. Nothing's ever the same with other people. I know. I was married to Michael and it was quite a different marriage from ours. I know our marriage didn't work out for many, many reasons. But at least we had those five years. On the other hand, your marriage to Betsy Bethune blew up in no time at all. Relationships are always different.'

'That was no marriage! It was not like ours!' he exclaimed. 'Betsy was no wife to me.'

'I realize that.'

'Have I upset you?'

I shook my head and asked, 'Who is she?'

He smiled, and it was such a beatific smile I was startled again; his demeanour was so out of character today. And I couldn't help thinking that whoever she was she must be someone unique.

'You'll meet her,' he ventured. 'And you'll like her, love her even. And she'll love you, I know that. You'll be great friends.'

'But who is she?' I pressed.

'She's a doctor. A scientist, actually. Very brilliant.'

'How old is she?'

'About your age. No, a bit younger, by a couple of years.'

'American?'

'No . . . I met her in Africa.'

'Is she African?' I asked.

'No, she's European. I'm going to be meeting her in Africa quite soon; she's working on a project there. We're going to India together, then we're coming here for Christmas. That's why I hoped you'd be here, to meet her. However, I hope we can get together in France in the new year. Can I bring her to meet you at Vieux Moulin?'

'Of course.'

'And if it's not too much to ask of you, I hope you'll be present at our wedding. We want to be married in the spring. You will be there, won't you, darling? I want you there.'

Flabbergasted though I was, I found myself agreeing. 'Of course, Sebastian. You know I'll be there, if that's what you want.'

'I do, Vivi, I do.'

I sat up, blinking in the sunlight and pushing my hair out of my eyes. And I asked myself the most potent of questions: *Why would Sebastian Locke commit suicide when he was about to marry the love of his life?*

# Eleven

Half an hour later I was sitting with my friend Marie-Laure on the terrace of her home, Château de Beauvais, telling her about the autopsy report.

She listened patiently, as attentive as she always was to my words, and when I had finished she said nothing, simply sat there, digesting what I had told her.

Finally, after a few minutes, she murmured softly, '*Mon Dieu*, how terribly sad. What a waste.'

'Yes, it is. And I can't help wondering why Sebastian would commit suicide when he was about to marry the love of his life.'

She stared at me in surprise. '*He was?* How do you know?'

'He told me,' I answered, and proceeded to repeat the conversation Sebastian and I had had the day we lunched together in New York.

'You say he was euphoric that Monday,' Marie-Laure murmured thoughtfully, 'yet five days later, on Saturday night, he killed himself. It is obvious, is it not, Vivienne? Something must have happened during the course of that week, and whatever it was caused him to do this most terrible thing to himself.'

'Or he was murdered,' I said.

'You don't mean that, do you?' She looked at me askance.

'Well, it's a possibility, isn't it? According to the autopsy report he was full of barbiturates and alcohol. But someone could have doctored his drinks – the way they make a Mickey Finn.'

'What is that? A Mickey Finn?' she asked, sounding puzzled.

'It's a combination of alcohol and chloral hydrate, and it usually knocks people out, makes them unconscious. It can also be poisonous.'

'So, you think Sebastian was given this . . . Mickey Finn?'

'No, no, you're misunderstanding me, Marie-Laure,' I said quickly, and explained, 'a Mickey Finn is not necessarily lethal, and anyway I was just using that as an example. What I'm trying to say is that he might have consumed a quantity of alcohol that had been tampered with, you know, laced with barbiturates.'

'Now I see what you are getting at. But who would want to do that? Who would want to murder Sebastian?'

'That's the problem, I don't really know,' I answered glumly. 'Although he *has* antagonized a lot of people over the years, and even quite recently. He told me that himself the last time I saw him.'

'Who did he antagonize?' she asked.

'Mainly foreign governments. Or rather, *members* of foreign governments, people whom he suspected of being overly bureaucratic, who were slowing down his aid programmes with what he considered to be their unnecessary red tape. Or those whom he believed to be corrupt. He just swept them to one side in that imperious way of his and plunged ahead, doing his own thing. In the process he performed innumerable miracles, of course. He may have been a bit of a maverick, and stubborn, independent, wilful and domineering, but he did get things done. Unlike anyone else ever has.'

'I understand what you're saying, *chérie*. But surely you don't *really* believe a foreign government would send somebody to *kill* Sebastian, do you?'

'I don't know . . . Maybe. More peculiar things happen every day of the week. We certainly read about them in the papers, see a variety of bizarre incidents on the television news.'

'It would be a bit risky, I think,' Marie-Laure replied, nodding to herself. 'After all, he was the world's greatest philanthropist. One of the most prominent men alive today. His killer, or killers, would be condemned by the entire world.'

'Terrorists are condemned, but that doesn't stop terrorism,' I pointed out. 'And besides, killers have to be caught to be condemned.'

'Very true,' Marie-Laure agreed, and rose. She walked up and down the terrace at the back of the château, deep in thought.

I sat watching her, thinking what a truly good friend she had always been to me. When I had phoned her earlier, to say I wanted to come over to discuss a problem, she had dropped everything she was doing in order to receive me, to listen to me.

She was a small woman, diminutive really, and

although she was forty she was like a young girl with her slender figure, dark, bobbed hair and fringe, and an exceptionally pretty face. She was also one of the most capable people I knew, running the château and its lands, which she had inherited from her father, being a supportive wife to Alexandre and a devoted mother to her two children, François and Chloé.

She and I had met thirteen years ago, when Sebastian and I were first working on the old mill, and we had taken to each other at once. There had been times, over the years, when I had wondered what I would have done without her friendship.

Marie-Laure stopped pacing finally, came and sat down on the garden seat next to me. Staring into my face, she took hold of my hand, and said carefully, 'I don't believe Sebastian was murdered. I think you must accept the facts, accept the autopsy report, accept that he took his own life.'

'But he didn't have any reason to do that,' I persisted quietly.

'Perhaps he did. How do you or I know? How does anyone know about another person, Vivienne? How do we know what goes on in someone else's mind?' She shook her head, and went on, 'We have no conception. There is one thing, Vivienne . . .'

'Yes?'

'Could it have had something to do with the woman he was in love with?'

'What do you mean exactly?'

'Maybe she broke off her engagement to him,' Marie-Laure suggested, her dark-brown eyes intent and alert as they fastened on mine.

'That's a possibility. I suppose anything can happen in a relationship. But I don't think she did that, no, no, no,' I answered.

'Don't be so emphatic, *chérie*. Women have been known to change their minds. They do it all the time.'

'No woman in her right mind would dump Sebastian Locke!' I exclaimed.

'You did, Vivienne,' she retorted, throwing me a wise and knowing look.

'No I didn't. We separated by mutual agreement . . . we loved each other, we just couldn't live together.'

'Let us consider this,' Marie-Laure began. 'The woman, who was younger than you, apparently, finds herself growing more and more nervous about the age difference between them. She gets . . . how do you say it . . . the cold feet, no? And so she ends their relationship.'

'All right, it could happen, I'll grant you that. But even if she did break it off with him, he wouldn't kill himself over it. Not Sebastian. I just know he wouldn't. Honestly, it's not a good enough reason for me, Marie-Laure, it really isn't. Sebastian was tough and resilient. He had a strong character, and he had many things in his life which were of vital importance to him. His work at Locke Industries, the Locke Foundation, and all of the charities he was involved with. He was constantly travelling the world, dispensing aid. So many people depended on him, and he *knew* they did.'

'I was always aware that he took his responsibilities

seriously. It was one of the things I've always admired about him,' she said.

I bit my lip, pondering, then endeavoured to explain more fully to her. 'Listen to me, Sebastian would never kill himself over a woman, no matter how much he loved her. He was far too sophisticated, too strong a man for that. Don't forget, he never had any problems getting a woman. He had five wives altogether, including me. My mother was his mistress, and God knows how many other mistresses he had over the years. Furthermore, there's no doubt in my mind that women were falling at his feet right up to the time of his death. That's the kind of man he was. Women couldn't resist him. And I can't begin to tell you how fantastic he looked the day we had lunch earlier this month, better than ever. He was full of vitality and that fatal charm of his was wholly intact. He was irresistible, in fact.'

Marie-Laure nodded slowly. 'What you say about him is true. I remember his charisma, his great sex appeal, and certainly you knew him better than anyone. So, I cannot argue, your reasoning is valid. Therefore it must have been something else which caused him to take that most fateful step.'

'Correct. But what could have pushed him over the edge?' I asked.

'I cannot even attempt to make a guess,' she answered. 'I just do not know. However, what we both know is that it wasn't a health problem, because the autopsy would have revealed any fatal disease. The police have done a thorough investigation and ruled out foul play, so we know that it was not murder. Anyway, *chérie,* that is too far-fetched an idea for me to even contemplate.'

'What you're saying is that you believe he actually did kill himself. Am I correct, Marie-Laure?'

'Yes, you are. What other conclusion is there? We just don't know *why* he did it, that's all.'

Marie-Laure and I stared at each other. We were both at a loss.

Eventually, she said, 'Let us admit it, *chérie,* we will never know the reason. The only person who could tell us is . . . dead.'

# Twelve

Driving back to Vieux Moulin from the château, I replayed everything Marie-Laure had said, and as I did I began to feel much calmer.

My dear old friend usually made great sense, and this afternoon had been no exception. I realized she had helped me to adjust to the fact that Sebastian *must* have killed himself. Very simply, there was no other explanation for his death. In the beginning, murder had crossed my mind, but only fleetingly really; I had attributed his fatal collapse to natural causes, either a heart attack or a stroke. This was the reason I had been so shocked by Jack's phone call. Suicide had been the furthest thing from my mind.

But Marie-Laure had reminded me that we never really know anybody, however close to them we are, or know what goes on in their minds. People could do surprising things. In essence, she had helped me to put matters in a better perspective, and I began to relax for the first time since Sebastian's body had been found.

By the time I arrived at the mill it was almost six-thirty. The sun was sinking low behind the ragged line of dark hills, the pale blue sky of earlier fading into an iridescent pearly grey. As I swung off the dirt road and into my driveway it was already dusk.

Once I'd parked the car, I went inside and raced straight to my bedroom without even letting Phyl know I was back. I didn't have much time to get ready before Kit arrived to pick me up for dinner.

In my bedroom, I pulled off my blue jeans and sweater, slipped into my dressing gown and refreshed my makeup. After brushing my hair and spraying on perfume, I dressed quickly in beige wool culottes, a cream silk shirt and black-and-beige shoes. Taking a black blazer out of the wardrobe, I slipped this on and made my way to the kitchen.

Phyl was standing at the old farm table, filling a wine cooler with ice cubes, and she glanced up as I walked in.

'There you are, Mrs Trent, I thought I heard you come in a short while ago. This is for the Sancerre. Should I open it now, do you think?'

'Hi, Phyl, why not.' I glanced at my watch. 'Mr Tremain will be here shortly, he's usually on time. You know, Phyl, it's turned quite coolish. I think it would be better if we had drinks inside tonight. In the library, I guess.'

'Good idea. Shall I light a fire?'

'No, thanks anyway. It's hardly worth it. We'll be going out for dinner in half an hour.'

'There're a couple of messages for you, over there on the dresser,' she said.

I strolled across the floor, took the messages from underneath the small, old-fashioned flat iron that served as a paperweight, and read them quickly. Renny Jackson, my book editor in London, had called to tell me she would be in Aix-en-Provence next weekend, and could we have lunch. She said she would ring me again on Monday to make the date. The other message was from Sandy Robertson, one of the editors I worked with at the London *Sunday Times*. Nothing important, Phyl had scribbled. He will phone you tomorrow.

'Are you sure Mr Robertson doesn't want me to call him back now, Phyl?'

'Oh yes, quite positive. He said he was just leaving the office, that he'd only phoned up to have a social chat with you.'

'I see.' I crumpled the messages in a ball just as the doorbell clanged loudly.

'That must be Mr Tremain,' Phyl said.

'I'll get it,' I told her and hurried out.

When I opened the door and greeted Kit a split second later, I was surprised to see how fit and well he looked, despite his arduous painting schedule of the last few months.

'Aren't you a sight for sore eyes!' he exclaimed, beaming as he stepped into the hall.

He swept me into his arms and hugged me tightly, not giving me a chance to say anything.

When he finally released me, he kissed me lightly on the lips and held me at arm's length, his expression appraising. 'You look great, just *great*, Vivienne.'

'So do you.' I smiled at him. 'And you don't look a bit done in, as you claimed you were.'

'I am, though. But just knowing you'd returned put the starch back in me, and cheered me up no end,' he replied, grinning at me. Slipping his arm around my shoulders, he walked me across the hall, his happiness at being with me palpable.

'Since it's turned cool tonight I thought we'd have drinks in the library,' I said. Looking at him, I added, 'It's lovely to see you, Kit.'

'And you. I feel as if you've been gone for ever. Now that you're finally here I hope you're going to stay, Viv.'

'Yes, I am, thank God. I've got to dig into my book again, finish it by March.'

We met Phyl in the doorway of the library; Kit greeted her in his usual breezy, friendly fashion, before ushering me inside the room.

Turning to me he said, 'This is my favourite spot in the whole house, you did such a wonderful job on it.'

'Thanks,' I said and went to the table where Phyl had placed the wine cooler holding the bottle of wine and two glasses. I poured.

'Cheers,' Kit said, touching his glass to mine. 'Welcome home, fair lady. You've been missed.'

'I've missed you too, Kit.'

'I hope so,' he answered and lowered himself into a chair near the big picture window which overlooked the gardens.

I sat down on the sofa opposite, and as I leaned back against the soft leather and looked across at him I was surprised to discover how much I really *had* missed him. I had not realized it until this moment.

Christopher Tremain was an attractive man by anybody's standards. Of medium height, he was slender, wiry in build, with a shock of dark-blond hair above a surprisingly unlined college-boy face. Since the first day I'd met him I'd always thought of him as looking like the All-American Hero, racing across a football field clutching a ball. Forty-two years old, he was a New Yorker, as I was. He had lived in France for eighteen years, where he was idolized as one of the great modern impressionist painters of his generation, and had moved to Provence from Paris two years ago.

Intelligent and exacting grey eyes stared back at mine staring at him. He said, 'What's wrong? Do I have a dirty mark on my face?'

I shook my head. 'No, I was just thinking again how truly fit you look, in the best of health. Certainly much better than you did just before I left in July.'

'I feel better. It's the work, I guess. All that painting, the supreme physical and mental effort seems to have regenerated me.'

'I know what you mean, work is a great turn-on for me, too.'

'Viv . . . look, there's something I want to say –' He stopped.

'What?' I asked swiftly, detecting an odd note in his voice. 'What is it?'

'I want to get this out of the way before we go to dinner. When I was getting ready a bit earlier I had the news on, and CNN had a flash about Sebastian. I guess the autopsy report's been released by the Connecticut State Police –' Again he cut himself short and looked at me worriedly.

'It has. Jack called me from New York this afternoon as soon as he knew. The Chief Medical Examiner's verdict is suicide, barbiturate poisoning. You must know that though, surely they had it on CNN.'

'Yes, they did.' He hesitated, before adding, 'It seemed odd to me.'

'*I* thought so. In fact I drove over to see Marie-Laure earlier, to discuss it with her. She knew Sebastian a long time, and knew him quite well.' I let out a long sigh. 'We tossed it around for ages, and there doesn't seem to be any other explanation for his death. We finally agreed on that, we'd no alternative.'

'I know how upsetting his death must have been to you, and I'm sorry I wasn't there to comfort you,' he expressed with genuine sincerity.

'I'm okay, Kit. It was a bit of a shock at first, and Jack's news today knocked me for a loop. But as Sebastian would have said, life has to go on.'

'Life's pretty unpredictable,' Kit said, putting his drink down on the coffee table in front of him. 'One never knows what's in store, what terrible shocks there are around the next corner.'

Rising, he came and joined me on the sofa, stretched one arm along the back, and drew closer to me. 'I want to help you, Vivienne, help you to cope, to make things easier for you, if I can. I'm here if you need me.'

'I know that. I'm fine, honestly I am.'

'Is it all right, Viv? Between *us*, I mean.'

'Of course it is, Kit.'

'So I *can* assume we're picking up where we left off in July?'

'Oh yes,' I answered quickly. I was beginning to

realize that I not only wanted to resume our relationship, but needed it, needed him.

He leaned forward, took my face between his hands and kissed me passionately. I returned his kisses with the same ardour.

'Oh God, Viv, I want you, I want to make love to you,' he whispered against my hair, when we finally drew apart. 'It's been so long since we were together, I can't stand it. Let's go to bed now, before we go out to dinner.'

I touched his face gently. 'Later Kit. We've got all the time in the world, you and I.'

He shook his head. 'No we don't. Who knows what tomorrow will bring? We've got to grasp today, live it hard, take life with both hands. Oh darling, I want you so much.'

'Later, Kit,' I said again. Leaning closer to him, I kissed him quickly and added, 'Let's go to dinner and afterwards I'll come home with you.'

He looked at me swiftly, his eyes suddenly intense as he asked, 'Will you stay the night?'

I nodded. 'I want to see the paintings for the exhibition, especially the last one, the big canvas.'

'Oh, so it's my work that interests you, is it, and not me?' he laughed.

'Both,' I answered and laughed with him.

When we had made our date for tonight, Kit had promised to take me out on the town. And, true to his word, he did.

We went to the best four-star restaurant in the vicinity, Le Moulin de Lourmarin. He had ordered champagne in advance, and it was served the moment we were seated at the table.

With our dinner, a marvellous veal stew, we had one of the best of our local wines, a Châteauneuf-du-Pape from a nearby vineyard, Domaine de Mt-Redon.

Quite apart from the delicious food and wines, Kit himself was in top form. He was amusing and expansive throughout the meal, talking about his work, his exhibition in Paris, and then he filled me in on the local gossip, told what had been happening during my stay in Connecticut. He kept me laughing and highly entertained for several hours.

Later, over coffee, he suddenly said, 'Will you come to Paris with me in November, Viv? Come to the opening of my show?'

'Oh, Kit, I've got such a lot of work to do yet on my book,' I began and paused when I saw the look of genuine disappointment settling on his face.

'Please, Viv, it's important to me that you're there.'

'Then I'll come,' I said, making a sudden decision. 'It's at the end of the month, isn't it?'

'Yes, Friday the twenty-fifth of November. Why?'

'It's just that the last part of the month is better for me. It gives me a chance to get back into the book. I'll work like crazy for the next few weeks, so that I can take a long weekend off to be with you in Paris.'

The look of pleasure which crossed his face told me what my acceptance meant to him, and I was touched. I said, 'Thanks for asking me, Kit, I know your show's going to be a huge success. And I can't wait for my private preview of the paintings tonight.'

'And I can't wait for you,' he said, leering at me

wickedly. Then grinning, he added, 'But I honestly think it's better to view the canvases tomorrow. In the daylight.'

'Oh you do, do you?' I answered, raising an eyebrow.

I stood at the bedroom window, looking out towards the ancient castle of Lourmarin, waiting for Kit. There was a full moon and it illuminated the castle's Renaissance bulk, its stark towers, and brought a silvery sheen to the time-weathered stones.

I had always loved the view from his bedroom and tonight there was something special about it, something different. Perhaps it was the play of brilliant moonlight on those ancient ramparts and the rolling fields where the castle stood. Or maybe it was the dark sky, littered with bright stars and fast-moving clouds that occasionally scudded across the face of the moon to obscure it.

Or perhaps it was because *I* was different tonight.

I was more relaxed and at ease with myself in a way I had not been for a very long time. *I was glad to be with Kit*. That had registered with me hours ago. I had forgotten how good he made me feel with his warmth and attentiveness and loving gestures. This was nothing new. He had always treated me well, beautifully really. I'd just forgotten in the three months I had been away.

Suddenly he was there, standing behind me, resting his hands on my shoulders. Lifting my hair, he kissed the nape of my neck. Then slowly he turned me around to face him.

He was wearing a white towelling robe, and he handed one to me. 'Please, darling, get undressed, let's go to bed,' he murmured.

But as I started to move away he pulled me back into his arms and kissed me. It was a long hard kiss and when he released me, he said in a low, urgent voice, 'Hurry, I can hardly wait, Viv, I've missed you so much.'

A few minutes later I returned wearing the towelling robe and joined him on the bed. We lay side by side for a second, holding hands, watching the sky turning colour, and I was happy to be next to him, to savour this moment of rare peace and intimacy. Then in a sudden movement Kit pushed himself up on one elbow, lay on his side, regarding me intently. 'You're beautiful, Vivienne,' he said and opened my robe, began to stroke my breasts, my stomach and my thighs, his hands moving over me lightly. Finally he bent over my body, kissing every part of me, until he finally arrived at the core of me. And it was here that his mouth lingered. I relaxed and let him love me as he wanted to, in the way he always had.

# *Part Two*

## JACK

### Duty

# Thirteen

I first came to the Château d'Cose when I was seven years old. If a small boy of that age could fall in love with a house then *I* did.

In those days I did not understand why I loved it so much. All I knew was that I felt at home. Its vastness did not frighten me. Nor was I intimidated by its grandeur. I was at ease in the great rooms. Or roaming through the meadows and woods of the estate.

Deep in my soul, I knew that I *belonged* at the château. For ever. This was my place. I never wanted to leave. When I had to, I was sad for weeks afterwards. I could not wait to return. We came back every summer. It was never long enough for me.

My father gave me the château and its lands just after he married Vivienne in 1980. I was stunned when he told me. I did not believe he meant to go through with it. I kept thinking he would back off at the last minute. To my surprise he did not.

Sebastian had grown bored with the château. He was no longer interested in the vineyards and the winery. But that was my father. He soon grew bored with things. And with wives.

After he and Vivienne split up, Luciana and I

started to call him Henry behind his back. After Henry the Eighth who had six wives. The name quickly deteriorated into Hank.

Luciana and I had secret names for a lot of people when we were kids. Vivienne was VTG. This stood for Vivienne the Great. My father thought she was just that. So did I. But Luciana detested Vivienne. So VTG was a derogatory name to her. Never to me. I laughed up my sleeve.

My half-sister also hated Vivienne's mother, Antoinette Delaney. I didn't. I loved her. I thought she was beautiful. Her hair was full of sunlight, her green eyes the same colour as the emeralds my father constantly gave her. She had a pale, pale skin. When she was angry it turned bright pink. In summer she got freckles on the bridge of her nose. I liked her freckles. They made her real, less ethereal.

Antoinette was always very kind to me. She loved me a lot. As much as she loved Vivienne. I knew this because she told me, told me I was like the son she had never had.

I wouldn't allow Luciana to give Antoinette a nick-name. Not unless it was flattering. We never did agree on that. And so she was never called anything behind her back. She was only ever referred to as Antoinette.

But I had my own name for her. She was my Special Lady. And she was *exactly* that. Truly special. She worked wonders in my young life, turned it completely around. And she helped to make me feel whole.

Then she went and fell down the cellar steps at

Laurel Creek Farm. She broke her neck and died.

I was twelve and it broke my heart. I'm not certain that I've ever recovered from her death. There has been a void in me since then. No one has been able to fill it.

My twelfth year was hell.

Antoinette died. And my father started to lecture me about Duty. It was my Duty to look after Luciana when he was away. It was my Duty to study hard. In order to go to Exeter and Yale. It was my Duty not to let the family down. It was my Duty to follow in his footsteps. My Duty to run Locke Industries and the Locke Foundation one day. And it was always Duty in a grand way. With a capital D.

I was still only twelve when Cyrus joined the act.

Whenever we went to see him in Maine it was *duty duty duty*. Not surprisingly, I began to hate that word. I determined that I would never do my duty. Not ever. But of course I did. Like the Pavlov dog, I had been brainwashed. I submitted to their will. And I did their bidding. After a fashion.

The Inheritance, as I called the château in those days, was deeded to me when I was only sixteen and attending Exeter Preparatory School. It was merely a small part of my vast inheritance, my grandfather and father being billionaires.

I sometimes thought of the château as a consolation prize. My father had married Vivienne, the woman of my dreams. I had always planned on marrying her myself. Not unnaturally, I was devastated when they tied the knot.

I suspect that Sebastian realized this. Hence the

château. Of course, gifting it to me when he did saved inheritance taxes as well.

Once the château was mine, I flew to France whenever Exeter broke for vacation. I was thrilled to be at d'Cose several times a year, instead of only in the summer months.

Sebastian and Vivienne were also there a lot in 1980 and 1981. They got on my nerves. They were forever billing and cooing. Luciana and I christened them the Lovebirds. They made me want to vomit.

The Lovebirds were preoccupied with the pile of rubble Sebastian had bought for her in Lourmarin. They were transforming it into a house. Eventually it was finished and they called it Vieux Moulin. I thought it was an imprudent waste of money. But I said nothing. It was none of my business. And, after all, *I* now owned the château. The house of my dreams, if not the girl.

I never did understand the attraction that heap of old stones held for Sebastian. An old mill, for God's sake. But then I never did understand my father. Now it was too late. He had been dead and buried for five months.

When I graduated from Exeter at the age of eighteen I went to Yale. Just as I was supposed to. Doing my Duty. I was following in the footsteps of those other Lockes who had gone before me. The first was my great-great-grandfather, Ian Lyon Locke. I would probably be the last, since I had no son.

I considered Yale to be a nuisance. It was preventing me from getting on with my life. All I wanted was to live at my château in Aix-en-Provence. I had been learning about my vineyards and my winery from Olivier Marchand, who had run everything for years. First for Sebastian. And then for me. It was my whole existence.

At twenty-two I became master of my own fate.

After graduating from Yale, I moved to the château permanently, where I worked alongside Olivier. I was passionately consumed by the land. My land.

I was also passionately in love.

When I was twenty-three I married her.

Everyone thought she was eminently suitable. She was, when it came to pedigree. Eleanor Jarvis Talbot had the right lineage. She was Boston Old Money. Except that they didn't have any. Not any more. This didn't matter to me. I had more than enough for both of us. Millions. In trust from my mother.

Eleanor was a lovely pale blonde. Tall and willowy. And highly over-sexed. I slept with her on our first date and continued to do so all through the last year I was at Yale.

Her cool, refined looks belied her sizzling nature. She was hot. Perhaps this was part of the attraction. She looked like a lady, behaved like a whore. When I was with her I was forever turned on just thinking about what we would do later. Actually, all we ever did was screw. Day and night, whenever we could. I was in seventh heaven, as they say. I couldn't believe my luck.

The family thought she was Miss Right. So did I. We were confused. Eleanor turned out to be Miss Wrong.

From the very beginning the marriage floundered.

Maybe it was partly my fault for not making her understand how much the château, the winery and the running of the estate meant to me.

We honeymooned in Morocco. I will never know what that country is really like. Not unless I make a return visit. I spent all of my time in bed. On top of Eleanor. Gazing down into her limpid grey-blue eyes. Or lying on my back. Staring up at hotel ceilings as she mounted me enthusiastically. She liked to do that. The dominant position appealed to her. 'Let *me* fuck *you*,' she would say and she did. Over and over and over again.

Then we came home to the château. And things changed. They had to change. I had a real life at the château. I had work to do. It was my Duty. But I cherished my duty in this particular instance. I was bound to the land and the winery.

The endless screwing had to lessen. But it didn't stop entirely. Unfortunately, Eleanor was like a rabbit. She was inordinately miffed when she couldn't get it all the time. Whenever she felt like it. She said I didn't love her. I believed I did. But she wore me out. I was exhausted. I needed a rest from all that unimaginative mindless fucking. I soon realized I had very little to say to her. Almost nothing at all.

This aside, she had no idea how to run a great château. Being a châtelaine meant nothing to her. Nor was she interested in learning how to be one. Her curiosity about what I did all day was nil. Her involvement in my working life was non-existent. Then, after a year of marriage, another problem developed. She became fixated on my father. She couldn't stop talking about him. His presence seemed to ignite her. She became overly animated, abnormally effervescent, almost raucous. In his absence, a despondency set in. She sulked. Threw tantrums.

Eleanor still wanted to screw me endlessly. But my interest in her was waning with rapidity. Her preoccupation with Sebastian sent a message loud and clear. I knew she really wanted to screw my father instead of me. Or as well as me. Whichever. This knowledge proved disastrous for our sex life. It rendered me impotent.

We divorced.

It was costly, but worth it.

And fortunately, despite our sexual marathons, there were no children from this regrettable union.

A glutton for punishment, I married my second wife when I was twenty-six.

I met Jacqueline de Brossard in Aix-en-Provence. She was the daughter of a minor baron and lived in a nearby château. What attracted me to her initially was her familiarity with château life. And her knowledge of the land. Plus her gorgeous body. Her looks were plain. However, her splendid French chic and great style more than compensated for this inadequacy.

Jacqueline de Brossard appeared to be the perfect mate. Ideally suited to me. We shared similar tastes. In most things we were compatible. Nevertheless, our marriage scarcely outlasted the year. She had two all-consuming interests in her life. Spending my money was one of them. Infidelity the other. My second wife apparently did not wish to bed my father.

As far as I knew. Merely every other man that crossed her path.

We divorced.

I vowed never to marry again.

I was now living in sin.

My paramour was an Englishwoman. Her name was Catherine Smythe. She was educated. Brainy. A bit of an intellectual. Fifty years ago she would have been termed a blue-stocking. Catherine was an Oxford graduate. A historian of some repute. She had taught history, written about it, lectured on it.

I thought she was outrageously good-looking. Red-haired, green-eyed, pale-complexioned.

There were moments when Catherine reminded me of my Special Lady. Like the Special Lady's daughter Vivienne, Catherine was older than me. By five years. That didn't matter. I've always preferred older women.

Catherine and I met in Paris. In August 1994. She was staying with an English journalist friend of mine, Dick Vickery. I assumed they were romantically involved. My assumption was incorrect. They were just good friends.

She and I became more than just good friends in a matter of days. I liked brainy women. They stimulated me. Turned me on. Catherine was much better than a mindless screw. She was the ultimate.

She came to stay with me for Christmas. It was then I asked her to move in with me. She agreed. We saw the old year out together, greeted the new one in. Drinking champagne on the château's ramparts. Toasting each other. Getting drunk together.

It seemed to me that 1995 held wonderful prospects. Especially with Catherine on the premises. Indefinitely.

'I can't promise you marriage,' I'd said to her over Christmas.

'Marriage!' she had cried indignantly. 'Who's interested in marriage? Certainly not I. I've no desire to be legally bound to any man, present company included. I love my independence. I don't aim to lose it.'

So that was that.

I had met my match.

Seven months after our first encounter this clever woman still fascinated me. Apparently I still fascinated her.

I moved away from the trees. Striding out, I headed for the château looming up in the distance, a great mass of stone.

It gleamed palely on this February morning. Watery sunlight glanced off its many windows. The grey-tiled rooftops and turrets were dark smudges against the hazy blue sky.

I paused, looked towards the château across sweeping green lawns, a formal garden and, just beyond the garden, the wide stone terrace.

It was the perfect spot from which to view the eighteenth-century edifice at any time of day. This morning it looked spectacular in the soft light, with the mist rising off the lawns.

I filled with satisfaction, knowing it was mine.

I glanced at my watch. It was almost nine o'clock. Time for breakfast with Catherine.

I found her in the library. She had been working there since seven.

'Aren't you a love,' she said, looking up as I came in. 'Bringing me breakfast, no less. Spoiling me.'

'Your turn tomorrow.' I put the large wooden tray on the coffee table in front of the fire and sat down.

She joined me a moment later. We sat drinking large cups of *café au lait* and eating warm, freshly-baked croissants spread with butter and home-made raspberry jam.

'Jack, these are lethal.'

'You say that every day.'

'Three minutes on the lips, six months on the hips,' she muttered, shaking her head. 'I simply must go on a diet tomorrow.'

'I like you the way you are.'

'I'm getting fat, living here with you, Jack.'

'Want to leave?'

'No, of course not, you fool,' she replied swiftly, affectionately, laughing as she spoke. 'This place is compelling.'

'I thought it was me.'

'It is. You *and* the château. Jack, I've come across something really fascinating, in one of the old books I found. I think I know where the name Château d'Cose might have come from.'

I pricked up my ears. Leaned forward. I was suddenly more alert. The origin of the château's name had always baffled Sebastian. Olivier Marchand had been unable to throw any light on it. Neither had any of the old-timers who had worked here for years. Documentation barely existed. It was a mystery.

'Speak,' I said. 'Tell me, Catherine.'

'As I mentioned, the book is old. It carries a series of paintings of about thirty famous people from the fifteenth, sixteenth and seventeenth centuries. The spelling of those periods, reproduced in the book, is quaint –'

'What do you mean by quaint?' I interrupted.

'For example, Rabelais is spelled *Rables*. Buckingham, as in the Duke of, is spelled *Boucquin can*. The Queen of Spain is *la Reine Despaigne*, instead of *d'Espagne*. And the Queen of Scotland, which correctly is *la Reine d'Écosse*, shows up as *la Rene de Cose*. I think that d'Cose, the name of this château, is a bastardization of *de* Cose, and somehow refers to Scotland.'

I stared at her. 'That would be peculiar. An odd coincidence. *If* you're right. Malcolm Lyon Locke, the founding father of the dynasty, was a Scotsman. Is there any reference to my château in the book?'

'No. None at all. As I just said, it's a picture book really, showing different paintings of . . . well, shall we call them celebrities of the day. Rabelais, the Duke of Buckingham, Mary Queen of Scots, etcetera, etcetera. And, of course, the spelling of the latter's name caught my eye at once.'

'Keep digging. Maybe you'll find something else that makes reference to Scotland. Maybe this was her place?'

Catherine shook her head. 'I doubt it. Mary was

mostly in the Loire Valley when she was growing up. And after she married the Dauphin of France, she was at Chenonceaux, the home of the king. She was with Henry II, his mistress Diane de Poitiers, his wife Catherine de Medici, and their son Francis II, who was the Dauphin. The *petite Reinette d'Écosse* she was usually called in those days, the little Queen of Scotland. Poor sad thing she was in the end. And she met such a grisly death. Had her head chopped off –'

The ringing of the telephone next to Catherine's elbow interrupted her. Reaching for it, she said, 'Château d'Cose. *Bonjour.*'

There was a moment of silence before Catherine went on, 'Oh hello, Vivienne, how are you?'

# Fourteen

I took the phone from Catherine, sat down in the chair she had vacated.

'Hi, Viv,' I said. 'How're things?'

'Fine, thanks. Jack, I'd like to come over to see you.'

'When?'

'This morning.'

'That's impossible,' I said quickly. I'd caught something in Vivienne's voice. I knew when to protect myself from her.

'What about this afternoon then? Or this evening?' Vivienne pressed. 'It's very important. Really it is.'

'Viv, I can't. Not today. I got problems. Stuff to deal with.'

'You can spare half an hour. Surely. For *me*.'

'Can't, Viv. Olivier has people coming. We'll be tied up. All day. Winery business,' I lied, improvising as I went along. I'd known her for ever. Since I was six. Something was troubling her, I could tell. It echoed in her voice. Instinct made me keep her at arm's length. Otherwise she'd rope me in.

'I really need to talk to you, Jack,' she murmured in a warmer, softer voice. 'About something which concerns us both.'

Viv could beguile when she wanted to, didn't I know that. Swiftly, I said, 'It'll have to wait.'

'Not necessarily. Perhaps we can talk on the phone.'

'I don't know when.'

'We can do it right now, Jack. Listen to me for a moment, please.'

'But –'

'No buts, Jack. I've finished the Brontë book, as you know, and now that I'm not so concentrated on my writing, the matter of Sebastian's death has broken through into my consciousness. It does –'

'Oh God, Viv! Not that old turkey! *Again*. Let it drop!'

'I won't, I can't. Listen to me. Sebastian's death does not sit well with me, not at all.'

'He committed suicide,' I snapped.

'I accept that. But I need a reason *why* he did it. I need to know. Only then, when I have a resolution, will I be at peace about it. And at peace with myself.'

'No one can give you a reason. Only Sebastian knows. He took that secret to the grave with him.'

'Not necessarily,' she said.

'What do you mean?'

'I've been thinking –'

'What about?' I cut in, groaning inside. How well I knew that tone of hers. It spelled trouble.

'About his life. What he was doing in the last six to eight months of it. Who he was with. And just as importantly, how he was behaving. You know, what frame of mind was he in? Was he troubled? Or happy?'

'He was happy. The day you had lunch. So you claim.'

*'He was.'*

'How can you be so sure?'

'That's a stupid question, Jack. I knew him intimately. He *was* happy. Look, I remember how I felt that day, truly I do. And I was pleased for him, pleased he was about to start a new life.'

'He was?' I was startled. 'What do you mean by a new life?'

'There was a woman, Jack, a new woman in his life. He was in love, and he was planning to marry her.'

Flabbergasted, I exclaimed, 'You gotta be kidding!'

'I'm not. He told me he was planning to marry in the spring. In fact, he wanted me to meet her and he invited me to the wedding.'

'That's sick,' I said.

'No, it's not. We were always close. Very, very close. Anyway, don't digress.'

Ignoring this admonition, I asked, 'Who was the woman?'

'I don't know. He didn't tell me her name. That's the problem. If I knew who she was, I could go and see her. Obviously *you* never met her, since you sounded so surprised when I mentioned her.'

'I didn't even *know* about her.'

'Did Luciana?'

'No. I'm sure. She would've told me.'

'*Someone* must have met her, Jack, and that's what I'm leading up to. I want to talk to people who worked with Sebastian on the charities in Africa.'

'Why the African charities?'

'Because Sebastian said he met her there,' Vivienne explained. 'He said she was a doctor. A scientist. I want to talk to a lot of people who were involved in his life and activities, in order to get a better perspective about him in that six-month period.'

'People might resent that. They might clam up,' I pointed out. 'They *are* very loyal to him. To his memory.'

'I know. But I have the perfect reason. I'm writing a profile about him for the *Sunday Times* Magazine. Sandy Robertson okayed it last night. I'm planning an in-depth profile about the world's greatest philanthropist . . . who was probably the last of the breed. That's one of the reasons I wanted to see you, Jack. I'd like to get your impressions of him during those last few months last year.'

'Vivienne, that's ridiculous! Why can't you just let it drop?'

'I can't. I wish I could. Rationally, intellectually, I do accept his suicide. Emotionally, I cannot. At least, I can't accept that he would kill himself when he was so happy, so positive about the future. It just doesn't sit well with me, I keep telling you that. There's something wrong here, something terribly amiss. Something strange must have happened after we'd lunched on that Monday. I just know it in my bones.'

'And you aim to find out? Is that it? Hey, Viv, I have the perfect reason. The lady dumped him.'

'Perhaps she did. That's certainly a possibility, I

won't argue with you there, Jack. But I don't believe Sebastian would take his life because of a woman, not the Sebastian I know.'

'And I know nothing. I can't help. Not with the profile.'

'You might think of something, if you rack your brains. If you really think hard about it, think back to those months last summer.'

'I doubt it.'

'The day of the funeral, Cyrus suggested I should write a book. A biography of Sebastian.'

'The keeper of the flame! Is that your new role, honey?'

'Don't be sarcastic, Jack, it doesn't become you. And I might do it. I just want to be sure I can be absolutely objective about Sebastian. Writing the profile will give me a good idea about that. It'll be a sort of test.'

'Who are you planning to interview, Viv?' I asked.

'His colleagues at Locke Industries and at the foundation. One person will lead to another, that's how it usually works. I'll soon understand who knew him best, knew certain sides to him. I hope to talk to Luciana, too.'

'Viv, you know better!' I exclaimed. 'You'll only get a flea in your ear.'

'We'll see.'

'Take my word for it, honey.'

'Jack?'

'Yes?'

'You were in New York last month for the board

meeting at Locke Industries. I just wondered if anyone mentioned anything to you. About the new woman in his life.'

'No.'

'Mmmm. Interesting. Perhaps they didn't know about her.'

'You got it, kid.'

'Jack, you will help me with the profile, won't you? It's so important to me. Important that I write this, and I do believe it will help me to come to terms with his death.'

'Okay,' I agreed reluctantly. And against my better judgement. 'But there's nothing I know. I hardly saw him last year.'

'You might think of something that would give me a clue about his moods, his behaviour in those final six months of his life.'

'I gotta go. I'll call you. Next week.'

'I won't be here. I'm leaving for New York in a couple of days, Jack. I want to start the interviews with some of my old friends at the foundation. It'll be a beginning.'

'Have a good trip. *Ciao*.'

''Bye, Jack. I'll be in touch, we'll talk soon.'

*'Merde!'* I said as I slammed the phone down and sat back in my chair, scowling.

'What is it, Jack? What's wrong?' Catherine asked in that calm voice of hers. A voice I had grown accustomed to these past few months.

'It's Vivienne. She's off the wall.'

'That's a curious statement to make about someone

so balanced, and as down-to-earth and rational as she is,' Catherine countered.

'She's not rational. Not down-to-earth,' I exclaimed heatedly. 'Not when it comes to Sebastian. She's obsessed with him. He's been dead five months and she's still ranting and raving. About his death. I wish she'd just shut the hell up. Let him rest in peace. I can't stand her when she's like this.'

'Like what?'

'Playing the keeper of the flame.' I laughed, added, 'She's carrying a torch,' and laughed again at my play on words.

Catherine did not appear to be amused. She wore a concerned expression.

'From what you've told me, she adored him and you hated him. Never the twain shall meet,' Catherine murmured. 'You're poles apart when it comes to Sebastian Locke. You'll never agree about him.'

'True enough, sweetheart. Vivienne's got a problem. Not enough to do. Her book on the Brontës is finished. Delivered. Now it's Sebastian. She's focused on him. Again. *Merde!*'

Catherine regarded me thoughtfully for a second or two, then said slowly, 'Do you mean she's going to write a book about your father, darling? Is that what you're trying to tell me?'

'Not a book. A profile. For the London *Sunday Times*. The magazine section. The editor she works with okayed it. But there might be a book. My grandfather, the old coot, suggested it. At the funeral. Can you beat that. Jeez! She might do it too. Bet she does. *Merde! Merde! Merde!*'

'Jack, for heaven's sake, why *are* you so upset? You're being quite childish. Irrational, actually.'

'I'm not.'

'Whenever your father is involved I'm afraid you are very irrational, darling.'

'Vivienne wants to probe. Dig into his life. The last year of it. *I need to know*. That's what she said. She also said, *I need to know what he was doing. Who he was with. What he was like. His moods. His demeanour. I have to understand him. I want to pinpoint the reason he killed himself*. That's what she just said to me.'

'How does she propose to get this information?'

'She's going to talk to people. Interview them.'

'Who exactly?'

'People who worked for him. With him. At Locke Industries. At the foundation. Me. Luciana. God knows who else.'

'And she's going to write about her conclusions, is that it?'

'Not exactly. She won't dwell on the suicide. Not in the article. Knowing her, she won't mention it. If she does, it'll be one line. The way she felt about him, still feels, it'll be a glowing profile. Flattering. She'll only show his good side. Understanding him, understanding the last few months of his life. That's what's important to her. This is purely personal.'

'I see. But I really can't quite understand why you're so upset.'

'I wish she'd let it rest. I don't want constant reminders about him. He's dead. Buried. I don't want her digging him up.'

'I do think you're being just a little bit silly, darling.

You just said she won't write anything bad about him. And I agree with you. From what you've told me, Vivienne's extremely loyal to Sebastian, and to his memory.'

'She's still in love with him.'

'Oh I don't think so, Jack, really I don't. Vivienne's too alive, too sexual and too sensual a woman to be still hooked on a dead man, from what I've observed of her, at least. Good Lord, no. She believes that life is for the living. It seems to me that she's batty about Kit Tremain. He's her life now, you know, not Sebastian Locke. Trust me on this. I know what I'm talking about, and I know I'm right.'

'I guess you are.' I immediately changed the subject.

# Fifteen

'There was another woman,' I said, staring across the dinner table at Catherine.

She stared back at me, and then said, with a light, amused smile, 'I'm sure there were lots of women before me, Jack. Quite apart from your two wives. I wouldn't expect it to be otherwise. You're a very attractive man.'

'No. No. I'm talking about Sebastian. There was another woman in his life. Just before he died. A new woman,' I explained. 'I knew nothing about her. No one did. But he told Viv. The day they had lunch. That fateful week he killed himself. He told Viv he was planning to marry her.'

'Who was she?' asked Catherine, looking at me alertly.

I shrugged. 'No idea. Viv never asked her name. He never gave it. Just said she was a doctor. Viv mentioned it this morning on the phone. Not before. Don't know why she didn't. I forgot to tell you.'

'Presumably he was happy then. How odd that he took his life when he did.'

'That's what Viv thinks.'

'On the other hand, the nameless woman could

have terminated their relationship,' Catherine remarked.

I smiled at her. 'That's what *I* think.'

'What did Vivienne say?'

'That he wouldn't have taken such a drastic step over a failed love affair.'

Catherine seemed to mull this over before saying, 'Well, I tend to agree with Vivienne.'

'But you didn't know him,' I protested.

'No, not personally, and you haven't told me much about him. Only odd snippets. But I was quite aware of him long before I met you, Jack,' she pointed out. 'All the money he gave away to charity. Those huge donations to Bosnia last year. *Everyone* was aware of him. And naturally I'd read a lot about him. A great deal of space was devoted to him in the press.' She paused to take a sip of her red wine. 'He had half a dozen wives, didn't he?'

'Five.'

'Same thing, more or less. He was rich, handsome, famous, so he had a lot going for him. He was sophisticated, I assume? Worldly?'

'Very.'

Catherine nodded her head. 'I think Vivienne's right. He wouldn't kill himself over a woman. He was too experienced. Anyway, I'm quite sure he could have had any woman he wanted.'

'True. Women were mesmerized by him. He and I didn't get on. I've told you that. But I've got to give the devil his due. He was a magnet to women. They fell over themselves to meet him. Fell at his feet. He didn't encourage that. He was very off-hand with women. But he had *it*. Presence. Charisma. Glamour. Sex appeal. And a fatal charm. Look, he was lethal. As a man. And unpredictable. Even a little crazy, in some ways.'

'Mad, bad and dangerous to know,' Catherine mused.

'That about sums it up. You've got a good turn of phrase, sweetheart.'

'Oh, it's not *my* phrase, Jack. Another woman said it long before I was born. In the early part of the nineteenth century, to be exact.'

'Who?'

'Lady Caroline Lamb. She wrote it in her diary, the first time she met Lord Byron, the poet. What she meant, of course, was that Byron was emotionally dangerous. He was already something of a legend in London. Great fame had come to him early, after *Childe Harold* was published in 1812. Women schemed to meet him, squabbled over him. Although he was more chased than the chaser. Later Lady Caroline Lamb completed the phrase when she added, "That beautiful pale face is my fate." When she met Byron he had acquired a reputation in the London social world. A reputation for being dangerous and irresistible. Legend and rumour played a big part in all of this, of course. They can be very potent stimulants.'

'Mad, bad and dangerous to know,' I repeated. 'Yes, that fits Sebastian to a T.'

'And no one knew about Sebastian's most recent conquest?' Catherine asked.

'I don't think so. I didn't. Neither did Luciana. She would've told me. Curious that he kept it a secret.'

Catherine merely nodded, said nothing.

There was a little silence between us.

Eventually I said, 'Do you believe in good genes and bad genes?'

'I'm not sure.' Catherine raised an eyebrow. 'What are you getting at?'

'Could the compulsion to commit suicide be *genetic?*'

'I just don't know. Why do you ask?'

'Sebastian's half-sister Glenda killed herself years ago. His half-brother Malcolm did the same. In my opinion. He was in a boating accident on Lake Como. Supposedly an accident. It wasn't, I'm sure. Aunt Fiona, Sebastian's other half-sister, became a drug addict. Disappeared. Years ago. She could be alive. Most probably dead though. *Bad genes?*'

'I simply can't answer that, Jack. But how awful, how terribly tragic.'

'Yeah. I'm the last. The last of the Mohicans.'

Her brow lifted again. Her expression was quizzical.

I grinned. 'I'm the last male of the dynasty. Unless I spawn an offspring. Which is unlikely. And Luciana won't ever have kids.'

After a moment of looking thoughtful, Catherine asked, 'Don't you find that sad, Jack?'

'What?'

'That you're the last of a great American family.'

'Not particularly. And I don't think any of them were that great. Least of all Cyrus and Sebastian.'

'Why do you hate *them* so much?'

'Do I?'

'That's the way it's sounded to me, whenever you've spoken about them these few months I've known you.'

'Sebastian was never a father to me. He was incapable of it. Incapable of loving me. Or anyone else,' I replied, and realized my voice sounded shrill.

'Vivienne says he loved *her*.'

'*She* likes to think that! But he *didn't*. He was nice to her. Nicer than he was to the other wives. But he didn't love her. He couldn't. It wasn't in him. Oh, yeah, he gave lip service to it. But it *was* only that. Trust me.'

'Why couldn't Sebastian love anybody?'

'How the hell do I know?' I swigged some of my wine, lolled back in the chair. 'Something missing in his genes?'

She ignored my question, asked one of her own instead. 'What sort of childhood did your father have?'

'God only knows. Awful, I suspect. His mother died giving birth to him. Cyrus brought him up. With a nanny. Then Cyrus remarried. He once told me his nanny *and* his stepmother were hard women.'

'It could be disassociation,' Catherine muttered, almost to herself.

'What does that mean?' I leaned over the table, my interest quickening.

'It's a psychiatric term. Let me try and put it very simply, as best I can, the way it was once described to me. When a child receives no love, no nurturing at birth and in the very first years of life, that child usually grows up removed from association with others. Thus, the child cannot love because it has not been loved. It doesn't know *how* to love anyone. You'd have to talk to a psychiatrist to get a proper medical explanation of it in detail. But in my opinion, disassociation could very well be the explanation for your father's behaviour, his inability to love, if this was the case.'

'It was. Take my word for it,' I said.

# Sixteen

Catherine and I lay together in my great fourposter bed, sipping cognac.

I was enjoying the closeness, the intimacy.

Earlier, I had turned off the lamps. The only light came from the fire burning in the hearth. It filled the room with a warm glow. The intermittent crackling of the logs was the only sound. Except for the faint ticking of the clock on the mantle. It was peaceful here.

I was relaxed. At ease with myself. I frequently was when I was alone with Catherine. I was glad I had found her. Glad she was here at the château.

She had lived with another man once. Years ago. She'd told me all about him. It hadn't worked out. Not in the end. When we met in Paris there was no one of importance in her life. That was lucky for me. We were well suited. I liked her braininess. The way her mind worked intrigued me. I couldn't stand dumb women. I'd known a few of those. Too many.

I closed my eyes. Drifting. Thinking. Mostly about Catherine. There was never any pressure with her. Or from her. She allowed me to be me. To be Jack. To her I was her friend. Her lover. I was not the son of the famous Sebastian Locke. I was not John Lyon

Locke, the last of the line in a great American family, head of Locke Industries and the Locke Foundation. She did not know that side of me. Nor did she care about it.

Catherine often heard me on the phone with the president of Locke Industries. And with those others who ran the company for me. As they had done for my father. Sometimes I spoke to my assistants at the foundation in front of her. But she paid scant attention to my phone calls. Nor was she curious about my other business interests.

Fortunately she loved the château and the winery. This pleased me. I had started to share my thoughts with her about the wine business. She always listened attentively. She understood my love of the land. My land, my vineyards.

Another aspect of her character was her lack of interest in my wealth. Catherine seemed to be as disdainful of money as Sebastian had been. Material things did not matter to her. This did not trouble me. I only wished she would let me spoil her. Give her gifts occasionally. But she found it hard to accept things from me. Unless it was a book. Or something else that was inexpensive.

She interrupted my thoughts of her when she said softly, touching my shoulder, 'Jack, are you asleep?'

'No. Only dozing. Well, half-dozing.'

'I've just thought of something.'

'What?'

'Did the mysterious woman in your father's life show up at his funeral?'

'No.'

'I wonder why not? Don't you think that's peculiar?'

'Not really,' I answered. 'The funeral was small. A family affair. In Cornwall, Connecticut. It was strictly private. *Verboten* to anybody not close. Or closely connected to him.'

'I see. I'll tell you something, though. If I were in love with a man and engaged to be married to him, and if that man died unexpectedly, I'd be in touch with his family immediately,' she exclaimed. 'Even if I hadn't met them, even if they didn't know about my existence. I would want to be with them, to share my grief. And I would certainly want to be at his funeral.' Catherine paused, bit her lip. 'It's strange, Jack, it really is when you think about it. I mean, that she hasn't been in touch with you or Luciana, if only to express her sympathy, give you her condolences.'

'She hasn't,' I said. 'But she could have been at the memorial service for all I know. Hundreds of people were. It was held at the Church of St John the Divine in Manhattan. Since a public announcement had been made, the world at large knew about it. And came.'

Catherine sighed. 'And because you never met her, you wouldn't have known whether she was present or not.'

'Precisely.'

'Do you mind if I ask you something else? Something a little more personal?'

'Shoot.'

'Had your father changed his will?'

'No. Why?'

'I just wondered. Often people who are about to commit suicide put their affairs in order.'

'His affairs *were* in order, Catherine. Already had been for years. He was made that way. Mr Efficiency. That was Sebastian.'

'No legacy left to a woman you'd never heard of?'

'No. His will was made three years ago. Nothing was changed in it. If there *had* been a legacy to a person I didn't know, I'd have made it my business to find out about her.'

'Yes, of course you would, darling. I'm beginning to realize these are stupid questions. I can be such an imbecile at times. Oh dear.'

She fell silent.

So did I.

She moved her head and the firelight danced in her long hair, turned it into a shimmering cascade of flame around her pale face. She moved again, turned her head the other way, exposed her white neck. Catherine had a swanlike neck, as Antoinette Delaney had had.

In a rush of words, I said, 'You've often reminded me of someone, of my Special Lady, but never more so than you do tonight, Catherine. It's uncanny.'

'Your Special Lady? Who's that?' This was asked softly, but I noticed that her face had tightened.

'Her name was Antoinette Delaney. She was Vivienne's mother. I loved her from the first moment she came into my life. When I was six. She was like a mother to me. Kind, warm, adoring.'

'And I remind you of her?' she asked, sounding slightly incredulous. 'Am I motherly?'

I laughed. 'She was very beautiful. Like you. You have her colouring. The same red hair, white skin, green eyes. She was as tall as you are. As willowy and graceful.'

Catherine smiled.

I said, 'I've not told you this before . . . but my own mother died when I was two. Of bone-marrow cancer. Sebastian married Christa about two years later. They had Luciana together. But Christa was an alcoholic. Sebastian put her in a clinic. To dry out. She never came back to live with us. He didn't want her around us. Or anywhere near him. I think he despised her.'

'So Antoinette was a friend of your father's? Or was she his lover?'

'Yes, his mistress. We were together for six years. All of us. In Connecticut, and here at the château. They were wonderful years. Whatever I am today, she helped to make me. Any good there is in me comes from her. From her influence. And her love.'

'That's such a lovely thing to say. So touching. She must have been quite unique. No wonder you call her your special lady. But why was she only with you for six years?'

'She died.'

'Oh Jack, I'm sorry. How tragic. She can't have been very old. What did she die of?'

'She had an accident. At least everyone said it was an accident. She fell down the basement steps at Sebastian's farm. She died instantly. She broke her neck.'

'Why do you say "everyone said it was an accident" in that peculiar tone of voice, as if you don't think it was?' Catherine's eyes fastened on mine.

I didn't respond. I looked away.

'Do you think she was murdered?'

'I've never known what to think,' I said at last, turning to her. 'It seems odd that she was going into the basement. In the early hours of the morning. And if she was pushed, who could've done it? Who would've wanted to anyway? Sebastian was in Manhattan. On business. Aldred was at the farm. He was my father's estate manager. We were there. Luciana and me. And her nanny. And the housekeeper. Sebastian arrived at about seven, from New York. He said he'd come up early to go riding with Antoinette. But I've often wondered about that.'

'Are you suggesting that Sebastian pushed her?'

'I don't know.' I'd never confided this to anyone else before. I took a deep breath. Then I plunged. 'He might have,' I muttered.

'But why?'

'I don't know.'

Catherine shook her head slowly. 'Shades of Amy Robsart.'

'Who's Amy Robsart?' I asked.

'She was married to Lord Robert Dudley, and on September the eighth in the year 1560 her body was found at the foot of the staircase in Cumnor Hall, where she was then living. Her death caused a terrible flurry at the time, became something of a *cause célèbre*, and in fact, it rocked the whole of England. You see, Robert Dudley was the closest friend of Queen Elizabeth the First. They were actually childhood friends. He was her dearest and most beloved companion. Never far from her sight. After she became Queen of England she bestowed many honours on him. He had a very high rank at court, and he was her Master of the Horse –'

'And rumoured to be the Queen's lover. If I remember my British history correctly,' I volunteered.

Catherine nodded. 'That's right. Amy's death was a mystery, and some people tried to implicate Robert Dudley. Even the Queen was under suspicion briefly. But since he was at court with Queen Elizabeth he couldn't have pushed her himself.'

'But he might have hired someone to push her . . . is that what you're getting at?'

'More or less. Certainly the stakes were high enough.'

'In what sense?'

'With his wife's death, Robert Dudley was a free man . . . free to marry Queen Elizabeth.'

'Would that have been possible?'

'Constitutionally, yes. And she did love him. Just as he loved her. But Elizabeth Tudor didn't want to marry anyone. Not really. She didn't want to share her power. In any case, I don't think he was involved or implicated in his wife's death. Neither was the Queen. She was far too smart to be a party to that kind of thing. As you know, I earned a doctorate in English history. What you don't know is that I specialized in the Tudors. In my opinion, Amy Robsart Dudley killed herself. I've actually written about this.'

'And she did it because of her husband's involvement with the Queen?'

'No. Amy was known to have cancer of the breast. She was ill, and she may have grown despondent. Anyway, that's my considered opinion. She did herself in by throwing herself down the stairs.'

'Antoinette wasn't ill,' I remarked, thinking out loud. 'The autopsy would have brought that to light. If she had been. So I suppose her death *was* an accident.'

'I think it must have been. I didn't know your father, but I doubt very much that he would commit such a crime. Or hire someone to do it for him. Why would he? What motive did he have? He wasn't married to Antoinette. If he'd wanted to break up with her, he could have done so easily enough. He could have left her. It's as simple as that. He didn't have to resort to murder.'

'I guess you're right.'

Catherine moved closer to me, put her arms around me and held me tightly. 'Don't let something like this haunt you, as I believe it has been doing for years and years.'

'Off and on,' I admitted.

After a moment Catherine got out of bed, and went into the bathroom.

I lay there thinking about my father. I wished she had not brought him up. Certainly not tonight. Not now. The discussion had been going on half the day. Ever since Vivienne's phone call this morning.

I groaned under my breath. I was sick of it all. And I was relieved that Vivienne was going to New York later this week. When she was pounding someone else about Sebastian Locke she was leaving me alone. Vivienne maddened me at times.

Catherine came back, gliding across the floor. She got into bed, curling up against me, kissing me lightly on the cheek.

'You don't want this, do you, darling?' she asked as she took the brandy balloon out of my hands and put it on her bedside table.

'Well,' I began, but she stopped the flow of words with her lips.

She began to kiss me, lightly at first, but then the kisses became hot, fervent, passionate. Her tongue grazed mine as she slid it into my mouth. I kissed her hard, wrapping my arms around her body, pulling her on top of me as I did.

We stayed locked together for several moments. Then I broke away, cupped a hand under one of her breasts and brought my mouth down to the nipple. I heard the soft groan in the back of her throat as I kissed her breast.

Eventually Catherine pulled away and trailed her mouth across my chest and on to my stomach. Then she slithered down in the bed. She crouched over me, touching me everywhere. Caressing the most vulnerable parts of me. I heard my own groans as she began to make love to me. She was a versatile lover. The most imaginative I'd known. Mindless sex was not her bag. Thankfully.

Her long hair trailed across my thighs and her mouth was suddenly on me, encircling me. I closed my eyes. Her warmth and softness enveloped me. Usually I became a potent lover within seconds, whenever she did this. Tonight nothing happened. I remained flaccid.

The foreplay was going on far too long. I soon began to realize that. She was growing tired. Suddenly, mortified and angry with myself, I stopped her ministrations. Gently I pushed her away.

Catherine was startled. She gaped at me.

'Be back in a minute,' I muttered and stumbled into the bathroom.

I locked the door and leaned against it.

I was breathing hard. That awful, familiar sick feeling was engulfing me. I knew it well. For a moment I thought I was going to vomit. Bring back the brandy. I felt nauseous, dizzy. I steadied myself. The feeling finally passed as I stood there in the darkened bathroom, gripping the door jamb.

I was impotent. *Again*. So far, until tonight, it had only happened twice with Catherine. At the beginning of our relationship, but not since. I had begun to believe that my problem had been cured. Apparently not. *'Merde,'* I whispered. I snapped my eyes shut. *'Merde,'* I said again.

Eventually the panic subsided. I grew calmer inside. Switching on the light, I crossed the room. I splashed cold water on my face, dried it, stood staring at myself in the mirror.

The image I saw reflected there was not Jack. It was a pale imitation of Sebastian Locke. I resembled him greatly. There was no denying whose son I was. Even though I had his features, mine were less distinct. They were not so well defined. Not so sculpted as his had been. True, my eyes were also blue.

But diluted, watery. His had been blindingly blue. Brilliant in his tanned face. My complexion was pale. I always looked washed out. His dark hair had been thick and wavy. Mine was dark, too. And straight. I was not in the least bit dashing and dynamic, as he had been. Nor was I loaded with his kind of irresistible sex appeal.

I bet *he* was never impotent, I thought, continuing to stare at myself with a degree of disdain. I bet *he* had a permanent erection.

I hated being a faded, carbon copy of that man. I hated being his son. I hated him. I hated the memory of him.

After gulping a glass of cold water, I steadied myself, pushed the anger down. Deep down inside. Buried it again. Taking total control of myself, I pushed open the door. Slowly I walked back into the bedroom.

Catherine had put on her robe. She was crouched in front of the fire, staring into the flames. Looking pensive, lost. I took my silk robe from the bottom of the bed, slipped into it. Went to join her by the fireside. I sat down next to her on the rug.

'I'm sorry,' I said quietly, taking hold of her hand. 'Too much wine. Followed by too much cognac.'

She was silent. She merely lifted her head and stared at me.

Again I said, 'Sorry.'

'It's *all right*, Jack, really it is,' she murmured in her softest voice. She smiled, and instantly the worried expression in her eyes evaporated. Lifting her shoulders in a slight shrug, she went on, 'We've many more nights together, I hope . . . hundreds of nights. We do, don't we, Jack?'

'Yes. I won't drink so much in future. It won't happen again,' I promised. I wondered if I was whistling in the dark.

Leaning forward, she kissed me lightly on the lips and touched my face. 'Don't look so concerned, so upset. It's of no consequence.'

But it is to me, I thought. I said, 'You're a beautiful woman, Catherine, a very desirable woman . . .'

Leaning back, Catherine looked into my face. Then she kissed me. I returned the kiss. When we drew apart she touched my mouth lightly, traced the line of my lips with her finger. Then she lay down with her head in my lap, gazing up at me unwaveringly.

Her eyes did not leave my face. I stared back at her intently. Wondering what was going on behind that lovely face.

After a moment or two, she said, 'You're *very* special to me, Jack. You've given me so much in the last few months. Love, warmth, understanding, tenderness and passion. You must know how much I love you,' she continued, her voice low, vibrant. 'You must know I'm in love with you, Jack.'

'Yes,' was all I dared to say.

I noticed a little smile playing around her mouth as she reached up with both arms. She placed them around my neck tightly and pulled me down to her. Kissing her swiftly, I broke free of her embrace. I was afraid. Afraid of being inadequate. I lay alongside her, resting on one elbow, staring into her face once more. She fascinated me.

'What is it, Catherine?' I whispered. 'You look as if you have a big secret.'

'I don't have one, though.'

'But you're wearing a secretive sort of smile.'

'Not secretive. Smug, perhaps.'

'Why smug?'

'Because I have you. Because I'm with you. Because you're the best lover I've ever had. Oh Jack darling –' She did not finish. She broke off, sighing deeply, contentedly. 'I've never felt like this before. It's never been like this for me. Never ever. Not with any other man. You excite me so much. I want you. I want you to make love to me. *Now.*'

'Oh Catherine . . . sweetheart . . .'

'Make love to me, Jack. *Please.*'

'Catherine, I don't know . . .'

'Don't be afraid,' she whispered and took off her robe, sitting up to do so, turning to smile at me.

She looked more ethereal than ever in the light from the fire. Her hair was a burnished coppery mass shot through with red and gold, tumbling down over her smooth white shoulders.

'Come to me, Jack,' she said, reaching out for me. 'Take me. Make me yours again. I want to give myself to you. I want you. Only you, Jack.'

I felt the heat slowly rising in me. Desire began to throb through me as she spoke. Shrugging off my robe, I almost fell into her outstretched arms. I pushed aside my fear of failing her. I was going to take her. Love her as I had never loved her. Or any other woman.

I lay on top of her long, lithe body, fitting mine to

hers. I kissed her neck and her breasts. I pushed my eager, trembling hands into the cloud of her red hair.

And as I continued to kiss her neck, her shoulders and her face, she began to whisper to me. Her whispered words were tantalizing, erotic. They drove me on. Filled me with excitement.

It was not long before I found myself fully aroused. I was able to slide into her swiftly. Catherine clung to me. Her fingers pressed into my shoulder blades. She wound her long legs around my back and locked her ankles. I slipped my hands under her buttocks. Brought her closer to me. Finally I was truly joined to her.

I forgot everything. Everyone. I could think only of Catherine.

# Seventeen

'I understand why you never want to leave this place,' Catherine said, linking her arm through mine as she gazed out across the landscape. 'It's extraordinary. Breathtaking really. And quite magical.'

'Yes, it is,' I agreed. I was pleased with her. She had expressed my sentiments exactly. Captured in a few words what I felt about the estate.

Catherine and I stood on top of a hill, the highest point on my land. We were above the vineyards which grew on the slopes of the hillsides. They stopped short at the château's gardens. To the right of the château were the woods; to the extreme left were the fields and the château's farm. The Home Farm it was called.

Just beyond the farm was the winery. There were many buildings clustered together, with vast cellars underground. It was here that the grapes were turned into wine.

I glanced around.

I saw the panoramic view as if through Catherine's eyes. And it *was* a magical sight. The sky was a pure, pale blue. Very clear, blameless, without cloud. It was a bright, sun-filled afternoon. Almost balmy.

Hardly any wind. It was only the middle of March. But spring was already here in Provence.

The land had undergone a change lately. I had noticed its sudden metamorphosis. New grass sprouting on the lawns. Tender green sprigs bursting open on the trees. Spring flowers shooting up in the gardens, brightening the many borders. They were vivid rafts of colour against the dark soil.

I took a deep breath. The air here was clean, pure, bracing.

Turning to Catherine, I said, 'I promised to show you the vineyards. Weeks ago now. So come on. Let's go. I think there's finally something to see.'

Taking hold of her hand, I led her along the narrow path that cut down through the first slope.

'Look!' I exclaimed. I was suddenly excited and bent down, hunkering close to the vines. 'The buds are appearing. Here! And here!' I pointed them out to her.

Catherine crouched down to look. She said, in a surprised voice, 'But they're so tiny, Jack. I can't believe they become grapes.'

'They do.'

'How does that happen? I know nothing about vineyards. Please explain to me.'

'I'll give it a try. First, let me tell you about the *cycle* of the vine. It begins with the winter rest. In February and March the sap rises. Now this –' I broke off, pointed to a bud. '*This* tiny thing is what we call a spring bud. In April the budbreak occurs. That means the bud opens more fully. A few weeks later the leaves appear. By May the leaves open and spread out more fully. In June the vines will have started to flower. Later these flowers turn into very, very small grapes. Through July and August we will see their growth. Late August, early September, they start ripening. Finally, in October, the grapes are mature. In November the leaves fall. The cycle starts all over again. The winter rest begins, etcetera.'

'It all sounds very simple,' Catherine said, looking at me. 'But I'm quite certain it isn't, is it?'

'No, it's not. It's much more complex. Especially the tending of the vines. The nurturing of them through the winter months. And the rest of the year. I tried to make it easy for you to understand.'

'Thank you, and presumably the grapes are picked when they are ripe.'

I nodded. 'That's when the *vendangeurs*, the grape harvesters, come to pick them. *Porteurs*, the grape carriers, take the grapes away in *běnatons*, those big baskets you've seen lying around. They move them to the end of each row in the vineyard. From there the *běnatons* are carried to the winery, and the grapes are put in the cellars ready for vinification.'

'Is the picking done by hand?'

'Yes. Olivier and I prefer it to mechanized harvesting. That's become popular in some parts in France. But it would be difficult here. On these slopes. Also, there's less chance of damage when the grapes are hand-picked.'

'What happens next in the process?'

'The wine is made, of course. It's stored in huge vats and casks in the *cuverie*. The vat room. I think I showed it to you. When I took you down into the *cave*, the big wine cellars, at Christmas.'

She nodded. 'I remember.' She tilted her head to one side. 'How do you know so much about wine-making?'

'I don't know *that* much,' I said. 'I've still got a lot to learn. But it was mostly Olivier. He taught me. He started me out. When I was sixteen. When Sebastian gave me the château. Fourteen years later I don't know half he does. Even though I went to the University of Toulouse to study the science of wine and wine-making. Oenological training in France lasts for four years. I *did* get my diploma. But I'm not up to Olivier's standards. Not yet. He's one of the best oenologists around. Considered to be a great wine scientist and wine-maker.'

'He seems very dedicated from what I've observed,' Catherine remarked.

'Over the years he's been improving everything. From the vintage of our red wines to the bottling of it. He's made immense progress in the last ten years. Because of Olivier Marchand our label, *Côtes de Château d'Cose*, is now considered to be a superior appellation.'

'And he's your partner, you said the other day.'

'Not my partner. I've given him a piece of the business. He deserves it. All the years he's devoted to the winery. To the château. The running of the entire estate.'

We began to walk down the slopes, heading towards the château.

After a moment or two, Catherine said, 'What

made your father buy the estate in the first place? I'm very curious about that. Was he interested in wine?'

'He liked it. Especially champagne. Veuve Clicquot. But he was just doing a good turn for somebody. As usual.'

'What kind of good turn?'

'A good turn for a widow woman. The widow of the man who owned Château d'Cose. About thirty years ago Sebastian was in Africa. Kenya. He met a Frenchman in Nairobi. A man called Pierre Peyfrette. Through a mutual friend. Over the years they became close. Sebastian often stayed here. About twenty-three years ago Pierre was killed. In a car crash. Driving down here from Paris. His widow Gabriella was at a loss. Didn't know what to do about the winery. The running of it. They had no sons to inherit. Just a young daughter. About my age. Gabriella wanted to sell the property, but there were no takers. Nobody was interested. It wasn't making money. Not in those days, anyway. So Sebastian took it off her hands. Bought it from Gabriella. Paid her very well. Maybe even too much. But it helped her start her life over. She moved to Paris with her little girl.'

'I see. Did he ever run it? I mean the way you're running it now, Jack?'

'Good God, no! Not Sebastian! He found Olivier Marchand. Put him in charge. What a wise move that was. I was seven when I first came here. And I fell in love with the château.'

'It's your home,' she said very simply, in a quiet voice, her expression full of understanding. 'You belong here. You love the winery and the vineyards.

You're very, very lucky, you know. You've found your true place in the world, found the work you want to do, your vocation. Found the life you want to lead. So many people don't. Not ever.'

'But you have, Catherine. You know what you want,' I said. 'Know where you're going. You're like Vivienne in certain ways. You both have a vision. Immense focus. You're a very functioning woman. And hard-working, thank God. I can't abide idle women.'

'Neither can I. It's impossible for me to relate to them. I've nothing in common, nothing to say. I always knew I wanted to read history at Oxford, and later lecture and write about it after I earned my doctorate. I was fortunate in that I had a flair for writing as well as a studious nature.'

'How's the book coming along? You've certainly been hard at it these past few weeks. Working like a regular little eager beaver.'

She laughed, her face lighting up. 'I find this place so conducive to work. And actually, in some ways, the book's proving easier to write than I thought.' She shook her head. 'Except that I'm not sure who's going to read it.'

'A lot of people,' I asserted. 'Take my word for it.'

Catherine laughed again. 'I can't. I don't believe there is anyone around who is interested in Fulk Nerra, count of Anjou, war lord and predator, known as the Black Hawk, founder of the Angevin dynasty and the Plantagenet line. Perhaps it only matters to me that the house of Anjou continued on its unrelenting course for well over a century, culminating in 1154 when Fulk's descendant Henry Plantagenet, count of Anjou, was crowned King of England, married Eleanor of Aquitaine, and sired a son who became the famous Richard Coeur de Lion.'

'I'm interested,' I reassured her. I meant what I said. 'You're a good story-teller. Even though you're dealing with facts not fiction. You've intrigued *me* when you've talked about the French–English connection. It sounds as if Henry and Eleanor had a real soap opera going. All their lives.'

'That's one way of putting it,' Catherine replied with a laugh, looking amused. 'And I suppose their lives together did have sort of . . . operatic overtones, what with their competitive, quarrelsome sons, Eleanor's scheming and meddling, Henry's philandering, and his constant banishment of her. He was always shoving her off to one of their many castles.'

'It would make a helluva good film,' I pointed out.

'Somebody beat me to it. A screenwriter. James Goldman. He wrote *The Lion in Winter*, which was all about Henry Plantagenet and Eleanor of Aquitaine.'

'Peter O'Toole and Katharine Hepburn! That's right! I saw it. And it *was* a nutty family. Dysfunctional. Just like the royals today. I guess it's all in the genes.'

'Not in this instance. The Windsors are not descended from the Plantagenets,' Catherine replied. 'They are of German descent through Queen Victoria and her consort Prince Albert. He was her cousin and all German. So was she, as a matter of fact. Her mother was a German princess and her father the Duke of Kent. He was descended from the

Hanoverian kings who were invited to rule England because of their Stuart connection. In a way, Victoria was born because of the scramble by the brothers of George IV to produce an heir. But going back to the Plantagenets, they were eventually eclipsed by the Tudors. When Elizabeth the First died, the throne of England went to her distant relative, James Stuart, King of Scotland.'

I laughed. 'Whatever you say, Catherine. But I bet a lot of people *will* read your book. Because you tell it all so well. Make it sound so . . . modern.'

'I guess human nature doesn't change much, Jack. Anyway, the Plantagenets were very colourful. But don't forget, I'm not really writing about them, but about Fulk Nerra. Nobody's interested in him. Except for me and my editor.'

'Don't be so sure. Listen, far be it from me to tell you what to write. But get more of the Plantagenets into the story. I guarantee it'll be a bestseller.'

'From your mouth to God's ears, darling,' she said, still laughing.

We had reached the bottom of the slopes where the vineyards grew, all thirty-three acres. I paused, took hold of Catherine's arm affectionately. 'I've got to work for a few hours. With Olivier. What about you? Are you going back to do more on your book?'

'For a while, and then I thought I would go riding. I think a good gallop across the fields will do me good. Blow a few cobwebs away. Would you mind awfully if I rode Black Jack? He's quite easy for me to handle.'

'I told you before, you can ride any horse in the stable. Of course you can take Black Jack.'

Leaning into me, she gave me a resounding kiss on the cheek. 'Thank you. Have a good afternoon. Don't work too hard.'

I smiled at her. 'Nor you.'

She was walking away towards the château when I called after her, 'Catherine!'

She swung around. 'Yes? What is it?'

'How about dinner in Aix tonight? We've been cooped up here far too long.'

'That's a lovely idea, darling.'

'I'll make a reservation at Clos de la Violette. Is that okay?'

'Only perfect.' She waved and went on her way.

I strolled towards the winery. As I passed the Home Farm I slowed. I almost went in to see Madame Clothilde. She ran the farm, as her mother had done before her. I had known her since I was a little boy. She had been a teenager then. Her husband Maurice was one of our vignerons, who worked in the vineyards. But he also helped out on the farm, along with their daughter Hélène and son Vincent.

She always made me very welcome, whipped up a *café au lait* in an instant. Brought out a warm brioche or a slice of *tarte tatin*.

My mouth watered, but I hurried on. Olivier was waiting for me. He wanted me to take a look at some bottles of wine. Quite a lot of bottles. He thought there might be something wrong with them. I wondered if they were bottle-sick. I hoped it was only that. Wine that was bottle-sick usually rectified itself if left to its own devices.

# Eighteen

'There's a thin veil on the surface of this batch of wine,' Olivier said when I found him in the bottling plant.

'*Maladie de la fleur*,' I exclaimed as I walked over to join him. I was referring to the flower disease which was the most frequent form of spoilage of wine. It was the yeasts which created the scum, or veil, on top of the wine.

'You're right, Jacques,' Olivier responded. 'But fortunately it is only the young wine which we made last year. Not so bad after all. And not too much of it either, only a couple of casks. Hardly a great tragedy.'

I nodded and said, 'On my way over here I wondered if the wine might just be bottle-sick.'

'No, more than that. And this spoilage *is* only minor.'

'We'll have to ditch the wine,' I asserted.

'Probably. However, let us not dwell on it, since we rarely have any spoilage. There's another reason I wanted to see you, Jacques, about something much more important. I want you to come with me to the *cave*.'

'Okay, let's go.' Turning on my heel I led the way.

I knew he had a pleasant surprise for me. I could tell from his face.

Together we went down into the cellars.

These covered an immense area undergr ɔund. It was here that the wine was brought to maturation and also sorted in casks, vats and bottles.

There was a small wine-tasting area at one end of the red-wine maturation cellar, and this was where Olivier was heading. Racks of wine had been arranged to create a two-sided corner. There were several chairs grouped around a small table. On this stood the mandatory white candle in its holder, a box of matches, various implements and a fresh white linen napkin neatly folded.

Olivier had already placed a bottle of wine and two glasses on the table. The first thing he did was light the candle.

I stood watching him. He was tall, and he stooped over the table slightly as he began to open the wine. Olivier was my mentor, teacher and friend. He was a good-looking man in a quiet, understated way. At sixty he was twice my age. But he looked much younger than his years. Maybe because he was a happy man. He loved his wife, his children and his work. And the *bastide* where he lived with his family. This charming old country house, part of my property, was situated across the fields near the orchards. He and his wife Claudette had made it a warm, welcoming home.

I watched Olivier opening the bottle. As usual I was struck by the way he worked on it. Delicately. Carefully. Like a surgeon. After cutting the red metal capsule around the neck of the bottle he removed it. This was so that he could see the wine in the bottle neck later. He then removed the cork, his movements smooth, gentle. I knew he did not want to disturb the sediment. Once the cork was out, he smelled both ends. Next he wiped the neck of the bottle inside and out with the white napkin. Finally, holding the bottle above the candle's flame, he peered at the colour of the wine in the neck and nodded to himself.

A smile of pleasure came to his face. 'Ah, Jacques, you are going to be pleased with this. I know you are.'

After pouring two glasses, he handed one to me.

We raised our glasses to each other.

'*Santé*, Jacques,' he said.

'*Santé*, Olivier.'

We both sipped.

I rolled the wine around in my mouth, savouring it. How delicious it was. Soft, velvety, yet full-bodied. I held the glass up to the light. The wine was a deep red colour. A beautiful red. Bringing the glass to my nose, I sniffed. Immediately I detected the perfume of violets. And something else, something not quite discernible.

'It's the red you put down in 1986,' I said, grinning at him. 'You used three grapes to make it. The Mourvèdre, the Syrah and the Cinsaut. The first two for their deep red colour and hint of violets in the taste. The Cinsaut also for its depth of colour as well as the softness it brings to the other two.'

Olivier beamed at me. 'Correct. Well done, Jacques. It has aged well, don't you think?'

'You bet. You've created a wonderful wine. A *great* wine. Looking back, I remember how good the weather was that year. You said the wine would have a wonderful lifespan because of that.'

'Thankfully, I was right. I think, though, that we must start shipping,' he said. 'The wine is ready. It must go out.'

'I'm in favour. So let's do that. And let's have another glass of it. I'm sorry I didn't bring Catherine with me. She'd have enjoyed tasting this.'

Olivier filled my glass.

I raised it to him. 'Here's to you, Olivier. Congratulations.'

'Ah, Jacques, do not congratulate me in this manner. We both worked on the wine.'

I laughed, shook my head. 'Oh no, we didn't. I was all of twenty-one. Knew nothing. Green behind the ears. I was still at Yale nine years ago. This is *your* wine. You created it, made it. You deserve all the credit for it, Olivier.'

'*Merci*, Jacques. You are very generous, as usual.'

For the next couple of hours I worked at my desk in my office in the winery.

There were accounts to study, figures to go over. I had been putting the job off for days. But I knew I had to get the paperwork out of the way. Today was as good a time as any. Gritting my teeth, I buckled down to it.

I worked until four o'clock. Finally it was all done. After putting the account books away, I picked up the phone, dialled the restaurant in Aix. I made a reservation for dinner.

When I left the office a few minutes later I took with me the half-finished bottle of wine Olivier had given me. I wanted Catherine to taste it. I was proud of this wine. Proud of Olivier for having created it.

I walked out of the front door and into the sunshine, into the most glorious afternoon. I strolled along slowly, glancing about as I did. Everything looked so well kept. This pleased me. I wanted the estate to be in good order.

The château ahead of me stood on flat ground. It was surrounded on three sides by gently sloping hillsides clad in vineyards. They rose up behind the vineyards like a giant flaring collar. Or, as Catherine said the other day, a huge Elizabethan ruff. The gardens and the fields were spread out in front of the château, splendid now in the golden light of the fading day.

To me this was the most idyllic spot in the world. I had always been happy here. Even when I was married, my difficult wives had not been able to ruin it for me. I had simply tuned them out. Tuned in to the land and the vineyards. Gone my own way. And I never wanted to be any place but here.

Out of the corner of my eye I saw a sudden flash of colour. I veered to my left, made for the wooden fence at the side of the narrow road where I was standing.

Leaning against the fence, I scanned the horizon. Then I saw it again. That flash of bright blue. Suddenly I could see Catherine in the distance, saw the flowing red hair, vivid against the blue sweater she was wearing.

Catherine was galloping across one of the fields, her hair streaming out behind her. She was a good horsewoman. I knew that. But for a reason I didn't immediately understand I held my breath. When she took the first hedge I cringed. I was worried. She was going to be thrown. Just as Antoinette had been thrown that day at Laurel Creek Farm.

I gripped the edge of the fence tightly, losing my grip on the bottle as I did. It fell on the grass. I left it there. I simply stood numbly staring at the figure in the distance. Waiting for her to fall off her horse . . .

The clock stopped. Its hands rolled back. I was pulled into my childhood.

A terrible memory I had kept locked inside me for twenty-two years broke free. It rose at last to the surface of my mind.

I was eight years old again. I was back at Laurel Creek Farm.

I was playing in the field with my red ball and bat when it happened. Antoinette was riding towards me, taking the hedge. And then she was off the horse, sailing through the air, falling, falling.

I dropped my bat and ball and ran as fast as I could. 'Antoinette! Antoinette!' I cried. I was afraid. Afraid she was dead. Or badly hurt.

She had been thrown by Tyger Bright just as she jumped the hedge. Now she lay there in a crumpled heap. Her face was the colour of chalk. Her hair, spread out around her face, looked more fiery than ever against those pale cheeks.

Her eyes were closed. My fear spiralled. My teeth began to chatter. *I thought she really was dead*. I knelt down next to her. Touched her face with my hand. She didn't stir. Yes, she *was* dead. Tears came into my eyes.

'Antoinette. Oh Antoinette. Speak to me,' I whispered, bringing my face close to hers. But I knew she wouldn't speak again.

'Get out of the way, Jack!' Sebastian shouted, bringing his horse to a shuddering standstill, jumping down on to the grass. 'You can't do anything. You're just a little boy.' Pushing me to one side, he knelt next to her, touched her face, as I had done.

'Run, Jack,' he said urgently, looking up at me. 'Run to the kitchen. Ask Bridget to bring a damp facecloth. And find Aldred. Tell him to come here.'

I was immobilized. I stood there staring at Antoinette.

'What's wrong with you! Do as I say!' my father screamed. 'Are you an imbecile? Go to the house, boy. Get Aldred. I need a man here to help me, not a child.'

I ran. All the way back to the farm. I was panting when I found Bridget in the kitchen. 'Antoinette fell. Off her horse. Wet cloth. My father wants a wet facecloth. Take it to him please, Bridget.'

Before Bridget could say anything to me, Aldred appeared. 'What's wrong, Jack?' he asked quietly. 'It's not like you to cry. Speak to me, child. What's wrong?'

Bridget said, 'Mrs Delaney's had an accident. Her horse threw her. Jack says Mr Locke wants a damp facecloth.'

'He wants *you* to go,' I said, tugging at Aldred's sleeve. 'He needs a man to help. Not a child. That's what he said.'

Aldred stared at me for a moment, frowning, but made no comment. He turned and raced out of the kitchen. Bridget followed him. I ran out of the house after them.

'I'm afraid to move her,' I heard my father say to Aldred as I staggered up to them a few moments later. 'That could be dangerous. Something might be broken.'

'Here, Mr Locke, let's put this damp cloth on her face,' Bridget said. 'It'll revive her. Yes, she's sure to come around in a few minutes.'

'Thank you, Bridget,' Sebastian said, taking the cloth from her. He placed it on Antoinette's forehead.

Aldred and my father spoke softly together. I couldn't hear them. I knew they didn't want me to know what they were saying.

She was dead. And they didn't want to tell me. I began to cry again. I pressed my balled fists to my streaming eyes.

'Stop that at once, Jack!' Sebastian said sharply, in a harsh tone. 'Don't be such a big baby.'

'She's dead,' I said and began to sob.

'No, she's not,' Sebastian snapped. 'She's just unconscious.'

'I don't believe you,' I wailed.

'It's all right, Jack,' Antoinette murmured, finally

opening her eyes, looking straight at me. And only at me. 'Don't cry, my darling. It was just a little tumble. Really, I'm fine, angel.'

I was so relieved I sat down hard on the grass.

'Where do you hurt, Antoinette?' my father asked, searching her face. 'Can you straighten out your legs?'

'I think so,' Antoinette said and did so as she spoke.

'Are you in any kind of pain, Mrs Delaney?' Aldred asked.

'None whatsoever. I just feel rather shaken up, that's all.'

'Let's get you upright, darling,' Sebastian said. 'Do you think you can sit?' he asked, looking at her in concern.

'I'm sure I can. Help me, please, Sebastian, would you?'

He did so. Once she was upright, she moved her head from side to side, stretched out her arms somewhat tentatively. Then she stretched her legs again.

'I'm sure there's nothing broken. I'm not really hurt, perhaps just a bit bruised,' Antoinette remarked with a light laugh. 'Although as I say that I think I might have sprained my ankle. I suddenly feel a twinge or two, can you help me to my feet, Sebastian?'

A moment later my beloved Antoinette, my Special Lady, was standing in front of me. She was alive. Not dead. My tears ceased instantly when she looked down at me, rumpled my hair and smiled. 'You see, Jack darling, I'm as good as new.'

However, she had sprained her ankle. At least she said it felt funny. So my father lifted her in his arms and carried her all the way back to the farm.

He took her up to her bedroom and came out after a few minutes. Bridget was sent in to help her undress. Later Dr Simpson came to examine Antoinette's ankle. 'Just to be sure it's not broken,' my father told Luce and me. 'And also to be sure she hasn't hurt herself in any other way.'

After supper I went to Antoinette's room and tapped on the door. My father opened it. He refused to let me in to say goodnight to her. 'Antoinette's resting,' he said. 'You can see her tomorrow, Jack.' Without another word he closed the door in my face.

I slumped down on the floor next to the grandfather clock in the corner of the upstairs hall. I would wait until he left. Wait until he went to bed. Then I could creep in to kiss her cheek, to say goodnight.

I must have fallen asleep in the darkened hall. It was the sounds that woke me. The groaning. The moaning. And then the strangled cry. A split second later I heard Antoinette's voice. 'Oh God! Oh God!' she exclaimed. There was a little cry again. 'Don't –' The rest of her sentence was muffled.

I scrambled to my feet, ran across the hall. I burst into her bedroom. It was dim, shadowy. But I could see my father in the light from the bedside lamp. He was naked. He was on top of Antoinette. Holding her face in his hands. He was hurting her. I knew it.

'Stop it! Stop it!' I screamed. I flew at him, grabbed hold of his leg.

My father was strong, very athletic. He moved

swiftly. Jumping off the bed he grabbed hold of me, lifted me up and carried me across the floor. As he marched out of the room with me I looked back. Antoinette was covering her naked body with the sheet.

She saw me staring and blew me a kiss. 'Go to bed, darling, that's a good boy,' she said and smiled at me lovingly. 'Sweet dreams.'

I cried myself to sleep. I was just a little boy. Only eight. And so I couldn't help her. I couldn't protect her from my father. He was back in her room hurting her. I couldn't do anything about it.

The next morning Antoinette was present at breakfast as she usually was. It seemed to me that she had never looked so beautiful. She was quiet. Lost in her thoughts. Whenever I looked at her she smiled at me in that special way she had. My father glowered at me over the rim of his coffee cup. I waited for him to chastise me about my behaviour the night before but he did not. He didn't even mention it.

Later, when we were alone, Antoinette gave me lots of hugs. And she kissed the top of my head and told me I was the best boy in the whole world, her boy, and that she loved me very much. She asked me to help her cut flowers for the vases, and we went out to the garden and spent the morning together.

I blinked several times and took a deep breath as Catherine came cantering up to the fence.

'Are you all right?' she asked, leaning forward, peering at me over Black Jack's head.

'Yes. Why?'

'You look a bit strange, that's all.'

'I'm okay.' I bent down, retrieved the bottle of wine from the grass. I regretted that I had dropped it so clumsily.

'Olivier has produced a remarkable wine,' I confided. 'Possibly a *great* one. The weather was excellent in 1986. The grapes were good. I wanted you to taste it. But I've probably ruined it. Dropping the bottle the way I did.'

'Let's try it anyway,' she answered. She gave me a wide smile, saluted and added, as she rode off, 'See you in a couple of minutes.'

I walked up to the château, my mind still on Antoinette and Sebastian. I had not thought of that awful incident since it happened. It had lain dormant for twenty-two years. But now that I had finally remembered it I understood everything. Understood that this was when I had first begun to hate my father.

# Nineteen

A week later I got the shock of my life.

After my usual morning walk through the woods, I returned to the château. In the kitchen I found Simone, my housekeeper. She was preparing the breakfast tray for Catherine and myself. After exchanging a few words with her I carried the tray to the library.

Since the advent of Catherine in my life, I always ate breakfast there. I didn't mind. It was a pleasant room overlooking the woods. Catherine loved it. She invariably worked on her book at the big library table under the window.

Catherine had not come down yet. I poured myself a *café au lait*, took a warm croissant out of the basket, spread butter and home-made strawberry jam on it.

I was munching on the croissant when Catherine came in, apologizing as she did.

'Sorry I'm late. Oh good, I see you've started,' she said, joining me in front of the fire. Sitting down on the sofa opposite, she poured coffee for herself.

After a moment, she went on, 'Did you have a good walk, darling?'

'Yes.'

'What's it like out today?'

'Sunny. As you can see. Not as mild as yesterday. But a nice day. For a good gallop.'

'Oh I don't think I'll go riding,' she responded. 'I don't think riding would be good for the baby, do you?' Putting the cup down, she looked at me.

'*Baby!* What baby?'

'Our baby, Jack.' She tossed back her flowing red hair and beamed at me. 'I was going to tell you tonight, tell you properly over dinner. It just popped out now. I've suspected I was pregnant for the past week. And the doctor in Aix-en-Provence confirmed it yesterday.'

I sat frozen in the chair, gaping at her.

At last I managed in a strangled voice, *'You're having a baby?'* I was not only shocked but incredulous.

All smiles, she nodded. 'Yes. Isn't it wonderful?'

I was speechless. Words failed me.

She went on quickly, 'I never realized I would feel this way, not that I ever thought much about children. I didn't care whether I had a child or not. But now that I *am* pregnant I'm just thrilled to bits. Terribly excited. It's really wonderful news, isn't –' Her voice faltered and abruptly she stopped. She stared hard at me. After a moment she said, 'You don't think it's good news, do you?'

'No, I certainly don't. It's horrendous. A baby was never part of our plan.'

'But Jack –'

'You were supposed to be taking care of yourself. You said you were using a diaphragm,' I rasped. I glared at her. 'What happened? Did you suddenly stop?'

'Of course I didn't!' she cried. She was irate. 'Something must have gone wrong.'

'*Merde!*'

'It can, you know.'

'It shouldn't have, though. Marriage was never part of our deal. I told you I would never get married again.'

'Who wants to get married?' she shot back angrily. 'Not I, Jack. *I've* always told *you* that. I cherish my independence. And this is not about marriage. It's about a baby. Our child. Unexpectedly, I find myself pregnant, and I'm pleased about it . . . I'm looking forward to having the baby.'

'You can't have it! Do you understand me? *You can't have it!*'

'Are you trying to tell me I should have an abortion?' she demanded. Her face had gone deathly white.

'You've no alternative!' I snapped.

'Oh but I do. I can have the baby.'

'I don't want it, Catherine.'

'I do, Jack. And I have no intention of terminating my pregnancy. I thought you'd be as happy as I am.'

'*Happy!* Don't be such a fool! This is a disaster.'

'It needn't be. We don't have to get married, darling,' she began in a softer voice. 'We can live together, just as we have been doing these past few months. And we can bring up our baby together, here at the château. It's a wonderful place to raise a child, Jack. And honestly, matrimony doesn't have to figure in it, not at all.'

'No way! Absolutely no way!'

'A lot of people do it, Jack. They –'

'I'm not a lot of people. I don't want this child. Don't you understand that? I'm not interested in this baby,' I spluttered.

'I'm going to have it, whatever *you* say. You can't stop me,' Catherine said, her voice hardening. There was a sudden change in her. She had acquired a defiance that brought a tautness to her face, and her body had stiffened. Her resoluteness took my breath away.

'If you have this baby we can't be together,' I threatened. 'It's the end of our relationship.'

'That's fine by me!' she cried and jumped up. Her eyes blazed in her white face. 'I will not get rid of my baby. And if you don't want to live with me and bring it up, then I'll live alone. I'll have the baby and bring it up myself. I don't need you. Or your bloody money, Jack Locke! I have enough of my own. I'm quite self-sufficient. In every way!'

'So be it,' I said coldly, also standing.

She glared at me, her fury apparent.

I stared her down.

Neither of us spoke.

'I'd better leave,' she exclaimed in a curt, clipped tone. 'I can be packed in half an hour, an hour at the most. Please be kind enough to order a cab for me. To take me to Marseilles. There are plenty of planes to London daily. I don't want to hang around here for longer than is necessary.'

'Consider it done!' I answered angrily. My voice sounded harsh to me.

Catherine walked across the room. She turned at

the door. In a voice that dripped ice, she said, 'You're afraid to be a father. You're afraid because you believe you can't love a child. And all because your father couldn't love you.'

I opened my mouth. No words came out.

She threw me one last pitying look. Turning on her heel she left, slamming the door behind her.

The chandelier rattled.

Then there was silence.

I was completely alone.

I did as she asked and ordered a car for her. Then I went to my office in the winery. I had work to do. But I also wanted to avoid Catherine. I didn't want to say goodbye. I didn't want to see her again. Not ever. Not as long as I lived.

Anger was fulminating inside me. I tried to shake it off. Work was the answer. I sat poring over the papers which had arrived by courier from Locke Industries in New York yesterday. Concentration eluded me. I pushed them away from me, sat back in my chair and closed my eyes.

Trying to calm myself, I made an effort to focus on my business affairs. I was not particularly successful. Emotions were crowding in, getting in the way.

I was angry. And hurt. I felt betrayed by Catherine. She had let me down by getting pregnant. It was irresponsible on her part. We'd had more than one conversation about birth control. She knew my feelings about children. I'd never wanted any when I was married. So why would I want them out of wedlock?

Suddenly her last words echoed in my mind. Had she spoken the truth? Did I really believe that I couldn't love a child because my father had never loved me? I had no answer for myself. How could I have an answer to an unanswerable question?

Catherine had said I was irrational about my father. But this was not the case. I was very rational when it came to Sebastian. I knew where my feelings of antipathy sprang from. My childhood. He had never tried to help me when I was growing up. Never ventured to teach me anything. He had never made an effort to be a real father. Like other boys' fathers did. He had always left me to my own devices. Left me with Luciana and Vivienne. We had never indulged in any masculine pursuits. Or exchanged confidences. All he had ever talked about was my duty. And he had never loved me.

At least Catherine hadn't tried to convince me I was wrong about that. Instead she had given me a psychological explanation. *Disassociation*. That is what she had called it. She said it sprang from lack of bonding in the first years of a child's life. She ascribed Sebastian's inability to love to this condition. It made sense. His mother had died in childbirth. He had never bonded with Cyrus. He had said as much once. I knew he had hated my grandfather.

But *I* didn't suffer from disassociation. I had known mother love for two years. Those crucial years of a child's life. Then Christa had come along. She had been there to love me. And after Christa went away there was my Special Lady. Antoinette Delaney.

I sighed under my breath. Catherine might be right

about my father. But she was totally wrong about me. Wasn't she?

Oh what the hell did it matter what she thought or said or did. She was out of my life. Or would be within the space of the next hour. It was regrettable really. I had cared about her. We had been good together. Built a good relationship. She had gone and ruined it. But then women usually did. In my life at least.

# Twenty

'Good God, where did you spring from?' I exclaimed. I stared at the door, startled to see my unexpected visitor. Her sudden arrival was a mixed blessing. Part of me was glad. The other part angry.

'New York,' Vivienne said, laughing. She stepped into my office and closed the door behind her. 'I got back to Vieux Moulin yesterday. I was going to phone you, but then I decided to surprise you instead.'

'You succeeded.' I got up, went to hug her. We strolled across the floor together. She sat down in the chair next to my desk and went on, 'You do look busy. All those papers. Oh, dear, I do hope I haven't interrupted you.'

'It's okay, Viv. I'd just about finished anyway. I've been hard at it all day. Locke Industries can be very demanding at times. Even long distance.' I glanced at my watch. 'It's almost five. I might as well pack it in now. Let's go and have a drink.'

'It's a bit early, isn't it?' she demurred.

'Not necessarily. Depending on how you look at it. Here in Aix it's five. But in Rome it's already six. The cocktail hour. Anyway, I'm not offering you any old drink but a very special one. So you can make an exception. Start drinking early for once. I want you to taste our new wine. Created by Olivier. In 1986. It's just matured. Come on, kid. Let's go down to the *cave*.'

'I'd love to,' Vivienne agreed, suddenly enthusiastic. She followed me out of the office.

Within minutes we were standing in the wine-tasting corner of the red-wine maturation cellar. I ushered Vivienne to a chair. Then I took a bottle of the vintage 1986 red out of a wine rack and showed it to her.

'It was good weather that summer and fall. If you remember, Viv,' I explained. 'And the wine is excellent. It's aged well. Olivier mixed three different grapes. It has a wonderful taste. Very soft on the palate.'

'I can't wait to try it,' she replied and smiled up at me. 'Go on then, open it. Let me taste your triumph.'

'Olivier's triumph,' I said.

I felt her eyes on me as I handled the bottle. I did so carefully. Slowly. I followed the steps taught to me by Olivier years ago.

Once I had poured a glass for each of us, I raised mine. 'Here's to you, Viv.'

'And you, Jack.'

She took a sip and then another. After a moment she nodded. 'It's wonderful. Like velvet on the tongue. And there's just the right hint of violets. Congratulations.'

'Thanks. But I told you, it's Olivier's wine. Not mine.'

Vivienne drank a little more, pronounced it the best

wine ever created at the château and said, 'I'd like to order some of it, if I may.'

'Sure. I'll give you a couple of cases. Tonight. Before you leave.'

'I want to pay for them, Jack.'

'No way. What's mine is yours. You should know that by now.'

'Thank you. That's sweet of you. Anyway, don't stand there, come and sit down with me.'

I did as she asked, groaning under my breath. I knew her so well. Better than I knew myself, at times. And I could tell from her expression what was on her mind. She was about to launch into a long recital. About her trip to New York. About Sebastian. About the damned profile.

Wanting to get it over with, I broached the subject. 'How's the profile on Sebastian coming along?'

'Very well, in certain respects. I talked to a lot of people at Locke Industries. To the president and his vice president.'

'What did Jonas and Peter have to say?'

'Only good things, of course. I spent a lot of time with Madge Hitchens at the foundation. In all the years she went to Africa with Sebastian she never met any women with him. And certainly not last year. At least none that he might have been romantically involved with.'

'She actually said that?'

Vivienne nodded. 'Yes, she did, and, in fact, no one knows anything at all about a new woman in his life. Nor did anyone know he was planning to get married this spring.'

'Except you.'

'That's right.'

I laughed out loud.

Vivienne stared at me. 'Why're you laughing like that?'

'Maybe she didn't exist. Doesn't exist.'

'What do you mean?'

I laughed again. I knew I sounded cynical. I couldn't help myself. I said slowly, 'Maybe this woman was an invention on his part.'

'That's ridiculous. Why would he invent a new woman, tell me he was in love, say he was getting married this spring?'

'To light a fire under you, Viv. Get you going.'

'Now why on earth would he want to do that?' she exclaimed.

'To make you jealous. That's what I'm trying to say.'

'That's preposterous. Very far-fetched indeed.'

'Not necessarily. Not when I really think about it.' I gave her a knowing look. 'Sebastian always cared about you the most. More than the other wives. You meant more to him than your mother ever did. Also –'

'I really find that hard to believe,' Vivienne cut in. 'He loved my mother very much.'

Ignoring her comment, I said, 'He could have wanted to start up with you again. Why not? Once you were very special to him. His favourite. Yep, that's it.' I laughed more loudly than before. 'He wanted to get you back. So he made himself look highly desirable. By inventing a new woman in his life.'

'That's a ridiculous premise on your part –'

'I bet I'm right,' I interrupted. 'He *did* make you jealous that day. Admit it.'

'No, he didn't,' she protested indignantly.

'It's me you're talking to, Vivienne.'

She was silent.

I sat drinking my wine for a few minutes. Neither of us spoke. I realized that I had hit the mark. He *had* made her jealous when they had lunch at Le Refuge. That was typical of him. He had always been very clever when it came to women. And at pushing the right buttons.

After pouring more wine for us both, I murmured, 'Why don't you fly to Africa? Go to every place he visited without Madge. The last year of his life. You'll discover he was there alone. I mean without a lover. Without a new woman. And *of course* Madge Hitchens was his only companion in the places he usually went to. Madge and some of the others from the charities.'

Vivienne said, 'During lunch at Le Refuge, when I asked Sebastian questions about his new girlfriend, his fiancée, because that's what she was, he said she worked in Africa. That she was a doctor. A scientist. It's more than likely that she was working in a laboratory somewhere. Maybe even somewhere isolated. I'm quite certain she didn't travel around with him. Why would she when she had a job? And *that* is the explanation, in my opinion.'

'So you do believe she existed?' I asserted.

'Exists,' Vivienne corrected.

I shrugged. 'Who's to know? I still think it's odd.

That no one met this woman with him. It's not at all in character.'

'What do you mean exactly?'

'Sebastian liked to show his women off. You should know that better than anyone. He loved a beautiful woman on his arm. Certainly, you were the prime example, Viv.'

'If that's a back-handed compliment, thank you,' she responded, and smiled at me.

'You're welcome, honey.'

'Jack?'

'Yes?'

'Do you trust me?'

'You know I do, Viv.'

'And my judgement?'

'Sometimes,' I hedged.

'Look, you must trust me now. I know *instinctively* that Sebastian meant every word he said to me. He wasn't trying to make me jealous, so that he could get me interested in him again. He *knew* me, and he certainly knew that would be the wrong way to go about it,' she explained quietly. 'Let me put it to you very simply. He *was* telling me the truth that day over lunch. He *had* met a young woman in Africa, had fallen in love with her. He loved her in a way he had never loved before. He said that in those exact words. He was going back to Africa to meet her. They were travelling on to India together. They were going to spend Christmas in Connecticut. At the farm. And then he was bringing her to France. To Vieux Moulin. To meet me. And you, I'm sure. They were going to be married here in France. This spring. I honestly and truly believe that this is exactly the way it was.'

I realized how serious Vivienne was. I said, 'Okay. Let's just say you're right. But why does it matter? You don't need this woman to write your profile. You knew him better than anyone. She can't add anything.'

'That's true, yes. I could start writing the piece tomorrow. But you've forgotten something. I want to know *why* he killed himself.'

'Oh, Viv, *honey*. You're never going to know.'

'I'm going to make a damned good try at finding out.'

'How?'

'I'm going to find the woman.'

*'How?'*

'I'm not sure. But I will. Believe me, I will.'

'Why?'

'I want to talk to her. Interview her.'

*'Why?'* I asked again.

'Because in my opinion she's got something to do with his death.'

I stared at her. 'You gotta be kidding.'

'No, Jack, I'm not. I think that she's somehow connected to his suicide. And before you say it, not because she might have jilted him either.'

'Then what?'

'I don't know. Not yet.'

'Why are you suddenly so focused on this woman?'

'Because in his very predictable life she was the only thing that was different.'

I nodded slowly. 'That's true. But you'll never find

her,' I remarked. I meant this. I thought Viv was wasting her time.

'We'll see. In the meantime, rack your brains for me, darling, and maybe you'll remember something, even a small thing could be pertinent.'

'I'll try. But I already told you. I didn't see much of him last year.'

Vivienne finished her wine without further comment. A bit later she said, 'I'm getting tiddly here, drinking on an empty stomach. And I've got to drive back to Lourmarin.'

'I'll feed you,' I said. 'Stay to dinner.'

'Why not? And thanks, I'd love to see Catherine. How is she?'

I cleared my throat. 'She's not here, Viv.'

'Oh. Where's she gone?'

'I don't know.'

Vivienne frowned. 'I'm not following you, Jack.'

'She's left me. Gone back to England. At least she went to Marseilles. Early this morning. To catch a plane home to London.'

'Oh, Jack, darling, I am sorry,' Vivienne commiserated. 'You two seemed so well suited. Perfect together. I thought you'd found the right woman at last. Whatever happened?'

'She got pregnant.'

'So?' Vivienne asked, raising an eyebrow.

'We disagreed. About the baby. She wanted it. I didn't. She dug her heels in. We argued. She said she was going to have it. No matter what I thought or said. In the end we had a screaming row. She left.'

'And you let her go?'

'Yes.'

'How could you be so stupid! So dense!' Vivienne cried, staring at me aghast. 'How could you let that marvellous woman escape?'

I flinched under her critical gaze. 'Look, Viv, I don't want to get married,' I said finally. 'And I certainly don't want to have kids. She fully intends to have this baby. Against my wishes. When she said she was leaving I didn't stop her. Anyway, it's for the best. It wouldn't have worked. Not in the long run.'

Vivienne regarded me for a prolonged moment. Then she said in a low but vehement voice, 'You're a damn fool, Jack Locke. You've just made the biggest mistake of your life.'

# *Part Three*

# LUCIANA

## Pride

# Twenty-one

I once heard my brother Jack tell Vivienne I was fragile, and I was astonished to hear him say such a thing. How totally wrong he was in his assessment of me.

I am not a fragile woman.

On the contrary, I'm one of the strongest people I know, mentally and physically. Certainly my father always understood this; that's why he called me a true Locke born and bred.

Sebastian saw in me the personification of the Lyon Locke character, and even said I was a genuine throwback to Malcolm Lyon Locke, that great Scotsman who was the founding father of our dynasty.

It is true, I have inherited many of the traits that made our family great. I have an iron will, determination, dedication, discipline, immense stamina and a proclivity for hard work.

I am also unrelenting, and ruthless in business, and my husband Gerald says I'm a born trader with ice water in my veins when it comes to wheeling and dealing.

My father called me an accomplished dissembler and one of the cleverest liars he had ever met. He assessed me as being rather better at prevarication than his father Cyrus. Sebastian had been laughing when he said this to me, and I know he had meant it as a compliment. Although when he told Vivienne I was a liar he probably made it sound derogatory, and there is no doubt in my mind that he *did* tell her. He had always confided everything in her, ever since she had come into our lives when she was twelve and I was only four.

Nevertheless, he *was* proud of me, proud of my talents and skills, especially my negotiating skills. I had come to understand, early on, that he wished I had been born a boy. He would have much preferred to have had two sons to carry on in his footsteps, rather than just one.

However, in the end, the fact that I was a girl did not deter him when it came to the family business. As soon as I was old enough he steered me into Locke Industries in New York.

For several years now I have been running the British division of Locke in London, and the last time I spoke to my father, just before he died, he told me I had done a superlative job. He was very proud of me. 'You're a chip off the old block, Luce. Well done, darling!'

In the course of this discussion, over dinner at his townhouse in Manhattan, he suggested that I might enjoy coming back to the New York office. It was there that I had started my business career after graduating from Yale. He said he had a special position for me: executive vice president in charge of all the women's divisions of the company.

I had been toying with the idea ever since. I still toyed with it. Certainly it was very tempting. All I had to do was tell Jack and he would arrange it. He had been at dinner that night, had noticed Sebastian's enthusiasm and mine, and had commented on it. My husband had no objection; in fact, Gerald rather fancied the idea of moving to New York where he would be able to work at the US branch of his family's investment bank.

If the truth be known, *I* should be head of the company, not Jack. My brother was supervising the business long distance, as my father had done for many years of his life. It wasn't very satisfactory, in my opinion, even though the CEO was competent, and had been hand-picked by Sebastian ten years ago.

I was a hands-on manager and therefore I believed I would be better for the company. I longed to run Locke Industries instead of Jack, and there was no doubt in my mind that he would welcome this change.

My brother genuinely loved the château and the vineyards more than anything else in his life. Certainly he was good at running the estate. I was proud that he had made such a huge success of the winery, and that his label was now a superior appellation. He had done it by himself, with the help of Olivier Marchand, and *chapeau!* to him.

No one could convince me that Jack was really interested in Locke Industries. He was chairman and did what he did only because it had been drilled into him for years that this was his chief role in life. Duty,

duty, duty had been the eternal cry from Sebastian and Cyrus. Deep down within himself I think he probably hated Locke Industries. I loved the company; I lived for it.

An hour ago Jack had phoned from Aix-en-Provence. He had cancelled the trip to London he had been planning to make this coming weekend. I was feeling somewhat put out with him because of this. I had been looking forward to talking to him about Locke Industries and business in general.

Now our chat would have to wait until next month, when he had promised to come to the birthday party I was planning for Gerald.

At this moment Gerald was in Hong Kong on business; he would be returning later this week. The thought of my husband prompted me to get up from my desk and walk across the office. I paused at the mirror hanging on the wall above a seating arrangement of sofa, chairs and a coffee table.

I stood in front of the looking glass for several moments, regarding myself, wondering what Gerald would think of my new image.

At first he would be extremely angry because I had cut off my blonde hair. He loved my long golden tresses. But he would eventually get used to this short, cap-like cut which was more up to date. Also, the hairstyle made my head look neater, smaller and therefore more balanced to my slender body.

Even my figure had changed, if only slightly, in the three weeks Gerald had been away. I had put on weight. Not much, only four pounds, but it was enough to make me look less emaciated. The weight gain had played havoc with my clothes and most of them no longer fitted me. They would have to go. I had ordered several new suits for work and they would be delivered to me next week.

I was pleased about my weight gain. Not only did I look better, I felt better. The pounds had started to come on quite naturally in December because unexpectedly I had started to eat properly again.

It was not that I had consciously dieted over the years; I never had. Very simply, I had never had much of an appetite. Not since I was twenty, when I lost my taste for food. That was when Sebastian had teased me about my weight, and told me I was fat. 'A regular little butter ball,' he had added a trifle scathingly, and the next day I had stopped eating correctly. In essence, I had brainwashed myself not to feel hunger, and in the process I had been starving myself for years.

For a long time Gerald had wanted a child. Now, so did I. I felt the timing was right. After all, I was twenty-eight and Gerald was thirty-three. We were both the perfect age to start a family.

*I wanted heirs*. Sons and daughters who would rejuvenate the declining dynasty that the Locke family had become. I wanted *my* children to carry on, to lead the family into the twenty-first century, to expand our fortune and carry on the tradition started generations ago.

Turning away from the mirror, I hesitated, and then on an impulse I left my office and hurried down the corridor to the boardroom.

I went in and closed the door behind me, switching

on the lights as I did. On the walls hung the portraits of the men who had made our family great.

In all truth, I did not need any reminders of my impressive heritage. This had been imprinted on my brain since I was a child, and I was filled with immense pride to be a Locke, to come from such a long line of brilliant entrepreneurs.

My father had always termed them robber barons, and in the most derisive way, but I never thought of them as such. They were my idols, whether they were robber barons or not.

Occasionally I liked to study their portraits. These were copies of the originals which hung in the boardroom in New York. I had had them copied for the London boardroom by a prominent artist, who had, in my opinion, painted portraits much superior to the originals. Their likenesses invariably inspired me to greater heights.

Viewing the images of my ancestors had now become something of a ritual with me. Each man fascinated me; I wished I had known them all.

I always started out with the founding father, Malcolm Trevor Lyon Locke. As I stood gazing up at his face now, I wondered, as I so often did, what kind of man he had really been, my great-great-great-grandfather.

Physically he looked like a nineteenth-century version of Sebastian. Or rather my father had resembled him, and it was easy to see where Sebastian's good looks had come from, and Jack's as well. Malcolm had the black hair, fresh complexion and bright blue eyes of the typical Scotsman.

I knew all about him. He was a legend in the family. Born in Arbroath, a small fishing village and seaport on the east coast of Scotland near Dundee, he had sailed for America in 1830. He had been nineteen years old when he set forth to seek his fortune.

As the story goes, Malcolm soon discovered that the streets of New York were not paved with gold as he had been led to believe. And so he moved to Philadelphia.

A blacksmith by trade, Malcolm was enterprising and something of an inventor, always tinkering with bits of machinery and farm tools. Whilst he worked as a blacksmith, he started his own tool shop and small forge on the side, and operated them in his spare time.

It was in 1837 that the first steel plough with a self-scouring mouldboard was invented. One year later, in 1838, Malcolm, who had himself been experimenting with ploughs, came up with an invention of his own.

Malcolm Locke created a mouldboard of chilled cast iron which scours best with the least friction. It changed his life, and set him on the road to becoming a millionaire. In fact, it was the beginning of the family fortune and Locke Industries, although in those days it was called the Locke Tool Company, so named by Malcolm.

From the portrait of Malcolm I moved on, stood in front of the painting of Ian. He was the eldest son of Malcolm and his wife Amy MacDonald, and Ian had been born in that propitious year of 1838.

When he was old enough, Ian went into the

business with Malcolm, who by this time not only manufactured mouldboards but all kinds of farm machinery and implements as well. The Locke Tool Company grew and prospered under Ian's steady if uninspired guidance.

Ian's first son Colin was born to him and his wife Georgina Anson in 1866. I peered at his face. Colin did not look like Ian or Malcolm, but he had inherited the latter's genius for invention and his pioneering spirit.

When he was in his late twenties Colin went to Texas to drill for oil. He did not make a lucky strike and eventually returned to Philadelphia and the family business.

However, his experiences in the oil fields had prompted him to tinker around with drilling bits. Also, he worked on numerous other inventions in his tool shop. But mostly, when he had time, he tried to improve on the fishtail bit, which was most commonly used for drilling. He knew from experience that it constantly broke.

It was some years later, when he was in his early forties, that Colin came up with a drilling bit which would change the Locke Tool Company yet again.

After years of frustration and numerous different versions, he finally invented a bit that would drill through rock and quicksand. It was formed like two pine cones, one moving clockwise, the other counterclockwise. These revolving cones, moving in opposite directions, had 170 cutting edges.

It was 1907 and Colin Locke's drilling bit was revolutionary. He was one year ahead of Bo Hughes, who invented a similar bit in 1908 and formed the Hughes-Sharp Tool Company.

I looked at Colin's portrait intently.

My great-grandfather was not as good-looking as the other Locke men who had gone before him. He had blond hair and dark brown eyes, and it was obvious to me where my colouring had come from. Colin appeared quite dolorous in the painting. Sebastian had actively disliked him, almost as much as he had disliked his father.

It was Colin Lyon Locke's invention that formed the basis of an even greater fortune for the family and the Locke Tool Company.

His famous drilling bit was sold all over the world, even as he continued to perfect it for several years. It is not possible to drill for oil today without using it, and the bit brings in hundreds of millions every year, just as it has since the day Colin invented it.

My grandfather's portrait hung next to that of his father. Cyrus, born in 1904, was the first child of Colin and his wife Sylvia Vale.

Grandfather was now in his ninety-first year. Whenever I thought of him I saw a white-haired old man in my mind's eye. Here, in this portrait, he was young, in his late thirties, and attractive enough in a sombre, glowering way. His hair had been a light brown and he had black eyes. He seemed out of place with his ancestors. To me he did not look like a Locke at all.

I thought again of the man I had seen at Sebastian's funeral and an involuntary shiver ran through me. How terrible old age was. Once Cyrus had been dominant, domineering, tough and ruthless. He had run Locke Industries with an iron hand.

Now he was nothing. He had no power or influence in the company where he had once been king. He was just a frail little old man who looked as if a puff of wind would blow him over.

I moved on from the painting of my grandfather. The one next to it, the last one, was of Sebastian Lyon Locke.

My father.

And what a beautiful man he had been. So handsome. The eyes so brilliantly blue, the hair as black as jet. And his features were as arresting as his colouring was, finely sculpted and well defined. No wonder women had dropped like flies at his feet. I couldn't blame them. He had been a gorgeous specimen.

Five wives he had had. But only two children by two of them. I wondered, as I had so often wondered lately, why he had not had more offspring.

His first wife, Josephine Allyson, had been Main Line Philadelphia and an heiress in her own right. She was the mother of Jack and had died when he was two. She had left him all of her money, millions, which had been held in trust until he was twenty-one.

My father's second wife had been my mother Christabelle Wilson. When he married Christa he had been the grieving widower, or so I had been led to believe.

I was the result of their brief union.

When I was small my mother was sent away to dry

out in a clinic in New Haven. She never came back to live with us. I saw her from time to time, but it was Sebastian who brought me up.

After he divorced my alcoholic mother, he took up with Antoinette Delaney, Vivienne's mother. Their love affair never became more than that, because she was married to Liam Delaney who was wandering around the South Seas.

Sebastian's relationship with Antoinette ended when she fell down our cellar steps and broke her neck. If she had lived I suppose she could have divorced Liam for desertion at some point, and married my father. I know he wanted to formalize their love affair. He told me this once. And he was certainly broken up about her death.

My father's third wife was Stephanie Jones, who had only a very short sojourn with us. She had worked with Sebastian as one of his assistants at the Locke Foundation. Jack and I both liked her. She had been intellectual and rather quiet, but lovely looking, a cool, refined blonde who reminded me of Grace Kelly. Stephanie had always been kind to Jack and me, and we were sad when she was killed in a plane crash.

Then along came the great Vivienne.

My father was married to her the longest. Five years. It seemed like an eternity to me. I know he made her pregnant and that she had a miscarriage. Sebastian told me that himself. He was heartbroken about the loss of the baby.

I suppose it was inevitable that he would marry Vivienne. He had always favoured her when she was growing up, and he became her guardian after her mother died. He paid her school fees and supported her financially, and she was always with us during school vacations and special holidays.

My dislike for Vivienne was quite intense. I couldn't stand her really, and I was glad when they finally split up. I always thought my father deserved better.

His fifth and last wife was Betsy Bethune, a career woman. To me she was the most unsuitable person he could have married. She was far too busy being a famous concert pianist to be a good wife to my father and I was not in the least surprised when he divorced her. I had never understood why he had married her in the first place. It was an enigma.

I stared hard at the painting of my father, studying his face intently.

Yet again I asked myself why he had killed himself. It just didn't make sense to me. He had seemed perfectly all right when I was staying with him in New York. In fact he had not been gloomy as he so often was. He was much more relaxed, even happy, that week before he took his life. I wished he hadn't done it. I missed him so much.

I had always loved my father, even though he preferred Jack to me in many ways. He had always devoted so much of his time and energy to Jack, but I suppose that was natural, since Jack was his only son and the heir apparent.

Vivienne had come between my father and me from the moment she had arrived on the scene with her unbearable mother. She stole my father from me when I was a child, but I managed to get part of him back when I was grown up.

After all, I was his real child, his biological child, with genuine Locke blood running through my veins. When I was a teenager he saw in me the second son he had always wanted. That was one of the reasons he had given me so much power in Locke Industries later on. Of course he knew I was a good businesswoman, practical and efficient like him; he knew, too, that I would not let him down. He was also aware of how much I cared about the company.

Yes, my father had loved me. He had made that very clear in his will.

'I give and bequeath to my dearest and most beloved only daughter Luciana . . .' Those had been his words before the bequests to me had been listed.

My father had left me half of his personal fortune and many of his prized possessions. Most of all, I cherished the priceless art collection of post-Impressionist paintings, especially all of those Van Goghs, which he had given to me. That gesture in itself was another expression of his love.

I sighed to myself as I took one last, lingering look at the portrait of Sebastian. Then I walked out of the boardroom, turning off the lights and closing the door behind me.

# Twenty-two

My secretary Claire had placed a pile of faxes on my desk in the short time I had been visiting my ancestors in the boardroom. They were mostly from Locke Industries in New York.

I read them all carefully, dealt with those that needed a response and made notes on the others. After signing a batch of letters, I went into the adjoining office and gave everything to Claire.

Returning to my desk I made half a dozen calls to Locke in New York, settled various bits of business and then looked over my appointments for the remainder of the week.

Tomorrow I had a date for lunch at Claridge's with Madge Hitchens from the Locke Foundation. She was on her way to Africa on behalf of the foundation, and she had stopped off in London for a few days to see her daughter Melanie who was attending the Royal College of Art.

Other than Madge I had no other special engagements, just routine work all day, and that night Gerald would be arriving from Hong Kong.

Closing my appointment book, I put it away in my desk, then went in to say goodnight to Claire.

*

The London offices of Locke Industries were situated in Berkeley Square, and I paused for a moment when I came out of the building.

It was six o'clock and still light, a pleasant evening at the end of March, and I decided to walk home to Belgravia. I made for Charles Street, which would take me into Curzon Street, and from there I could head into Park Lane and Hyde Park Corner.

I liked walking in London, looking at the old buildings, enjoying a feeling of the past, and of history and tradition; it was my favourite city. My father first brought me here with Jack when he was fourteen and I was twelve. Of course I fell in love with the place, the people and the culture, not to mention the manners of the British. They were so polite and civilized it was a pleasure to be around them.

It was the summer of 1979, and my father had come to London ostensibly to sell his apartment in Mayfair. But after he had put this on the market, he then turned round and bought a house in Eaton Square.

I was with him the day he viewed the house for the first time, and I'm not certain who liked it the most, Sebastian or I. Jack had absolutely no interest in it whatsoever. He was simply marking time until we left for the Château d'Cose in Aix-en-Provence, the only place he ever wanted to go. He had loved the château intensely for seven years. It was his grand passion.

In any event, the house was duly purchased, decorators were sent in, and we came back at the end of the year to spend Christmas at our new home in London. A great deal of care and money had been spent on it, and Colefax and Fowler had done a superb job, had created elegance, a warm ambience and great comfort. It was a real home, not a design statement, and Sebastian in particular was pleased with the finished result.

For me the trip was marred by Vivienne's presence, but I was so happy to be in London I managed to disguise my displeasure behind a fraudulent smile. This I fixed to my face permanently.

I also managed to make myself scarce that winter, rushing off to the Victoria and Albert, the British Museum, the Tower of London, Madame Tussaud's, and my favourite place of all, the Tate Gallery. I loved to wander around looking at the paintings, especially the Turners.

When we were growing up, Jack was always telling me that Sebastian was after Vivienne. He said it was a campaign, called it the Gradual Seduction of Vivienne, making this sound like the title of a play or movie. Jack insisted Sebastian was the fat cat waiting to pounce on the innocent virgin. But I didn't really agree with him; in my opinion, it was the other way round.

In fact, I had always believed that Vivienne was after my father even when she was a teenager, and when her awful mother was still alive. Her avid interest in Sebastian became more apparent than ever to me that Christmas of 1979, and she never let him out of her sight. She hung on his every word, and his arm, never gave me or Jack a moment alone with him.

At the time, I told Jack she was sleeping with

Sebastian, but he pooh-poohed the idea. My brother had had a crush on Vivienne the Great for as long as I could remember, so I suppose he had not been able to support the thought that our father was where *he* wanted to be – in her arms.

I remember I wasn't too crazy about this thought myself, since she had long endeavoured to drive a wedge between my father and me. As Sebastian's lover she would have a greater opportunity to do that, and knowing her she would take advantage of that situation.

I was smart enough to realize that I couldn't change the situation, if it did indeed exist. For this reason I involved myself in my own activities and let them get on with it. I advised Jack to do the same, but he persisted in hanging around the house. He called it 'keeping an eye on things'. I called it spying.

I came to know London well in those days, and the London house was my favourite place to be, after the Manhattan townhouse where I had grown up with Jack and Sebastian. Luckily for me, we spent quite a lot of time in England over the next few years. My father was becoming more and more involved with his African charities, and London made a good jumping-off point to that continent for him.

After he married Vivienne he seemed to lose interest in London and in the house. In fact, they stayed at Claridge's when they were on their honeymoon, and later that year he bought the old mill in Lourmarin. I was glad my father had done this, because it prompted him to give the château to Jack, and this made Jack so happy he was almost delirious.

I was twenty-three when I moved to my favourite city permanently. Sebastian gave me one of the top jobs at the London office, and I was in my true element at last, running some of the women's divisions.

Over the years Locke Industries had become a huge conglomerate. We no longer made Malcolm's ploughs, at least only a token number; instead we manufactured tractors and other kinds of farm machinery, as well as pick-up trucks, jeeps, golf carts and station wagons.

We had a building materials division that produced everything from doors and windows to floors and walls. We made prefabricated houses, garages and barns. Our bathroom division manufactured a decorator-designed line of baths, showers, toilets and all the accessories used in a bathroom. We even had a shower-curtain division.

This diversification had been started by my great-grandfather Colin and my grandfather Cyrus, long before it was a popular trend in business. Then my father had followed their lead when he was still running the company on a full-time basis, quite some time before he became so heavily involved with his charity work.

Over the years Sebastian had bought a number of corporations which he then proceeded to mould into the women's divisions of Locke Industries. He had purchased companies that manufactured well-known brands of clothing, undergarments, hosiery, shoes, swimwear, sports attire and leisure wear.

When my father sent me to work in London, five

years ago now, one of the first things *I* did was to buy a company specializing in cosmetics and body-care products. This led to several other acquisitions, but the first one quickly became a huge money earner, and I'm very proud of it.

For years I had believed myself to be a dyed-in-the-wool career woman, and I had never really given much thought to marriage, even though I'd had plenty of boyfriends. But I had only been in London a few months when I fell in love.

It was Thomas Kamper, a business acquaintance, who introduced me to his brother Gerald, with whom he worked in the family's merchant bank in the City.

Gerald and I hit it off immediately. His lean, dark good looks and candid blue eyes struck a chord in me, and within six months of our first meeting we were married. I was twenty-four and he was twenty-nine.

I am still not sure whether Gerald's mother Lady Fewston was very happy about her youngest son acquiring an American for a wife, but Sebastian was all for the union. He liked Gerald, approved of the short engagement, and as a wedding gift he gave us the house in Eaton Square. I was particularly thrilled about this, as joyful as Jack had been when he got the château.

I loved Gerald for a number of reasons, not the least of which was his attitude to women. He did not have much time for the idle and the indolent who had nothing to occupy their days, much preferred women like me who were strong, independent and had flourishing careers. Like my brother Jack, he was attracted to brainy women who had something to say for themselves.

Deep down I know that, despite my love for Gerald, I would have hesitated about marrying him if he had objected to my job. In fact, I would have probably had only a few dates with him and let it go at that.

It was necessary for me to go to work every day, necessary to my wellbeing and my sense of self. I needed to be busy, to accomplish something, to make a contribution in my own small way. And, after all, Locke Industries was in my blood, a huge part of my life. It always had been, and I wanted it for myself. I hoped one day to get it.

Suddenly I realized I was almost home. I had been walking so quickly I had reached Eaton Square in record time. As I put my latchkey in the door and turned it, the grandfather clock in the hall struck six-thirty.

# Twenty-three

'When Vivienne said your father was planning to get married this year, I was completely taken aback,' Madge Hitchens said, looking at me intently across the lunch table. 'I didn't know anything about it, Luciana, did you?'

I stared at her without answering. I was stupefied to hear this.

Madge said, 'I can tell by the expression on your face, and your silence, that you didn't. You look as surprised as I was when she told me.'

Recovering my voice, I asked, 'Who on earth was he going to marry?'

'Vivienne didn't know her name. That's why she was asking me.'

I frowned and said quickly, 'Vivienne thought you would know because you travelled with Sebastian constantly, spent so much time with him.'

'Yes. But I wasn't aware of a fiancée. In fact, no one at the foundation was.'

'How come Vivienne knew?' As I asked this question I realized it was stupid of me to even pose it. Vivienne had always been a kind of confidante to him.

'Sebastian told her,' Madge replied, confirming my thought.

'But he didn't tell her the woman's name, Madge.' I shook my head. 'How like Sebastian that was. However, he must have told her something else, surely?'

'He did. He told Vivienne she was a doctor. A scientist. At least, so I gathered. He also said she lived and worked in Africa.'

'What's Vivienne's interest in her now that my father's dead?'

'She's writing a profile about Sebastian and she wants to interview her.'

'I see.' I smiled faintly at Madge. 'Well, at least we don't have to worry about the tone and content of the story, Madge dear. It's bound to be flattering, since Vivienne's writing it.'

'Oh I'm sure it will be.'

'Who's Vivienne writing it for? Did she tell you?'

'Yes,' Madge said, nodding. 'The magazine section of the *Sunday Times*. As I told you earlier, she was in New York for several weeks, interviewing people at Locke Industries and the foundation. From what I gather, everyone spoke beautifully about Sebastian. But then why wouldn't they? He was a unique man, and those who worked for him and with him revered him. They still do. I think Vivienne's premise for the profile is very accurate.'

'And what is it?' I asked curiously.

'She's focusing on the idea that he was the world's last great philanthropist.'

'The Last Great Philanthropist,' I repeated. 'Not a bad title, not bad at all.'

'Your father was a great man, Luciana. In the eighteen years I knew him, a day didn't go by that I didn't marvel at him. He could win men's hearts by the sheer force of his personality, and he commanded energies beyond the average. And I've never known anyone with his strength of will. He was formidable in so many ways, and such a compassionate man as well.'

'Yes, he was everything you say,' I agreed. 'And I've always believed that he could have been anything he wanted, even if he hadn't been born who he was. He was so brilliant, he would have succeeded at anything he did.'

'He certainly had an extraordinary aura,' Madge remarked. 'It served him well when he was dealing with some governments in Third World countries. They were awed, bowled over by him, and ultimately he brought them around to his way of thinking. Which brings *me* to another point, Luciana.'

'Tell me, Madge.'

'Even though Jack is now running the foundation and administering the money as your father did, he won't go on any field trips. I wonder if you could influence him to come to Africa with me later this year?'

'You must be joking! He won't listen to *me*, Madge! Or anyone else, for that matter. Jack's very stubborn, surely you know that after all these years. Why, he grew up at your knee, as I did.' I shook my head and finished, 'He won't go to Africa. Or anywhere else, I'm afraid.'

'Don't you think we could work on him, Luciana?'

I laughed hollowly. 'We could try, but I'm not sure it would do any good. He never wants to leave that vineyard of his.' I took a sip of water, and continued, 'Madge, I think we ought to look at the menu and order lunch, don't you?'

'Of course.' She eyed me for a long moment and then said, 'I'm glad to see you've put on a bit of weight. You've been far too thin for far too long.'

I smiled at her. 'I know. I suddenly got my appetite back.'

Once we had ordered, I took up the subject of Jack again, and his involvement with the foundation. 'Jack doesn't mind giving away the money, Madge,' I explained. 'He's not a bit tight-fisted, and he knows it goes to help people in need. However, he doesn't want to be personally involved with the charities. He doesn't know how to deal with people the way Sebastian did. Don't ask me why, he just doesn't.'

'Perhaps I could edge him into it,' Madge began and stopped short, pursing her lips. 'You know, I always felt that Jack hated living in your father's shadow. Maybe that's the problem.'

'It could be,' I agreed. 'He's so much like Sebastian and in so many ways, but he does his damnedest to be completely different. It's as if he doesn't want to be my father's clone.'

'I'm sure he doesn't.' Madge gave me a hard stare, and asked, 'Do you think Sebastian was *really* engaged to someone?'

'It's possible.' I shrugged. 'But he never told *me*.'

'Or anyone else, except Vivienne. So if it was true, why *did* he keep it a secret?'

'Perhaps he didn't,' I said thoughtfully. 'Maybe she worked in a remote area. You know what *he* was like, jumping around all over the map. I could never keep track of him, could you?'

'Not all the time, no, and certainly he and I were often in different parts of Africa. Indeed in different parts of the world. But it is a mystery, isn't it? By the way, I think I ought to alert you . . . Vivienne plans to come to London to see you, Luciana, to interview you for the piece.'

I merely nodded and stored this bit of information away.

At this moment the waiter arrived with our first course and I let the subject of Vivienne sink. To my astonishment I was hungry, and I even found my mouth watering as the waiter served me. I was about to eat Morecambe Bay potted shrimps for the first time in years, and I was actually salivating.

'*Bon appétit*,' I said to Madge, picked up a thin slice of buttered brown bread and took a bite, then dipped into the potted shrimps with relish. I'd first eaten them in 1979, here at Claridge's, where Sebastian had often brought us for lunch and occasionally for dinner. I had sworn off them years ago, because the shrimps were potted in pure butter, but I could enjoy them with impunity today since my aim was to actually put on weight.

'I hope I get a chance to see Gerald,' Madge murmured, as she dug a fork underneath a Colchester oyster.

'He'll be back from Hong Kong tonight. Perhaps

you'd like to have lunch with us in the country on Sunday?'

'That would be great, Luciana, thank you. He's such a nice man, and he was very kind to me at the memorial service in New York, very comforting.'

'That's Gerald. I'm afraid he still feels badly that he wasn't able to come to Sebastian's funeral in Connecticut, but his father had just undergone surgery and he didn't want to leave him,' I said.

'He told me all about it, and I could well understand his feelings.'

'Would you like to bring Melanie with you?' I asked, smiling at her. 'Or would it be too dull for her?'

'Of course it wouldn't. I'm sure she'd love it. Thank you.'

'She's doing well at the Royal College of Art?'

'Spectacularly. And loving every minute of it,' Madge replied, and went on talking about her twenty-year-old daughter for the next few minutes.

As I listened to my father's former colleague and dear old friend of the family, I couldn't help thinking how well she looked. Madge had gone to work as Sebastian's administrative assistant when she was forty-two, when Melanie was just two years old. Eighteen years later she didn't look much different than she had then. Her hair, which came to a widow's peak on her forehead, was still as black as coal, her heart-shaped face smooth and unwrinkled. At sixty she looked much younger.

'You're staring at me, Luce,' she said, regarding me with her head on one side. 'Is something wrong?'

'How rude. I'm sorry. But I was actually admiring you, Madge, thinking how wonderful you look . . . the same as you did the first day I met you, when I was all of ten.'

'Kind words will get you everywhere,' she answered with a laugh. 'And I feel wonderful.'

'Sebastian always said you were very fit, the fittest person he knew. He even mentioned it the last time I was with him in New York . . . just before he died.'

Madge stared at me, and then unexpectedly blurted out, 'I miss him so much, Luce.' Her fine grey eyes filled with tears, and she cleared her throat several times.

I reached out and took hold of her hand resting on the table. 'I know you do. So do I.'

There was a silence, and then finally recovering herself, she gave me one of her penetrating stares and said quietly, 'I dwell on his suicide a lot. I can't imagine why he did it. I've racked my brains for a reason.'

'Perhaps there isn't one, Madge,' I said, squeezing her hand. 'At least not one that we could understand.'

# Twenty-four

'Gerald, listen to me. Please don't go to sleep. *Please,*' I said. 'I want to talk to you about something and it's very important.'

Stifling a yawn and rousing himself, my husband responded in an apologetic voice, 'Sorry to be so sleepy, darling, I'm afraid I'm still suffering from the time change. But talk to me, please do, I'm all ears, I promise.'

Pushing myself up on one elbow, I looked down at him and said, 'I've stopped using birth control pills, so you may well have made me pregnant tonight. Isn't that an exciting thought?'

Gerald sat upright in bed and gaped at me. 'Good Lord, darling, when on earth did this extraordinary change of heart occur?'

'I've been thinking about having a baby since December, Gerald. The time *is* right, don't you think?'

'I certainly do! I'm all for it, you know that. Good lord!' he exclaimed, '*a baby*. What a wonderful idea.' He gave me a boyish grin. 'Perhaps we *did* make one, we were certainly passionate enough, if that counts for aught.'

He leaned back on the pillows, gave me a long

penetrating look and added, 'Well, well, well, so you want to be a mother, Luciana. What was it that actually wrought this unexpected change in you?'

'The fact that the Locke dynasty is on the wane has been bothering me for a long time,' I said. 'And the only way to rectify that is for us to have children. *Heirs,* Gerald. Heirs to follow in our footsteps. Mine and yours. I know you want children, and that your father wants grandchildren to go into Kamper Brothers. After all, your family business is one of the oldest merchant banks in England, just as the Locke family is one of the oldest dynasties in America. We can't let the Lockes and the Kampers become extinct, now can we?'

'Perish the thought,' he said with a dry laugh. 'And how many children are you planning for us to have, my sweet?'

'At least four,' I answered. 'Two for me, I mean two to go into Locke Industries, when they're old enough, and two for you for the bank.'

'Sounds a bit cold-blooded when you put it that way, don't you think?' he murmured, giving me an odd look.

'It may sound it,' I said. 'But it isn't, not really, Gerald. I'm just being practical, that's all, and maybe we'll only have two or three. Perhaps we might have six, though. Who knows? There's some luck attached to it, I'm sure, but as far as I'm concerned, the more the merrier.'

'Forgive me if I seem a trifle startled, but this is indeed something of a switch on your part. Quite a switch actually. You were always so much against having children.'

'You've always led me to believe you wanted them. Don't tell me you've changed your mind. You haven't have you?'

'No, no, not at all, Luce. I'm delighted about your decision, couldn't be more pleased if I tried. I suppose you'll want to continue working, and have a nanny for the baby?'

'The answer to both questions is a decided *yes*, and surely that doesn't matter to *you*, Gerald. You've always understood about my work.'

'No, it doesn't bother me at all.'

'And *you* were brought up by a nanny.'

'Yes, thank heavens. My Nan was wonderful and I loved her very much when I was a child. I still love her. Pity she's retired, she would have been perfect for Bertie.'

'Bertie?'

'Yes, Bertie the baby. Our baby. Sounds sweet, doesn't it?'

I laughed. 'Not Bertie, darling. We're not going to call him that. He'll be named Sebastian after my father, Horatio after yours. So, in fact, his full name will be Sebastian Horatio Lyon Locke Kamper.'

'Good Lord, that's a hell of a mouthful for a little baby.'

'But he's going to grow up and be a tycoon and run Locke Industries. And anyway, he'll be known as Sebastian Locke Kamper. That doesn't sound too bad, does it?'

'It seems you've got it all worked out,' Gerald

answered. 'Well, there's one thing I do know for certain, poppet.'

'What's that?' I asked, gazing into his vivid blue eyes. I loved him a lot.

'We're going to have rather exciting times these next few years, trying to make all the babies you want.'

I laughed, reached up and kissed him on the cheek. 'I'm sure that won't worry you.'

'Of course it doesn't, I'm mad for you, Luce.'

'You're the sexiest thing, Gerald.'

'Thanks for the compliment, and let me return it. So are you.'

'Thank you. Gerald?'

'Yes, darling?'

'There's something else I want to talk to you about.'

'I'm wide awake now, so go ahead, I'm listening.'

'It's about Locke Industries,' I began and then hesitated. 'Are you sure you're not too tired?'

'I'm all right. Tell me what's troubling you.'

'I'm not really troubled,' I answered quickly. 'Just concerned about Locke Industries.'

'In what sense?'

'Jack's not really interested in running the business. He does what he does because he has to, and he was brought up to understand that he had to do his *duty*. God knows, that was drilled into him all his life. But he doesn't *love* Locke Industries the way I do. And I feel I should be running the company in his place. He could still have the title of chairman.'

'Are you trying to tell me that you want to be CEO

and president?' Gerald asked, his voice rising slightly.

'Well,' I began and paused when I saw the concerned expression settle on his face. 'Don't you think I could do the job?'

'Don't be silly, Luce, of course you could do it. But it's awfully demanding, and all-consuming. Quite frankly, I think Jonas Winston is a wonderful businessman and a great CEO and he's done a fine job for ten years, performed extremely well. Don't forget, he was hand-picked by Sebastian. And Peter Sampson is a darned good second in command. I –'

'Do you think I can't run Locke because I'm a woman?'

'That has nothing to do with it!'

'Then why are you looking so worried?'

'You're my wife. I want to spend time with you, Luciana. Obviously I don't mind if you have a career, in fact I'm proud of you, your achievements. You know that. But I'm not sure I'd want you spending eighteen hours a day at Locke headquarters in New York.'

'I wouldn't be doing that.'

'Of course you would. You're a hands-on person, that's your style of management. I doubt you'll change.'

'Maybe Jack would be happy if I became chairman in his place,' I said, thinking aloud. 'That's a much less demanding job. And it would be much better for the company than having him making decisions from France. You wouldn't mind if I were chairman, would you, Gerald dear?'

'No. But Jack might.' He threw me a knowing look.

I shrugged.

Gerald said softly, 'And how many decisions do you think Jack really makes? Mostly he approves of what Jonas Winston thinks should be done, the decisions which Jonas has already made. They discuss them, of course, but Jack listens to Jonas, I'm positive of that. He'd be a fool not to listen when Jonas is sitting there in full command of the company. I absolutely believe this is exactly the way it is. Trust me on this, Luce, please.'

'I'm not sure you're right,' I began, but paused. I knew he was correct in everything he'd said.

'Look here,' Gerald exclaimed, 'I'm going to give you a bit of advice. It's the same advice I give to friends and colleagues who come and discuss a problem with me, a problem they have with someone else. I always tell them they're talking to the wrong person. I point out that they should be talking to the person they're at odds with, not me, because that's the only way they'll get any satisfaction, resolve the problem.'

'So you're telling me I should go and talk to Jack?'

'Yes, I am, darling, if you want to pursue this matter further.'

'And what if Jack is relieved and happy that I want to take over from him? How would you feel about that? And also, Gerald, would you really move to New York?'

'Like a shot! Of course I would. Move to New York, I mean. I'd be happy living there. I could run our Wall Street office, we could live in that magnificent townhouse of your father's that's now yours and is standing empty. And we could spend weekends at Laurel Creek Farm. I'm sure your brother would be happy if we made use of it in his absence. As for you taking over the chairmanship from Jack, that would be perfectly all right with me as long as you were not killing yourself at Locke Industries.'

'I wouldn't be doing that!' I exclaimed. 'Not as chairman.'

'No, I don't think you would. You have more sense than that.' He grinned at me in that boyish way of his and added, 'It's absolutely necessary that we have some free time together, in order to make all those babies you say you want.'

'I do want them, don't doubt that, Gerald.'

'I don't. Now if Jack's not amenable to giving up the chairmanship, which he may not be, then you could suggest something else to him. You could offer to become joint chairman, share the responsibility with him.'

'Yes . . . I guess I could . . .'

'Let's just suppose that Jack agrees to your proposal. How do you think Jonas would feel about it?'

'I don't think he'd mind. He's always liked me, admired me even, and we got on well when I worked with him at Locke in New York. I don't think I'm wrong in saying that both he and Peter Sampson respect me.'

'And certainly you don't have any shareholders to answer to, since Locke is a privately held company with all of the shares in the hands of the Locke family.'

'Except for Vivienne Trent. She has some shares. Sebastian gave them to her years ago when they were married,' I reminded him.

'Good Lord, Luce, that's not a problem! Vivienne would never fight you in any way.'

'Want to bet?'

'No, I certainly do not. And in any case, it's not even a fair bet, since she doesn't own enough shares to make a bit of difference one way or the other.'

'That's true.'

Gerald yawned and stretched. 'I'm frightfully sorry, poppet, but I think I do have to go to sleep now. I feel as if I've been awake for four or five days, I'm so tired. It's the Hong Kong time difference getting the better of me at last.' He leaned over, kissed me lightly on the lips. 'But at least I had strength enough earlier to make love.'

'And perhaps make a baby,' I murmured.

He smiled at me. 'I hope so, I really do. Goodnight, sweet.'

'Goodnight, darling,' I said and turned out the light.

Within seconds Gerald was fast asleep, breathing deeply. Poor thing, he really was exhausted after the long flight from Hong Kong, plus the time difference. He had arrived last night, looked fatigued and yet he had insisted on going to the bank this morning.

Not unnaturally, his jet lag had caught up with him later in the day. He had succumbed to it this afternoon, had fallen asleep in the car as I had driven us down here to our small country house in Aldington in Kent.

I lay next to Gerald in the darkness, trying to fall asleep, but my mind was racing, working overtime. Mostly I thought about Jack. I cared about him and I knew he cared about me; he had looked after me when we were little, had always been my champion. And despite his ridiculous infatuation with Vivienne I knew he was always on my side when it came to the crunch. We may have had different mothers, but our father had made sure we were close and caring.

We had been through a lot, seen a lot when we were children. I had shared Jack's hurts, as he had shared mine, and I suffered with him when Sebastian and Cyrus were forever brainwashing him about doing his duty at all times.

In the last few years I had felt sorry for him. My brother had had such rotten luck with women. No wonder he had turned to drink at one point. His first wife had become obsessed with our father; his second wife had turned out to be a nymphomaniac panting to get into any man's trousers. And now he had quarrelled with his girlfriend Catherine Smythe. I had met her with Jack twice, and I was not particularly enamoured of her.

When Jack told me two weeks ago that he had broken up with her and sent her back to London I was not in the least surprised. Those two were totally unsuited to each other and I had predicted to Gerald that they were bound to split up in the end. She was far too intellectual and highbrow for my down-to-earth Jack.

At least my brother had the vineyards to consume him. They gave him immense pleasure, and he relished the success his label had become in recent years. Earlier this week he had told me on the phone that he would never get married again, and I believed him. Furthermore, even if he changed his mind, and did tie the knot again one day, he would never have children. He disliked them far too much, found them irritating.

Therefore it really was up to me to provide a new generation of Lockes, my own Lockes who would take the family into the twenty-first century. I fell asleep thinking about this.

The following morning after breakfast, I went into the den and telephoned Jack at the Château d'Cose. He seemed glad to hear my voice, and pleasantly surprised when I told him I wanted to visit him.

'Is Gerald coming with you, Luce?' he asked.

'No, I'm afraid he can't. As you know he's been away for three weeks, and he's a lot of work to catch up on.'

'How long can you stay?'

'Two days, that's all. I need to talk to you about a few business matters, quite aside from wanting to see you, Jack. I really was disappointed that you cancelled your trip to London this weekend.'

Ignoring this, he said, 'When are you coming?'

'On Wednesday morning. Is that all right?'

'It's fine.'

We said goodbye and hung up.

# Twenty-five

As planned, I left London very early on Wednesday morning.

Several hours later I was being driven out of the airport in Marseilles, headed in the direction of Aix-en-Provence.

I had not visited the château for some time and I had forgotten how beautiful Provence was. Now as we drove up through the Bouches-du-Rhône I leaned back against the car seat, occasionally glancing out of the window, enjoying the scenery.

It was a pleasant spring day. Sunlit fields, vineyards and olive groves under a fine blue sky brought back a rush of childhood memories, and for a few seconds I was transported to another time.

I had first come to Provence when I was five years old, and I recall how confused I had been by the foreign language and this strange new place full of voluble people and unfamiliar sights.

I had clung to Jack's hand tightly, my eyes as big as saucers as I had taken everything in. But I had not been afraid. Quite the contrary. I remember that, like Jack, I had been excited about seeing the castle my father had recently bought. And when we had finally arrived at the Château d'Cose, Jack and I had been impressed.

Together, hand in hand, we had wandered around the great house, peering into its vast rooms, traversing its endless corridors, and exploring its dusty attics. We had been awed by it all.

We had spent many happy times at the château for the next few years, even though Antoinette Delaney and Vivienne had invariably been with us on our vacations in France. My father had wanted them with us and who was I, a mere five-year-old, to protest.

*Vivienne*. I wondered what to do about her.

Madge Hitchens had warned me she wanted to interview me for the profile of my father she was writing. No doubt she knew I was coming to Aix. Jack wouldn't have been able to keep that to himself. He told her everything. Like my father he had made her his sole confidante, a role which went all the way back to their childhood in Connecticut.

There was no question in my mind that she would come bearing down on me whilst I was staying with Jack. I at once decided to beat her to the draw. I would call her and make a date before she had a chance to phone me. I didn't particularly relish the idea of seeing her, but knowing her as I did, she would persist in hounding me until I talked to her. I might as well get it out of the way. And on my own ground.

The last time I had seen Vivienne was at Sebastian's memorial service at the Church of St John the Divine in Manhattan.

She was miffed with me after our run-in at the farm

following my father's burial; I was angry with her. She had tried my patience, playing the grieving widow the way she had during the course of that morning. Divorced from Sebastian for a number of years, Vivienne had been another man's wife and then his widow. I had seen no reason for her to adopt the role of widow at Sebastian's funeral, since she was merely an ex-wife.

Jack had said I was wrong, pointing out that Vivienne was genuinely grieving, reminding me that Sebastian had been her guardian after her mother had died. I'd quarrelled with Jack that day too; we had all been on edge, I decided later, and immediately smoothed it over with Jack.

I made up my mind to be civil and cordial with Vivienne when I saw her at the château. For undoubtedly I *would* see her.

Simone, Jack's housekeeper, and Florian, his houseman, were hurrying down the front steps of the château even before the car had drawn to a standstill.

A second later, as I alighted, they came rushing forward to greet me, their faces all smiles.

'*Bonjour, madame,*' they said in unison.

'*Bonjour*, Simone, Florian,' I responded, smiling back.

The driver had now taken my small case out of the boot and when she saw it, Simone exclaimed, 'Monsieur Locke said you would be here only two days. I see that is so from your luggage. *C'est dommage, Madame Kamper, c'est dommage.*'

'Next time I hope to stay longer, Simone,' I murmured, following her up the steps into the château. She had worked here for fifteen years and I had always been a special favourite of hers.

Jack came striding into the hall at this moment, saying apologetically, 'Sorry, honey. I was on the phone. Paris.'

'Hello, Jack,' I answered and smiled up at him.

He hugged me affectionately and then held me away from him. 'Luce. You're different.' After a sharp and appraising look, he went on, 'Cut your hair. Put on weight. Great! You look great.'

'Thank you, Jack. You don't look so bad yourself.'

Grinning at me, he put his arm around my shoulder and walked me into the small sitting room next to the library. It was a cosy room and I had always liked it.

He said, 'Let's have a chat. And a drink. Before lunch. I have a new wine. Special. You must try it, Luce.'

'I would love to, and tell me, darling, how've you been? I hope you're not too down in the mouth about the split with Catherine Smythe.'

'Not at all. Good riddance.' He walked over to the console table, where he kept a tray of drinks and glasses, and proceeded to open a bottle of wine. 'We were not suited, not right together. I'm glad she's gone,' he muttered dismissively.

Sitting down on a chair near the fire, I studied him for a moment.

I could not help thinking how much he resembled Sebastian this morning. He was wearing a vivid blue turtleneck sweater which emphasized the colour of his eyes. With his head of thick dark hair and finely chiselled features, he was the spitting image of our father.

I almost said this and then instantly bit back the words, knowing they would offend him. He hated me to tell him he looked like Sebastian, and he forever went out of his way to dress quite differently.

Our father had been such an elegant, fashionable and impeccably tailored man; Jack was just the opposite, favouring old sweaters, frayed shirts, baggy corduroys and worn jackets which he had Florian endlessly patch and repair. I was really quite ashamed of his clothes. That was why I usually gave him sweaters and shirts, ties and jackets for birthdays and Christmas. He never seemed to buy anything for himself.

Jack would never admit it, but I knew he dressed this way on purpose, and that he revelled in looking slightly rumpled. I had long ago discovered that comparisons with Sebastian infuriated him, and yet they were almost unavoidable. There was no question whose son he was, they looked so much alike.

Glancing at me across the room, Jack started to give me details about the new wine, how it had been put down nine summers ago, and how it had turned out to be a jewel of a red, probably the best ever produced at the château.

As I listened, I began to realize that Jack spoke more fluidly and in longer sentences as he discussed the wine and Olivier, and how the latter had created it.

It struck me suddenly that this was because he was

relaxed and talking about something which he genuinely cared about. Usually words came out of my brother's mouth in short staccato bursts, an abrupt speech pattern that had developed when he was about eight or nine years old. In those days, he frequently stuttered, an affliction that had upset all of us, not only Jack. I think this was why he began to speak in those short bursts. To avoid stuttering. At least that was my theory.

Carefully, Jack carried my glass of wine over to me, then went back to get his own. Standing in front of the fire, he raised his glass and said, 'Here's to that great man whose name is Luciana.'

I stared at him, a brow lifting as I did.

'That's what Voltaire said to Catherine the Great. It's a compliment.'

'I realize that,' I said. 'Thank you.' I then took a sip of wine, and nodded. 'It's lovely, Jack, and not too heavy. Congratulations.'

Beaming at me, Jack sat down on the sofa and asked, 'What did you want to talk to me about, Luce?'

I took a big swallow of wine and said, 'Locke Industries?'

'What about Locke?'

'The running of the company *specifically*, Jack.'

'Jonas is a great CEO. No problem there. Sebastian hand-picked him. Jonas hand-picked Peter Sampson. Our profits are high. We've never done better. What's your problem?'

'I don't have a problem. I agree with you, I think they're both terrific and Locke *is* in great shape. What

I'm trying to say is that I'd like to be more involved in the running of it.'

My brother stared at me. 'Want to move, Luce? Run the women's divisions. In New York. Like Sebastian offered. Is that it?'

'I might want to move to the New York headquarters, and take up the offer Sebastian made before he died, yes. But what I'm talking about right now is being involved at a higher level, a corporate level.'

'Not following you, kid.' My brother eyed me.

'I'd like to have a hand in the running of Locke Industries, not just the women's divisions.'

'That wouldn't work! It wouldn't sit well, Luce. Not with Jonas. Nor with Peter. Interference. That's how they'd see it. Wouldn't blame 'em.' He shook his head vehemently. 'No, no, it wouldn't work.'

'Because I'm a woman, is that it, Jack?' I asked quietly, staring him down.

'You know better than that. For this reason: *you need more experience*. You're not old enough to handle a company like ours. It's too big.'

'Oh come on, Jack, don't say that. You know very well that Sebastian thought a lot about my ability, my practicality and efficiency. He had great things planned for me at Locke.'

'He did. That's true. But you're not experienced enough. Neither am I. Luce, *I* wouldn't know where to begin. Nor would you. Down the road a bit maybe. Not now, honey.'

I sighed. 'I don't want you to think I don't have faith in Jonas, because that's not so. I happen to believe he's a genius and so does Gerald.'

'He's proved it to me. Look at the balance sheet,' Jack said in a voice that sounded tough.

'Have *you* ever wanted to run Locke Industries, Jack?'

He shook his head. 'No. But you know that. I just told you how I felt. I wouldn't know how. Not even Sebastian wanted to run it. Not full-time. Not in the end. And he helped to make it what it is. Tough job, Luce, real tough.'

'You don't really like being chairman, do you?' I gave my brother a penetrating stare. 'Isn't it a bit of a bore having to go to New York every two months? Having to deal with Jonas on a daily basis?'

'I don't talk to him every day,' Jack cut in, frowning. 'What're you getting at?'

'If you want to step down, I wouldn't mind being chairman, Jack. Really I wouldn't. You've never been interested in the company, you much prefer to be here running the vineyards.'

He threw back his head and roared, his laughter echoing around the small room. 'I always knew you were ambitious. But Jesus, Luce! Trying to take the chairmanship! *From me*. That beats everything.'

'I'd only take it if you didn't want it. Or share it with you, if you felt like doing that. You know, to ease your burdens.'

My brother began to laugh again, shaking his head. 'I gotta hand it to you, kid. You got chutzpah.'

'I'm being realistic. I love the business. You don't. I'd make a terrific chairman.'

'Maybe. But it's *my duty*. To be chairman. I was brought up to do the job. And I will. Remember

Cyrus and Sebastian drilling it into me? Night and day. Duty. Duty. Duty. That's all they talked about to me. Don't let the family down. Run the business. Look after your sister. Be a dutiful son. Dutiful grandson. Dutiful heir. Dutiful Locke.'

'Yes, I remember,' I murmured. 'They gave you a hard time, Jack darling, I know that.'

'So leave it alone. And don't forget something. Sebastian laid it all out. In his will. In the division of shares.'

'I know he did. Drop it, Jack. Forget I brought it up. But in case you ever do want to retire from the chairmanship, I'm ready to take over.'

'You'd have to, Luce. That's the way the will's laid out. The way Sebastian wanted it. There's no one else.'

I nodded, and continued, 'Jack, there's something else I want to say. Look, I promised to talk to you on Madge's behalf. She wants you to go out on a few field trips. To Africa, for the charities.'

'No way! Absolutely not!' he exclaimed. 'I've told Madge that. Several times. I'm giving away the same amount of money. As much as Sebastian did. I'm even willing to fund more charities. New ones she brought to me. But no travelling. Not for me. No trips to Zaire. Or Zambia. Or Somalia. Or Angola. Or Rwanda. Or India. Or Bosnia. Or any of the places Sebastian liked to wander around. Indifferent to disease, bombs, bullets. Indifferent to chaos, murder, revolution. Whatever. Absolutely no bloody way! *I'm* not insane. He *was*.'

'All right, all right, don't get so excited. It was only

a suggestion on Madge's part, well, a request really. And I already told her that I was quite sure you wouldn't do it.'

'Damn right I won't.'

'Jack, did you tell Vivienne I was coming to stay with you?'

'Yes. Why? Does it matter?'

'No, of course not. I understand from Madge that she wants to . . . sort of interview me for the profile she's writing about Sebastian.'

'Yes, she does.'

'Then I'm going to phone her later and invite her over to the château. How about tonight? Does that suit you?'

'Sure. Invite her to dinner. If you want.'

'I will,' I said.

Locke Industries before lunch. Jack had not erupted angrily, as Gerald had predicted he would before I left London this morning. However, my husband had been right about one thing: Jack had no intention of giving up what was his birthright.

It was not often my judgement was flawed when it came either to business or my brother, but in this instance it had been. However, Jack had taken it well, and no harm had been done to our relationship. He knew I liked to take control, be in charge. Also, he no longer overreacted now that he'd stopped his heavy drinking.

After taking off my suit and putting on a dressing gown, I carried my laptop to the bed and spent the next hour working.

Vivienne arrived punctually a couple of minutes before six, and Florian led her into the small sitting room where I was waiting.

There had always been a certain amount of animosity between us, and since neither of us was a hypocrite we made no pretence of great friendship by hugging and kissing. Instead we greeted each other rather formally and shook hands.

I sat down in my usual chair near the fire.

Vivienne took the one opposite, and said, 'You look very well, Luciana.'

'Thank you, so do you,' I replied, trying to be nice.

Then taking control of the situation in my usual way, I got straight to the point before she had a chance to say anything. 'How can I help you? What do you want to know about Sebastian that you don't already know?'

She looked uncertain for a moment, then cleared her throat and said, 'I was hoping you could tell me what he was like the last year of his life. You saw him more than Jack and I, didn't you?'

'Yes. He was in London around this time last year. Early April, actually, and I spent a few days with him at the office. He came back in May. It was a weekend and he drove down to Kent on the Sunday, to have lunch with us at Goldenbrooke. He was very much himself on those two visits, by that I mean low-key, slightly remote, even a bit melancholy. Still, that *was* par for the course, right? He was a moody man, Vivienne, as you well know. Certainly we witnessed his mood-swings and temperament when we were growing up.'

'He could be morose,' Vivienne concurred. 'Often on the edge. He seemed to be carrying the burdens of the world on his shoulders.' She gave me a hard stare, asked, 'Did he tell you if he had any special plans? For the future?'

I shook my head. 'No, he didn't.'

'Can I come in?' Jack asked from the doorway. 'Or am I interrupting?'

Vivienne exclaimed, 'Hello, Jack. No, you're not interrupting. Come and join us.'

Jack strolled in, gave her a peck on the cheek, then went and opened the bottle of Veuve Clicquot which stood in a silver bucket on the console. 'How about a glass of bubbly, you two? Or would you prefer something else?'

'Champagne's fine,' I said.

'Thanks, Jack, I'll also have a glass.' Vivienne turned back to me and went on, 'So Sebastian was being Sebastian right to the end?'

'You're not going to dwell on his suicide in the profile, are you Vivienne?' I demanded, my voice suddenly turning sharp.

'I'm devoting exactly *one line* to it, that's all, Luciana. I am only interested in writing a profile of him as he was. So there were no new ventures on the horizon? Either at Locke Industries or the Locke Foundation?'

'Not that I know of,' I responded and glanced at my brother. 'Did Sebastian tell you anything about his future?'

'Nope. It was business as usual with him. And there was nothing different on his agenda. I've already told Viv that.'

Looking across at her, I said swiftly, 'Just before Jack came in, I was about to mention that Sebastian was in good spirits when Jack and I were staying with him last October. This stuck in my mind, because I hadn't seen him happy very often in my life.'

'I noticed that too,' Vivienne murmured quietly.

'I didn't witness this happiness,' Jack muttered as he brought us our flutes of champagne. 'If you two agree he was, who am I to argue? There must be something to it.'

We all said cheers and raised our glasses.

I said, 'There's more to this than just the profile, isn't there? You could easily write it without talking to either of us or anyone else.'

Vivienne sat back, crossed her legs and nodded. 'Certainly. But I told you, I want to get an all-round picture of him. Sebastian as seen through many eyes.'

'Vivienne, I'm not stupid. Madge told me about the so-called girlfriend. But you're wasting your time because I know nothing about her. No one does. You're the only one he confided in.'

'If she exists,' Jack murmured as he came to join us. He hovered in front of the fireplace, sipping his drink.

'Oh, she exists all right.' Vivienne sounded so confident that I stared at her swiftly.

Jack murmured, 'Maybe you're right, Viv. But you'll never track her down. How can you? You don't have a name.'

'Oh but I do have a name. Actually I just found it. I know who she is, Jack. I hope to interview her within the next couple of weeks, and perhaps she might be able to shed some light on Sebastian's suicide.'

'What do you mean by *that* exactly?' I asked.

'She might have a clue *why* he did it,' Vivienne answered.

'Oh for God's sake! Forget all that nonsense, Viv!' Jack exclaimed. 'I want to know who the hell she is. And how you managed to find her. Jesus! Talk about a needle in a haystack!'

'Let me first tell you *how* I found her,' Vivienne said. 'This past weekend I was going through an old appointment book, checking a date for Kit Tremain, when the diary fell open to a day last July. Monday, July the eleventh, 1994. I'd made a note that I'd spoken to Sebastian that morning. He'd called me from Paris. As I stared at the page I started to remember our conversation. He'd told me he was staying at the Plaza-Athénée, that he was in Paris to attend a special dinner with a friend of his. It was a medical dinner. I asked him if he'd like to come to Lourmarin for a few days, and he said no, he couldn't, that he had to go to Zaire for the Locke Foundation. Anyway, once I'd remembered this conversation, I realized I had something to go on at last. A real *clue*. The medical dinner. It was the key to me. Since Sebastian was a very well-known figure, I was quite sure he would be listed as one of the important guests attending the dinner. In press reports, if there were any.

'Following my hunch, I flew up to Paris for the day on Monday morning. I went straight to *Le Figaro* and asked an editor I knew there to arrange for me to have access to their back-issue files for July 1994. He did. Unfortunately, there was nothing in the newspaper about the medical dinner, so I grabbed a cab and shot over to *Paris Match*. I have a friend on the magazine, Patrick Brizzard, a photographer I've worked with in the past. Patrick helped me to go through last year's July issues, and I found what I was looking for, a brief mention of the dinner in the society pages. And there, staring at me as large as life, was a photograph of Sebastian. He was accompanied by a couple of French doctors. Male. And a French scientist. Female. His girlfriend, the one he told me about.'

'Not necessarily,' Jack said. 'She could've been anybody.'

'Not the way she was looking at him and he was looking at her!' Vivienne put down her glass and stood up. 'Excuse me a moment, I left my briefcase in the hall.'

Alone with my brother, I said, 'Maybe Vivienne's stumbled on to the real thing.'

Jack shrugged. 'Could be.'

Vivienne came back carrying her briefcase. She took out a copy of *Paris Match* and a black-and-white photograph. 'I was able to get this back-issue through Patrick, who also made me a print of the photo. If those two people are not involved with each other, then I don't know a thing about human emotions,' she finished, handed them to me and sat down.

I regarded the photograph first. There was my father, looking impossibly handsome in an immaculately tailored dinner jacket. He was flanked by a couple of men on his left; on his right, a woman stood next to him. She was gazing up at him, rather than at the camera, and he at her. They had eyes only for each other; it was perfectly obvious how they felt. Even though I hated to admit it to myself, Vivienne was correct about their feelings. They looked as if they were in love.

Jack, who was leaning over my shoulder, said, 'She's a good-looking woman. She reminds me of somebody. I don't know who. So tell us, Viv. Who the hell *is* she?'

Before Vivienne could respond, I glanced at the caption in the magazine and read aloud, 'Doctor Ariel de Grenaille of the Institut Pasteur.'

'I called the institute yesterday when I got back to

Lourmarin,' Vivienne said. 'And she does indeed work there. Except that she's not in Paris at the moment. She's involved in a special project. *In Africa*. Since yesterday I've been trying to arrange a meeting with her, through the institute. However, she's unavailable, according to them. She's heading up some sort of experiment on a highly infectious disease. Quite literally she's in a sort of . . . quarantine. They won't even say where she *is* exactly. For the last twenty-four hours I've been trying to get in touch with her family.'

'I've always said you're like a dog with a bone. You just won't let go of something when you get your teeth into it,' Jack remarked. 'Or was it luck that you managed to find her?'

'Not luck. I'm a damned good journalist, Jack, and that's the reason I found her,' Vivienne shot back.

'I agree,' I said, glancing at Vivienne. Although I had disliked her most of my life, I had to admit she was a true professional. I had almost come to understand how much she had really loved my father. Her unswerving pursuit of the truth about his death had convinced me.

# *Part Four*

# ZOË
## Truth

# Twenty-seven

I am an old woman.

I must admit that to myself today, for it is the truth. Until very recently I thought I had escaped it, thought old age had passed me by. I felt so strong, so vigorous, so full of zest. But lately I have grown decrepit and worn out. It is as if all the life has been drained out of me, leaving only a fragile shell of a woman.

When one is young one never thinks of growing old, pays no mind to age. Youth lies to us, blinds us, gives us a false sense of immortality, makes us believe we are supreme, unbeatable, everlasting. How frightening it is to learn that we are only too mortal, vulnerable, and that in the end we must die. To be no more, to cease to exist, boggles the mind.

Last week, on April the sixth, I celebrated my seventy-third birthday. That evening, when I sat looking at myself in the mirror of my dressing table, I saw myself objectively for a fleeting moment.

What I saw startled me, made me suck in my breath in shock. Surely the image staring back could not be me, was not me, surely not. No, this woman was not *me*.

*I* was the great Zoë, they said, the beautiful Zoë, the woman every man desired. I had been irresistible to men all my life, with my chestnut hair and sky-blue eyes, my height and grace, my hour-glass figure and perfect breasts and my long, long legs.

Last Thursday the woman in the mirror had only the remnants of her great beauty left – the fine blue eyes and the high cheekbones. The chestnut hair was no longer thick and luxuriant, owed its rich colour to the skill of the hairdresser. The height and the legs and the elegance had not diminished with the passing of time, but the figure had thickened.

But oh how glorious I had been once, when I was in my prime. I had reigned supreme. My beauty had been extolled far and wide. Men had worshipped me, fought over me.

Charles came to Paris last week for my birthday. 'You look so very, very beautiful,' he said to me that night, lifting his crystal flute of champagne to me, toasting my birthday. Well, beauty *is* in the eye of the beholder. *Charles*. My son. My pride. My joy. *Ma raison d'être*.

He came from Normandy with his wife Marguerite and they took me for a celebration dinner at the Tour d'Argent, my favourite restaurant. I have always been entranced by the views from its floor-to-ceiling windows, breathtaking views of the River Seine and the *bateaux mouches*, Notre Dame Cathedral and the glittering sky, panoramic vistas of this city which I made my own long ago. Forty-five years ago this month.

I came to Paris in April 1950.

The chestnuts were in bloom in the Bois de Boulogne, gaiety filled the air and Paris was still rejoicing that the war was over. Love, laughter, life lived to the fullest – those were the things we cared about then.

Five years after I had chosen this city to be my home I met Édouard. I fell in love. I loved him so much, I loved him until the day he died. I would have done anything for him. Anything at all. And I did.

When we are grown old and horrendous things happen to destroy the fabric of our existence, age makes it easier to cope in so many ways. We have acquired understanding, wisdom is ours, and we have life's experiences to draw on and sustain us.

But in our youth when trouble comes to plague us we have few weapons with which to combat it, no ready references, no old knowledge stored in our bones, no inner resources to see us through. It overwhelms; it can destroy us.

I know this and I know it well.

It was in my early life that great trouble came to me. My life was difficult, terrible. Unconscionable things were done to me when I was young, destructive acts were perpetrated against me.

I suffered alone. I had no one to help me. No one to rescue me. No one to ease the pain. No one to console me. I sank low in my despair. I did not want to live. I thought that death was my only means of escape. I wanted to end my pain. But I did not take my life. I found courage and strength within myself. I lived again. I came back up. Slowly. I rose higher. I soared.

And ultimately I became the incomparable Zoë.

The woman all men wanted. The woman with the world at her feet.

Édouard wanted me from the first moment he set eyes on me. He was not solely driven by lust, although he lusted after my beautiful body, that is the truth. He wanted love from me as well. Love and devotion. I gave them to him willingly. He accepted them and returned my feelings in full measure. He adored me. He placed me on a pedestal. He made me his wife.

He gave me dignity, my husband.

Édouard died nine years ago at the age of eighty-nine. He never looked his age, nor was he senile in his latter years, but quite strong and robust to the very end. He died peacefully in his sleep, went gently out into the dark night, as gently as he had lived.

The king is dead. Long live the king, the saying goes.

Charles inherited it all. The ancient title, the château and estates in Normandy, the bulk of the family fortune. Charles hardly seemed to care about these material trappings of life. Heartbroken, he long grieved for his father. They had been close, inseparable, the best of friends since he had been a small boy.

Charles had his own son now, my grandson Gérard, who was six and would one day inherit the title. I had ensured the line, at what great cost no one would ever know. Nor should they.

The morning after my birthday last week, we had taken breakfast together, my son and I. He had looked at me at one moment, and said, *'Maman*, you are a great lady. *Une femme avec grand courage.'*

I had smiled faintly as I thanked him for his compliment.

Yes, I was of good courage, he was correct in that, and if I was a great lady, *une grande dame*, then it was because I had made myself one. I had not been born great. Nor had I been born a lady. But I had been born with courage.

Life is hard. It is meant to be hard. To test us, to test our mettle, to break us, or make us. And the lessons of life are equally hard. Yet if we are astute and *quick* then we only have to learn those lessons once.

When I was first married to him, Édouard told me that I had the face of a madonna. I smiled and thanked him and kissed his cheek.

Later, when I was alone, I peered at myself in the looking glass, searching my face: not a line, not a blemish, not a sign of pain nor a mark of sorrow. How could it be that all the anguish I had suffered did not show?

I could not answer that. Perhaps if they cut me open all the suffering I had endured would be visible on my heart.

It was Édouard who made my life livable. He gave me the greatest of all gifts, the gift of happiness. And slowly, with infinite love, he erased much of my pain.

I missed him. I was lost without him. Alone. Lonely. Devastated by his death, I lived on because I had taught myself to survive years ago when I was a young girl. I knew no other way to be. But I was only marking time, waiting for the day I died, when we would be reunited in another life, the afterlife.

The antique ormolu clock on the white marble mantelpiece began to chime, startling me out of my reverie. I glanced across at it, saw that the golden hands were sitting at three o'clock on the enamel face. Then I looked down at the document on the desk. I placed it in the envelope, put that in the small letter case and locked it. I sighed to myself, returned the case to the drawer of the desk.

I had frequently wondered whether there was a grand design, as Édouard had believed, a pre-ordained reason for all the things that happen to a person in the span of a life.

Was *I* part of some great cosmic pattern? Had Édouard been interwoven into it? Were he and I simply pawns of Fate, pawns who fulfilled their destinies when they came together, were joined as man and wife?

Once Édouard had said that what must happen *will* happen. Nothing can stop it. 'Fate rolls along inexorably,' he had said to me. 'And you Zoë are my fate. And I am yours, don't ever doubt that.'

My eyes settled on his photograph in the gold frame on my desk. It had been taken forty years ago, the year we met and married. He had been fifty-eight then, twenty-five years older than me, but so vital and alive.

I looked into his eyes and my own filled. Oh Édouard, I said to him silently, help me, give me strength.

# Twenty-eight

I have lived in this house for forty years. I came here as a bride, and when I leave it finally, for the last time, it will be in a coffin.

It is then that the house will pass to my son Charles. He will live in it when he visits Paris from Normandy, just as his father and his ancestors did, and one day it will pass to my grandson Gérard.

Our family home has always been regarded as one of the most beautiful houses in the city, the finest *hôtel particulier*, as this type of grand Parisian house is called. It is located on an elegant street, the Faubourg Saint-Germain, in the fashionable seventh *arrondissement* on the Left Bank, a district I have always liked.

Those many years ago when I came to live in Paris, I found myself drawn to the Left Bank, preferring it to the Right, for it seemed to have more gaiety and spirit, a marvellous sense of *joie de vivre* that made me feel buoyant and full of life.

And I am still captivated by its quaint streets and wide boulevards, the small, enticing tree-shaded squares, the little cafés, the antique shops and art galleries.

Now, as it was then, the area is a haven for writers, artists and the students of the Sorbonne, who all roam around the *quartier*, gather at the Café Flore and the Café Deux Magots, to while away the time and watch the world go by, as I once did when I was young.

In contrast, the seventh *arrondissement* also has a historic façade, visible in the architecture of gracious old houses like mine, the museums and the public buildings. Whenever I wish, I can easily walk to the Rodin Museum or the Hôtel des Invalides, which houses Napoleon's tomb.

It was Édouard who first took me there, who explained so much about the Emperor, and gave me my first lesson in French history. I constantly learned from him; knowledge was yet another of the gifts he gave me.

Or if I feel like it, I can stroll leisurely across to the Luxembourg Palace, to meander for a while through its beautiful gardens, sifting through my memories as I walk. For it is here that I brought my children when they were young, to run and play and be with other children. Those were the truly joyous days of my life, the golden days of their youth.

There is so much life, so much excitement out there on the streets of the Rive Gauche. Yet here, behind the high garden walls, my house is quiet, grown still, now that I am widowed and my children are raised and gone.

When children are small, one never thinks about the day they will spread their fledgling wings and try to fly. No mother ever thinks that day will really come. But it does, and they go with hardly a backward glance. There was no real surprise in this for me. I had always told Édouard that children are only ever lent to us. When the time comes they must be given to the world.

The lovely, gracious rooms in my house are still the same, filled with priceless antiques, paintings and *objets d'art*, extraordinary possessions my husband's family accumulated over the centuries, and to which he added throughout his lifetime.

Once these rooms rang with voices and laughter, but they have now been silent for some years. I no longer entertain as Édouard and I once did so brilliantly, with such panache.

For many years I was considered to be one of the great Parisienne hostesses, renowned for my table and my distinguished guests.

Only the finest quality in food and wines was acceptable to Édouard, who was a perfectionist, and our guests were of the highest quality too – ministers from the French Assembly, politicians, and prize-winning writers. And the upper crust of Parisian society, *le gratin*, the most closed and impenetrable circle of the élite, a circle open only to those of the same ilk.

I was in mourning for Édouard for several years, but eventually I put away my widow's weeds and began to entertain once more but on a smaller scale.

Without him by my side I soon lost the taste for it. There was no purpose in it any more. I had always done it for him, to please him. I brought the world to him, to entertain him, and he had applauded me for it, loved every moment of it. Once he was no longer here to share them the luncheons and dinners palled on me, became meaningless, irrelevant.

The back of the house opened on to a large garden, one of the few left in Paris.

Now I stood in the small salon looking out towards that garden on this glorious April afternoon. The gardener had turned on the antique fountains, five of them in all, each one placed in a different part of the garden. From where I was standing I could see them easily.

Jets of water spraying upward into the air caught the sunlight, and yet again I realized how clever Édouard had been to add those fountains years ago. They looked so cool, refreshing and pretty in the bright air, and the sound of water was never far from my ears when I was outside.

He had kept the rest of the garden simple. Green lawns were edged by wide borders of perennials in the palest of colours, and encircling the entire garden were tall trees which stood just inside the high stone walls.

The trees were very old, had been planted by Édouard's grandfather in 1850, and were mostly horse chestnuts. Their wide and spreading green canopies were cool and inviting on hot summer afternoons or sultry evenings.

Édouard had made the garden beautiful for me, because he knew what it meant to me. I enjoyed sitting out there under the chestnut trees reading. I was a voracious reader and it was Édouard who had encouraged in me the love of books, which I had harboured since being a child. But there were no books available to me in those grim days and no time at all to read. They had worked me too hard and taken away my privacy, and much else besides.

This afternoon there was no time either for reading or going out into the garden. I had a job to do; I must do it well, in order to protect those things which I held dear.

Turning away from the window, I moved back into the room. The small salon was decorated in the palest shade of watery green, with a marvellous Aubusson on the floor and eighteenth-century French furniture placed in intimate groupings.

There were two large, gilded mirrors above the console tables on either side of the fireplace, and I caught sight of myself in one of them as I crossed the salon.

I paused to stare.

And to assess.

Earlier, I had changed into a tailored suit of navy-blue wool and a white silk shirt. A pearl choker encircled my throat and pearl studs shone at my ears. My only other jewellery was my plain gold wedding ring and a watch.

I decided that I looked rather austere but business-like, which was exactly how I wished to appear.

I nodded, satisfied.

There was a light tap on the door and Hubert came in quickly. Inclining his head, he said, 'Comtesse?'

'Yes, Hubert, what is it?'

'Do you wish tea to be served in here, Madame? Or in the grand salon?'

'I think in here would be preferable, Hubert. Thank you.'

He nodded again and disappeared as quickly as he had arrived, gliding off on silent feet. Édouard had hired him as a junior houseman twenty-five years ago and he was still here. But now he was the senior butler and in charge of my household.

I sat down on a straight-backed chair to wait for my guest. And as I waited I asked myself how to deal properly with a loose cannon. I had no idea. I pondered this.

Suddenly I had no further time for thought. I heard the sound of footsteps on the marble floor of the foyer, and a moment later Hubert was opening the door of the salon.

I rose and turned to face the door expectantly.

'Madame,' he said, 'your guest is here.' He ushered her into the salon, and went on, 'Madame Trent, I would like to present you to the Comtesse de Grenaille.'

I stepped forward, arranged a polite smile on my face and stretched out my hand. 'Good afternoon. I'm very pleased to meet you, Mrs Trent.'

The young woman smiled at me and grasped my hand firmly in hers. 'And I am pleased to meet you, Countess. It is so very kind and gracious of you to see me.'

I nodded, extracted my hand and waved it in the direction of the seating arrangement near the french windows to the garden.

'Shall we go and sit over there? In a few moments,

Hubert will serve tea, but we can chat whilst we're waiting, I think.'

'Thank you,' Vivienne Trent said, and followed me across the room.

She took a seat on the small sofa.

I sat down on the same straight-backed chair as before, which I preferred, and said, 'When the Institut Pasteur telephoned me, they said you wished to talk to me about my daughter Ariel. Something to do with an article you are writing about the late Sebastian Locke.'

'That's true, Countess, yes. I am writing a profile about him for the *Sunday Times*. I am calling it "The Last Great Philanthropist", and it will deal with the essence of the man, what made him tick. I will touch on his great achievements, his compassion and generosity to the world's poor and suffering. It'll be a very positive story. Very upbeat, actually.'

'I see,' I murmured. 'However, I am not quite sure how I can help you. My daughter is away, and I didn't know Mr Locke.'

'But your daughter did, Countess. Didn't she?'

I hesitated, but only fractionally, and then I nodded. 'Yes, she did.'

'I would like to talk to her about him, get her impressions of him as a man who set out to work miracles in the world.'

'I don't believe she is available at the moment. In fact, I am quite certain she's not.'

Vivienne Trent looked crestfallen, and then she leaned forward, rather urgently I thought, and said, 'I want to be very open and straightforward with you,

Countess. I am not only a journalist writing a story about him, but a member of the Locke family.'

I merely nodded.

Mrs Trent said, 'If I may explain?'

'Of course, please do,' I answered.

'I knew Sebastian from the age of twelve. My mother had a relationship with him for six years. When she died, when I was eighteen, he became my guardian. He sent me to college, to Wellesley actually, and looked after me in general. He and I were married when I was twenty-two and he was forty-two. We were married for five years and remained friends after our divorce. It was an amicable one.' She paused and looked at me intently.

'I see,' I murmured.

'Anyway, Countess, I'm telling you this because I want you to understand that my profile of him will be laudatory. It won't be critical of him, I'm not about to write a "warts and all" portrait of him. Quite the opposite. And of course it would only be laudatory about your daughter, Dr Ariel de Grenaille.'

'I understand,' I responded. 'Thank you for explaining. But I don't know how much my daughter could contribute, even if she were available. And as I did just tell you, she's not.'

'I think she could contribute quite a lot,' Mrs Trent said swiftly. 'After all, she was the last woman he was involved with. Personally involved with on an emotional level.'

I stared at her but said nothing. I just sat there, waiting, wondering what she would say next.

There was total silence in the room for several

minutes. I knew Vivienne Trent was expecting me to make a remark, but I remained silent.

Finally, it was she who broke the silence. Clearing her throat, she said, 'Countess de Grenaille, Sebastian told me he was going to marry your daughter.'

'He said that?'

'Yes, he did.'

'When did he tell you this?'

'Last October, early October. On the Monday of the week he died.'

'You were his confidante, Mrs Trent? Or did other members of his family know of his intentions?'

Vivienne Trent shook her head. 'No one else knew, Countess, because *I* was his only confidante.'

When I said nothing, she asked, with a slight frown, 'Didn't you know they were planning to marry?'

'Oh yes, Ariel had told me. You must have been *extremely* close to him if he confided in you, Mrs Trent, even after your divorce.'

'I was. Sebastian trusted me implicitly.'

'What did he tell you about Ariel?'

'Not a great deal *about* her, only that she was a doctor, a scientist, working in Africa. But he did speak to me about his feelings for her, the depth of his feelings.'

'Did he now. How extraordinary. Unusual really, under the circumstances.'

'I don't think so,' she said.

'But you were once his wife. Was it not upsetting for you to hear that he loved another woman? To be told that he was going to marry her?'

'No, not at all!' she exclaimed rather fiercely. 'I cared about him. I loved him. I wanted him to be happy, to have love and companionship in his life, just as he would have wanted that for me. Did want it, actually. As I've said, we were very, very close.'

'I realize that you must have been.'

'Countess de Grenaille, I know your daughter is working in Africa. I would like to go and see her. Could you possibly arrange this for me?'

'That is very doubtful, Mrs Trent. She *is* unavailable.'

'The Institut Pasteur said the same thing. The person I spoke to indicated she was working with infectious diseases. And explained that Dr de Grenaille was in some kind of . . . *quarantine*.'

'That is correct, she is.'

'Could you explain what it is she is doing exactly?'

'I'll try,' I answered. 'Ariel is a virologist. Currently she is working with viruses that are known as hot viruses.'

'In a laboratory in Africa?' Mrs Trent asked, leaning forward eagerly, her expression alert, questioning.

I nodded. 'Yes.'

'Whereabouts in Africa?' she pressed.

'Central Africa.'

'Could you be more precise, please, Countess?'

'Zaire. She is working in Zaire.'

'With those hot viruses?'

'Yes, Mrs Trent, I just said so. That is what she does. She has been working on them for the past seven years, especially the filoviruses.'

'What are they?'

'Sometimes they are called thread viruses – filo is the Latin word for thread. They are highly contagious and deadly. *Lethal.*'

There was a knock on the door and Hubert came in, carrying the tea tray.

'Excuse me, Madame,' he said placing the tray on the small antique table in the centre of the seating arrangement, and glanced across at me. 'Shall I pour the tea, Madame?'

'*Oui, merci*, Hubert.'

'It sounds like very dangerous research,' Vivienne Trent murmured.

'It is the most dangerous work in medical science today,' I replied. 'The slightest little mistake, the merest slip on her part, and she could infect herself. She would die, of course, if that happened. There are no known vaccines.'

# Twenty-nine

We were silent, she and I, as we sipped our lemon tea, but after a few seconds Vivienne Trent put down her cup and said, 'I think I've read about the hot viruses. They're rare, aren't they?'

'Very, but so lethal I can hardly bear to think about them,' I responded. 'As I explained a moment ago, there are no vaccines against them, no known cures. They kill in a matter of a few days, and in the most devastating ways.'

'How do they kill?'

'You don't want to know,' I answered and drank a little tea.

Vivienne Trent did not press me. She asked quietly, 'And they come out of Africa, am I correct?'

'Yes, you are.'

'Where from exactly?'

'Various areas. I'm not really an expert, you know,' I said, giving her a slight smile.

'But surely your daughter has discussed her work with you? Told you about it?' she asserted, and a dark brow lifted.

'Yes, she has talked to me from time to time.'

'Then you must know more than the average person, Countess, a person like me.'

'I suppose I do.'

'Countess de Grenaille, forgive me if I sound as if I'm prying. I'm not, really. I'm just trying to understand about your daughter's work. For my profile of Sebastian. Their emotional involvement aside, I can see that she must have had quite a lot in common with Sebastian, in that the foundation funded medical research there, fought disease. And, of course, he did love Africa, had so much knowledge about it. They must have got on very well –' She broke off, reached for her handbag. 'Would you mind if I made a few notes? Just for background information.'

Briefly, I hesitated, and then before I could stop myself I acquiesced. 'No, I don't mind, that's perfectly all right, Mrs Trent.'

'Thank you so much.' She offered me a warm and very winning smile, took out a notebook and pen, closed her bag, and went on. 'You said the viruses come from various areas in Africa. Did your daughter ever tell you anything about their actual source?'

'Ariel and the other doctors and scientists working in this field of medicine believe that the viruses come out of the rain forests of Africa. According to Ariel, the viruses have probably been around for hundreds of millions of years. However, they've been undetected. Undiscovered. My daughter explained to me that because the tropical forests are now being destroyed in a very systematic way, the viruses are beginning to . . . come out. *Emerge*. And they've gone into the human population.'

'But how does that happen?' she asked, her voice

rising, her intelligent eyes fixed more intently on mine than ever.

'Scientists have discovered that the monkey can act as a host for the viruses, other monkeys get infected and become carriers. Ariel told me that the viruses have somehow managed to mutate, have changed their genetic structure and moved from monkeys to humans.'

'Oh, my God, that *is* frightening!' she exclaimed. Her voice was full of sympathy when she added, 'It must be extremely worrying for you, Countess, knowing that your daughter is working with these deadly viruses, handling them constantly.'

'It is,' I answered, and then found myself unexpectedly confiding in her. 'I'm afraid for Ariel. Always afraid. And afraid of the viruses. I try very hard not to think about her work, what she's doing. She's talented, you know, and very skilled. And she is careful, cautious –'

I broke off, reached for my cup of tea, reminding myself that I had not intended to have a long discussion with Vivienne Trent. But she was extraordinarily disarming. Her soft, sympathetic manner was effective, and I had begun to relax with her. I felt at ease. From the moment she had walked into the small salon I had detected something special in her, something fine and decent. Instinctively, I knew she was trustworthy, a good person. Besides which, we were only talking about Ariel's work. Not that there was much else to discuss anyway.

'That's quite a pressure on you, Countess de Grenaille,' Mrs Trent was saying. 'Living with that kind of . . . *apprehension*. About someone you love, I mean. I know only too well. Years ago, when I was married to Sebastian, and he went off alone to places that were in turmoil, in the midst of revolution or upheaval, I could barely sleep for worrying about him. I was always quite certain he was going to catch a bullet, or get blown up. Or be kidnapped by rebel troops. I also worried that he would catch some deadly disease. He used to wander around Africa quite unconcerned for himself, and my heart was very often in my mouth, the risks he took.' She smiled and shrugged lightly. 'But nothing ever did happen to him. I used to tell him that he had a guardian angel sitting on his shoulder.'

I nodded but made no comment. I hoped my daughter had a guardian angel sitting on her shoulder when she was working in the laboratory. Night and day I lived with the knowledge that if she made the slightest error she would endanger her life.

Vivienne Trent cut into my thoughts, when she said, 'There's been quite a lot written about hot viruses in the past few years, quite aside from the AIDS virus, I mean. Isn't one of the more deadly ones called Marburg virus?'

'Yes. It's from the filovirus family I told you about.'

'Is she working on that?'

'Not any more.'

'What is she working on, then?'

'A virus called Ebola Zaire. It's the deadliest, the worst. It kills in nine out of ten cases.'

'Oh my God, how ghastly.'

'It is.'

'What are the symptoms?'

'A lot of bleeding . . . terrible bleeding . . . haemorrhagic fever –' I let my voice trail off. The horror of it was always too much to contemplate.

Vivienne Trent seemed to be digesting my words. Then she looked across at me and said, 'What prompted Dr de Grenaille to become a virologist?'

'Ariel was always interested in viruses and in Africa, and one day these two interests merged.'

'So she always wanted to be a doctor, did she?'

'Not a doctor practising medicine, but a scientist, even when she was quite a young girl.'

'I can certainly understand her interest in Africa,' Mrs Trent said and confided, 'I went there with Sebastian on our honeymoon, to Kenya, and I fell in love with the place. I often went back to other parts of Africa with him, on foundation business, and it never ceased to fascinate me. Does your daughter feel that way?'

'Yes, I think she does. My husband's uncle had business interests and holdings in French Equatorial Africa, the French Congo, as it was known years ago. Ariel loved to sit and listen to his tales when he visited us. In 1973, when she was about twelve, he invited us all to the French Congo. We started out in Brazzaville, and then travelled all over Africa. She too fell in love with its beauty and its mystery, its sense of timelessness.'

Mrs Trent nodded, remarked casually, 'So your daughter must be about thirty-three?'

'Yes. Thirty-four at the end of April.'

'I hope you don't mind me asking this, Countess, but was Dr de Grenaille ever married before?'

'No, she wasn't. She's always been very dedicated to her work. She once told me that she had been so busy looking into the lens of a microscope all her life she hadn't had time to look up and find a man.'

Vivienne Trent smiled. 'I do wish I could meet her –'

'I told you earlier, that's not possible,' I cut in swiftly, sounding a little more sharp than I had intended. 'She's in a laboratory that's been isolated, contained if you like, for safety. She's involved in a very special project at this moment. She and her team work long hours, and the work itself is very difficult, quite debilitating in a variety of different ways. For one thing, they wear special clothes. Biological suits –'

'Do you mean space suits, the kind astronauts wear?' she interrupted.

'Something like that. Plus helmets with windows, boots, and several pairs of gloves. Between the danger, the intensity of the work and the complicated clothing, it's a very stressful environment, as I'm sure you can imagine.'

'I can,' Vivienne Trent said. There was a small silence. She leaned back against the sofa looking reflective. 'Doctors like your daughter are the true heroes, Countess, so very selfless in so many ways,' she said at last. 'You must be awfully proud of her and the contribution she is making. After all, she is endeavouring to create a safer world for us to live in.'

'Thank you, Mrs Trent, that's very kind of you to

say so. And yes, it's true, I am proud of Ariel. Very proud.' I paused, shook my head. 'But I'm also very worried a great deal of the time,' I finished with a pained smile.

'I can well appreciate why. Did your daughter meet Sebastian through her work? I imagine she must have done.'

'You're correct in that. In fact, she sought him out, went to see him. She wanted his foundation to fund a special project. A medical project some friends of hers were working on in Zaire.'

'And did he?'

'Of course. Would you expect otherwise?' I looked at her pointedly.

She laughed. 'No. He was always so generous, and especially when it came to medical research.'

'From what I know of him . . . have learned about him, he was a very good man, I think.' As I said this I realized Vivienne Trent's eyes were focused on a table at the other side of the room.

Following her gaze, I exclaimed, 'Ah, I see you are interested in photographs of my family . . . of my husband Édouard, my son Charles, and my Ariel. She's the young woman in the photograph standing next to theirs.'

She said, 'She's very lovely. May I go and take a closer look, Countess?'

'Please do.'

Rising, she walked across the room. I watched her staring at the photograph of Ariel, fully understanding her interest in my daughter. She then peered at the pictures of my husband and my son. It was then that I felt the first stab of pain, a pain so fierce I closed my eyes and sucked in my breath, trying not to gasp out loud. I had not suffered from the pain for several weeks now and it took me by surprise.

'Countess, Countess, is there something wrong?' Vivienne Trent was saying.

I opened my eyes as she drew to a standstill next to my chair.

Taking a deep breath, I explained, 'I'm afraid I'm in pain quite suddenly, Mrs Trent.'

'Can I help you? Perhaps I can get you something.' Bending over me, her face taut with concern, she asked, 'Are you ill? Do you need medication of some kind?'

I was moved by her consideration and reached out, touched her hand resting lightly on my arm. 'I'll be all right, thank you. But I will have to bring our talk to a close now.'

'Yes, of course, I do understand. You've been very generous with your time, Countess. In fact, I think I may have overstayed my welcome. When we spoke on the phone, you did say an hour and I think I've been here a bit longer than that.'

'I enjoyed meeting you,' I said. I was feeling faint, and when the stabbing pain attacked again I winced.

Vivienne Trent could not fail to notice this and exclaimed, 'Oh, Countess! I know you're ill! I must go and fetch your butler. Don't you think I should do that?'

I could only nod. Then I managed to say, 'There's a bell over there, near the console. You just have to push it, and Hubert will be here in an instant.'

She did this and then returned to my side, hovering over me. 'I wish I could help you in some way, make you feel better, Countess.'

'I'm afraid that's impossible, Mrs Trent,' I said. 'You see, I have cancer. I'm dying.'

# Thirty

It is foolish for an old woman to fall under the spell of a younger one. Both women are bound to get hurt.

Inevitably the younger woman will grow bored, resentful of the older woman's wisdom and the burden of her age. And the old woman will feel hurt and abandoned when she is eventually rejected.

I suppose it is only natural that young feet want to keep running, doing, experiencing, while old feet have a tendency to slow.

I knew all this, had known it for a long time, and yet I had allowed myself to fall under the spell of Vivienne Trent. Fortunately, the negative aspects did not feature in our particular case. And for one simple reason: I was not going to be in this life very long; therefore, there was no time for either of us to cause pain to the other.

My doctors had told me several months ago that there was nothing more they could do for me. They had allowed me to leave the hospital so that I could spend what time I had left in my own home.

I had not told Charles or Ariel, or anyone else, how close the end was for me. There was no point. They could do nothing to help me. In one sense,

I was being self-protective. I had long realized that I would not be capable of dealing with my children's emotions if they knew I was dying. I did not have the strength.

I yearned for peace and quiet, needed to spend what short time I had left leading as normal a life as possible. It was important for me to go about my business whenever I was able to do so with my dignity and pride intact.

Although I had not confided in my children, I had told Vivienne Trent the truth. I had done this one week ago today, the afternoon we were having tea. The words had been said without any thought on my part, nor did it matter that I had uttered them.

I felt quite comfortable that she knew I was facing imminent death. In part this was because she was a stranger. However, I had also witnessed her display of genuine concern for me: she had shown me compassion.

The fact was I trusted this young woman.

I had seen something fine and good and essentially honest in her that day. And in the past week she had proved that I was correct in my judgement of her.

A day hadn't gone by without her telephoning me to see how I was feeling. She had sent flowers and books she thought I might like. Two of the books were her own, books she had written herself.

One of them was about Napoleon and Josephine and the early years of their marriage, and the other was a biography of Catherine the Great of Russia. They had been most revealing of the author in so many different ways.

Every day for the past few days, Vivienne had come to tea at four o'clock, just to sit with me and keep me company. She had told me a great deal about herself, her life, her houses in Lourmarin and Connecticut, entertained me in such a delightful way that she had managed to take my mind off my illness.

Thankfully I've come to feel much better in the last twenty-four hours. The pain has finally lessened. I'm almost free of it again.

Never once in this last week had Vivienne asked me a single question about Ariel and her relationship with Sebastian Locke. Nor did she mention the profile she was writing about him.

It is possible to know a person for a whole lifetime and not know them at all. Yet I knew Vivienne Trent the very first day we met, knew her as if we had been intimate friends for many years.

She was an endearing young woman, very beguiling, and crept under one's skin. I could understand why a man like Sebastian Locke had loved her as a young girl and later when she was a grown woman.

Vivienne was intelligent, sincere, warm and loving, and she did not have a bad bone in her body. What is more, she seemed to be totally without cynicism.

In certain ways she reminded me of my daughter.

They were rather similar in character – responsible, caring, dedicated and disciplined young women with good values and a sense of purpose.

But Vivienne was much more worldly, more sophisticated, and certainly more lighthearted than Ariel.

My daughter had always had an unusual aura about her, one which many mistook for aloofness. It was, in fact, an aura of isolation, something which is not uncommon in the truly gifted, who *are* different, who do seem somewhat removed from us lesser mortals. It is as though they live on another plane altogether.

Ariel's work had always dominated her life. She had had little time for anything else most of her adult years. Until Sebastian Locke came into her life. Now that he was dead I was thankful that she had her work as a virologist to fall back on. Dangerous work in so many ways, but it had always consumed her, was something she loved and was excited by. And it would get her through this difficult period in her life.

I longed to see her again before I died, the beautiful child of my heart. But I feared I would not. Unless she finished her current project sooner than expected and came home to Paris.

It was not possible for me to tell her how ill I really was. If I did, if I said I needed her, she would drop everything in Africa and come running to me. But that would be such a selfish act on my part.

She had been mine for thirty-three years and had given me so much pleasure and joy, fulfilled so many of my dreams and hopes for her. And she had been a good daughter. Therefore my impending death did not amount to much in the overall scheme of things.

I knew Ariel loved me, knew that I would live on in her heart and memory long after I was dead. Just as Édouard did. Like most girls she had been close to her father, and Édouard had adored her. She would have her memories to sustain her. She and her brother were also close. They would always be there for each other.

As for Charles, he would hurry to me when I finally told him the truth, and he and Marguerite would stay with me until the end.

But the pale rider on the pale horse had not come to take me yet. I believed I still had a few weeks left on this earth. I had felt so much better today. The medication had finally alleviated the severe pain which had attacked me so savagely last week. I was back on my feet again, able to cope.

I was determined that Vivienne and I would have tea outside in the garden today. I had told Hubert as much. He had agreed that it was warm enough, and I could see him now from my bedroom window. He was arranging cushions on a garden seat, and Josie, the maid, was covering a small table with a white linen cloth.

Glancing at my watch, I saw that it was three forty-five. Vivienne would be here promptly at four. She was never late.

'Could I ask you something rather personal, Countess Zoë?' Vivienne said carefully, her eyes smiling.

'You can ask me anything, Vivienne,' I said, 'And I'll certainly answer you if I can.'

'Are you French?'

'Yes, I am. Why?'

'You speak such perfect English, but I detect a slight accent. It's one I can't place. And you don't sound like most French people do when they're speaking English. I just wondered if you had been born somewhere else?'

'How clever of you to pick that up. You must have a good ear.'

'So you're not French, then?'

'Yes, I am, by nationality, Vivienne. I became a French citizen many, many years ago. But I was born in America. Of Irish parentage, actually. My mother and father emigrated to America with their parents when they were small children. They both grew up in New York. They met each other there and married.'

'How amazing! You're an Irish-American, then.'

I nodded and said, 'Originally, yes. But why do you sound so surprised?'

'You're so French. You have such chic, such great style, what I call true French style, the way you look and dress, and yet you're not French at all –' She cut herself off and shook her head. 'I shouldn't say that! Of course you're French. After years of living here, absorbing the culture, the mores and manners of the French, and being married to a Frenchman, how could you not be?'

'Funnily enough I feel very French, Vivienne. And what you're hearing in my voice is a slight lilt I think. The Irish lilt I picked up from my mother when I was growing up. But do you know, I didn't even realize it was still in evidence when I spoke English.'

'It's faint, but it's there,' she answered.

'Let me explain. When I first came to Paris I fell in love with the city, long before I met Édouard and fell in love with him. I knew I wanted to live here, nowhere else would do for me, once I'd seen the city of light. So I immediately started to take French lessons, knowing that I must speak the language if I was going to settle in Paris. I'm glad I stayed, France has been good to me. I've never regretted moving here.'

'Did you come to France from America?' Vivienne asked.

'No, from London. I had been living there through the war years.' I picked up the teapot and filled her cup and then my own.

'Thank you,' she said, sat back in the wrought-iron garden chair, and glanced around the garden. It seemed to me that she was lost in thought.

I studied her. She appeared to be preoccupied, as if she were troubled, and after a moment, I said, 'Are you all right? Is everything all right with you, Vivienne?'

'Yes, of course, why are you asking?'

'You look so very preoccupied, even a little worried,' I replied.

'Countess Zoë . . . there is something I feel I must say. I was going to mention it yesterday, but it was already getting late and I didn't want to tire you. I hesitate to bring it up even now.'

'You can. I'm perfectly fine,' I reassured her. 'I told you earlier, the medicine has worked wonders for me in the last twenty-four hours. So why don't you tell me what's on your mind? Why don't you unburden yourself?'

'It's like this –' She stopped somewhat abruptly, sighed and looked away, but eventually she brought her gaze back to mine.

Her clear, green eyes were filled with such intelligence, candour and honesty they almost took my breath away.

She said in a low, serious voice, 'There's something I want to tell you, to explain.'

I nodded.

'Last Tuesday, when I first met you, I was very drawn to you. In the hour I was here, I felt as if I knew you, as if I'd always known you. When you collapsed I wanted to help you. I couldn't bear to see you suffering. I've been coming to see you ever since because I cared. As we've talked these past few days, and come to know each other, it's seemed to me that there's a bond between us. It's hard to explain, because we did meet only a week ago. But I really mean what I say. I do feel close to you, Countess Zoë.'

'I know you do, Vivienne, and I feel that way myself. There is a bond. As though something is pulling us closer together.' I patted her hand. 'I wish we'd met a long time ago. You're a very special young woman, Vivienne, and you've become quite dear to me in only a few days. I want you to know that you've been a comfort to me this past week. You have helped me to pull through that little crisis.'

'I'm so glad!' she exclaimed, looking pleased. She took hold of my hand, held it tightly in hers for a moment.

'You remind me so much of Ariel,' I confided, smiling at her. 'I wish you had known each other. I think you would have been friends. Good friends.'

'That's what Sebastian wanted. He said that last

October when he told me he was going to marry her. He'd hoped I would be spending Christmas in Connecticut. He wanted me to meet Ariel then, and he was so disappointed when I explained I was going to be in France. He said he would bring her to Lourmarin in the new year, that he knew we would like each other, that we'd love each other when we met. He explained that he wanted me to be at their wedding in the spring. Actually, I had a strong suspicion he wanted to have it at Vieux Moulin.'

'And how would you have really felt about that, if he had suggested it?' I asked, my eyes resting on her thoughtfully.

'I would have been pleased,' she responded. 'And I would have made them very welcome, given them a lovely wedding. I genuinely cared about him. He was my only family. But then you know that.'

'Yes,' I said softly. 'I do.'

'Countess Zoë?'

'Yes, Vivienne?' I looked at her alertly, detecting something different in her voice. I braced myself.

'I don't want to upset you, and I know *you* know that. I truly hope you don't think I've been coming to see you this past week because I have an ulterior motive. And, I'm quite certain you accept that I'm very sincere in all that I've just said to you. But I *have* to ask you something.'

'Then ask me, my dear.'

'I would still like to meet Ariel. Won't you arrange that for me, please, Countess Zoë?'

'Vivienne, I cannot.'

'An hour, two at the most, that's all I need with

her. I could fly to Zaire. Talk to her for a short while, and then leave. I'd leave immediately, you have my promise. *Please,*' she pleaded.

'Vivienne, *no*. I cannot arrange it.'

'What harm would it do?' she asked.

'More than you could possibly imagine!' I exclaimed and hated the fact that my voice had risen sharply, but I couldn't help myself.

Swiftly, I went on more softly, 'When Ariel heard the news of Sebastian Locke's death she was devastated. She was ill for several weeks. A little later she even took herself out of her own research project, for her own safety. She was slow in recovering from the news of his death and she was afraid she might make an error in her experiments that could cost lives. His death affected her very deeply. And to have you go there *now,* only seven months later, to interrogate her, to ask questions about their relationship, about his attitude and mental state in the last few weeks of his life, would only open up wounds. Wounds which have just begun to heal. The kind of work Ariel does is so stressful, so dangerous, I don't want her to be distracted by any emotional upsets.'

I paused and looked at Vivienne intently. 'Try to see it from my point of view, my dear. I want Ariel to concentrate on her work, so that she doesn't make any fatal mistakes. In short, I want her left alone. By you. By anyone else who might cause her more grief. There's nothing she can tell you that you don't already know. You can write your profile without meeting her, please believe me you can.'

'I understand how you feel, Countess Zoë, understand everything you're saying. I've only persisted about seeing her because I thought Ariel might have a clue.'

'A *clue*?' I repeated.

'Yes, a clue to why he killed himself.'

'I doubt it very much. She can't give you an explanation about his death, Vivienne.'

'She loved him, he loved her, and he was so *happy* that last week of his life,' Vivienne murmured. 'Really happy, Countess Zoë.' She looked at me and shook her head. Her expression was sad. 'I knew him so well, and for so long, there was no way he could ever have fooled me. Not about anything. That awful gloominess, that moroseness of his, was absent. He was positively glowing. So why would he want to kill himself when he was on cloud nine and planning to marry your daughter?'

'Vivienne dear, listen to me. No one ever really knows why people do these awful, tragic things to themselves, take such terrible and irrevocable steps.'

'His suicide has never made sense to me,' Vivienne said softly, almost to herself. 'The reason I wanted to see Ariel was because I had hoped she might be able to help me understand it.'

'How would she have been able to do that?'

'I've always had an uncanny feeling that Ariel was somehow involved. Please don't misunderstand, Countess Zoë, I mean *indirectly* involved. I know she was in Africa when he took his life in Connecticut.'

'But why do you think she would know anything?' I probed.

'Because his relationship with her was the only

thing in his life that was *new, different*. His lifestyle was very predictable. His pattern didn't change very much. For years he had lived the same way.'

'And how was that?' I asked curiously.

'He went from Manhattan to the farm in Connecticut, and then back to Africa. Or to some other part of the world where he felt he was needed. He did his work there, returned to the States, stayed a while, attended to business at the foundation and Locke Industries, and went off again. But then he met Ariel in Zaire. He fell in love, made plans to marry her, but suddenly killed himself. To me there is something very strange at work here. I believe that something unusual occurred that week he was in New York. Between the Monday when we had lunch and the Saturday when he killed himself. But it's a mystery. I can't begin to imagine what it was.'

'Maybe his life had simply become unbearable,' I suggested quietly.

'What do you mean by that, Countess Zoë?'

'Isn't that why people kill themselves, Vivienne? Because their lives have become unbearable. They simply don't want to live any longer,' I ventured.

Vivienne was silent. I could feel her pain.

After a moment she leaned forward and said, 'I want to explain something else to you, Countess Zoë. I loved Sebastian from the age of twelve. I will always love him, and part of me will always belong to him. But writing the profile of him is not very important to me in the long run. It was an excuse in a way. When I got the idea, I ran with it, thinking that it might help me to understand his death, even come to grips with it. Oh yes, it would be satisfying to write lovely things about him. But there is something much more pressing than my hero worship of him.'

She paused, took a breath and went on, 'I need to know *why* Sebastian Locke took his life. For myself. It was an act so out of character, so alien to his nature. And I won't have any peace of mind until I know. I think it will haunt me for the rest of my life. I needed to solve this terrible riddle right from the beginning, which is when I got the idea for doing the profile. I thought that talking to people who had known him might help, that I might eventually turn up the truth. And that's really why I wanted to see your daughter. Not to write about their relationship. But, selfishly, for my peace of mind.'

'Thank you for your honesty, Vivienne. Ariel was just as perplexed as you, baffled by his suicide. And perhaps one day you *will* meet her, when her wounds have healed completely.'

Vivienne nodded, let out a deep sigh, then she said in a low voice, 'I just want to close this book and move forward, Countess Zoë, get on with my life.'

'I understand your motivations and what drives you. And don't think for a moment that I'm angry, because I'm not. But I must say again that whatever you might think, my daughter couldn't possibly enlighten you.'

'You sound so sure.'

'I am.'

Vivienne's tone was deflated when she said, 'You were my only chance. I thought you were the one person who could help me get to the truth of it all through Ariel. I thought she held the key.'

For a moment I could not think. My mind froze. I simply sat there in my beautiful garden, shivering slightly from the light breeze now blowing up, staring into those unflinching, honest green eyes that held mine.

And as I looked into the lovely face of this sincere young woman I made a momentous decision.

I knew she had integrity, that honour was an essential part of her character, and so I knew in my bones that I could trust her.

I rose. 'Let us go inside, Vivienne dear. It's growing chilly,' I said.

She nodded and stood up, took hold of my arm solicitously and helped me into the house.

Once we were seated in the small salon, I leaned back against the soft cushions of the sofa and regarded her for the longest moment.

Finally, taking a deep breath, I said, 'I am going to tell you a tale, a familiar tale that's as ancient as the hills . . . a tale of a man, a woman and another man . . .'

# Thirty-one

'I was twenty-eight and a rich young widow when I visited Paris for the first time, Vivienne.

'Paris instantly captivated me and I decided to move permanently to France. For numerous reasons, I was determined to leave London for good. Suffice it to say that I believed it to be imperative for my wellbeing to do so.

'After several weeks in Paris I returned to London, put my house in Mayfair and its contents up for sale, gave my solicitors power of attorney to deal with my business affairs and returned without delay to France.

'Within several weeks I had rented a furnished apartment on the rue Jacob on the Left Bank, hired a student to teach me the language and begun my search for a proper dwelling place, one of charm, elegance and permanence. My French teacher, a young woman of good family, was instrumental in helping me to find the perfect apartment on the Avenue de Breteuil – large, airy and light-filled. Whilst it was being appropriately decorated and furnished I settled down to my studies, and at the same time acclimatized myself to Paris and the French way of life.

'Even though I say this myself, I was quite beautiful

when I was young, Vivienne. I had great *allure*. I suppose that is the best word to use. My looks were glamorous, not so much exotic as lush. Men found me irresistible. I did not lack male companionship in Paris, and I had plenty of escorts to take me everywhere I wished to go.

'But I was well aware that women and not men were the key to my success in local society. Only women could propel me into the proper circles. Men might admire me, flatter me, lust after me, wine and dine me and fall in love with me. However, it was women who could open all the right doors; it has always been women the world over who run the social scene, make the decisions and issue the invitations. They can either make or break another woman, especially a newcomer to a city.

'I had no intention of allowing any doors to remain shut or be slammed in my face. Nor did I plan to let anyone break me. That had been done to me when I was a child. *Almost*. I would never let it happen again.

'Fortunately for me, I had a sponsor, a mentor, if you will, someone I had met in London several years earlier. She was a woman of a certain age and a socialite of some standing, regarded as one of the greatest hostesses in Paris, indeed in France.

'She was of fine lineage in her own right, had married into one of the grand titled families of France, and, like me, she was a widow.

'This accomplished and remarkable woman had been a friend of my first husband, the late Harry Robson. Because of his kindness to her during a most difficult time in her life, and their long-standing friendship, she took me under her wing when I moved to Paris in 1950.

'She was the Baronne Désirée de Marmont, attractive, elegant, charming and very knowledgeable about everything. It was she who taught me about eighteenth-century fine French furniture, Aubusson and Savonnerie rugs, tapestries, porcelain and art.

'I had developed a good sense of clothes by the time I arrived in Paris, but it was the baroness who instilled in me her own brand of chic, her incomparable stylishness. What you admire in me, that sense of style you've commented on, Vivienne, I acquired from Désirée de Marmont.

'The first thing she did was take me to her favourite couturiers, milliners and shoemakers, saw to it that I was dressed simply but elegantly in the height of fashion. It was her preferred interior designers who helped me to furnish and decorate the new apartment on the Avenue de Breteuil, again under her discerning eye. And it was she who found me the right butler, cook and housekeeper to run things for me. In short, she supervised every aspect of my life.

'Thus Désirée turned me into a chic and polished young woman with style, grace and sophistication, quite apart from my natural good looks. It was two years after my arrival in Paris that she decided I was "finished" and, therefore, finally ready to be launched into Parisian society as her protégée from London.

'And so, Vivienne, I began my life again. It was my fourth life. I had had three others, two of which I had tried hard to forget, to obliterate entirely. No one knew of this, not even Désirée. She was aware of one only, my rather pleasant but dull life as the wife of the Honourable Harry Robson, third son of a minor English lord.

'Désirée had one child, her son Louis, with whom she was not on the best of terms. Although she was still in her early fifties I became a surrogate child to her in many ways, like the daughter she had never borne.

'There was a special bond between us, rather like the bond we share, Vivienne. She was not only my mentor in those days, but my inspiration. I aspired to be exactly like her and in some ways I believe I succeeded.

'A good woman, kind, loving, witty, amusing and a wonderful companion, Désirée was part of that élite circle known as *le gratin,* the top crust. Yet despite this she was not in the least snobbish. I have observed in my long life that true aristocrats such as Désirée de Marmont and Édouard never are. In my experience it is the jumped-up no-accounts who tend to look down their noses at others.

'It was Désirée who introduced me to *Monsieur le Comte,* Édouard de Grenaille. The evening we met it was a *coup de foudre* as the French say, a thunderbolt. Or love at first sight, if you prefer. By this time I had already been living in France for five years. I was thirty-three and completely unattached. He was a widower with no children, also uninvolved, and fifty-eight years old. However, Édouard did not look his age, nor did he seem it.

'He was a good-looking man, debonair and dashing, and was imbued with continental charm. He swept me off my feet. Within the year we were married. I became *Madame la Comtesse*, the mistress of this house and a wonderful old château in Normandy.

'We were sublimely happy for the first two years. Then a problem developed in the marriage. I did not conceive. Childless and longing for an heir to carry on the line, Édouard began to change. He became depressed, bad-tempered and critical of me. Oh, not all the time, Vivienne, there were moments when he behaved like his old self, the Édouard of our courtship, and was kind, considerate. We had always enjoyed a good sex life, an active one, and we loved one another. But love and sex are not always enough. A marriage must be sustained by so much else besides.

'By the time our third wedding anniversary came around there was a genuine breakdown in our relationship. Édouard had grown more and more introverted, preoccupied as he was with his lineage and lack of an heir to carry on the family name. Somewhat irrationally he blamed me. Even though he loved me he took it out on me. For almost two years I ran to doctors and specialists in infertility, following Désirée's advice. The answer was always the same: there was nothing wrong with me.

'When I attempted to talk to Édouard about this, pass on the medical opinions I had received, he became angry and refused to listen. By now I was fully aware that he might not be able to face a simple fact: that he was sterile and unable to procreate.

'I feared for our marriage and I must admit I

was profoundly relieved when he decided to go to Brazzaville in French Equatorial Africa. He had a long-standing invitation to visit his uncle Jean-Pierre de Grenaille who owned vast estates there. I thought the break would do us both good. Édouard seemed to agree. He planned a long trip as he wanted to go on safari to hunt big game.

'It was the beginning of June 1960 when he set off for Brazzaville. Before he left he expressed the hope that our three-month separation would help to alleviate the strain between us.

'For the first two weeks Édouard was gone I spent my days undergoing further gynaecological tests. Once more the results were exactly the same as before. Three new doctors confirmed to me that there was no reason why *I* could not have a baby.

'By the end of June I was feeling miserable, low in spirits and overwhelmingly sad. I had had such a terrible childhood and youth. Suddenly it seemed to me that the past was repeating itself, albeit in a different way. I began to think that I was doomed to be unhappy, that life was not going to go right for me after all. I was also fearful that when Édouard returned from Africa our marriage would finally crumble completely, that we would end up either leading separate lives apart or divorcing. I was not sure which I thought was worse.

'The weather in Paris that summer was gruellingly hot and unbearable. Yet I had no wish to go to the château in Normandy by myself. Fitful, restless and constantly on the brink of tears, I went to see Désirée de Marmont, hoping that she might be able to both advise and console me. She knew why I had been troubled for so long, and was also aware that Édouard had seen fit to blame me for depriving him of an heir.

'When I arrived at her country estate in Versailles to spend the weekend she took one look at me and threw up her hands in alarm. She told me I was too thin and exhausted, insisted that I must take a vacation immediately.

'Vivienne, even now I remember so well what she said to me all those years ago. "Take yourself off to the Côte d'Azur, *ma petite*. Sunbathe, swim, relax, go for long walks, eat delicious food, shop for pretty things and indulge in a romantic interlude with a nice young man if the possibility arises." You can't imagine how shocked I was by her last suggestion. I was speechless.

'Then, somewhat indignantly, I told Désirée that I loved Édouard. She smiled. "All the more reason to have a little lighthearted affair. It will make you feel more relaxed, instil confidence in you again and when Édouard returns you will be in the right mood to work miracles. You can fuss over him, seduce him, make him feel virile, and believe me you will be able to put your marriage on a more even keel." Naturally I insisted that an affair was out of the question.

'But on the Sunday afternoon, just before I returned to Paris, Désirée took me on one side, told me again that I needed a change of scenery for my own good. "Go to Cannes, Zoë. Have some fun. And if there's a chance for a little flirtation, take it. What harm can it do? *None*. Providing no one knows about it. Just remember to be discreet, careful. And take the advice of an experienced woman, stay at one of the smaller hotels and use an assumed name." On the way back to Paris I pondered her words.

'I never intended to go to Cannes, Vivienne. But during the course of the next week the idea of a holiday in the sun became more and more appealing. On the spur of the moment one morning I telephoned the Hôtel Gray d'Albion in Cannes and made a reservation under the invented name of Geneviève Brunot, booked myself a seat on the Blue Train, packed a few simple clothes and left Paris for the south of France.

'Désirée had been correct about the change of scene doing me good. After three days of sunbathing, swimming, long walks and good food I was feeling much better and looking more like my old self.

'Cannes was busy that summer. The American Sixth Fleet stationed in the Mediterranean had just put into port. Hundreds of young ratings were on shore leave, mingling with the locals and the tourists. I managed to get lost in the crowds. There was a sense of jollity in the air, a feeling of festivity. Everyone seemed so young and gay and happy. I was infected with this spirit of *joie de vivre*. And of course I met a young man.'

I stopped speaking and looked across at Vivienne. She was sitting on the edge of her chair, facing me. Her eyes were glued to my face, and I knew she had been listening attentively.

I said, 'I'm afraid this is becoming rather a long story, longer than I'd intended. Can I offer you some sort of refreshment, Vivienne? Tea? Coffee? Or would you like a drink perhaps?'

'If you're going to have something, Countess Zoë,' she said with a small smile.

'I believe I will. I'm going to have a glass of champagne. Does that appeal to you, my dear?'

'That'd be lovely, thank you.'

'Would you mind ringing the bell for Hubert, please?'

'Of course not,' she answered getting up, crossing the room. After she'd done as I asked she glanced at the photograph on the console and said, 'This one is of you, isn't it, Countess Zoë? When you were in your thirties?'

I nodded. 'Yes, it is.'

'How beautiful you were.'

I merely smiled and glanced at the door as Hubert knocked and entered. 'Madame?'

'Hubert, we would like to have some refreshment. Please bring us a bottle of Dom Perignon and two glasses. Oh, and perhaps you'd better retrieve the tea things from the garden.'

# Thirty-two

Vivienne put down her flute of champagne, leaned forward and said, 'Please don't stop, Countess Zoë, please continue your story . . . you said you met a young man in Cannes . . .'

'I did, Vivienne. He was a nice young man, an American. For several mornings I had taken breakfast on the terrace of a small café not far from my hotel. He was usually there, drinking coffee and smoking a cigarette. He always smiled at me or nodded politely, and on the fourth morning when I arrived he spoke to me. He said good morning in French. I responded with a smile.

'A short while later I paid my bill and left the café. I had not walked very far when the young man caught up with me. In rather halting French he asked me if I was going to the beach. When I said I was, in English, he grinned and asked if he could join me.

'I hesitated for a moment. But he was so clean-cut, genial and polite I asked myself what harm there was in it. Also, I had only ever seen him alone at the café, never with any companions. It struck me that he seemed lonely, which was the way I was feeling at that moment in my life.

'He must have noticed my hesitation because he

excused himself for being rude, stretched out his hand and said, "Joe Anthony." Taking hold of his hand I shook it. "Geneviève Brunot," I said, and added that he was welcome to accompany me to the beach.

'We spent the morning sunbathing, swimming and talking generalities. He was rather quiet and didn't say very much about himself. But then neither did I. That day I was reserved, somewhat uncommunicative. He invited me to lunch at one of the small cafés on the beach, and I remember thinking how young, healthy and uncomplicated he looked as he ate his beefsteak, French fries and green salad with such gusto, savoured every mouthful of red wine.

'After lunch he walked me back to the Hôtel Gray d'Albion. On the way there he asked me to have dinner with him that night. Again I hesitated momentarily, and when I finally agreed to meet him later he looked so relieved and happy I was touched.

'And that is how it began, our little affair. The following morning we met at the café for breakfast and once again we went down to the beach together. That evening he took me to Chez Félix for dinner, then dancing afterward at La Chunga, a popular nightclub on the Croisette.

'By this time I had learned that Joe was only twenty-two years old. I was startled when he told me this because he appeared to be older and in fact was quite sophisticated. I did not dare tell him my age, admit to being thirty-eight. When he asked me how old I was I lied. I took off ten years and said I was twenty-eight. Joe believed me. It was true, I did look much younger than I actually was, everyone said that. However, I *was* forthright with Joe about my status, and from the very beginning he knew I was a married woman with obligations.

'That night at La Chunga, as he led me around the dance floor, holding me tightly in his arms, kissing my cheek and my hair, I realized I could not stop the inevitable from happening. I knew we were going to end up in bed together. Joe knew it too. There had been something special between us from the start of our friendship.

'We spent the next four days and nights together, and then unexpectedly I panicked. Much as I liked Joe, thought he was attractive and engaging, I realized that I was risking far too much by continuing the relationship. It struck me most forcibly that I had no alternative but to bring our brief romantic liaison to an end.

'When I explained to Joe that I had been called home because of a sudden emergency, he said he understood. Nevertheless, he looked disappointed when I said we could never meet again, was saddened when we took our leave of each other.

'Later that day I boarded the Blue Train for Paris and my real life there. Almost immediately I began to regret the affair and wished it had not happened. The more I thought about it the more I believed I had been foolish and irresponsible. Constantly I chastised myself. On the other hand, there was no way I could turn back the clock. Nor could I eradicate my adultery. I kept telling myself I was not the first person to have had an extra-marital affair. Hundreds of millions of people did it every day; it was part of being human. But this knowledge did not make me feel any better.

'I tried hard not to dwell on those few illicit days I had spent with Joe in Cannes and to some extent I succeeded. But there were awful moments when those guilty feelings returned, usually in the middle of the night when I tossed and turned and wrestled with my demons.

'And then at the end of July I had something else to occupy my mind, rather serious worries in fact. I had missed my period. As the days passed I grew more and more convinced I was pregnant with Joe Anthony's child. In August my body started to undergo certain changes, in particular my breasts were tender and enlarged. I missed my second period at the end of August. By my calculations I was about five or six weeks into my pregnancy.

'I was panic-stricken, floundering, and did not know which way to turn. I thought of confiding in Désirée and then changed my mind, although I've never been sure why I did so. She was my dearest friend, I trusted her, and I knew she would never betray my confidence. And yet I could not bring myself to speak to her of my affair with Joe.

'Perhaps I was a little self-conscious, even ashamed of myself, although I knew that Désirée de Marmont was a woman of the world and wise. She would never presume to pass judgement on me or anyone else. There was even one awful moment when I toyed with the idea of an abortion, but I dismissed this at once. It was far too repugnant to me.

'I am not a religious person. God was beaten out of me when I was young. When one suffers all kinds of abuse at the hands of adults it is hard for a child to keep her faith in God. As a young girl I used to ask myself why God was allowing such terrible things to happen to me, why God allowed such evil to thrive in this world. But I had no answers. I felt He had abandoned me. And I ceased to believe in God's existence.

'When I married Édouard I naturally had to give lip service to the idea of God because the de Grenailles were a devout Catholic family. However, it was only lip service. Imagine my surprise then, Vivienne, when one day at the end of August, when I was out walking, I found myself going into a church in the Latin Quarter. It was St Etienne du Mont, a place of worship I had not frequented before.

'To this very day I don't know why I went into that particular church on that particular afternoon. I did not go inside to pray. I simply sat there letting the silence envelop me. The interior was very beautiful with its vaulted ceiling, soaring pillars and stained-glass windows. But it was the quiet, the absolute peace that made the greatest impression.

'I sat there for a long time. A kind of lassitude settled over me. My thoughts had been on the baby the entire morning, and I had been worrying, wondering what to do. But now I closed my eyes, let go of those worries, finally relaxing. Then without warning I experienced a rush of the most intense emotion, a feeling of such enormous love for the child growing inside me that I was startled.

s glad to be alone for a few weeks, brium.

nont was leaving for Biarritz that gged me to go with her. At first I at the last moment I accepted her Ariel and the nanny with me.

, I met a man in Biarritz, Vivienne. f Désirée's, and he proved to be a nsiderate escort, taking me out to ives along the coast, and to the became good friends very quickly. as a local landowner, titled, and a wever, his wife never accompanied ited Désirée's house, and I got the s not a particularly happy marriage. ow attracted he was to me, and one cision. I would no longer resist his going to have an affair with Patric. s desperate for a son. I was going to

ow Charles was conceived, Vivienne. nade my affair with Patric sound very en cold-blooded. But it wasn't, not I do admit it was a conscious art, desiring as I did to get pregnant. tric was a kind man and loving, and l womanly again, and desirable, and s and despair soon fled. I felt better a long time. I admit it was different r with Joe Anthony. Joe and I had each other's arms unwittingly, almost This was more calculated, it's true, but





'Almost at once everything became crystal clear. With great clarity I saw right into the heart of things. I knew what I was going to do. When the baby was born it would be a de Grenaille. It would bring joy and happiness back into my marriage, and Édouard would love the baby as much as I already did. The baby was the solution to everything.

'A short while later I rose and walked slowly down the aisle, confident at last that everything was going to be all right. Just before leaving the church I paused to put money in the collection box. It was then that I discovered the church contained the reliquary of Saint Geneviève. I could not help thinking what a curious coincidence that was.

'Almost overnight my feelings of guilt and remorse disappeared, and that wonderful sense of *rightness* remained with me. Édouard returned home from Brazzaville on the first day of September. From the moment he walked in I was convinced everything would work out. He was in such a wonderful frame of mind, Vivienne, my heart lifted even more than it had in church. He looked brown and fit, and he was full of good humour, gave the impression of being glad to be home. One of the first things he did was to apologize to me for his churlish behaviour over those many, many months before.

'That weekend we drove to the château in Normandy, and in the tranquillity of our lovely old bedroom we made passionate love. It was as if Édouard were trying to exonerate himself for his unfairness and unkindness to me during the past few years.

His passion did not lessen that weekend and he kept avowing his love for me.

'Édouard made me radiantly happy that weekend, and my feelings for him were reinforced. I understood how deeply I loved my husband and how much he meant to me. A month later I was able to tell Édouard I was pregnant. Of course he was overjoyed. And for my entire pregnancy he was loving, tender, devoted and considerate, and he could not do enough for me. I was completely content and happy as I carried the child to full term.

'Of course there were days when I had sudden misgivings, Vivienne. I am not devious by nature and occasionally my deception troubled me. But whenever I experienced a slight twinge of guilt, I focused all my thoughts on Édouard. I reminded myself I was about to give him the child he had wanted throughout his adult life.

'His first wife had failed him. I had not. I was going to present him with the heir he craved. I had ensured the family name and title. The de Grenaille line would continue. Édouard would never know that the child was not his. In any case he would be a good father, and thus would make the child his through his love, there was no doubt in my mind about that.

'I was certain that Joe Anthony was already back in the States, had disappeared into oblivion. Joe did not know my real name. I was Geneviève Brunot to him. Therefore I was safe. The baby was safe. I would never set eyes on Joe Anthony again. Or so I thought.

'My baby was born eight months after Édouard and I had enjoyed our passionate reunion at the family

I liked Patric and I knew how much he cared about me.

'Once Édouard had a son in his arms at long last he reverted to his old self, became the lovely man I originally married. He adored the children and he adored me. He became an exemplary father and husband, and we settled into domestic bliss.

'The next twenty years were the best years of my life, Vivienne. I never looked back. I never thought about Joe Anthony. Or Patric Langalle. Édouard and our children were my whole existence. I was content. At peace. The happiness I had dreamed of years ago was mine at last. I even forgot about my terrible childhood and horrendous things which happened to me in my early life. I was a good wife, a good mother, and I revelled in these roles.'

I paused and looked across at Vivienne. 'I may have shocked you . . . admitting that I let Édouard think Ariel and Charles were his children.'

'No, you haven't!' she exclaimed, shaking her head. 'Not at all. You gave your husband everything he wanted, Countess Zoë, made him happy, brought joy into his life. He had those children from birth, so they *were* his. Besides, just because a man pumps sperm into a woman, gets her pregnant, doesn't mean he's a father. It's what a man does after the child is born that matters. From what you've told me, the count loved Ariel and Charles very much, and that's what is important, surely?'

'Thank you for saying that, Vivienne,' I replied, and continued, 'from the moment Charles was born there was never another cross word between Édouard and myself. We were so close, like one person, and our happiness was the thing I treasured the most. Yes, life was finally as I had dreamed it could be.

'Then out of the blue in the spring of 1983 my whole world fell apart.' I stopped, took a sip of champagne.

Vivienne asked quickly, 'What happened?'

'I received a letter from a man called Sam Loring, a stranger. He wrote that he was visiting Paris from Chicago, that he was a friend of Joe Anthony and Geneviève Brunot and wished to see me. I was stunned. I did nothing for two days, and then I finally phoned him at the Hôtel Scribe, as he had requested.

'We met that afternoon in the lounge of the hotel. He was a tall, lean, grey-haired man with a craggy face and looked as if he was in his early seventies. I had never seen him before.

'With no preamble I asked him what he wanted with me. He repeated what he had written in the letter, that he was a friend of Joe Anthony and knew about my affair with Joe twenty-three years earlier. He told me I had used the name Geneviève Brunot and that I had been a guest at the Hôtel Gray d'Albion in Cannes.

'Naturally I denied everything. His response was cold. He said he was sure I would not want my husband to know about my adulterous affair, nor would I want aspersions cast on Ariel's legitimacy. I took an indignant attitude, a haughty stance and countered that he was talking nonsense. I got up to leave.

'Sam Loring pressed me to stay and brought out an old photograph. It was one of me and Joe Anthony taken at La Chunga all those years ago. Joe had his arm around me. I was looking up at him and smiling. I recognized at once that the photograph was definitely suggestive and therefore damaging. Sam Loring pointed out the date the photographer had stamped on the back of the picture. *July 1960*. I felt trapped.

'I asked Loring what he wanted exactly. But I knew before he answered that he was after money. And, more than likely, a great deal of it. I also knew that if I paid him to be quiet now I was exposing myself to further blackmail later. On the other hand, what alternative did I have but to pay?

'Whilst Loring could never prove that Ariel was not Édouard's child, the date on the back of the picture was damning, and this frightened me. Furthermore, I did not want Édouard questioning anything about Ariel. Or about Charles, for that matter. I had to protect my children. And my husband as well. He was no youngster; he was twenty-five years older than I, and at eighty-six a fit and healthy man. Nonetheless, I did not want him unduly upset.

'Sam Loring shocked me when he asked for a hundred thousand dollars for his silence. I told him I had no intention of giving it to him. I pointed out that I had no guarantee that he wouldn't demand more from me later on. His answer was that I would have to trust him. "Honour among thieves," was his comment.

'I laughed in his face. I also asked him why he had waited so long to seek me out, to tell me this extraordinary story, which nobody would believe anyway, I said. Loring answered that he was retired, had serious family problems, great financial difficulties, and that if he hadn't been so desperate he would never have been in touch with me.

'I then demanded an explanation about Joe Anthony. I asked how Loring knew him, how he had come into possession of the photograph taken in La Chunga so long ago.

'It was a curious story that he told me, Vivienne. But I believed him, I must admit that. Loring explained that twenty-three years ago he had been employed by an American businessman to run the security division of the man's company. In the summer of 1960 Loring was sent to Europe to follow his employer's son who was travelling through France and Italy alone. His assignment was to keep an eye on him, make sure he didn't get into trouble.

'The young man in question was Joe Anthony, of course. Loring confided that he had known about our affair from its very inception. He had seen us together on the beach, at the little café, at La Chunga, and entering and leaving my hotel. He also informed me that at the time he had hired a French detective to follow me, that the man had boarded the Blue Train when I did, that day I returned to Paris after saying goodbye to Joe.

'Apparently Loring knew within twenty-four hours who I really was and all about me. He even knew when Ariel was born and the hospital she was born in. Through the French detective, he had kept tabs on me for a few years thereafter, just in case Joe Anthony ever tried to get in touch with me again. As for the photograph, he had bought it from the photographer at La Chunga the day after it was taken and had kept it all these years.

'I told him I would get the money, arranged to meet him three days later, and left the Hôtel Scribe. In the taxi on the way home I told myself that Loring couldn't prove anything, that I would not succumb to blackmail, but the moment I walked into this house I knew that I would. I had far too much to lose.

'It took me several days to get the money together, mostly because I wanted to pay Loring in cash. Fortunately, my first husband Harry Robson had left me a very wealthy woman, and I used some of his inheritance to pay the blackmailer.

'When I met Loring at the end of the week I demanded the photograph in exchange for the money. And I made him promise he would stay away from me. But even as I was speaking I knew there were no guarantees. Wanting to get rid of him, to be done with it, I took a great chance that day.

'Sam Loring did give me his word, for what it was worth, and vowed that I would never see him again. Then he handed me the photograph.

'As he did so he said, "Good-looking guy, Joe Anthony was, wasn't he? Except that he wasn't Joe Anthony." When I asked him what he meant, Loring said, "Countess, you weren't the only one masquerading as another person, using an assumed name. So was Joe. His real name was Sebastian Locke."'

# Thirty-three

Vivienne was staring at me.

She looked stunned and very pale. She exclaimed, 'Oh my God! If Sebastian was Joe Anthony, then he was Ariel's father. Oh my God!' Sitting back in the chair, she shook her head as if denying this, and said again, 'Oh my God! *Oh no!*'

I had anticipated this reaction from her and I merely nodded and said, 'Yes,' very quietly.

'Did Sebastian find out, Countess Zoë? Is that why he killed himself?' Vivienne demanded. 'It must be so! Of course! He committed suicide because he discovered he was involved in an incestuous relationship, albeit unwittingly. That's it, isn't it?'

I did not answer her for a moment or two. There was a small pause before I said slowly, 'For you to understand everything, Vivienne, I must begin at the beginning . . . the beginning of my life . . .

'I was born on April the sixth 1922. My parents were Niall and Maureen Rafferty, and they christened me Mary Ellen. We lived in Queens, and the first few years of my life were happy. Things changed drastically for me and my mother when my father was killed in 1927. A construction worker by trade, he was hit by a steel girder on a construction site and died of head injuries.

'My mother struggled to support us for the next two years, but despite her valiant efforts she was not very successful at earning a living.

'However, she was a pretty if somewhat fragile-looking woman and when Tommy Reagan, an old friend of my father's, showed up one day she immediately set her cap at him. Tommy, known to be a hard-working, hard-drinking bachelor, fell for her and within a few months they were married.

'My stepfather had a steady job. He was one of the managers of a large and prosperous farm in Somerset County near Peapack, New Jersey. Along with a good salary he was provided with a house on the property, one he said was big enough for us, his new family.

'At first I thought everything was going to be wonderful, living in the country on a farm, having a man to look after us again. I soon discovered how wrong I was. Tommy Reagan resented me, detested having another man's child under his feet and, looking back now, I believe he was insanely jealous of my mother's love for me, the special place I had in her heart.

'Certainly he took it out on me whenever things went wrong and sometimes when they didn't. He was a hard man who did not think twice about hitting me at the slightest provocation.

'When they were first married he was careful, never struck me in my mother's presence, but as time went on and he recognized her dependence on him he grew careless. Or it could have been that what she thought no longer mattered to him. I've never been sure of that, Vivienne, although I do believe the gloss wore off their marriage rather swiftly.

'His attitude to me was unrelenting. His motto was spare the rod, spoil the child. I can assure you I was never spoiled if the number of beatings I received at his hands counted for anything.

'Tommy Reagan was an exceedingly strict disciplinarian, and the true example of a naturally vindictive man who turned into a tyrant when given a small amount of power. A bully and a coward, he only picked on the weak and defenceless, those who could not strike back.

'My mother and I were intimidated by him. I tried to keep out of his way as best I could. Almost always my mother had to back down whenever she attempted to defend me. I often heard her sobbing in bed at night, especially when he had been drinking.

'The fact was, my stepfather made me his whipping post and years later, long after I had left the farm, I began to understand how sadistic he had been.

'It was sad and unfortunate that after only three years of marriage to Tommy my mother developed a heart condition and became a semi-invalid. She was bedridden half the time. Her poor health infuriated my stepfather, and my life became even more miserable. Apart from hitting me whenever he felt like it, he turned me into a drudge. I was made to clean the house and cook for him, for us, since my mother was too debilitated most of the time. I was ten years old.

'I grew up quickly, Vivienne. By the age of thirteen I was already well-developed and looked older than

I was. Nubile is perhaps the best way to describe myself. My lush looks were in bud but had not yet flowered. However, my mother had already told me I was going to be a beautiful woman when I grew up.

'One day, during that summer of 1935, I caught the eye of the man who owned the farm. Suddenly, as I went about the property, he started to look at me more closely and longer than he usually had before.

'He became very friendly and invited me into the main house, mostly into his office, where he gave me candy and chocolates, ribbons for my long hair, old magazines and, once, a book. And soon his hands were all over me, on my breasts and up my skirt, between my legs and anywhere else he felt like putting them.

'Thus began my real misery, Vivienne. It was not long before he was unbuttoning his trousers, showing himself to me and making me touch him. There were times when he forced me to take off some of my clothes.

'Although I was terrified of him, there was nothing I could do to stop him from treating me in this way. My mother was ill; I did not want to upset her, make her feel worse by bringing my troubles to her. My stepfather was unapproachable and he would not have believed me anyway. Perhaps he even knew and turned a blind eye. He did not care about me, I was a nuisance. I tried to block everything out, made believe it never happened.

'The owner warned me that if I ever breathed a word to anyone about what he did in the privacy of his office he would get rid of us. He would fire my stepfather, turn us out without money or references.

'I blamed myself, thought it was my fault that he abused me the way he did, so freely, so wantonly. Just before he had started to waylay me, his mother had been visiting him and she told me that I was a lovely-looking girl. But then she added in a spiteful voice that my looks were bound to get me into trouble one day. She said they would only lead me down the path to hell where Satan was waiting to devour me. As far as I was concerned her son was Satan incarnate.

'I was fourteen when he raped me, in September 1936. Naturally, I was a virgin and since he had been overly rough with me, forcing me, I bled profusely.

'There was a bit of a commotion about this matter. He had not properly locked the door in his haste to violate me. The housekeeper walked in on us. Our dishevelled state, plus the blood on the hooked rug, left little to her imagination. She knew what had taken place and told him so. But like everyone else on the farm she was afraid of losing her job. So he continued to do whatever he wanted with me.

'It was not until the winter of 1937 that he made me pregnant. I was fifteen and more frightened than ever when I realized I had conceived. But times were hard, he was my stepfather's boss and we were dependent on him. Therefore, nothing much was said about my condition. My mother cried a lot. My stepfather blamed me.

'The owner of the farm was in his thirties and had never married. The idea of a child and a wife must have appealed to him. Much to Tommy Reagan's surprise, and mine, he married me because of the baby. The wedding took place at the farm. It was conducted by a local judge, and it was a simple affair, rather hurried.

'The odd thing was he immediately went away and left me living in the house with my mother and stepfather. When he returned to the farm unexpectedly a few months later, he installed me in the main house with him. He continued to have sex with me until it was impossible for him to do so because of my condition. But he rarely spoke to me and there was no warmth between us, no kindness in him. I dreamed of running away, but I knew I could not.

'The first day of June my labour pains started. I was in labour for almost two days and when the baby was finally delivered on June the third I was totally depleted. They told me that the baby had died.

'I was very ill for several months. Weak, exhausted and afraid, I did not want to get well. As long as I was sick in bed no one could hurt me. However, I knew I could not hide for ever. When I was finally back on my feet my stepfather told me I was being sent away by my husband to recuperate. It had been decided that I would go to London to stay with my mother's sister Bronagh. Apparently it had been my mother's idea to send me there, and miraculously my husband had agreed.

'I cannot tell you how relieved I was to be leaving. I did not see my husband before I set out for New York to board the ship, since he was in Canada on business. However, I knew he was paying for my passage to England and a few new clothes, and that he had provided three hundred dollars for my expenses in London.

'The thing that stays in my mind is what my mother said to me the day I left the farm. I've never forgotten her face, the way she looked at me, the sound of her voice. "Don't come back to this place, mavourneen," she whispered to me when I bent down to kiss her. She told me she loved me, and I remember thinking how happy she looked that morning. I knew I was witnessing her profound relief that I was making my escape.'

Lifting my glass, I took a sip of champagne and shifted on the sofa, making myself more comfortable.

Vivienne, who had been watching me alertly, exclaimed, 'You're not going to stop, are you, Countess Zoë? I want to hear the rest of your story. Please.'

'Then you shall, Vivienne,' I said. 'I am going to tell you everything . . . things no one else has ever heard.'

# Thirty-four

'It was in London that I started my second life, Vivienne. And it was much happier than my first, thanks in no small measure to my Aunt Bronagh.

'She was my mother's younger sister, and an actress. When she lived in New York she had worked with a small theatre company in Greenwich Village. And it was there that she met a young English actor named Jonathan St James. They had fallen in love, and when he returned to England in 1933 she had gone with him. They had been married for five years when I arrived to stay with them.

'The moment I walked into their little house in Pimlico my spirits lifted. It was a warm, cosy place, almost like a doll's house, and Jonathan St James made me feel welcome and at home. Like Bronagh he was in his late twenties and the two of them were full of vitality, high spirits and somewhat bohemian in their lifestyle. They were crazy about each other and the theatre, and both were working in plays in the West End. Naturally, they were in their element. Their happiness and gaiety was infectious and I soon felt much better, better than I had since my early childhood when my father was still alive. They were loving with each other, and with me.

'Slowly my health improved; my broken spirit began to heal. And Bronagh restored my soul. Sympathetic by nature, she had an understanding heart; gradually, I started to confide in her. Things came out slowly, little by little. Within three months she knew the whole story of my life, and she was enraged. "You're not going back there, Mary Ellen. I swear to God it'll be over my dead body if you do. Mary, Mother of Jesus! It's criminal, what's been done to you, sure an' it is, mavourneen." Jonathan, who by this time knew everything from Bronagh, agreed that I must not return to New Jersey under any circumstances.

'But no one seemed in much of a hurry to get me back, including my mother. Of course I knew that in her case she was protecting me, trying to keep me out of harm's way. She wrote to me regularly and never failed to tell me she loved me, and I did the same, sending her a letter once a week.

'At the end of six months in London I was a different person. Bronagh and Jonathan had truly worked miracles. They had cosseted and pampered me and it showed. I had put on weight; there was flesh on my bones at last. I had grown taller and my figure was willowy. The bloom was on the rose, as Bronagh kept saying to me.

'But most importantly, because of Bronagh and Jonathan I felt safe, more secure than I had for years. I was no longer cowed and scared, fearful of being beaten or abused. The fear I had lived with for so long finally diminished and I came to understand that one day it would vanish completely.

'Once I had believed that the only way out of my torment was to die. I had been a mere child of thirteen when I had contemplated suicide, Vivienne, that was part of the tragedy. You see, I had had no childhood.

'But I turned a corner during those first few months in London. I was aware that I could become a whole new person, have a new identity, start again.

'That summer Bronagh found me a job through a friend of hers. I became a dancer in a cabaret in the West End. Because of my height and slender figure I made the perfect showgirl.

'I loved it all – the glamour, the costumes, the crowds, the glitter of the footlights. I had found my true métier. The stage was mine. It meant everything to me. It became my entire world. I put death and heartbreak behind me; I reached out for life.

'Since I was living in a brand-new world I needed a brand-new name. Discarding Mary Ellen Rafferty, which only reminded me of my pain and humiliation, I invented a new one for myself.

'*Zoë Lysle*. That is who I became. With this new name I acquired a different persona. Zoë had never been touched or damaged; she was clean, pure, whole. And every night when I stepped out on to the stage in my fine feathers I was reborn. I soared.

'I missed my mother, I worried about her, and I had moments of sadness when I thought about my baby who had died at birth. But these moments were fleeting. After all, I *was* only sixteen. I had started my life again . . . as Zoë. I looked forward always, never back.

'I did not hear from my husband and I was relieved

he had remained silent for so long. When I had first arrived in London I had worried that he would eventually drag me back to America. But as the summer passed and there was no word from him I began to relax.

'Then on September the third 1939 Britain declared war on Nazi Germany. The world turned upside down. The war years in London were extraordinary – full of hardships and danger because of the constant air raids. But I came through them relatively unscathed.

'After America entered the war in 1941, American troops started to flood into Britain. Every time I saw a GI I was scared to look at his face in case it was my stepfather. But he did not show up in London, although I knew from my mother that Tommy had joined the US army.

'As for my husband, I didn't know what had actually happened to him. He had sold the farm in Somerset County, divorced me and had the legal papers sent to me in 1940, care of Bronagh. I never heard from him again.

'Being a showgirl I had many admirers and went out with some of them. But I was forever wary, always on my guard, determined that I would not be exposed to the heartlessness of others ever again.

'However, in 1943 I met an English officer in the Coldstream Guards. He was the Honourable Harry Robson, a captain in the army and the son of an English lord. Harry's father had been married three times and his last wife, Harry's mother, had been an American heiress with a railroad fortune at her disposal.

When she died in 1940 Harry had inherited everything.

'I was twenty-one when Harry and I started going out together. He was twenty-eight. Harry was bowled over by me the first time we met, and I was rather taken with him. He was pleasant to look at and the first kind man I had met other than Jonathan St James.

'Encouraged by Bronagh and Jonathan, I accepted Harry's proposal. We were married in 1944. At the time he insisted I retire from the stage and I was happy to do so. I had grown accustomed to men ogling me. But in all truth, Vivienne, there was often a knot of fear inside when I sensed instinctively that I had attracted someone who might be difficult to handle. Curiously enough, loving the stage though I had, I never missed it.

'And so my third life began, Vivienne. Harry and I had five years together. They were good years. I was devoted to him. I know I made him happy; he gave me security and protection and a great deal of love.

'Harry was crossing Oxford Street in 1949 when he was knocked down by a double-decker bus. He died of massive internal injuries a week later. I was grief-stricken. I had loved Harry, in my own way, and I knew I would miss this gentle, generous man who had been so good to me.

'After the funeral I went into mourning, kept to myself and wondered what to do with the rest of my life. I was twenty-seven and Harry had made me a wealthy woman. I was his sole heir.

'I had no wish to return to America. There was nothing there for me. My mother had died not long after I married Harry. It was a year after I was widowed that I decided to take a vacation in Paris. Almost at once I knew I would make it my permanent home. I did so and disappeared from the London scene for ever.

'I began my fourth life when I married Édouard, but then you know a good deal about that life, Vivienne, and what happened to me in the intervening years. As I already told you, Sam Loring showed up in Paris in 1983 and blackmailed me to the tune of one hundred thousand dollars because of my affair with Joe Anthony, or rather Sebastian Locke. I paid because I wanted to protect my family, even though I knew that it was risky to do so. Loring could come back at any time and demand more money.

'However, a few days after I had paid Loring I began to worry about another matter, one which had more serious implications than blackmail. I decided to go to America to check out something for myself. When I told Édouard that I had family business to attend to in the States he suggested I go alone. At eighty-six he did not feel like travelling any more.

'I flew to New York and went straight to the Pierre Hotel, where I had booked a suite. The following day I hired a private investigator to do the work I required. It did not take him long. Within forty-eight hours he brought me the information I needed.

'What I had dreaded and feared was true. For several days I was in shock and incapable of thinking straight. But as the shock receded I filled with enormous rage. For the first time in my life I wanted to kill somebody . . .'

I realized that I could not continue.

A wave of emotion swept over me, and I was held in the grip of that terrible fury I had experienced twelve years ago. I was trembling inside.

'The rage has never really left me,' I said at last, looking at Vivienne, holding her with my eyes. 'Nor have I ever lost the desire to kill that man.'

'Which man? Who do you mean, Countess Zoë?'

'Cyrus Locke.'

'*Cyrus*? But why? Because of Loring? Because Cyrus sent Loring to follow Sebastian all those years ago, when you met him in Cannes?'

'No, Vivienne, this has nothing to do with Loring. In a way he was a godsend, coming to me when he did. He helped me without even realizing it, helped me to avert a great tragedy.'

A puzzled expression crossed Vivienne's face. 'I'm sorry Countess Zoë, but I'm afraid I'm not following you.'

'Of course you're not,' I said and stopped.

My throat constricted, I could feel the tears welling behind my eyes and I had begun to shake uncontrollably.

Taking a deep breath, I clasped my hands together to steady myself, but my voice quavered as I said, 'Cyrus Locke was the owner of the farm in New Jersey. He was the man who abused me as a child and raped me when I was fifteen, the man who impregnated me, married me and then discarded me like a piece of worthless garbage. And he stole my child. He told me my baby had died, but that was not the truth. My son lived. My son Sebastian.'

As I said his name the tears crept out from under my lids and slid down my cheeks. I brought my shaking hands up to my face and the tears continued to fall unchecked.

Vivienne came and sat next to me on the sofa. She took me in her arms and held me close, endeavouring to comfort me.

And I wept as I had wept in 1983, on the night I had discovered the shocking truth. I felt as though my heart were breaking all over again, as it had done then.

# Thirty-five

Eventually I drew away from Vivienne, found a handkerchief in my pocket and blew my nose.

Then I looked at her.

She was white-faced, and I could see the pain in her eyes. Reaching out, I squeezed her hand. 'Thank you,' I said, and before she could ask any questions I went on, 'I'd like to finish my story, tell you the rest of it, Vivienne.'

She nodded. 'You must.'

'Armed with Sam Loring's information I grew suspicious when I began to focus on Joe Anthony's age –' I broke off. 'I always think of him as Joe, never Sebastian. Anyway, he was twenty-two and I was thirty-eight when we met in Cannes. Sixteen years' difference in age. My mind began to race. My baby had been born on June the third 1938. He had died the same day, according to Cyrus Locke and the midwife who had delivered the child at the farm in New Jersey. Had my baby lived he, too, would have been twenty-two in 1960.

'It was hardly likely that Cyrus Locke had fathered *two* sons in 1938. No, only mine, I reasoned. Especially since he had not married again for several years.

'The unthinkable was staring in my face. Was it

possible that my child had lived? Was it possible that Sebastian was not Hildegarde Locke's son, but mine? And if he were, then I had given birth to a child by my own son. My daughter Ariel.

'I was horror-struck, and naturally I denied it to myself for some time. But in the end intelligence took over from emotion, and I was convinced that Cyrus Locke had lied to me all those years ago. I was haunted by the knowledge that Sebastian and I had committed incest, although we had done so unknowingly. I felt as though I were living in a nightmare. Ariel fathered by my own son. My mind shut down whenever I thought of this.

'After a great deal of soul-searching I realized there was only one thing to do. I must go to New York and start digging for the facts. I had to know the truth for my own sanity. As I explained to you, I hired a private investigator and asked him to obtain certain documents for me. I also told him I wanted him to provide me with information about Cyrus Locke. I was vaguely aware that, after divorcing me, he had eventually remarried and fathered children. I had noticed the occasional item about him in newspapers over the years, but wanting to forget that painful period in my life I had paid little attention.

'Several days later the private investigator reported to me at the Pierre Hotel. He brought with him various documents and a detailed summary of Cyrus Locke's life.

'The most important document was a copy of Sebastian's birth certificate. And there in black and white was the date of his birth: June the third 1938.

The father's name was given as Cyrus Lyon Locke. The mother's name was Mary Ellen Rafferty Locke. *Me*. The place of birth was shown as Reddington Farm, Somerset County, New Jersey. As I had requested, the private investigator had also obtained a copy of my marriage certificate.

'The report about Cyrus Locke explained additional things to me. Apparently he had moved to Maine after selling the farm in New Jersey, and lived in a mansion he had owned since December 1937. Obviously he had bought this immediately after marrying me. There was no doubt in my mind that he took the baby to Maine with a nurse, installed them in that house and brought up the child himself until he remarried several years later.

'I think he always planned to do this, Vivienne. When he raped me he was thirty-three years old, unmarried and childless. Once he discovered he had made me pregnant, he married me to get the child. He did not want me. I was of no further use to him. But he did want an heir. The more I pondered it the more convinced I became this was the only explanation. Otherwise why would he have stolen my baby?

'That night at the Pierre Hotel my world was shattered. I was so devastated I was unable to function properly for almost a week. Finally I managed to pull myself together and flew back to France. I had a life there, a husband and family who adored me.

'But it was not easy for me to go on, and for some months I was desperately ill. The doctors were baffled, as was Édouard. I was not. I knew what was wrong with me. I carried a terrible secret in my heart. It was a secret I could not confide to anyone on this earth. It was the greatest burden I've ever had to bear, and I was concerned about Ariel. At twenty-two my daughter was beautiful and a brilliant student. Everyone predicted she would have an extraordinary career in medicine. I knew there had been no genetic damage; nonetheless, I fretted about her.

'It was Édouard who helped me to recover my health. He was no longer young, but he was a robust and active man, and he devoted all his time to me. He was always at my side, always encouraging me. And he was full of love.

'Gradually, I began to feel better. I stopped blaming myself. I accepted that I could not change what had happened so long ago; therefore, I must live with it.

'Once I was finally on my feet I put every ounce of strength and energy into loving Édouard, Ariel and Charles. I survived because I am a survivor by nature. In 1985 I received a letter postmarked Chicago. My heart missed a beat when I saw the name S. Loring on the back of the envelope. The letter was from Sam Loring's daughter Samantha. She had written to tell me her father had died. One of his last requests of her was that she write to let me know he had passed away. She told me that he thanked me for my aid in his time of need. So, my blackmailer was dead.

'When my beloved Édouard died in 1986 I felt that my life had come to an end, too. We had been very close for the last twenty-odd years of our marriage. He had been my great love and my cherished companion; he had been my whole life. Without him I believed there was no reason for me to exist. But I went on. I drew immense pleasure from Ariel and Charles, from my daughter-in-law Marguerite and grandson Gérard. As the years slid by I somehow managed to obliterate Joe Anthony from my mind and I put the past behind me.

'And then one night last September the past came back to hit me in the face. Ariel returned from Zaire, and she brought her fiancé to meet me. His name was Sebastian Locke.

'I will never forget that night, Vivienne. How I got through it I will never know. My mind was floundering, my senses swimming. Also, I saw what a wonderful man he was; I ached inside because I had been so cruelly deprived of my son.'

I leaned back against the cushions, feeling depleted, then I finally finished, 'And that is the story of my life. Now you know it all . . .'

Drawing closer, Vivienne took hold of my hand and held it in hers. 'You have moved me so much, Countess Zoë. My heart aches for you when I think of what you've suffered. I don't know how you've lived through it.'

'Very few people have an easy time in this world, Vivienne. What counts most is that we survive, endure.'

Vivienne was silent for a few moments and then she said in a voice so low I could hardly hear it, 'You told Sebastian, didn't you?'

'Yes, I did. What else could I do?'

'And that's why he killed himself, isn't it?' she whispered.

'Yes, Vivienne, I believe it is.'

'You must have told him after he and I had lunch together on that Monday.'

'Yes, that's so. I saw him on Wednesday.'

'You came to New York?'

I nodded. 'Ariel went back to Zaire. Sebastian flew to New York. I followed him. I telephoned him at the Locke Foundation, explained that I was in New York and had to see him urgently. He agreed. Why wouldn't he? I was the mother of the woman he was planning to marry.'

'Where did you meet?'

'At his townhouse. I was extremely distressed, in turmoil inside. But I managed to hide it. I plunged right into my story. I told him I had once been married to Cyrus Locke, that he was my son who had been stolen from me by his father. And then I told him I was also Geneviève Brunot. He was stunned, reeling from shock. And of course he didn't believe a word of it. Not at first.

'However, I had the documents to bear me out. His birth certificate. And my own. My marriage certificate. Ariel's birth certificate. And the photograph of Joe Anthony and Geneviève Brunot, taken at La Chunga in July of 1960. The thing that baffled him was that this woman confronting him with a most horrifying story was Geneviève, the pretty young woman he had known in Cannes. I convinced him she and I were the same person. I explained that I lied about my age, had dropped ten years because he was so young. I had too many pertinent details about those four days we'd spent together. He had no option but to believe me. I also showed him some other photographs of me which had been taken that year. They helped to convince him that I *was* Geneviève Brunot.

'When he asked how I had found out about everything, I explained how Sam Loring had contacted me in Paris, blackmailed me and told me of Joe Anthony's real identity. Before I could stop myself I confided some of the things I've told you today, Vivienne. About Cyrus Locke's abuse of me –'

I paused for a moment, then I said slowly, 'I destroyed Sebastian, of course. I know that. But I had to prevent a great tragedy from occurring. I told him he must never again see Ariel.'

Vivienne gave me a hard stare and shook her head. 'And later that week Sebastian took his life. But he needn't have done that. He could have broken off his engagement to Ariel, and he didn't even have to explain why he was doing so.'

'Yes, Vivienne, you're right.' I let out a long sigh, clasped her hand all that much tighter. 'All I knew that day was that I had to stop them marrying. I never imagined he would kill himself. But I should have known, I should have guessed when he said, "However am I going to live without her? She's the only person I've ever really loved." I wept when he said that and so did he.'

Vivienne was very still. Her eyes were brimming and slowly the tears ran down her cheeks. She could not speak. Neither could I. We just sat there holding each other's hands, caught up in our own thoughts.

After a while Vivienne roused herself. 'You told

me at the beginning that no one else knows any of this. Why did you tell me?'

'Because you had such a need to understand why Sebastian killed himself. I realized that if I didn't explain everything, you would be haunted by it for the rest of your days.'

'Thank you, Countess Zoë, for confiding in me,' she answered very softly.

'You know, Vivienne dear, I've never understood why it all happened . . . why I had to meet Joe Anthony in Cannes all those many years ago. Chance? Fate? I cannot explain . . . I don't think anyone could . . .'

'How tragic it is,' Vivienne murmured. She looked at me closely. 'I loved him so very much. Always.'

'I know you did . . . and that's another reason why you had to know the truth. The truth sets us free, Vivienne.'

# *Part Five*

# VIVIENNE

## Honour

# Thirty-six

Countess Zoë's house on the Faubourg Saint-Germain was very quiet when Hubert let me in. Quieter than usual, I thought as I followed him across the grand marble foyer.

'How is Countess de Grenaille?' I asked him as we went up the wide curving staircase together.

'A little better today,' he said. 'She has rallied again. She is a most remarkable woman, Madame Trent. And she is looking forward to seeing you.'

'As I am her, Hubert.'

He led the way down the corridor, opened the big double doors to her bedroom, ushered me in, excused himself and disappeared, as always the perfect butler.

I glanced towards the antique bed and saw to my surprise that it was draped in its silk coverlets and was empty.

'I'm over here, Vivienne, sitting near the fire,' Countess Zoë said in a voice that was stronger than I had expected. This morning, on the phone, she had sounded weak. I had been alarmed, worried for her health.

I turned to her and, smiling, I walked across the room in the direction of the fireplace. And I could not help thinking how well she looked. Hubert was right, she *was* remarkable. Her chestnut hair was stylishly coiffed and she wore makeup, expertly applied. I was again struck by the arresting looks of this seventy-three-year-old woman.

This afternoon she was wearing delphinium-blue silk lounging pyjamas, obviously couture, and sapphire earrings. The colour of the silk outfit and the sapphires exactly matched her wonderful eyes. From the first moment I met her I had recognized her great beauty, and there had been odd moments when she had seemed very familiar to me. Puzzled, I had not been able to fathom out why this was so. I knew now. She reminded me of Sebastian. It was her eyes, of course. Bits of sky, I thought, as his had been, and their mouths were identical. Sensitive, vulnerable mouths.

'I'm glad you're back in Paris, Vivienne, I've been longing to see you. Thank you for coming, my dear.'

'I was planning to run over today,' I answered, bending down, kissing her on both cheeks. 'I was just about to phone you and invite myself to tea, when you called the hotel.'

Smiling at me, she patted my hand resting on her arm. 'You've become very special to me, Vivienne.'

'As you have to me, Countess Zoë.' I was carrying a shopping bag of books; I placed them next to her chair and went on, 'These are for you. I hope you like them.'

'I'm sure I will, you seem to know my tastes very well. How kind you are, my dear. Thank you.'

I went and sat down on the chair opposite and looked at her expectantly.

'I wanted to see you because I have something for you.' As she was speaking she turned to the Louis XV end table next to her chair and picked up a small package. Leaning forward slightly, she offered it to me and added, 'This is for you, Vivienne.'

I was surprised, and as I took it from her I exclaimed, 'But Countess Zoë, you don't have to give me gifts!'

She laughed lightly. 'I know I don't . . . come along, open it.'

I did as she said, removing the ribbon and the gold wrapping paper. The small velvet box in my hands looked old, and when I lifted the lid I gasped, more surprised than ever. Lying on the dark red velvet was a heart-shaped brooch covered entirely with small diamonds and there was a slightly larger diamond set in the centre. 'Countess Zoë! It's beautiful! But I can't accept this, it's far too valuable!'

'I want you to have it. Harry Robson gave it to me when we were married in 1944 and I've always liked it. I think you will, too. It's a pendant as well as a brooch. If you look on the back you will see how it works. There's a little hook, so it can hang on a chain.'

'But this is something you should give to Ariel or your daughter-in-law.'

'Hasn't it occurred to you that you are my daughter-in-law? Or were, when you were married to Sebastian.'

I simply stared at her without speaking. And of course she was correct. But the brooch was obviously extremely valuable and I was reluctant to take it.

She continued, 'However, that is not the reason I

am giving it to you. I want you to have a memento, something special to remember me by . . .'

'Oh Countess Zoë, I'll never forget you, how could I! You're the most extraordinary person I've ever met in my whole life.'

'Please accept the brooch, Vivienne, you'll make me very happy if you do. It gladdens my heart to think that every time you put it on you'll be reminded of an old lady who has grown very attached to you.'

'You sound as if you're not going to see me again. And you are! Every time I come to Paris!' I exclaimed.

'I sincerely hope so. But let us be realistic, my dear. I am an old woman and I am very ill. You know that, Vivienne. I am not going to be on this earth for ever. But enough! Let us not get maudlin today. Please accept the brooch. Do it for me.'

'Well of course I accept it, Countess Zoë, and thank you very much. It's beautiful and you're very generous . . .'

I rose and went to kiss her. Then I looked down into her upturned face and said, 'Just so long as you know that I don't need the brooch to be reminded of you.'

'Yes, I do know that,' she replied. Her vivid blue eyes were suddenly sparkling.

I could tell she was happy and this pleased me. I took out the diamond heart and pinned it on the jacket of my suit. 'There, how does it look?'

'Dazzling,' she said, glanced over at the desk near the window, and went on, 'would you please bring me the letter case on the desk, Vivienne?'

Nodding, I did as she asked. Then I went and sat

down in my chair again. Leaning against the antique tapestry pillows, I watched her open the case and sort through the contents.

This woman had captivated me the moment I had entered her house and we had bonded almost instantly. I had fallen completely under her spell; there was something unique about her. She had an understanding heart, was intelligent, wise and brave. So very brave. When I thought of the painful things which had happened to her in her life, I wondered how she had ever stood it all, how she survived. It was miraculous that she had lived through those tragedies the way she had, so courageously. Zoë de Grenaille was indeed an indomitable woman. I was filled with admiration for her and I had grown to love her.

'Vivienne?'

'Yes, Countess Zoë?'

'This is Sebastian's birth certificate. Please burn it.' Handing the document to me, she continued. 'You can read it if you wish . . .'

I nodded, glanced down at the paper I was now holding. The facts were written there. They were exactly as she had told me. The names danced before my eyes. Cyrus Lyon Locke. Mary Ellen Rafferty Locke. Sebastian Lyon Locke. Reddington Farm, Somerset County, New Jersey. And Sebastian's date of birth, June the third 1938. How often I had celebrated his birthday with him on that date.

'This was the beginning . . . the beginning of a great tragedy,' I whispered.

'Burn it, Vivienne. Please.'

'Immediately.' I went to the fire, knelt in front of it and let the flames consume Sebastian's birth certificate.

'Now this one. My marriage certificate.'

I held the piece of paper that had legalized the union between Mary Ellen Rafferty and Cyrus Lyon Locke and a wave of anger swept through me. He was at the root of it. Cyrus Locke. How evil he had been. I tore the marriage certificate in half and dropped the pieces into the fire.

'This is the photograph taken at La Chunga in 1960,' Countess Zoë went on, handing it to me. 'Consign this to the flames as well.'

My eyes dropped to the picture. I was compelled to look at it, I could not help myself. It was a Sebastian I did not know who stared back at me. I recognized him immediately, there was no question who he was. But how different he looked from the Sebastian I had known. The older man. He was so young here, so untouched by life. And the Zoë next to him was the most glamorous of women. Her beauty was in full bloom. She looked glorious. No wonder she had been irresistible to men.

Conscious of her eyes on me, I placed the photograph on top of the logs and watched it curl and burn until it was no more, then I turned my head to look at her.

'You wished you could keep that, Vivienne,' she said slowly. 'And for a moment I almost told you that you could. But it's better to destroy everything. It's not that I don't trust you with the photograph, but –' Her voice faltered and she glanced away.

I said, 'I know you trust me. And you're right, it's better this way. You'll feel easier in your own mind.'

She sighed to herself and murmured, 'Let me see what else is in here. Ah yes, my marriage certificate from Caxton Hall in Westminster where I married Harry Robson. No need to destroy that. However, here is my own birth certificate. Please burn it.' Handing this to me, she settled back in her chair.

'Are you sure?' I asked. 'I mean, there's no real reason to throw this away, is there?'

She was thoughtful. Eventually she said rather softly, 'Ariel and Charles know that I was an actress when I was young, and that my name was Zoë Lysle. They're aware that I was widowed when I married Édouard, the widow of Harry Robson, supposedly my first husband. But they've never heard the name Mary Ellen Rafferty, and I want everything burned that could ever link me to the Locke family. Put it on the fire, my dear. Please.'

I did as she asked and then pushed myself to my feet.

Countess Zoë said, 'It was wise to get rid of the damning evidence. I wouldn't want Ariel or Charles to find it later. But I'm glad I told you everything, Vivienne. I think I've lifted a burden from you, taking you into my confidence, and it's lifted a burden from me, sharing my secret with you. That has weighed me down for twelve years; it's been a relief to speak of it with you.'

I got up and went and crouched next to her chair. Looking deeply into those startlingly blue eyes, I said, 'I will honour your confidence. I will never tell anyone as long as I live.'

Leaning closer, Countess Zoë kissed my forehead, touched my cheek gently. 'I know you won't reveal anything I've told you. You're such a fine person, so honest and loyal. And honour is bred in the bone with you. You could no more do a shoddy thing than Ariel could.' She paused and looked at me intently when she said, 'You've become like another daughter to me. I've grown to love you, Vivienne.'

'Thank you for saying those lovely things, Countess Zoë. I want you to know that I love you too.'

A smile touched her mouth and was gone in an instant. A sudden sorrow seemed to settle over her and her eyes filled with tears. Reaching for my hands, she said, 'It's as though I took a knife and plunged it into him. I'm responsible for Sebastian's death, Vivienne. I've lived with that ghastly knowledge for over seven months, and it's overwhelmed me. The sorrow is unendurable.' Tears rolled down her cheeks.

'Please, please, don't blame yourself,' I said. 'You had to tell Sebastian the truth. There was nothing else you could do. You couldn't let him marry Ariel. That would have been unconscionable.'

She fumbled in her pocket for a handkerchief. 'His death is a shadow on my heart,' she said.

I continued to console her and eventually she took hold of herself, became composed at last.

Hubert brought in the tea tray, poured for us and left.

We sipped our tea in silence for a while. It was Countess Zoë who spoke first. She said, 'Love is the only thing that's worth while in this terrible and incomprehensible world we live in. It's the only thing that makes any sense. Take the advice of an old woman who's seen almost everything and experienced much . . . don't make any compromises when it comes to marriage. Oh yes, you'll marry again, Vivienne, I'm absolutely certain of that. But you must only marry for love.'

'I know; there is no other reason, as far as I'm concerned.'

'When the right man comes along, you'll know it. You'll be swept off your feet, but you'll be very sure of your feelings, I don't doubt that.'

'I think I will, Countess Zoë.'

There was a faint smile on her face, but I could see the tears glittering in her eyes when she said softly, 'Oh, I don't doubt *you*, Vivienne. Not at all.' There was a pause before she finished, 'Your whole life is ahead of you. Live it well from this day forward.'

# Thirty-seven

I went straight from Countess Zoë's house to the restaurant where I was meeting Jack for dinner.

As I sat back in the cab, after giving the driver the address of Chez Voltaire, I wondered whether I should remove the diamond heart. It was still pinned to my jacket and looked wonderful against the black wool. I decided to leave it where it was.

Jack was already there when I arrived, and he rose as I was shown to the table. 'Well, aren't you a sight for sore eyes,' he said, kissing me on the cheek.

We both sat down. I looked across the table at him and said, 'And so are you, darling.'

He grinned at me. 'You're looking very nifty this evening, Viv. Very chic. Great suit. Who gave you the pin?'

'I've had it for ages,' I said evasively, now regretting that I had not taken it off in the cab after all.

'It looks very Sebastian to me,' he said, motioned to a waiter, and went on, 'what would you like to drink?'

'I'll have a glass of champagne, Jack, please.'

'Good idea, I'll have that too. I'm really off the hard stuff these days.' He ordered a bottle of Veuve

Clicquot, the waiter went away to fetch it, and Jack continued, 'So, have you tracked her down?'

'Who?' I asked, although I knew at once to whom he was referring. Ariel. She had been the subject of our last conversation at the Château d'Cose only a couple of weeks ago.

'The mystery woman in Sebastian's life. Ariel de Grenaille, of course,' he said.

'No, I haven't,' I replied. 'And I don't think I'm going to either.'

'Why not? You were so gung-ho about her . . . about speaking to her.'

'Well, I've spoken to her mother and Ariel is in Africa. I'm not planning to go there, Jack, I don't think it's worth it.'

'That's a change of tune! So what did you find out? From the mother, I mean?'

'Not a great deal. Ariel lives in Africa. That's where she was when Sebastian killed himself. So obviously she can't shed any light on the matter. She doesn't know any more than you or I do.'

'*Is* she a doctor?'

'Yes.'

'A scientist?'

'Yes, Jack, she works with hot viruses, such as Ebola and Marburg. That's what her mother told me.'

'Jesus! That's dangerous work.'

'Yes, it is.'

The waiter came with the ice bucket and champagne and proceeded to open the bottle. This put a stop to Jack's questions. But the moment we were alone again he continued to press me about Ariel de Grenaille.

'*Was* she engaged to Sebastian?' he probed, his curiosity apparent.

I answered, 'From what I understand, yes. They were planning to get married at some point this spring. About now. As he had told me, Jack. And that's it, there's nothing more to say. Except that you were always right. We'll never know why Sebastian killed himself. It's still a mystery.'

'So you're not planning to interview her for the profile?'

'No, I'm not. Cheers.' I touched my glass to his.

'Cheers,' he said and went on, 'is it a work in progress? Or have you finished it?'

I laughed. 'No, I haven't, not yet. But I'm going back to Lourmarin tomorrow, and I fully intend to add the final touches. All it needs is a good polish.'

'I'd hoped you'd be staying in Paris for a few more days,' he grumbled, sounding petulant. 'I thought you could keep me company. I'm here on wine business until the end of the week.'

'I'd like to, but I really must get back. I've such a lot to do, and my book on the Brontë sisters is coming out in the summer. I'll have to do a certain amount of promotion for it, travel a bit, and right now I need some time at Vieux Moulin. Quiet time. Alone.'

'Are you going to Connecticut in August, as you usually do?' he asked.

'Yes, why?'

'I might be there at that time. At Laurel Creek Farm.'

'I can't believe it! And I certainly can't believe you'd leave Château d'Cose!'

He began to laugh. 'I'm thinking of spending a couple of weeks there, I'm not planning to move *permanently* to Cornwall, Vivienne.'

I sat back in my chair and regarded him for a long moment. He looked well, thinner, and much better groomed than he usually was. I also realized he was in a good mood, almost benign, which was unusual for him. Taking a deep breath, I said, 'Jack, I want to ask you something.'

'Shoot.'

'I want you to look me in the eye and tell me you don't love Catherine Smythe.'

'Now you've gone and ruined the evening, Viv, and it's only just begun.'

'Do you love her?' I pressed. When he was silent I went on relentlessly, 'It's *me*, Viv, sitting here. Your oldest and dearest friend and you can't fool me. Look me right in the eye, Jack Lyon Locke and tell me that you don't love her.'

'I do, but –'

'No, no, no, Jack. No buts.'

'Who gave you that fabulous pin?'

'Don't change the subject.'

'Okay, okay. I love her. So what?'

'I saw Catherine two days ago. When I was in London working with my publisher.'

'You did!' He sat up straighter and stared at me intently. 'How is she?'

'She looks fantastic. She's got a wonderful peachy bloom about her. I must say there are some women who really blossom during pregnancy and she's one of them. She's in great spirits, happy about the baby, working hard on her book about Fulk Nerra, and planning to move into a new apartment.'

'When?'

'Well, she hasn't actually found one yet, Jack, but she's looking hard, and certainly she hopes to be settled in a new place before the baby's born.' I stared at him, waiting for a comment or a question, but he said nothing. He gulped down his champagne and looked around for the waiter, who came in a flash to fill his glass.

Once we were alone, I said, 'Catherine loves you very much, Jack.'

'Go and tell that to the marines,' he muttered in a truculent voice.

I answered softly, 'I know she does, and I also know that she'd like to be with you, with or without the benefit of marriage. In any case, she's very independent-minded about matrimony, but then you know that.'

'If she loves me as much as you say she does, then why did she betray me?' he asked in a sulky voice.

'How did she do that, Jack?' I murmured, frowning.

'She got pregnant when she knew I didn't want children.'

'I don't believe that was on purpose. From what she said, it was an accident. Let me ask you something, just out of curiosity. Why are you so against children?'

'I'm not against kids. I just don't want any of my own.'

'Catherine says you think you can't love a child. Because you believe Sebastian didn't love you.'

He offered me a sardonic smile. 'That was her parting shot to me, if I remember correctly. And she's off her rocker. Of course I can love a child . . .'

'Then why don't you go to London and get her, bring her back to France? You could have a good life together, darling.'

'No way, Viv. I'm better off alone.'

'*I* don't think you are. She also told me something else, Jack. She said that you confided things about Sebastian and she thinks he was suffering from something called disassociation.'

'Yeah. She spouted all that to me too! A lot of psychiatric mumbo-jumbo!'

'Not necessarily, Jack. There is such a condition, I've discussed it with a psychiatrist I know.' I paused, then slowly I continued, 'I think she's correct. Sebastian probably was afflicted with it.'

'Well, well, well, so the worm turns.'

'No, not at all. But I've thought a lot about him in the past few weeks, since I've been working on the profile of him for the *Sunday Times*, and I've come to see him differently.'

'Tell me. I'm all ears.'

'I believe Sebastian had a problem being intimate with us, loving us on a certain level. He just couldn't do it, the emotion wasn't there. Very simply, it was missing in him. And by *us* I mean you, me and Luciana. My mother. And probably all the wives. You see, he never knew mother love, had never bonded with *anyone* during the first years of babyhood when that is essential. And yet, conversely, he was a caring human being, Jack. Look how concerned he was about the world, how he wanted to help those in desperate need. It was possible for him to do enormous charity work, to "love" the world en masse, so to speak, because he didn't have to be *intimate* with all those people out there. He gave vast amounts of money, travelled the world making sure it was used properly. And gave the *impression* of being a "loving" man.'

Jack was listening to me, taking in my words, and I could see that I had reached him. I went on, 'Sebastian tried so hard, he did the best he could for us and he did care about us, Jack. In fact he always showed the three of us how much he cared, demonstrated it in so many different ways. He gave you the château because *you* loved it so much. It wasn't for tax benefits, as you've so often implied. He encouraged you to work with Olivier and learn the wine business. I know he expected you to run Locke Industries and the Locke Foundation one day, but he never said you couldn't do it long distance, the way he had always done. And he never once said you had to give up the winery. He spent time with you, he encouraged you to do so many things when you were young. Sebastian helped to make you what you are today.'

Jack was staring at me in astonishment. 'What do you mean, spent time with me? He never did that! He was forever travelling, always lumbering me with Luciana. And you, missy.'

I laughed in his face. 'Oh God, Jack, you sound like a maungy little boy. And for what it's worth, *I'm* the one who got lumbered with you and Luciana.' I leaned forward and grabbed hold of his hand resting on the table. 'Listen to me! Sebastian did the very best he could for you! *I know. I saw it.* And he did spend time with you. He taught you how to ride a horse, play tennis, row a boat and swim, and many other things. You've just blocked it out because you hate him for some unknown reason. Why, I'll never know. And I'll never know why you can't give him the benefit of the doubt.'

'You have always viewed him from a different angle. You see him differently than I, Viv!' he shot back.

'That's true to some extent, I agree. But I think I'm beginning to see him more realistically. I know I always idolized him. And idealized him, as well. I've suffered from a complaint called hero worship for years. But I'm getting over that. He wasn't perfect, I realize this. He was moody and difficult, and one of the most agonized men in the world. That's why he was morose and gloomy so much of the time. And I believe his agony sprang from his awful childhood. Being brought up by Cyrus Locke and some hideous nanny, and then acquiring a dreadful stepmother like Hildegarde Orbach must have been perfectly horrible. Foul. Poor little boy. When I think about his childhood my heart bleeds. Actually, in my opinion, he turned out very well under the circumstances.'

Jack was looking at me intently, digesting my words. He had an odd look on his face when he said,

'You seem to have worked out his psychology very well . . . do you really believe he suffered from dis-association, then?'

'Frankly, Jack, I do.'

He nodded. 'You said he couldn't love on a intimate level. Are you now telling me he couldn't love *you?*'

'Yes, I am. I don't think he loved me, not in the way you and I love people, Jack. Oh, Sebastian *said* he loved me. And I know he cared very deeply about me and my welfare, and that he was sexually involved with me. Very much so. But sexual passion can't be construed as love.'

'The worm *has* turned,' he said in such a soft voice he was barely audible.

'I see him in a new light,' I replied, 'I understand him better, that's all. And I don't love him any less than I ever did. My *view* of him has changed. Not my feelings for him. They're still exactly the same.'

'I see.'

'Try to give him the benefit of the doubt, Jack, can't you? I think you'd feel better if you did. You have no reason to hate him. He was a good father.'

He said nothing. He sat there staring at me across the table, and suddenly I understood without him saying it that I had got through to him. And I realized he respected me more than ever for being so honest with him.

I sipped my champagne. I, too, was silent.

Unexpectedly Jack exclaimed, 'But he always took what I wanted –'

'What do you mean?' I asked with a frown.

'My Special Lady, for one. Your mother. I loved Antoinette very much.'

I was so taken aback I gaped at him and my jaw dropped. 'Jack, my mother was a *mother* to you! She was a grown woman. They were heavily involved. She adored him. What on earth are you getting at?'

'I don't know . . . I always felt I was in some sort of competition with him . . . for her love and attention. And yours. I couldn't believe it when he married you. He took you away from me.'

'Oh Jack, I'm sorry. So very sorry you've been harbouring these awful feelings of . . . frustration and anger. And quite obviously for years. But Sebastian wasn't in competition with you, don't you see that? You were only a little boy. He was a man, and one who was lethally attractive to women.'

Jack sighed heavily. 'I guess the shoe was on the other foot . . . I suppose *I* was competing with *him*. Is that what you're saying?'

'I think I am, Jack, yes.' I leaned closer to him. 'I want you to do something for me. And for yourself. This is vitally important, so please pay attention, don't start looking around the restaurant in that way.'

He brought his gaze back to mine. 'I'm listening, Viv.'

'I want you to go to London. *Immediately*. I don't want you to waste any time. I want you to get Catherine and bring her back to Aix-en-Provence. I want you to marry her at once so that the baby is legitimate when it's born.'

'Why?'

'Because I want you to start your life all over again.

I want a new beginning for you, a new beginning for the Locke dynasty. The baby Catherine is carrying is the future of the dynasty. And Catherine herself is your future, Jack. You'll never meet anyone more suited to you than she. And she loves you so much.'

He sat very still, listening attentively to every word.

I smiled faintly. 'It's odd, you know,' I continued. 'I've just realized that Catherine loves you in exactly the same way I loved Sebastian.'

He lolled back in the chair, gave me a questioning look. And I couldn't help thinking that he looked so very much like his father at this moment. Levelling his blue eyes at me, he lifted a dark brow. 'And how is that?' he asked finally.

'With all her heart and soul and mind,' I answered.

# Thirty-eight

The quietness of the old mill at Lourmarin had been restorative, just as I had known it would be. That was one of the reasons I loved to come back to Provence, to bask in the stillness of my house, rediscover its beauty and the beauty of my gardens, to be at peace.

In the past two weeks the tranquillity had been a godsend. I had sifted through my troubled thoughts, brought order to the chaos in my mind.

And now at last it was all so very clear to me. I understood everything and I had finally come to terms with myself.

I had changed.

I would never be the same again.

And I would never see the world in quite the same way, either.

Elements beyond my control had wrought these changes in me – Sebastian's suicide, Countess Zoë's confessions, Catherine's insights, my new-found knowledge of those I thought I knew, but had not known at all. And my new understanding of myself. I realized that for the time being I wanted to walk alone. For one thing, it had now become clear to me that I could not make a commitment to Kit

Tremain. But I think I had always known that.

Jack and I had become closer than ever, perhaps because I had been so forthright about Sebastian and my revised perception of him. And somehow I had helped Jack to see the future more clearly than before.

Jack was at peace with himself at long last. He had resolved his hatred of his father; the turmoil in his heart had been vanquished. Jack had taken the advice I had given him in Paris. He had gone to see Catherine in London and brought her back with him to Aix-en-Provence. Between the two of us we had convinced her to become his wife.

They were married yesterday at the Château d'Cose.

It was a small wedding. We had all agreed this was the way it should be. Olivier Marchand and his wife Claudette were present, along with Madame Clothilde and her husband Maurice, and a few of the other old-timers from the estate, whom Jack, Luciana and I had grown up with.

Luciana and Gerald had flown in from London, and Luciana was so cordial with me that I was amazed. She seemed happier and healthier. The change in her was so remarkable that I wondered if she was pregnant.

Afterwards we were served lunch in the garden. It was such a lovely May day with the lilacs in full bloom and Catherine had made a beautiful bride in a pale pink dress and coat which set off her red hair. Jack had never been smarter in his life. He wore a dark blue suit, white shirt and grey silk tie and looked more like Sebastian than ever. I had never seen him so happy. I was thrilled for him, thrilled for them both. They were going to be all right, those two. I had no fears.

Rising, I left my desk and walked across the library to the french windows overlooking the gardens. I stood for a moment staring out, thinking what a lovely evening it was. Then, pushing open the doors, I stepped on to the terrace.

My eyes turned towards the distant horizon.

The sky was changing as the sun sank low in the west. The colours along the rim of the horizon took my breath away: vermilion and orange running into peach and gold, violet bleeding into amethyst, and lilac striated with the palest pink. It was the most glorious sunset I had seen in a long time.

The radiant light streaming out from behind the darkening clouds looked supernatural, as if it were emanating from some hidden source below the line of sombre hills.

Only the shrill ringing of the phone forced me to tear my eyes away from that extraordinary sky.

I stepped into the library and reached for the receiver. 'Vieux Moulin. Hello?'

'Madame Trent, *s'il vous plaît.*'

'This is she speaking. Hubert, is that you?'

'*C'est moi, Madame. Bon soir* –' He broke off, his voice trembling as he strived hard for control.

I knew what he was going to say, the news he had to impart, before he spoke again. 'Is it Countess Zoë, Hubert?' I asked quietly.

'Yes, Madame. She just died a few moments ago. She realized she was dying this afternoon. She asked me to let you know. "Telephone Madame Trent immediately, Hubert. She must be told at once." That is what she said to me. It was her last wish. She died gently, Madame. And she was at peace.'

'Was her son Charles with her, Hubert?'

'Yes. *Monsieur le Comte* was at her bedside with his wife and little son. And Mademoiselle Ariel. Monsieur finally overruled his mother last week and brought his sister back from Africa.'

'I'm so glad they were all with her,' I said, my voice shaking. I brushed the tears off my cheeks. 'Thank you, Hubert, for letting me know. Goodnight.'

'Goodnight, Madame.'

I replaced the receiver and went back to the terrace. I walked down the steps into the gardens Sebastian and I had planted so many years ago.

How beautiful they looked tonight. Many of the flowers had bloomed early this year. The borders were riotous with colour and the early evening air was fragrant with their mingled scents.

I stood looking out towards my lavender fields and the meadows far beyond. Everything was a blur. I could not see anything through my tears.

My thoughts were of Countess Zoë. She had shown me that the past was immutable. My past was Sebastian and part of me would always belong to him. But I had let him go . . . I had exorcized his ghost at last. And now I could get on with my life. Like Jack, I could start anew.

Countess Zoë had set me free.

BARBARA TAYLOR BRADFORD

# HER OWN RULES

*As always, for Bob,*
*with all my love*

# Contents

# PROLOGUE

## *Time Past*

# Prologue

The child sat on a rock perched high up on the river's bank. Elbows on knees, chin cupped in hands, she sat perfectly still, her eyes trained on the family of ducks circling around on the surface of the dark water.

Her eyes were large, set wide apart, greyish green in colour and solemn, and her small face was serious. But from time to time a smile would tug at her mouth as she watched the antics of the ducklings.

It was a bright day in August.

The sky was a piercingly blue arc unblemished by cloud, the golden sun a perfect sphere, and on this balmy summer's afternoon nothing stirred. Not a blade of grass nor a leaf moved; the only sounds were the faint buzzing of a bee hovering above roses rambling along a crumbling brick wall, the splash of water rushing down over the dappled stones of the river's bed.

The child remained fascinated by the wildlife on the river, and so intent was she in her concentration that she barely moved. It was only when she heard her name being called that she bestirred herself and glanced quickly over her shoulder.

Instantly she scrambled to her feet, waving at the

young woman who stood near the door of the cottage set back from the river.

'Mari! Come on! Come in!' the woman called, beckoning to the child as she spoke.

It took Mari only a moment to open the iron gate in the brick wall, and then she was racing along the dirt path, her plump little legs running as fast as they could.

'Mam! Mam! You're back!' she cried, rushing straight into the woman's outstretched arms, almost staggering in her haste to get to her.

The young woman caught her daughter, held her close, and nuzzled her neck. She murmured, 'I've a special treat for tea,' and then she looked down into the child's bright young face, her own suddenly serious. 'I thought I told you not to go down to the river alone, Mari, it's dangerous,' she chastised, but she did so softly and her expression was as loving as it always was.

'I only sit on the rock, Mam, I don't go near the edge,' Mari answered, lifting her eyes to her mother's. 'Eunice said I could go and watch the baby ducks.'

The woman sighed under her breath. Straightening, she took hold of the child's hand and led her into the cottage. Once they were inside, she addressed the girl who was sitting in a chair at the far end of the kitchen, reading a book.

'Eunice, I don't want Mari going to the river alone, she might easily slip and fall in, and then where would you be? Why, you wouldn't even know it had happened. I've told you this so often. Eunice, are you *listening* to me?'

'Yes, Mrs Sanderson. And I'm sorry, I won't let her go there by herself again.'

'You'd better not,' Kate Sanderson said evenly, but despite her neutral tone there was no doubt from the look in her eyes that she was annoyed.

Turning away abruptly, Kate went and filled the tea kettle, put it on the gas stove and struck a match.

The girl slapped her book shut and rose. 'I'll get off then, Mrs Sanderson, now that you're home.'

Kate nodded. 'Thanks for baby-sitting.'

'Shall I come tomorrow?' the teenager asked in a surly voice as she crossed the kitchen floor. 'Or can you manage?'

'I think so. But please come on Friday morning for a few hours. That would help me.'

'I'll be here. Is nine all right?'

'That's fine,' Kate responded, and forced a smile despite her lingering irritation with the teenager.

'Ta'rar, Mari,' Eunice said, grinning at the child.

'Ta'rar, Eunice,' Mari answered and fluttered her small, chubby fingers in a wave.

When they were alone, Kate said to her five-year-old daughter, 'Go and wash your hands, Mari, that's a good girl, and then we'll have our tea.'

The child did as she was bidden, and went upstairs to the bathroom, where she washed her hands and dried them. A few seconds later, she returned to the kitchen; this was the hub of the house and the room they used the most. It was good-sized and rustic. There was a big stone fireplace with an old-fashioned oven built next to it, lattice windows over the sink, wooden beams on the ceiling and brightly-coloured rag rugs covered the stone floor.

As well as being warm and welcoming, even cosy, it was a neat and tidy room. Everything was in its proper place; pots and pans gleamed, and the two windows behind the freshly laundered lace curtains sparkled in the late-afternoon sunshine. Kate took pride in her home, and this showed in the care and attention she gave it.

Mari ran across to the table which her mother had covered with a white tablecloth and set for tea, and scrambled up onto one of the straight wooden chairs.

She sat waiting patiently, watching Kate moving with swiftness, bringing plates of sandwiches and scones to the table, turning off the whistling kettle, pouring hot water onto the tea leaves in the brown teapot, which Kate always said made the tea taste all that much better.

The child loved her mother and this adoration shone on her face as her eyes followed Kate everywhere. She was content now that her mother had come home. Kate had been out for most of the day. Mari missed her when she was gone, even if it was for only a short while. Her mother was her entire world. To the five-year-old, Kate was the perfect being, with her gentle face, her shimmering red-gold hair, clear blue eyes and loving nature. They were always together, inseparable, for the feeling was mutual. Kate loved her child to the exclusion of all else.

Kate moved between the gas oven and the counter-top next to the sink, bringing things to the table, and when finally she sat down opposite Mari she said, 'I bought your favourite sausage rolls at the bakery in town, Mari. Eat one now, lovey, while it's still warm from the oven.'

Mari beamed at her. 'Oooh, Mam, I do love 'em.'

'Them,' Kate corrected softly. 'Always say *them*, Mari, not 'em.'

The child nodded her understanding and reached for a sausage roll, eating it slowly but with great relish. Once she had finished, she eyed the plates of sandwiches hungrily. There were various kinds – cucumber, polony, tomato and egg salad. Mari's mouth watered, but because her mother had taught her manners, had told her never to grab for food greedily, she waited for a second or two, sipped the glass of milk her mother had placed next to her plate.

Presently, when she thought enough time had elapsed, she reached for a cucumber sandwich and bit into it, savouring its moist crispness.

Mother and child exchanged a few desultory words as they munched on the small tea sandwiches Kate had made, but mostly they ate in silence, enjoying the food thoroughly. Both of them were ravenous.

Mari had not had a proper lunch today because Eunice had ruined the cottage pie her mother had left for them, and which had only needed to be reheated. The baby-sitter had left it in the oven far too long, and it had burned to a crisp. They had had to make do with bread and jam and an apple each.

Kate was starving because she had skipped lunch altogether. She had been tramping the streets of the nearby town, trying to find a job, and she had not had the time or the inclination to stop at one of the local cafés for a snack.

Kate's hopes had been raised at her last interview earlier that afternoon just before she had returned home. There was a strong possibility that she would get a job at the town's most fashionable dress shop, Paris Modes. There was a vacancy for a sales person and the manager had seemed to like her, had told her to come back on Friday morning to meet the owner of the shop. This she fully intended to do. Until then she was keeping her fingers crossed, praying that her luck was finally about to change for the better.

Once Kate had assuaged her hunger, she got up and went to the pantry. The thought of the job filled her with new-found hope and her step was lighter than usual as she brought out the bowl of strawberries and jug of cream.

Carrying them back to the table, she smiled with pleasure when she saw the look of delight on her child's face.

'Oh Mam, *strawberries,*' Mari said and her eyes shone.

'I told you I had a treat for you!' Kate exclaimed, giving Mari a generous portion of the berries, adding a dollop of cream and then serving herself.

'But we only have treats on special days, Mam. Is today special?' the child asked.

'It might turn out to be,' Kate said enigmatically. And then seeing the look of puzzlement on Mari's face, she added, 'Anyway, it's nice to have a treat on days which aren't particularly special. That way, the treat's a bigger surprise, isn't it?'

Mari laughed and nodded.

As so often happens in England, the warm August afternoon turned into a chilly evening.

A fine rain had been falling steadily since six o'clock and there was a dank mist on the river; this had slowly crept across the low-lying meadows and fields surrounding the cottage, obscuring almost everything. Trees and bushes had taken on strange new shapes, looked like inchoate monsters and illusory beings out there beyond the windows of the cottage.

For once Mari was glad to be tucked up in her bed. 'Tell me a story, Mam,' she begged, slipping further down under the warm covers.

Kate sat on the bed and straightened the top of the sheet, saying as she did, 'What about a poem instead? You're always telling me you like poetry.'

'Tell me the one about the magic wizard.'

Kate smoothed a strand of light brown hair away from Mari's face. 'You mean *The Miraculous Stall*, don't you, angel?'

'That's it,' the child answered eagerly, her glowing eyes riveted on her mother's pretty face.

Slowly Kate began to recite the poem in her soft, mellifluous voice.

*'A wizard sells magical things at this stall,*
*Astonishing gifts you can see if you call.*
*He can give you a river's bend*
*And moonbeam light,*
*Every kind of let's pretend,*
*A piece of night.*

*Half a mile,*
*A leaf's quiver,*
*An elephant's smile,*
*A snake's slither.*
*A forgotten dream,*
*A frog's croaks,*
*Firefly gleam,*
*A stone that floats,*
*Crystal snowflakes,*
*Dew from flowers,*
*Lamb's tail shakes,*
*The clock's hours.*
*But – surprise!*
*Not needle eyes.*
*Those he does not sell at all,*
*At his most miraculous stall.'*

Kate smiled at her daughter when she finished, loving her so much. Yet again, she smoothed the tumbling hair away from Mari's face and kissed the tip of her nose.

Mari said, 'It's my best favourite, Mam.'

'Mmmmm, I know it is, and you've had a lot of your favourite things today, little girl. But now it's time for you to go to sleep. It's getting late, so come on, snuggle down in bed . . . have you said your prayers?'

The child shook her head.

'You must always remember to say them, Mari. I do. Every night. And I have since I was small like you are now.'

Mari clasped her hands together and closed her eyes.

Carefully she said: 'Matthew, Mark, Luke and John, bless this bed that I lay on. Four corners to my bed, four angels round my head. One to watch and one to pray and two to keep me safe all day. May the grace of Our Lord Jesus Christ, the love of God and the fellowship of the Holy Spirit be with us all now and forever more. Amen. God bless Mam and keep her safe. God bless me and keep me safe. And make me a good girl.'

Opening her eyes, Mari looked at Kate intently. 'I *am* a good girl, aren't I, Mam?'

'Of course you are, darling,' Kate answered. 'The best girl I know. My girl.' Leaning forward, Kate put her arms around her small daughter and hugged her close.

Mari's arms went around Kate's neck and the two of them clung together. But after a moment or two of this intimacy and closeness, Kate released her grip and settled Mari down against the pillows.

Bending over the child, she kissed her cheek and murmured, 'God bless. Sweet dreams. I love you, Mari.'

'I love you, Mam.'

Wide rafts of sunlight slanted through the window, filling the small bedroom with radiance. The constant sunshine flooding across Mari's face awakened her. Opening her eyes, blinking and adjusting herself to the morning light, she sat up.

Mari had recently learned to tell the time and so she glanced over at the clock on the bedside table. It was nearly nine. This surprised the child; her mother was usually up and about long before this time every morning, calling her to come down for breakfast well before eight o'clock.

Slipping out of bed, thinking that her mother had overslept, Mari trotted across the upstairs hall to her mother's bedroom. The bed was empty. Holding onto the banister, the way she had been taught, she went down the stairs carefully.

Much to Mari's surprise, her mother was nowhere to be seen in the kitchen either. At least, not at first glance. But as she peered around the table she suddenly saw her mother on the floor near the gas stove.

'Mam! Mam!' she shouted, ran around the table and came to a standstill in front of her mother. Kate was lying in a crumpled heap; her eyes were closed and her face was deathly white.

Mari saw that there was blood on her mother's nightgown and she was so frightened she could not move for a moment. Then she crouched down and took hold of her mother's hand. It was cold. Cold as ice.

'Mam, Mam,' she wailed in a tremulous voice, the fear intensifying. 'What's the matter, Mam?'

Kate did not answer; she simply lay there.

Mari touched her cheek. It was as cold as her hand.

The child remained with her mother for a few minutes, patting her hand, touching her face, endeavouring to rouse her, but to no avail. Tears welled in Mari's eyes and rolled down her cheeks. A mixture of panic and worry assailed her; she did not know what to do.

Eventually it came to her. She remembered what her mother had always told her: 'If there's ever anything wrong, an emergency, and I'm not here, go and find Constable O'Shea. He'll know what's to be done. He'll help you.'

Reluctant though she was to leave her mother, Mari now realized that this was exactly what she must do. She must go to the police box on the main road, where Constable O'Shea could be found when he was on his beat.

Letting go of her mother's hand, Mari headed upstairs. She went to the bathroom, washed her face and hands, cleaned her teeth, and got dressed in the cotton shorts and top she had worn yesterday. After buckling on her sandals, she returned to the kitchen.

Mari stood over Kate, staring down at her for a moment or two, her alarm and concern flaring up in her more than ever. And then turning on her heels decisively, she hurried outside into the sunny morning air.

Mari raced down the garden path and out onto the tree-lined lane, her feet flying as she ran all the way to the main road. It was here that the police box was located. Painted dark blue and large enough to accommodate two policemen if necessary, the box was a great convenience for the bobby on the beat. Fitted out with a telephone, running water and a gas burner, it was here that a policeman could make a cup of tea, eat a sandwich, write up a report and phone the main police station when he had to report in or request help. These police boxes were strategically placed in cities and towns all over England, and were indispensable to the bobbies on the beat, especially when they were on night duty and when the weather was bad.

By the time Mari reached the police box she was panting and out of breath. But much to her relief Constable O'Shea was there. He'll help me, I know he will, she thought, as she came to a stop in front of him.

The policeman was standing in the doorway of the box, smoking a cigarette. He threw it down and stubbed it out when he saw Mari.

Taking a closer look at the panting child, Patrick O'Shea immediately detected the fear in her eyes and saw that she was in a state of great agitation. Recognizing at once something was terribly wrong, he bent over her, took hold of her hand and looked into her small, tear-stained face. 'What's the matter, Mari love?' he asked gently.

'It's me mam,' Mari cried, her voice rising shrilly. 'She's lying on the kitchen floor. I can't make her wake up.' Mari began to cry even though she was trying hard to be brave. 'There's blood. On her nightgown.'

Constable O'Shea had known Mari all of her young life, and he was well aware that she was a good little girl, well brought up and certainly not one for playing tricks or prone to exaggeration. And in any case her spiralling anxiety was enough to convince him that something *had* gone wrong at Hawthorne Cottage.

'Just give me a minute, Mari,' he said, stepping inside the police box. 'Then we'll go home and see what's to be done.' He phoned the police station, asked for an ambulance to be sent to Hawthorne Cottage at once, closed the door and locked it behind him.

Reaching down, he swung the child up into his arms, making soothing noises and hushing sounds as he did so.

'Now then, love, let's be on our way back to your house to see how your mam is, and I'm sure we can soon put everything right.'

'But she's dead,' Mari sobbed. 'Me mam's dead.'

# PART ONE

## *Time Present*

# One

Meredith Stratton stood at the large, plate-glass window in her private office which looked downtown, marvelling at the gleaming spires rising up in front of her. The panoramic vista of the Manhattan skyline was always eye-catching, but tonight it looked more spectacular than ever.

It was a January evening at the beginning of 1995, and the sky was ink-black and clear, littered with stars. There was even a full moon. Not even a Hollywood set-designer could have done it better, Meredith thought: there's no improving on nature. And then she had to admit that it was the soaring skyscrapers and the overall architecture of the city that stunned the eye.

The Empire State building still wore its gaudy Christmas colours of vivid red and green; to one side of it, slightly to the left, was the more sedate Chrysler building with its slender art deco spire illuminated with pure white lights.

Those two famous landmarks dominated the scene, as they always did, but this evening the entire skyline seemed to have acquired more glittering aspects than ever, seemed more pristinely etched against the dark night sky.

'There's nowhere in the world quite like New York,' Meredith said out loud.

'I agree.'

Meredith swung around to see her assistant Amy Brandt standing in the doorway of her office.

'You gave me a start, creeping in on me like that,' Meredith exclaimed with a grin, and then turned back to the window. 'Amy, come and look. It takes my breath away.'

Amy closed the door behind her and walked across the room. She was petite and dark-haired, a contrast to Meredith, who was tall and blonde. Amy felt slightly dwarfed by her boss, who stood five feet seven in her stocking-feet. But since Meredith always wore high heels she generally towered over most people, and this gave Amy some consolation, made her feel less like an elf.

Gazing out of the window, Amy said, 'You're right, Meredith, Manhattan's looking sensational, almost unreal.'

'There's a certain clarity about the sky tonight, even though it's dark,' Meredith pointed out. 'There're no clouds at all, and the lights of the city are creating a wonderful glow . . .'

The two women stood looking out of the window for a few seconds longer, and then, turning away, moving towards her desk, Meredith said, 'I just need to go over a couple of things with you, Amy, and then you can get off.' She glanced at her watch. 'It's seven already. Sorry to have kept you so late.'

'It's not a problem. You'll be away for a week, so I'll be able to take it easy while you're gone.'

Meredith laughed. 'You taking it easy would be the miracle of the century. You're a workaholic.'

'Oh no, not me, that's *you*! You take first prize in that category.'

Meredith's deep green eyes crinkled at the corners as she laughed again, and then pulling a pile of manila files towards her she opened the top one, glanced down at the sheet of figures and studied them.

Finally, she looked up and said, 'I'll be gone for longer than a week, Amy. I think it will be two at least. I've quite a lot to do in London and Paris. Agnes is very set on buying that old manor house in Montfort-L'Amaury, and you know she's like a dog with a bone when she gets her teeth into something. However, I'm going to have to work very closely with her on this one.'

'From the photographs she sent it looks like a beautiful property, and it's perfect for us,' Amy volunteered, and then asked, 'You're not suddenly off it, are you?'

'No, I'm not. And what you say is true, it *is* ideal for Havens. My only worry is how much do we have to spend, in order to turn that old house into a comfortable inn, with all the modern conveniences required by the seasoned, indeed pampered, traveller? That's the key question. Agnes gets rather vague when it comes to money, you know that. The cost of new plumbing is not something that concerns her particularly, or even interests her. I'm afraid practicalities have always eluded Agnes.'

'She's very creative though, especially when it comes to marketing the inns.'

'True. And I'm usually stuck with the plumbing.'

'And the decorating. Let's not forget that, Meredith. You know you love designing the inns, putting your own personal stamp on them, not to mention everything in them.'

'I do enjoy that part of it, yes. On the other hand, I must consider the costs, and more than ever this time around. Agnes can't put up any more of her own money, so she won't be involved in the purchase of the manor or the cost of its remodelling. And the same applies to Patsy in England: she can't offer any financial help either. I have to raise the money myself. And I will. Agnes and Patsy are somewhat relieved that I'll be taking care of the financing, but more than ever I'll have to keep a tight rein on the two of them when it comes to the remodelling.'

'Are you sure you want to go ahead with the new inns in Europe?' Amy asked. Until this moment she had not realized that Meredith would be doing all of the financing, and she detected a degree of worry in her voice.

'Oh yes, I do want to buy them. We have to acquire additional inns in order to expand properly. Not that I want the company to become too big. I think six hotels is enough, Amy – certainly that number's just about right for me, easy to manage, as long as Agnes is running the French end and Patsy the English.'

'Six,' Amy repeated, eyeing Meredith quizzically. 'Are you trying to tell me something?'

Meredith looked baffled. 'I'm not following you.'

'You said six inns are easy to manage, but with the

two new ones in Europe you'll actually own *seven*, if you count the three here. Are you thinking of selling off one of the American hotels?'

'I *have* been toying with the idea,' Meredith admitted.

'Silver Lake Inn would bring in the most money,' Amy remarked. 'After all, it's the most successful of the three.'

Meredith stared at Amy.

Suddenly she felt the same tight pain in her chest that she had last week, when Henry Raphaelson, her friendly private banker, had uttered the same words over lunch at '21'.

'I could never sell Silver Lake,' Meredith answered at last, repeating what she had said to Henry.

'I know what you mean.'

No, you don't, Meredith thought, but she remained silent. She simply inclined her head, dropped her eyes, stared at the financial breakdown, the costs of remodelling the manor in Montfort-L'Amaury, but not really concentrating on the figures.

She was thinking of Silver Lake Inn. No one really knew what it meant to her, not even her daughter and her son, who had both been born there. Silver Lake had always been her haven, the first safe haven she had known, and the first real home she had ever had. And Jack and Amelia Silver, the owners, had been the first people who had ever shown her any kindness in her entire life. They had loved and cherished her like a younger sister, nurtured her, brought out her potential – encouraged her talent, helped her to hone her business acumen, applauded her style. And from them she had learned about decency and kindness, dignity and courage.

*Jack and Amelia*. The only family she had ever had. For a moment she saw them both very clearly in her mind's eye. They were the first human beings she had ever loved. There had been no one to love before them. Except Spin, the little dog, and even she had been taken away from her just when they had become attached to each other.

Silver Lake was part of her very being, part of her soul. She knew she could never, would never, sell it whatever the circumstances.

Meredith took a deep breath and eventually the pain in her chest began to subside. Lifting her eyes, she remarked almost casually, 'I might have a buyer for Hilltops. That's why I've decided to go up to Connecticut tonight.'

Amy was surprised, but she merely nodded. 'What about Fern Spindle? Don't you think you'd get more for the Vermont inn than for Hilltops?'

'It's certainly a much more valuable property, Amy, that's true, valued in the many millions. But someone has to want it, has to want to buy, only then does it become viable to me.'

Amy nodded.

Meredith went on, 'Blanche knows I'm coming up tonight. I'm staying at Silver Lake, there's no point in having her open up the house for one night. Jonas will stay over and drive me up to Sharon tomorrow morning, to meet the potential buyers. After the meeting at Hilltops I'll come straight back to the city, and I'll leave for London on Saturday as planned.'

Picking up a manila folder, Meredith handed it to Amy. 'Here're my letters, all signed, and a bunch of cheques for Lois.' Leaning back in her chair, she finished, 'Well, I guess that's it.'

'No . . . you have e-mail, Meredith.'

Meredith swung around to face her computer on the narrow table behind her chair, peered at the screen.

Thurs. Jan 5 1995

Hi Mom:

> Thanks for cheque. Helps.
> Have a fab trip. Go get 'em.
> Bring back the bacon.
> Luv ya loads.
>
> JON.

'Well, well, doesn't he have a way with words,' Meredith said, shaking her head. But she was smiling, thinking of her twenty-one-year-old son Jonathan, who had always had the ability to amuse her. He had turned out well. Just as his sister had. She was lucky in that respect.

Left alone in her office, Meredith studied the figures from her French partner. She thought they seemed a bit on the high side, and reminded herself that Agnes was not always as practical as she should be, when it came to refurbishing: with her long scarves and trailing skirts she was bohemian but stylish.

Agnes D'Auberville and she had been involved

in business together for the past eight years, and their partnership had been a successful one. They got on well and balanced each other, and Agnes's flair for marketing had helped to put the inns on the map.

Agnes ran the Paris office of Havens Incorporated and oversaw the management of the château-hotel they jointly owned in the Loire Valley. But she was unable to participate financially in the acquisition of the manor house in Montfort-L'Amaury, although she was keen that they buy it. 'You won't regret it, Meredith, it's a good investment for the company,' Agnes had said to her during their phone conversation earlier that day.

Meredith knew that this was true. She also knew that a charming inn, situated only forty-eight kilometres from Paris, and within easy striking distance of Versailles and the forest of Rambouillet, was bound to be a money-maker, especially if it had a good restaurant.

According to Agnes, she had already lined up a well-known chef, as well as a distinguished architect who would properly redesign the manor house, help to turn it into a comfortable inn.

As for Patsy Canton, her English partner who had come on board ten years ago, the story was a little different in one respect. Patsy had fallen upon two existing inns for sale quite by accident. She believed them to be real finds.

One was in Keswick, the famous beauty spot in the Lake District; the other was in the Yorkshire dales near the cathedral towns of York and Ripon. Both were popular places with foreign visitors. Again, such an inn, with its good reputation already established, would more than earn its keep.

Unfortunately, Patsy had the same dilemma as Agnes. She was unable to put up any more money. She had already invested everything she had in Havens Incorporated; her inheritance from her parents had gone into Haddon Fields, the country inn Havens owned in the Cotswolds.

In much the same way Agnes did in Paris, Patsy oversaw the management of Haddon Fields, and ran the small London office of Havens. Her strong suits were management and public relations.

Meredith let out a small sigh, thinking about the problems she was facing. On the other hand, they weren't really insurmountable problems, and, in the long run, the two new inns in Europe were going to be extremely beneficial to the company.

Expansion had been her idea, and hers alone, and she was determined to see it through; after all, she was the majority stockholder of Havens and the Chief Executive Officer. In essence it was her company, and she was responsible for all of its operations.

Henry Raphaelson had told her at the beginning of the week that the bank would lend her the money she needed for her new acquisitions. The inns Havens already owned would be used as collateral for the loan. But Silver Lake Inn was not included. Henry had agreed to this stipulation of hers, if somewhat reluctantly, because she had convinced him Hilltops would be sold quickly. She hoped she was right. With a little luck Elizabeth and Philip Morrison would commit to it tomorrow. Of course they will, she told herself, the eternal optimist.

Pushing back her chair, Meredith rose and crossed to the lacquered console against the long wall, where she had put her briefcase earlier.

Tall though she was, she had a shapely, feminine figure and long legs. She moved with lithesome grace and swiftness; she was generally quick in everything she did, full of drive and energy.

At forty-four Meredith Stratton looked younger than her years. This had a great deal to do with her vitality and effervescent personality, as well as her youthful face and pale blonde hair worn in a girlish pageboy. This framed her rather angular, well-defined features and arresting green eyes.

Good-looking though she was, it was her pleasant demeanour and winning, natural charm that captivated most people. She had a way with her that was unique, and she left a lasting impression on all who met her.

Carrying her briefcase back to the desk, a glass table top mounted on steel sawhorses, Meredith filled it with the manila folders and other papers she had been working on all day. After closing it and placing it on the floor, she picked up the phone and dialled her daughter's number.

'It's me,' Meredith said when Catherine answered.

'Hi, Mom!' Catherine exclaimed, sounding genuinely pleased to hear her mother's voice. 'How're things?'

'Pretty good. I'm off to London and Paris on Saturday.'

'Lucky thing! Can I come with you?'

'Of course! I'd love it. You know that, darling.'

'I can't, Mom, much as I'd enjoy playing hookey in Paris with you, having a good time. I have to finish the illustrations for Madeleine McGrath's new children's book, and I've several book jackets lined up. Oh, but I can dream, can't I?'

'Yes, you can, and I'm so glad things are going well for you with your work. But if you suddenly decide you can get away, call Amy. She'll book your flight and get you a ticket before you can even say Jack Robinson.'

Catherine began to laugh. 'I haven't heard you use that expression for years, not since I was a kid. You told me once where it came from, but now I can't remember. It's such an odd expression.'

'Yes, it is. It's something I learnt when I was growing up in Australia. I think it originated in England and was brought over by the pommies. Australians started to use it, and I guess it became part of our idiomatic speech. Sort of slang, really.'

'Now I remember, and you told us that it meant *in a jiffy*.'

'Less than a jiffy, actually,' Meredith said, laughing with her daughter. 'Anyway, think about coming to Paris or London. You know how much I enjoy travelling with you. How's Keith?'

Catherine let out a long sigh. 'He's fantastic . . . yummy.'

'You sound happy, Cat.'

'Oh I am, Mom, I am. I'm crazy about him.'

'Is it getting serious?'

'*Very.*' Catherine cleared her throat. 'Mom, I think he's going to propose soon.'

For a split second Meredith was taken aback and she was silent at the other end of the phone.

'Mom, are you still there?'

'Yes, darling.'

'You do approve . . . don't you?'

'Of course I do. I like Keith a lot. I was just surprised for a moment, that's all. It seems to have progressed very quickly . . . what I mean is, you haven't known him all that long.'

'Six months. That's enough time, isn't it?'

'I suppose so.'

Catherine said, 'Actually, Keith and I fell in love with each other the moment we met. It was a *coup de foudre*, as the French are wont to say.'

Meredith smiled. 'Ah yes, struck by lightning . . . I know what you mean.'

'Is that how it was with my father?'

Meredith hesitated. 'Not really, Cat . . . Well, in a way, yes. Except we didn't admit that to each other for a long time.'

'Well, you couldn't, could you? I mean, given the peculiar circumstances. It must've been hell for you.'

'No, it wasn't, strangely enough. Anyway, that's an old, *old* story, and now's not the time to start going into it again.'

'Was it a *coup de foudre* when you met David?'

'No,' Meredith said, and thought of Jonathan's father for the first time in several years. 'We loved each other, but it wasn't a . . . crazy love.'

'I always knew that, I guess. It's a crazy love between me and Keith, and when he asks me I'm obviously going to say yes. You really *do* approve, don't you, Mom?' she asked again.

'Very much so, darling, and if he pops the question while I'm in London or Paris, you will let me know at once, won't you?'

'I sure will. And I bet we make you a grandmother before you can say ... Jack Robinson.' Catherine giggled.

Meredith said, 'You're not pregnant, are you?'

'Don't be silly, Mom, of course I'm not. But I can't wait to have a baby. Before I get too old.'

Meredith burst out laughing. 'Don't be so ridiculous, you're only twenty-five.'

'I know, but I want to have children while I'm young, like you did.'

'You always were a regular old mother hen, even when you were little. But listen, honey, I'm going to have to go. Jonas is driving me up to Silver Lake Inn tonight. I have a meeting at Hilltops tomorrow. I'll be back in New York tomorrow evening, if you need me. Good night Cat. I love you.'

'I love you too, Mom. Say hello to Blanche and Pete, give them my love. And listen, take care.'

'I will. Talk to you tomorrow, and God bless.'

After hanging up the phone, Meredith sat at her desk for a moment or two, her thoughts with her daughter. Of course Keith Pearson would propose, and very soon, Meredith was quite certain of that. There was going to be a wedding this year. Her face lit up at the thought of it. Catherine was going to be a beautiful bride, and she would give her daughter a memorable wedding.

Rising, Meredith walked over to the window and stood staring out at the Manhattan skyline. New York City, she murmured to herself, the place I've made my home. Such a long way from Sydney, Australia . . . how far I've come . . . I took my terrible life and turned it around. I made a new life for myself. I took the pain and heartbreak and I built on them . . . I used them as foundations upon which to built *my* strong citadel, in much the same way the Venetians built theirs on pilings driven into the sandbanks. And I did it all by myself . . . no, not entirely by myself. Jack and Amelia helped me.

Swinging around, Meredith stood gazing at her office.

Her eyes swept around the elegant room decorated in various shades of pale grey, lavender and amethyst. They took in the expensive silks and velvets used to upholster the sofas and chairs, the sleek grey lacquer finishes on the modern furniture, the French and American modern impressionist paintings by Taurelle, Epko and Guy Wiggins.

She saw it as if for the first time, through newly objective eyes, and she could not help wondering what Jack and Amelia would think of it . . . what they would think of all that she had accomplished.

Her throat tightened with a rush of sudden emotion, and she stepped back up to the desk and sat down, her eyes now lingering on the two photographs in their silver frames which she always kept there in front of her.

One photograph was of Catherine and Jonathan taken when they were children; Cat had been twelve, Jon eight, and what beauties they had been. Free spirits and so finely wrought.

The other picture was of her with Amelia and Jack. How young she looked. Tanned and blonde and so unsophisticated. She had been just twenty-one years old when the picture was taken at Silver Lake.

Jack and Amelia would be proud of me, she thought. After all, they helped to make me what I am, and in a sense I am their creation. And they are the best part of me.

# Two

Whenever she came back to Silver Lake, Meredith experienced a feeling of excitement. No matter how long she had been absent, be it months on end, a week, or merely a few days, she returned with a sense of joyousness welling inside, the knowledge that she was coming home.

Tonight was no exception.

Her anticipation started the moment Jonas pulled off Route 45 North near Cornwall, and nosed the car through the big iron gates that marked the entrance to the vast Silver Lake property.

Jonas drove slowly down the road that led to the lake, the inn and the small compound of buildings on its shores. It was a good road, well illuminated by the old-fashioned street lamps Meredith had installed some years before.

Peering out of the car windows, she could see that Pete had had some of the workers busy with the bull-dozer earlier in the day. The road was clear, the snow banked high like giant white hedges, and in the woods that traversed the road on either side there were huge drifts blown by the wind into weird sand-dune shapes.

The branches of the trees were heavy with snow, many of them dripping icicles, and in the moonlight the white landscape appeared to shimmer as if sprinkled with a fine coating of silver dust.

Meredith could not help thinking how beautiful the woods were in their winter garb. But then this land was always glorious, no matter what the season of the year; it was so special to her that no other place in the world could compare to it.

The first time she had set eyes on Silver Lake she had been awed by its majestic beauty – the great lake shining in the spring sunlight, a smooth sheet of glass, surrounded by lush meadows and orchards, the whole set in a natural basin created by the soaring wooded hills which rose up to encircle the entire property.

She had fallen in love with it instantly, and had gone on loving it, with a glowing passion, ever since.

Twenty-six years ago this year, she thought, I was only eighteen. So long ago, more than half her life ago. And yet it might have been only yesterday, so clear and fresh was the memory in her mind tonight.

She had come to Silver Lake Inn to apply for the job of receptionist, which she had seen advertised in the local paper. The Paulsons, the American family who had brought her with them from Australia as an *au pair*, were moving to South Africa because of Mr Paulson's job. She did not want to go there. Nor did she wish to return to her native Australia. Instead, she preferred to stay in America, in Connecticut, to be precise.

It had been the middle of May, not long after her birthday, and she had arrived on a borrowed bicycle, looking a bit windswept, to say the least.

Casting her mind back now, she pictured herself as

she had been then – tall, skinny, all arms and legs like a young colt. Yet pretty enough in a fresh young way. She had been full of life and vitality, eager to be helpful, eager to please. That was her basic nature: she was a born peacemaker.

Jack and Amelia Silver had taken to her at once, as she had to them. But they had been concerned about her staying on in America without the Paulsons, had inquired about her family in Sydney, and what they would think. Once she explained that her parents were dead they had been sympathetic, sorry that she had lost them so young. And they had understood then that she had no real reason to go back to the Antipodes.

After they had talked on the phone to Mrs Paulson they had hired her on the spot.

And so it had begun, an extraordinary relationship which had changed her life.

Meredith straightened in her seat as the inn came into view. Lights blazed in many of the windows, a welcoming sight. She could hardly wait to be inside, to be with Blanche and Pete, surrounded by so many familiar things in that well-loved place.

Within seconds Jonas was pulling up in front of the inn. He had barely braked when the front door flew open and bright light flooded out onto the wide porch.

A moment later Blanche and Pete O'Brien were at the top of the steps, and as Meredith opened the car door Pete was already halfway down, exclaiming, 'Welcome, Meredith, you've certainly made it in good time, despite the snow.'

'Hello, Pete,' she said as he enveloped her in a hug.

She added, as they drew apart, 'There's nobody like Jonas when it comes to driving. He's the best.'

'That he is. Hi Jonas, good to see you,' Pete said, nodding to the driver, smiling at him. 'I'll help you with Mrs Stratton's bags.'

'Evening, Mr O'Brien, but I can manage. There's nothing much to carry.'

Meredith left the two men to deal with the bags, and ran up the steps.

'It's good to be back here, Blanche!'

The two women embraced and then Blanche, smiling up at Meredith, led her inside. 'And it's good to have you back, Meredith, if only for one night.'

'I wish I could stay longer, but as I explained on the phone, I've got to get back to the city after the meeting at Hilltops tomorrow.'

Blanche nodded. 'I think you're going to make a deal with the Morrisons. They're awfully keen to buy an inn, get away from New York, lead a different kind of life.'

'I'm keeping my fingers crossed,' Meredith said, shrugging out of her heavy grey wool cape, throwing it down on a bench.

'I know you'll like them. They're a lovely couple, very sincere, straight as a die, and quite aside from wanting to start a new business they love this part of Connecticut.'

'And why not, it's God's own country,' Meredith murmured. She glanced around the entrance hall. 'Everything looks wonderful, Blanche, so warm, welcoming.'

Blanche beamed at her. 'Thanks, Meredith, you

know I love this old place as much as you do. Anyway, you must be starving. I didn't think you'd want a proper dinner at this late hour, so I made some smoked-salmon sandwiches, and there's fruit and cheese. Oh, and I have a hunter's soup bubbling on the stove.'

'The soup sounds great. You make the best, and they're usually a meal in themselves. I'm sure Jonas is hungry after the long drive, so perhaps you'd offer him the soup too, and some sandwiches.'

'I will.'

Pete came in with Meredith's overnight bag and briefcase. 'Jonas has gone to park the car,' he explained. 'I'll take these upstairs.'

'Thanks, Pete,' Meredith said.

'I've put you in the *toile de Jouy* suite,' Blanche told her, 'because I know how much you like it. Now, do you want a tray up there? Or shall I bring it to the bar parlour?'

'I'll have it down here in the parlour, thanks, Blanche,' Meredith said, peering into the room that opened off the inn's large entrance hall. 'I see you have a fire going . . . that's nice. I think I'll make myself a drink. Would you like one, Blanche?'

'Why not? I'll join you in a vodka and tonic. But first let me go and fix a tray for Jonas. I'll be back in a few minutes.' She hurried off in the direction of the kitchen.

Meredith went into the parlour, glancing around as she strolled over to the huge stone hearth at the far end of the room. The fire burning brightly, the red carpet, the red velvet sofas and tub chairs covered in red-and-cream linen gave the parlour a warm, rosy feeling. This was further enhanced by the red brocade curtains at the leaded windows, the polished mahogany panelled walls, and the red shades on the wall sconces. It was a slightly masculine room in feeling, rather English in overtone, but there was a mellowness about it that Meredith had always liked.

The carved mahogany bar was to the left of the fireplace, facing the leaded windows, and Meredith now went behind it, took two glasses, added ice and poured a good measure of Stolichnaya Cristal into each one. She smiled to herself when she noticed the small plate of lime wedges next to the ice bucket. Blanche had second-guessed her very accurately. Her old friend had known she would have her drink in here. The bar parlour had always been a favourite spot of hers in the inn, as it was with everyone, because it was so intimate and cosy. And conducive to drinking. Jack had been smart when he had created it.

Once she had made the drinks, Meredith went over to the fireplace. She stood with her back to it, enjoying the warmth, sipping her vodka, relaxing as she waited for Blanche, whom she thought had never looked better. If there was a tiny fleck of silver in her bright red hair, she was, nonetheless, as slim as she had been as a girl, and the merry dark brown eyes were as lively as ever. She's wearing well, Meredith thought, very well indeed.

The two women, who were the same age, had been friends for twenty-four years. Blanche had come to Silver Lake Inn two years after Meredith had taken the job as receptionist. She had started as a pastry chef in the kitchens, had soon been promoted to chef, since she was an inspired cook. Blanche had enjoyed working in the kitchens until she married Pete, who had always managed the estate for the Silvers, and became pregnant with Billy.

By then Meredith was running the inn, and she offered Blanche the job of assistant manager. Blanche had been delighted to accept the offer at once, glad to be out of the heat, relieved not to lift heavy pots and pans, and thrilled to be able to continue working at the inn.

These days she and Pete ran Silver Lake Inn together and were responsible for its overall management as well as the upkeep of the entire estate. *She's been good for this place*, Meredith mused, her thoughts centred on Blanche for a moment. *She's as passionate about it as I am, and it shows everywhere, in everything she does.*

Blanche interrupted her musings, walking rapidly into the bar parlour, saying, 'By the way, you're not going to believe this, but we're rather busy this coming weekend. All the rooms are taken. And several suites. Unusual for January, I must say, but I'm not complaining.'

'I'm delighted. In some ways it's not that surprising. A lot of people do like being in the country in the snowy weather, and this place has such a great reputation. Thanks, in no uncertain terms, to you and Pete. I do appreciate all you both do, Blanche.'

'We love the inn, you know that.'

'By the way, Catherine sends her love to you and Pete.'

Blanche smiled. 'And give her ours. How is she, Meredith?'

'As wonderful as always, and doing so well with her work; she's turned out to be a fine illustrator. And of course she's madly in love.'

'With Keith Pearson?'

Meredith nodded. 'She told you?'

'Yes, when you were all here at Thanksgiving.'

'I think it's become rather serious.'

'Are we looking forward to a wedding?' Blanche asked, staring at Meredith quizzically.

'I think so . . . I'm pretty sure.'

'You will have it here, won't you?'

'Where else, Blanche? Cat was born here, grew up here, and so I'm certain she'll want to be married here. And it is the perfect setting.'

'Oh, I can't wait to start planning it!' Blanche cried, taking a sip of her drink. 'Cheers. And here's to Cat and the wedding.'

'The wedding,' Meredith said and lifted her glass as Blanche was doing. She wondered if it was bad luck to drink to something so prematurely.

'*Marquees*. We'll have to have marquees,' Blanche said, gazing into space, obviously already envisioning the reception.

'But they'll no doubt get married in the summer,' Meredith pointed out.

'Yes, I know. June probably, every girl wants to be a June bride. But it *can* rain up here at that time of year, you know that as well as I do, and it's best to be safe. Oh it'll be great, though. We'll do wonderful flowers and table settings. And a special menu.

Oh, it's going to be fabulous. Leave it all to me.'

Meredith laughed. 'I'm happy to, my darling Blanche.'

'Good.' Blanche sipped her drink, and then suddenly she looked across at Meredith and said, 'Do you ever hear from David?'

'David Layton?' Meredith asked, slightly surprised.

'Yes.'

'Rarely. Why do you ask?'

'I thought of him just now ... have you forgotten that you married him here and that I did the entire wedding?'

'No, I haven't,' Meredith said slowly, and began to shake her head. 'Funny, isn't it ... how someone's name is rarely, if ever, mentioned, and then it comes up twice in one day.'

'Who else mentioned David?'

'Catherine. When we were talking on the phone earlier this evening. She asked me if I'd been crazy in love with him, or words to that effect.'

'And what did you say?'

'I told her the truth. I said that I hadn't.'

'Of course not. You were only crazily in love once, and that was with her father.'

Meredith was silent.

'Have you ever wondered what your life would have been like if he hadn't –'

'I really don't want to discuss it,' Meredith snapped, cutting in peremptorily. Then she bit her lip, looking chagrined. 'I'm sorry, Blanche, I didn't mean to bite your head off like that, it's just that I prefer to leave that particular subject matter alone tonight. It's been a long day and I don't really feel like delving into the tragedies of the past.'

Blanche smiled gently. 'It's my fault. I brought it up and I shouldn't have ... now you're looking sad ... I've upset you.'

'No, you haven't, I promise you, Blanche.'

Deeming it wiser to change the subject, Blanche put down her drink and said, 'By the way, we're going to have to order new carpet for the *toile de Jouy* suite, and the blue room. There's been some leaks this winter, and the carpets are damaged. I hate to tell you this, but there's also been a leak in your bedroom in the house. I'll show you tomorrow. I'm afraid you'll have to replace the carpet there as well.'

'These things happen, Blanche. We know that from years of experience. And even after we put in new roofs last year. I'll call Gary at Stark tomorrow, before I go to London. He's got everything on the computer, so it won't be a problem.' Meredith frowned. 'The carpets were from the standard lines, weren't they?'

'Yes, I'm sure,' Blanche said, and then began to walk towards the door. 'It's getting late. I'm going to the kitchen to bring you that bowl of soup.'

Meredith put down her glass and followed her. 'I'll eat in the kitchen, Blanche, it's much easier.'

# Three

Hilltops, the inn Meredith owned near Sharon, was built on top of a hill, as its name suggested. The site was the highest point above Lake Wononpakook, and the views from the inn's windows were spectacular: endless miles of lake and sky and wooded hills, with hardly another structure in evidence on the expansive land.

The inn started out as a mansion, the summer retreat of one of America's great tycoons, who built it in the late 1930s, sparing no expense. He and his family spent summers there until his death in the mid-1960s, when it was sold.

When Meredith bought it in 1981 it had been an inn for almost twenty years, and it was already well established. But it was her stylish refurbishing and the two new restaurants she created which gave it a certain *cachet*, and put it on the map.

Hilltops evoked images of Switzerland in her mind, and turning to Paul Ince, who was the manager of the inn, she said, 'I feel as if I'm looking down on Lake Geneva this morning, Paul.'

He laughed and answered, 'I know what you mean. I always get the sensation of being in the Swiss Alps myself, especially in winter.'

Meredith had arrived at Hilltops fifteen minutes earlier, and the two of them stood together in the inn's lovely old pine-panelled library, waiting for the Morrisons to arrive for the meeting.

Glancing out of the window again, Meredith murmured, 'All this snow. It really came down this year, but it doesn't seem to have affected business, does it?'

'No, not at all, Meredith. Well, I shouldn't say that. As you know, we did have a few problems last week, and had to close the restaurants for a few days. But we soon got rid of the snow, once the bulldozer was up on the main road here. When it was shifted we were fine.' He paused, turned to her. 'And we are fine,' he reassured.

'What are your bookings like for the weekend?' she asked.

'Pretty good, twelve out of the fifteen rooms are taken. And both restaurants are almost full. Local trade as well as the hotel guests.'

Paul cleared his throat, briefly hesitating, and then said, 'I know you'll be able to sell this place, Meredith. Whether it's to the Morrisons or someone else, because it's such a good buy. And I just wanted to say this now . . . I'm really going to miss working with you. You've always been great, such a wonderful boss.'

'That's nice of you to say so, Paul, thank you. And I've enjoyed working with *you* all these years. I couldn't have done it without you. You're definitely a big part of the inn's success, you've put so much of yourself into it, built up the business so well. And as I told you earlier, if the Morrisons do end up taking it over, I'm sure they'll want you to stay on. If *you* want to, that is.'

'I do, and when they were over here last weekend they indicated they felt the same way.'

'What're your feelings about them? About their intentions, Paul?'

'They're more than interested, Meredith. I'd say they're extremely keen to get their hands on Hilltops, as I told Blanche the other day. It's apparently what they've wanted for the last few years . . . a country inn in Connecticut, far away from the hectic pace of New York City and the rat race of Wall Street and Madison Avenue. New careers for them both. New life styles for them and their kids.'

'I didn't know they had children,' Meredith said, frowning. 'Does that mean they'd want to live in the cottage? Your cottage?'

Paul shook his head. 'No, Mrs Morrison's indicated that they're going to keep their house in Lakeville. But if they did want the cottage, Anne and I could always move into the inn until that apartment over the garage was made habitable.'

Meredith nodded her understanding; she walked over to the fireplace, where she sat down, poured herself another cup of coffee. 'Do you want a second cup, Paul?'

'Yes, please.' Paul joined her by the fireside.

They sat in silence for a few minutes, drinking their coffee, lost in their own thoughts. It was Meredith who spoke first, when she said, 'As you know, the asking price for the inn is four million dollars, and so far I've not budged from that figure. Between us, I would come down a bit, just to make the sale. What's your assessment of them, regarding the price?'

'It's hard to say,' Paul replied, looking thoughtful. After a moment or two's reflection, he went on, 'I'd stick to your guns for a bit and see what happens. But just be mentally prepared to accept three million.'

She shook her head. 'No way, Paul, I've got to get three and a half million, at least. Anyway, the inn's worth that . . . in fact, it's worth four. My real-estate people actually valued it at four and a half.'

'But you've always said to me that someone's got to want to buy a property to make it a viable holding, an asset.'

'I know, I know, but I really do need three and a half million dollars for my expansion programme,' Meredith said, putting her cup down with a clatter. 'The two inns in Europe are going to cost money, and I'd like to have something left over from this sale for operating costs and to plough back into Havens.'

'Look, Meredith, I'm sure the Morrisons are quite well placed. He's worked on Wall Street for years, and she's been one of the partners in an ad agency on Madison Avenue. In any case, when you meet them, talk to them, you'll be able to judge for yourself what the freight can bear.'

'Too true . . . why try to second-guess?'

There was a knock on the door, and as Paul called, 'Come in!' it opened.

The receptionist looked in and said, 'Mr and Mrs Morrison have arrived.'

Paul nodded. 'Show them in, Doris, please.'

Several seconds later Paul was introducing

Elizabeth and Philip Morrison to Meredith. Once the handshakes were over they all sat down in the chairs near the fire.

Meredith said, 'Can I offer you something? Coffee, tea, mineral water, perhaps?'

'No, thank you,' Mrs Morrison said.

Her husband shook his head and murmured something about just having had breakfast. Then he began to speak to Paul about the weather, the snow on the roads, and the drive over from Lakeville, where they owned a weekend home.

Mrs Morrison looked across at Meredith and said, 'I love the way you've decorated Hilltops . . . it's so charming and intimate. It reminds me of an English country house.'

'Thank you,' Meredith said, smiling at the other woman. 'I like decorating, creating a look, an ambience. And lots of comfort for the guests, of course. I think an inn should be a haven; that's why I called my company Havens Incorporated.'

Elizabeth Morrison nodded. 'Very apt, very apt indeed. And I think all your little touches are wonderful. The hotwater bottles in silk cases, the special reading lights by the bed, the cashmere blankets on the chaises, little luxuries like that make all the difference.'

'That's what I believe,' Meredith murmured, 'and that's my policy in all of the inns we own.'

'We've always wanted to run an inn like this,' Mrs Morrison confided. 'And now's the time to do it, when we're both still young. Also, we want to get out of the city, bring up our three children in the country. The city's become so violent, hard to take.'

'I understand. I raised two children in Connecticut, and I've always felt lucky that I was able to do so. As you know, since you've been residents up here for a few years, there are plenty of good schools. Yes, it's a great spot for a family.'

Elizabeth Morrison was about to say something else when she caught her husband's warning look; she simply cleared her throat and sat back in her chair, having suddenly become a mere spectator at this meeting.

Meredith, who missed nothing, noticed this infinitesimal exchange. She understood immediately that Philip Morrison did not want his wife saying any more. Nor did he wish her to sound too enthusiastic about the inn. He wanted her to play it cool. As he had been doing all along. He was obviously ready to deal.

Not giving him an opportunity to start the ball rolling, Meredith jumped in with both feet.

Staring directly at him, fixing him with an appraising eye, she said, 'I know you've been back to look at Hilltops many times now, and that you both like it. The question is, do you really want to buy it?'

'Yes,' Philip Morrison said. 'At the right price. For us, that is.'

'The price is four million dollars, Mr Morrison. I think my real-estate lawyer in the city has already told you that.'

'He did. But as I told Mr Melinger, it's a bit steep for me.'

'Actually, the inn *is* worth four million dollars, even

more if the truth be known,' Meredith pointed out. 'As a matter of fact, its true value is four and a half million dollars. You can check that with the real-estate people, both here and in the city. It just so happens that I'm willing to take less because I'm expanding my company. Otherwise, I'd hold out for the *proper* price, I can assure you.'

'I'll give you three million,' Philip Morrison said, glanced at his wife, and added, 'That's all we can pay, isn't it, Liz?'

Momentarily startled to be drawn into this exchange, she looked nonplussed. Then she said quickly, emphatically, 'We're selling our Manhattan co-op and hoping to get a mortgage on the Lakeville house, and by cashing in some of our other assets we can raise three million. But that's it.'

Meredith gave her a long and thoughtful look but made no comment. Leaning forward, she picked up her cup of coffee and took a sip.

Morrison said, 'What do you say, Mrs Stratton? Will you accept three million?'

'No,' Meredith said, looking him right in the eye. 'I can't. As I told you, when I first decided to sell Hilltops my original price was four and a half million dollars, because that *is* its true value. It's in perfect condition. New roof, new plumbing and new wiring in the last few years, among many other major improvements. And there's a great deal of land attached to the inn. I only came down in price because it was suggested I do so by my advisers, in order to sell now. But I must stick at four million.'

'Three million and a quarter,' Morrison countered.

Meredith pursed her lips and shook her head. 'Four.'

'Three and a quarter,' he offered again.

Meredith let out a small sigh and gave the Morrisons a slow, resigned smile, glancing from one to the other. 'I tell you what, I'll take three million, seven hundred and fifty thousand.'

'I just can't do it,' Philip Morrison said.

'But it's a bargain,' Meredith stated quietly. 'If you consider that the proper price is really four and a half million, I've just come down by three-quarters of a million dollars.'

Philip Morrison smiled wryly. 'But we've always been talking *four* million, not *four and a half*, Mrs Stratton, let's not forget that, shall we?'

Meredith made no response.

She rose and walked across to the bank of windows overlooking the lake, and stood there staring out at the view for a few moments.

Finally, when she swung around, she said, 'You want the inn. I want to sell it. So I'll tell you what I'll do, *I'll* compromise. I'll sell it to you for three point five million.'

The Morrisons exchanged pointed glances.

At last he said, 'I'd like to do it, but I just don't think I can. I can't raise any more.'

'You could go to your bank,' Meredith suggested, 'and get a loan – or better still, a mortgage on the inn.'

Philip Morrison stared at her. But he remained silent.

'I can introduce you to the right bank,' Meredith volunteered, wanting to conclude the deal.

'Do you think they would give me a mortgage on the inn?' he asked, taking the bait.

'I'm pretty certain, yes. There's something else I'll do. I'll have my real-estate lawyer structure a reasonable payment schedule, one that won't cripple you.'

Elizabeth Morrison said, 'That's very decent of you.'

Meredith answered, 'I want to make the deal and I don't want to take advantage of you. You want to make the deal and I'm sure you don't want to cheat me.'

'Never! We're not people like that!' the other woman exclaimed indignantly.

'I must say, you're making it very tempting,' Morrison muttered, directing his gaze at Meredith. 'Making it hard to resist.'

'Then don't resist, Mr Morrison,' Meredith said.

He got to his feet when she drew to a stop next to his chair.

Meredith thrust out her hand. 'Come on, let's not haggle. Let's make the deal. It's good for us both, beneficial to us both.'

He hesitated only fractionally. Then he took her hand and shook it. 'All right, Mrs Stratton, you've got a deal. Three and a half million dollars it is.'

Meredith nodded and smiled at him.

He returned her smile.

Elizabeth Morrison came over and shook Meredith's hand.

Paul Ince, who had been on tenterhooks throughout this negotiation, congratulated everyone, then said, 'I think this calls for a toast. Let's go to the bar and I'll open a bottle of Dom Pérignon.'

'What a great idea, Paul,' Meredith said, leading the way out of the library.

On the drive back to New York City, Meredith gave only fleeting thought to Hilltops. She had accomplished what she had set out to do; she had sold the inn for the amount she wanted, and she was well satisfied. Three and a half million dollars would meet her expansion needs more than adequately.

Before leaving the inn, she had settled everything. Arrangements had been made for the Morrisons to meet with her real-estate lawyer, who would draw up the necessary documents next week. She had also set up an appointment for them to see Henry Raphaelson. The banker had sounded amenable during the phone call, had assured her he would endeavour to work things out with the Morrisons.

And so she turned her thoughts to other matters as Jonas drove back to Manhattan. Mostly she focused her attention on her trip to England, and on the purchase of an inn there. She was confident she would like one of the two Patsy Canton had found. With luck, she would be able to bring that bit of business to a conclusion fairly quickly, so that she could go to Paris to see Agnes D'Auberville.

Patsy had invited her to lunch on Sunday, so that they could go over business matters and map out a plan, and in so doing save time. The general idea was that they would travel to the North of England on Monday, going first to Cumbria. After looking at the inn located in the Lake District they would drive down to Yorkshire to see the one in the dales.

When she had asked Patsy which of the two inns she preferred, her partner had been somewhat evasive. 'The one in Keswick needs much less done to it,' she had said and then clammed up.

When Meredith had pressed her further, Patsy had refused to make any more comments. 'I want this to be your decision and yours alone,' Patsy had murmured. 'If I give you my opinion now, before you've seen either hotel, I'll be influencing you, setting you up in advance. So don't press me.'

It had been Patsy's suggestion that, if she had no reason to return to London, she should fly to Paris from the Leeds–Bradford Airport. 'There're lots of flights to Paris from there and also from Manchester.' Meredith had agreed that this was a great idea, since it would save so much time.

Leaning back against the car seat, she closed her eyes, thinking of the packing she still had to do, trying to decide what clothes to take. Unexpectedly, she thought of Reed Jamison and the dinner date she had made with him. The mere idea of seeing him filled her with dismay. But she knew she must keep the appointment if she was to break off with him.

It was never on, she thought, sitting up, glancing out of the window. Their relationship had never really lifted off the ground, although lately he seemed to believe otherwise. In an effort to make herself feel better, she adopted a positive attitude, assured herself that it was going to be easy. He would understand. After all, he was a grown man.

But deep down Meredith felt she was wrong. Instinctively, she knew he was going to be difficult. Her dismay turned into apprehension.

# Four

'I know you thought I was being stubborn the other day,' Patsy Canton said. 'When I wouldn't discuss the inns with you, but –'

'More like evasive,' Meredith interrupted.

'Not evasive, not stubborn, either. Just cautious. I didn't want you to get any preconceived ideas, especially from me, before you saw the inns. But now I can give you a sort of – *preview*, shall we say. The owner of the inn near Lake Windermere sent us a batch of photographs. They arrived yesterday. Let me get them for you.'

Patsy pushed herself out of the chair, walked across the small red sitting room of her house in Belgravia, where she and Meredith were having a drink before lunch on Sunday.

In her late thirties, she was an attractive woman, more handsome than pretty, almost as tall as Meredith and well built. Her hair was blonde, cut short, and it curled all over her head; her grey eyes were large and full of intelligence. But it was her flawless English complexion that everyone commented on.

Pausing at the small Georgian desk, Patsy picked up a large envelope and walked back to the sofa, where she sat down next to Meredith.

'Ian Grainger, the owner of Heronside, is rather proud of the pictures. He took them himself, last spring and summer.' So saying she handed the envelope to Meredith, who pulled out the photographs eagerly.

After a few seconds spent looking at them, she turned to Patsy and said, 'I'm not surprised he's proud of them. The pictures are beautiful. So is Heronside, if these are anything to go by.'

'Very much so, Meredith. In a way, the photographs don't really do the inn and the grounds justice. There's such a sense of luxury in the rooms, you feel pampered just walking into one of them. The whole inn is very well done, lovely antiques and fabrics, and I know you'll like the decorative schemes, the overall ambience. As for the grounds, they're breathtaking, don't you think?'

Meredith nodded, shuffled through the pictures again and picked one of them out. It was a woodland setting. The ground was carpeted with irises and rafts of sunlight slanted down through the leafy green canopies of the trees. Just beyond were brilliant yellow daffodils growing on a slope, and, far beyond this, a stretch of the lake could be seen – vast, placid, silvery, glistening in the sun.

'Look, Patsy,' Meredith said, and handed it to her partner. 'Isn't this gorgeous?'

'Yes, especially the slope covered in daffodils. Doesn't it remind you of Wordsworth's poem?'

Meredith stared at her.

'The one about the daffodils. Don't you know it?'

Meredith shook her head.

Patsy confided, 'It's one of my favourites.' Almost involuntarily, she began to recite it.

> *'I wandered lonely as a cloud*
> *That floats on high o'er vales and hills,*
> *When all at once I saw a crowd,*
> *A host, of golden daffodils;*
> *Beside the lake, beneath the trees,*
> *Fluttering and dancing in the breeze.'*

'It's lovely,' Meredith said.

'Didn't you learn it at school?'

'No,' Meredith murmured.

Patsy went on, 'I like the last verse best of all. Would you care to hear it?'

'Please,' Meredith replied. 'You recite poetry extremely well.'

Once more Patsy launched into the poem:

> *'For oft, when on my couch I lie*
> *In vacant or in pensive mood,*
> *They flash upon that inward eye*
> *Which is the bliss of solitude;*
> *And then my heart with pleasure fills,*
> *And dances with the daffodils.'*

'It's really beautiful,' Meredith said, smiling at her. 'It's very peaceful . . . serene.'

'That's how I feel about it.'

'I think I've heard that last verse before. *Somewhere.* But I'm not sure where,' Meredith murmured. 'Not at school, though.' For a moment or two she racked her brain, but try though she did, she could not remember. And yet the poem had struck a chord in her memory . . . The fleeting memory remained elusive.

Patsy remarked, 'Unfortunately, I don't have any pictures of the inn near Ripon. The Millers, who own it, did have a few photos, and they were very good, too. Yet somehow they didn't quite capture the spirit of the place, its soul. You'll have to judge it cold, when we get there.'

'That's no problem.' Meredith looked at her closely. 'But you *do* like Skell Garth don't you?'

'Oh yes, Meredith, very much, otherwise I wouldn't be dragging you there,' Patsy quickly reassured her partner. 'The setting is superb, the landscape awe-inspiring, picturesque, actually. And from the inn there's a most fabulous view of Fountains Abbey, one of the most beautiful ruins in all of England. Yes, Skell Garth is a unique place.'

'Skell Garth,' Meredith repeated. 'You know, when you first mentioned it, I thought it was such an odd name.'

'I suppose it is. Let me explain. The Skell is a river which flows through Ripon and through the land on which both the inn and the abbey stand. Garth is the ancient Yorkshire word for field, and many of the local farmers still refer to their fields as garths.'

'So the name actually means *the field of the River Skell*. Am I correct?'

Patsy laughed, delighted with Meredith's astuteness. 'You're absolutely correct! I'll make a Yorkshirewoman of you yet.'

The two friends and partners sat talking about the

inns for a while, as they sipped their white wine, and then they moved on, became involved in a long and involved discussion about their business in general.

It was Patsy who brought this to a sudden halt when she jumped up, exclaiming, 'Oh my God! I smell something awful. I hope that's not our lunch getting burnt to a cinder.'

She flew out of the sitting room and ran downstairs to the kitchen.

Meredith charged after her.

Patsy was crouching in front of the oven, looking at the roast, poking around in the pan with a long-handled spoon.

'Is it spoiled?' Meredith asked in concern as she walked in.

'Fortunately not,' Patsy said, straightening. She closed the oven door and swung to face Meredith, grinning. 'A couple of potatoes are singed around the edges, but the lamb's okay. It's the onions that are a bit scorched. They're *black*, actually. Anyway, everything's ready, well, *almost*. I hope you're hungry . . .'

'I'm starving. But you didn't have to go to all this trouble, you know. I was quite happy to take you out to lunch. Or have you to the hotel.'

'I enjoy doing this occasionally,' Patsy assured her. 'It reminds me of my childhood growing up in Yorkshire. And anyway, Meredith, it's not often you get a traditional English Sunday lunch, now is it?'

Meredith chuckled. 'No, and I'm looking forward to it.'

# Five

It was a windy afternoon.

A few stray leaves danced around her feet, and her full-length cream tweed cape billowed occasionally as she walked briskly through Green Park.

Meredith did not mind the wind. It was sunny and this counteracted the sudden gusts, the nip in the air, and she was glad to stretch her legs after sitting so long over lunch with Patsy.

It had been fun to visit her old friend and partner, and to catch up with everything, both business and personal. Also, Meredith always enjoyed going to Patsy's little doll's house, which is the way she thought of it. Situated in a mews in Belgravia, the house had four floors; it was charmingly decorated, very much in the style they used in the inns. This was a lush country look, which was built around good antique wood pieces, a mélange of interesting fabrics skilfully mixed and matched, vibrant colours carefully co-ordinated to each other plus a selection of unusual accessories.

As Meredith walked on, her thoughts settled on Patsy, of whom she was extremely fond. It was her New York banker, Henry Raphaelson, who had introduced them in 1984. Henry had known Patsy from her teenage days, since he had been for many years a close friend and business associate of her father, until his death a merchant banker in the City.

Patsy and she had taken to each other at once, and, after several constructive meetings they had decided to go into business together, opening a London office of Havens Incorporated.

In the ensuing years, Patsy had been good for the company, a great asset. She was as solid as a rock, hardworking, dependable, devoted and loyal. While she was not as visionary or as imaginative as Agnes D'Auberville, Patsy more than made up for these minor shortcomings because she was loaded with common sense. Also, her talent for public relations had worked well for Havens. There wasn't a hotel in England that received as much publicity and press attention as Haddon Fields in the Cotswolds, and all of it was positive. In fact, they had never had a negative write-up in the entire ten years the inn had been open.

When Meredith had expressed an interest in opening an hotel in France, Patsy had taken her to Paris to meet Agnes D'Auberville. The two young women had attended the Sorbonne at the same time, and they had been good friends since those youthful days in Paris.

Agnes, like Patsy two years earlier, had been looking to invest inherited money in a business she could be involved in on a full-time basis. And so she had jumped at the chance to open a Paris branch of Havens Incorporated, and had plunged enthusiastically into the creation of the inn situated in the Loire Valley.

Meredith and Agnes had found the Château de Cormeron, which stood on the banks of the beautiful

Indre river in the centre of the Loire Valley. After purchasing the château, they had spent almost a year getting it into proper shape and turning it into an inn. Many of the rooms had needed new floors, some new ceilings; they had had to install central heating and air conditioning; almost all of the plumbing had to be replaced, as had the wiring. Once this had been done, they had set about decorating it in the appropriate style, mostly using French country furniture, wonderful old tapestries, luxurious traditional fabrics and unique accessories culled from local antique shops.

They had put a tremendous amount of energy, effort, talent and money into its remodelling and redecoration, but the transformation was so stunning they both knew it had been well worth it.

And much to their gratification, it had proved to be a tremendous success as a small hotel. Château de Cormeron was close to many of the great châteaux of the Loire, such as Chinon, Chenonceaux, Azay-le-Rideau, Loches and Montpoupon, all open to the public and especially popular with foreign visitors.

Well-heeled tourists gravitated to their charming little Château de Cormeron, seeking its luxury, comfort and superlative service, which was becoming renowned, its bucolic surroundings and its proximity to so many famous châteaux. And the fact that the hotel boasted one of the finest restaurants in the Loire region did it no harm.

Agnes D'Auberville had become as good a friend as Patsy, as well as a most dependable business partner, and all three women enjoyed a good relationship.

Like Meredith, Patsy was divorced with two

children, twin boys of ten who were away at boarding school. Agnes, who was thirty-eight, the same age as Patsy, was married to Alain D'Auberville, the well-known stage actor, and they had a small daughter, Chloe, who was six.

I've been lucky with them, Meredith thought, as she completed her circle around Green Park and went out into Piccadilly. We all balance each other very well, and they've both done a great deal to make Havens work in Europe, been instrumental in its success.

Coming to the Ritz Hotel, she stood at the kerb, waiting for the lights to change. Once they did, she crossed Piccadilly and headed back to Claridge's on Brook Street.

Meredith had always liked walking around London, and she was thoroughly enjoying her stroll, feeling invigorated by the brisk air and the exercise. Turning down Hay Hill, she went up into Berkeley Square. But as she crossed it, she couldn't help thinking that the little park in the centre looked a bit bleak today, with its bare trees and patches of dirty snow on the shrivelled brown grass.

On the other hand, she took great pleasure in looking at the lovely old buildings in Mayfair, which was the area of London she knew best. She had been coming here for twenty-one years, ever since her marriage to David Layton in 1974. Twenty-three she had been at the time, and so young in so many ways; yet in others she had been rather grown up.

England had made a lasting impression on her. She felt comfortable on its shores, and she enjoyed the British people, their idiosyncrasies as well as their good manners and civility, not to mention their great sense of humour.

David Layton had been a transplanted Englishman, living and working in Connecticut when she met him. After their wedding at Silver Lake, he had brought her to London to meet his sister Claire, her husband and children.

Meredith had liked David; she had loved him well enough to marry him, and she had felt regretful that their marriage had floundered. Their genuine attempts to make it work had come to nothing, and in the end divorce had seemed to be the best, the only, solution.

The one good thing that had come out of this rather dubious and tenuous union was their son Jonathan. The sad thing was, David never saw his son these days. He had moved to California in the 1980s and had never made any effort to come East to see Jonathan. Nor had he ever invited Jonathan to visit him on the West Coast.

David's loss, Meredith muttered under her breath: she couldn't help wishing that things were different, for her son's sake at least. But Jon didn't seem to care that he was so neglected by David and he never mentioned his father.

Being a single parent all those years had been a strain on her at times, Meredith was the first to admit it. But Jon had turned out well, and so had her darling Cat. And so it had been worth it in the end . . . the hard work, the sacrifices, the endless compromises, the cajoling, the bullying and the unconditional loving. Being a good mother had taken its toll on her life, but she was proud of them. And of herself in a funny way.

Those years of bringing up Cat and Jon alone, plus creating and developing her business, had left her little time to meet another man, let alone become involved with him. There *had* been a few boyfriends over the years, but somehow her children and her work had intruded, got in the way. Deep down, she had never really minded. Her children had been her whole world, still were.

Circumstances had been right when she had met Brandon Leonard four years ago. But he had been a married man. In no time at all, she had come to understand that not only was he *not* separated, as he claimed, but that he had no intention of ever leaving his wife, or getting a divorce. Simply put, Brandon wanted his wife. He also wanted a mistress. Since she was not a candidate for the latter role, she had terminated their friendship, and in no uncertain terms.

Then this past September, on a trip to London, Patsy had taken her to the fancy opening of an exhibition of sculpture at the posh Lardner Gallery in Bond Street.

And there, lurking amongst the Arps and the Brancusis, the Moores, the Hepworths and the Giacomettis, had been Reed Jamison. The owner of the gallery.

Tall, dark, good-looking, charismatic. The most attractive man she had met in a long time. And seemingly very available. 'Beware,' Patsy had warned. When she had asked her what she meant, Patsy had said, 'Watch it. He's brilliant but difficult.' Again she had pressed Patsy, asked her to elucidate. Patsy then answered her enigmatically, 'Save us all from the brooding Byronic hero. Oh dear, shades of Heathcliff.'

Meredith had only partially understood, and then, before she could blink, Reed Jamison, having taken one look at her, was in hot pursuit.

Drawn to him initially, she had fallen under his spell; but gradually, over the following months, she had begun to feel unexpectedly ill at ease with him. And she had begun to pull away from the relationship within herself.

On his last visit to New York, in late November, she had been turned off. He had been morose, argumentative, and possessive. Furthermore, she had detected a bullying attitude in him and this had alarmed her.

Tonight she was going to tell him that she could not see him again, that their relationship, such as it was, had come to an end. She wasn't looking forward to it, but she knew it must be done.

'Why bother?' Patsy had said over lunch earlier. 'Have dinner with him tonight. Say nothing. Tomorrow we're going to the Lake District and Yorkshire. And then you're off to Paris. Don't make yourself sick over this. Avoid a troublesome confrontation.'

'I have to tell him it's over,' Meredith had answered. 'Don't you see, he'll be in my life, pestering me, circling me, until I make it clear I don't want him anywhere near me.'

'What went wrong?' Patsy had asked curiously.

'Reed went wrong. He's just too complex a man for me.'

'I hate to say I told you so,' Patsy had murmured.

'It's all right, you can say it, Patsy. Because you did warn me, and you were right about him all along.'

They had then gone on to talk about other things,

but now Meredith could not help wondering if maybe Patsy was right. Might it not be infinitely easier to have dinner with Reed and say nothing?

Maybe I should do that, she thought as she turned into Brook Street.

'Good afternoon, madame,' the uniformed doorman outside Claridge's said as she went up the steps.

'Good afternoon,' she responded, smiling pleasantly, and pushed through the door which led into the hotel.

Martin, one of the concierges, greeted her as she crossed the lobby, making for the lift.

'Meredith!'

She stopped in her tracks, freezing as she recognized the cultivated masculine voice.

Slowly turning, she pasted a smile on her face as she moved towards the man who had called her name. 'Reed! Hello! But you're a bit early aren't you?'

He smiled and leaned into her, put his arm around her waist, drawing her closer. He kissed her cheek. 'I'm here having tea with friends.' He jerked his head in the direction of the salon, which opened off the lobby, and indicated a group of people at one of the tables. Afternoon tea was being served and a string quartet played.

'Darling, it's lovely to see you,' he went on, staring deeply into her eyes. 'I've missed you, but then I told you that on the phone this morning. I was actually just coming out to ring you up in your room, to invite you to come down and join us, when I saw you heading for the lift.' He took hold of her arm firmly, and drew her towards the salon.

Meredith resisted and held her ground, shaking her head. 'Reed, I can't. It's so nice of you to invite me, and thank you, but there are a number of things I must do before dinner.' Peeking at her watch, she added, 'It's almost five. We're still meeting at six-thirty, aren't we?'

'Of course. Unless you want to make it earlier. Look, do join us now,' he pressed, and once more tried to draw her into the salon.

Meredith said softly, 'Please, Reed, don't make a scene here. I just can't have tea. I've some phone calls, and I must change for dinner.'

He let go of her arm abruptly and stepped away from her. 'Very well,' he said, sounding suddenly grudging. 'Don't get frightfully dressed up. I'm taking you slumming tonight.'

Giving him a fraudulent smile, she murmured, 'I'll see you in a short while, Reed.' Not giving him a chance to say another word, Meredith spun around on her heels and walked rapidly to the lift.

Once she was inside her suite, she threw off her cape and unbuttoned the jacket of her cream trouser suit, then went through into the bedroom. Pulling open the wardrobe door, she looked at her clothes hanging there, settled on a black trouser suit for dinner, wishing deep down inside herself that she had never met Reed Jamison.

# Six

At precisely six-thirty there was a knock on the door of the suite, and Meredith knew it was Reed Jamison.

Walking out of the bedroom into the sitting room, buttoning her jacket, she arranged a pleasant smile on her face before opening the door.

'Not too early, I hope,' Reed said, kissing her on the cheek.

'Exactly on time,' Meredith murmured, and stood back in order to let him walk into the suite. 'I'll just get my bag and coat and we can be off.'

'Oh, but it's far too early for the restaurant, darling. Why don't we have a drink here first?' He put his overcoat on a chair and sauntered into the middle of the sitting room. After giving it a sweeping glance, he went to the fireplace where he draped himself against the mantel, striking an elegant pose.

'All right,' Meredith said, trying to be gracious, although she couldn't help wishing he had not come up to the suite. She had fully expected him to phone her from the lobby. Pressing the bell for the floor waiter, clearing her throat, she asked, 'What would you like?'

'Scotch and soda, please, my dear.'

'Where are we going for dinner?' she asked, making small talk.

'Aha, that's a surprise!' he exclaimed.

'You said we were going slumming.'

'I'm taking you to a wonderful Chinese restaurant, rather off the beaten track. But you'll enjoy it. The place has tremendous local colour, and the food is the best Chinese in London. Genuine, too, not the bastardized stuff served in fancy West End restaurants.'

'I'm looking forward to it,' she murmured and then moved out into the hall of the suite as the waiter knocked and then let himself in. After ordering their drinks, she returned to the fireside and sat down.

Looking at her intently, shifting his stance slightly and leaning forward, Reed said, 'I'm really rather put out with you, darling.'

'*Oh*.' Meredith stared at him questioningly. 'Because I didn't want to come down to tea and meet your friends?'

'No, no, of course not. That didn't matter. But I am somewhat surprised that you went to lunch with Patsy when I had invited you to come over to the house.'

Meredith was taken aback. 'But Reed, Patsy and I had a lot of business to discuss. I told you last week, when I was still in New York, that I had many things to attend to on this trip, and –'

'Oh *really*!' he cut in with a sardonic laugh. 'You could have dealt with Patsy on the phone, surely.'

'No, I couldn't!' she shot back, her voice rising in exasperation. She was irritated with him; she realized, yet again, that he did not really take her work seriously. Suppressing a rush of impatience, she went on more calmly, 'We had business to discuss, and I was anxious to see her.'

'But not anxious to see me.'

'Reed, don't be –'

There was a loud knock and the waiter entered with the tray of drinks. Meredith got up, thanked him, and handed him some of the coins she kept in the ash tray for tips. After giving Reed his drink, she picked up her own, and sat on the sofa.

'Cheers,' Reed said and took a swallow of his scotch and soda.

'Cheers.' Meredith merely touched the glass to her lips, then put it on the coffee table. She had no desire to drink tonight.

Once again Reed looked at her; this time he was smiling.

She was relieved the awkward moment had passed. It struck her that he seemed less morose tonight, and certainly he was in a better mood than he had been earlier, when she had run into him in the lobby.

'Have you told Patsy you're planning to move to London within the next few months?' he asked.

Meredith gaped at him. 'What makes you say that, Reed? I'm not moving anywhere.'

'When I was in New York in November you certainly indicated that you intended to live in London.'

'No, I didn't.'

'Oh Meredith, how can you say such a thing! I practically proposed to you, and I told you it was hard for me to go on like this any longer, that we couldn't continue our affair if we were separated by the Atlantic Ocean. I made it quite clear I wanted you here with me. Very much so. And you certainly acquiesced.'

'Reed, that's not true, I didn't!'

'You did!'

'You imagined it, Reed. Never in a million years would I lead you to believe such a thing.'

He stared at her incredulously, sudden anger flaring in his dark eyes. 'I distinctly remember telling you that I needed you here with me in London. And you agreed to come.'

Meredith had no recollection of this at all and was about to say so when he came and sat down next to her on the sofa.

'What's wrong with you, darling? Why are you behaving like this?' he asked, moving closer, draping his arm along the back of the sofa. 'Don't be difficult, my dear, you know how I feel about you. I need you, Meredith, and I need you *here*. Not in New York, but living with me in London. I told you when I was in the States, and I assumed you would get rid of the business and move as soon as you could. Settle here permanently with me.'

'Reed, you've truly misunderstood. I don't know how that happened . . . but it did, somehow. And I've no intention of giving up my business.'

'Then don't, darling. If you want to work you can, although it's really not necessary. I can support us extremely well, you know that. Forget the gallery, that's not important, merely my hobby. Just remember that I do have a very large private income from my trust. Monty might be inheriting the old man's title when he dies – after all he's the eldest son – but I've got Mummy's money.'

Meredith sat gazing at him mutely. She was at a complete loss for words, and filled with acute dismay.

Suddenly, unexpectedly, Reed pulled her into his arms. He was a tall man, well built and strong, and he caught hold of her hard, held her in a vice-like grip, pressing his mouth on hers.

She struggled, managed partially to push him away, and pulled herself up on the sofa, straining to extricate herself from his arms.

Unexpectedly, Reed let go of her as abruptly as he had grabbed her. Giving her an odd look, he said in a quiet, icy voice, 'Why did you pull away from me as if I'm suddenly a leper? What's wrong?'

Meredith bit her lip, said nothing. Then she sprang to her feet, hurried over to the window and stood looking out.

A cold silence filled the room.

Meredith was shaking inside. She wanted to get this over. Be done with him. End the whole thing as gracefully as she could. But he was being difficult – and worse, imagining things which hadn't happened.

After a moment or two, when she was calmer, she turned to face him and said slowly, in her kindest voice, 'Reed, listen to me . . . things are . . . well, not right between us any more. They haven't been for weeks.'

'How on earth can you say that! We had a wonderful time in New York. Only a month ago, unless I'm sadly mistaken.'

Meredith shook her head, her dismay intensifying. She wanted to be considerate, to let him down lightly, yet she knew within herself that she must make her feelings absolutely clear to him. 'It wasn't wonderful, Reed, at least not for me. I realized you and I were completely incompatible, not suited to each other at all. I began to feel ill at ease with you, and I certainly knew our relationship was on the skids, that it couldn't possibly work.'

'That's not so, and you know it. If you lived here and we weren't conducting our relationship long-distance, everything would be entirely different. Please move to London to be with me, Meredith.'

'Reed, I've just told you, as far as I'm concerned we don't have a future together. And anyway I have such a huge commitment to my business.'

'Oh don't go on so, Meredith. I can't believe for one moment that you're such a dyed-in-the-wool career woman as you claim to be. I couldn't love that kind of woman, and I do love you.'

Meredith was silent.

He repeated, 'I love you.'

'Oh Reed, I'm so sorry . . . but I just don't feel the same way.'

'That's not what you led me to believe,' he said softly, his eyes narrowing.

'I admit I was infatuated with you last fall, that's true. But it *was* an *infatuation*, nothing stronger or more lasting. I can't make a commitment to you, I just can't.'

'It's been so good between us, Meredith. Why are you saying these things?'

Taking a deep breath, Meredith plunged in. 'I've come to understand that you don't take my life seriously. Not my personal family life with my children, and certainly not my work. I will not deny my children's existence for you, or anyone else for that matter, and I will never give up my work. It's far too important to me. I've put too many years and too much effort into my business.'

'You're not living up to my expectations of you, Meredith,' he said, his voice suddenly grown cold and disparaging. 'Not at all. I thought you were different. I thought you were an old-fashioned woman with old-fashioned values. What a miscalculation on my part. I can't believe my judgement was so flawed. Or perhaps you simply deceived me.' He raised a dark brow.

Slowly, and in a cold tone, Meredith answered, 'You know, you've just put a finger on something of vital importance, Reed. I *feel* the weight of your expectations, and I just can't handle that. I began to realize in November that you believe you come first in my life. I'm afraid you don't. The reason I wanted to see you tonight was to explain this, to tell you about my feelings and to bring our relationship to an end.'

Reed Jamison was speechless. In all of his forty-one years he had never been discarded by a woman. He had always been the one to end affairs or start them, controlling, manipulating, pulling the puppet's strings and getting his own way.

He continued to stare at Meredith. She was the only woman who had ever bested him, and a terrible rage began to fulminate in him. He leapt to his feet, glaring at her. He shouted, 'I'm glad I found out what kind of woman you really are! Before I made the terrible mistake of marrying you!'

Without another word Reed strode across the room, picked up his coat and left, banging the door behind him with such ferocity that the chandelier rattled and swayed on its chain.

Meredith ran to the door and locked it; she leaned against it for a few seconds. She was shaking. Calming herself, she walked over to the desk, sat down and dialled Patsy's number. It rang and rang. She was just about to hang up when she heard Patsy saying, 'Hello?'

'Patsy, it's me. Reed was here, and I told him it was over between us. He's gone ... he marched out in a fury.'

'Well, that's a relief. That you told him, I mean. And naturally he left in high dudgeon. He's not used to getting dumped unceremoniously. That's part of his problem, you know. He's always been spoilt by women, and he thinks he's God's gift to everything that walks in skirts.'

'Yes, I know what you mean. He's also a male chauvinist pig, to use a very out-dated phrase. However, it is appropriate. That's something I guess I detected when he was last in New York. He doesn't take my business seriously, or my life. He's self-involved, and he just can't imagine why I'm not rushing over here to set up house with him. He said he wanted me to marry him.'

'He proposed! Good God! Well, I must say, you must've really got to him, Meredith, my girl. Ever since his divorce from Tina Longdon he's been a hit-and-run man.'

'I'm not sure what that means.'

'You know, the kind of chap who has an attitude ... *love me on my terms, darling. Thanks for everything.*

*Farewell*. Hit-and-run chaps, that's what we call them over here. I know several women who've suffered at Reed's hands.'

'Why didn't you tell me?'

'I did, Meredith – at least I tried to warn you as best I could. I did say he was a difficult man.'

'Actually, you said he was a brooding Byronic hero, or words to that effect, and I never did *really* understand what you meant by that.'

'Oh that's only the role he's adopted for years. In essence, it's a pose. But I suppose it has been rather effective, got him a long way with women. Not that he needs a pose, actually. His looks aside, he's charming most of the time, despite that smouldering manner of his.'

'All too true. But do you think women fall for that ... for that brooding thing?'

'Oh yes, I think so. Let's face it, *many* do. The smouldering eyes, the soulful expression, the moody demeanour can be appealing. There are a lot of women who go for the suffering, anguished Heathcliffs of this world. They want to change them, make them happy.' Patsy paused, then said, 'Wasn't that one of the things about him that attracted you?'

'No,' Meredith answered quickly. 'To tell you the truth, it was only this past November, in New York, that he turned morose and moody. It irritated me more than anything else.'

Patsy laughed. 'I bet it did! Anyway, the main thing is you don't sound any the worse for giving him the boot.'

Meredith also laughed. 'I'm not. Naturally, I'm not

thrilled about hurting someone's feelings. But it had to be done; Reed had to be told. I needed that closure.'

'I realize you did.'

'I thought it only fair that Reed knew exactly how I felt. And immediately. It was much better to clear the air, cut it off before it dragged on any longer. These kinds of situations can end in such bitterness.'

'Don't I know it!' Patsy exclaimed. 'Tony's been bitter about our divorce for years. Blames me, of course. Listen, do you want to come over for supper? Or we could go out if you like, if you don't want to be alone . . .' Patsy's voice trailed off.

'That's sweet of you, but I want to stay in tonight. I'll order room service and pack. You did say you were picking me up at six tomorrow morning, didn't you?'

'Yes. Sorry about that, but we do have to leave early. We'll be about four hours on the road, three and a half if the traffic's light. We'll spend a couple of hours in Keswick and then head down to Ripon. We've a great deal to do in one day. In fact, we might have to spend the night in Ripon.'

'No problem. And Patsy?'

'Yes?'

'I don't think I hurt his feelings too much, do you?'

'You may have. Don't underestimate the effect you had on him.'

'I've probably damaged his ego, that's all.'

'Oh definitely, Meredith, I'm certain of that. But I also believe that our Reed, the glamorous playboy, fell rather heavily for you. That's *always* been my opinion. Oh well, what can one do ... He finally met his Waterloo.'

# Seven

Meredith found it hard to fall asleep.

For a long time she tossed and turned until finally, in exasperation, she got out of bed. After putting on a warm woollen dressing gown, she went and sat on the sofa in the sitting room. Her mind was racing.

She had not drawn the heavy velvet draperies earlier and moonlight was filtering in through the muslin curtains which hung against the window panes. Everything had a silvery sheen from this natural light, and the room was peaceful.

Meredith leaned back against the silk cushions of the sofa, thinking of Reed. How unpleasant their parting had been, and how foolish she had been to get involved with him in the first place. She was forty-four years old; she ought to have known better.

How unlucky she was with men. Always.

No, that was not quite true.

There had been one man. *Once.* A man who had been exactly right for her. He was dead. He had died too young. Such an untimely death . . . that's what they had all said. And how truthfully they had spoken.

To die at the age of thirty-six was some terrible trick of God's, wasn't it?

Meredith had asked herself this question a thousand times. And she had striven hard to find some special meaning in that awful, untimely death. She had found nothing. There was no meaning in it. None at all.

And all she had been left with was a void.

Of course there had been Cat, just a toddler, and Amelia, poor Amelia, and they had shared that void with her, and the grief. How they had mourned him ... endlessly ... she and Amelia. His women. The women who had loved him.

I'll always mourn him, Meredith thought, the old familiar sadness rising in her, filling her throat. Oh Jack, why did you die? How many times had she asked herself that in the silence of her mind? There was no answer. There had never been an answer. Not ever in twenty-two years.

And how many times had she asked herself when she would meet another man like Jack? She never would, she knew that now, because men like him were amongst the very few. And they were already spoken for. Jack had been spoken for early on in his life, when he was only twenty-two. He had married that youthful love of his. *Amelia*. Then one terrible day she had been thrown by her horse. When she was only twenty-five and pregnant. She had lost the baby and been crippled for life, a paraplegic trapped in a wheelchair. But he loved her; he would always love and cherish Amelia and she would always be his wife; he had told Meredith that and she had understood. And she had loved Amelia and Amelia had loved her and Jack; and Cat – she had loved her, too. Amelia had given them her blessing in her own silent, smiling way, full of approval, and gratitude for their love and kindness and loyalty.

*Jack.*

Blond, blue-eyed, tanned. So quick and sprightly and energetic. Full of good humour, tall tales, laughter and life. No wonder she had fallen in love with him instantly, the first day she had set eyes on him. A *coup de foudre*.

So long ago now.

May of 1969.

She had been just eighteen.

Meredith closed her eyes. Behind her lids she could see his face. She remembered what had gone through her mind that day as she had stared back at him, held in the grip of his mesmeric gaze.

Such a beautiful face for a man, she had thought, such a sensitive mouth and those extraordinary eyes. Such a lovely blue. Bits of sky, she had thought then. His eyes are like bits of a summer sky.

Now tonight, so many years later, Meredith saw herself as she had been on that May afternoon . . . the images of the three of them floated before her. They were all so clear . . . so very vivid and alive . . . she and Jack and Amelia.

The decades fell away.

She tumbled backwards in time . . . tumbled back into the past.

'Can I help you?' the young man asked politely, getting up off the steps where he had been sitting, pulling off his tortoise-shell sunglasses, peering intently at her.

Meredith stared back at him. 'I'm looking for a Mr

Silver,' she answered, jumping off her bike, almost falling in her haste and sudden confusion. Unexpectedly she was feeling self-conscious in front of this handsome man, so well groomed and well dressed, wearing grey trousers and a dark blue cashmere sweater over his lighter blue shirt.

The man walked over to her, thrusting out his hand. 'Well, you've found him,' he announced, 'I'm Mr Silver.'

'Mr *Jack* Silver?' she asked, shaking his hand.

He nodded. 'That's right. And the only Mr Silver who's alive and kicking. That I know of, anyway. The rest are over there.' He indicated a plot of land behind him.

She followed the direction of his gaze and saw a small walled cemetery to the right of a copse of trees. 'You have your own graveyard?' she asked, sounding awed.

He nodded, and there was a questioning expression on his face as he asked, 'How can I help you?'

'I've come about the advertisement in the newspaper . . . for a receptionist.'

'Oh yes, of course. And whom might I be speaking to?'

'I'm Meredith Stratton.'

'Well hello, Meredith Stratton. Pleased to meet you!' he exclaimed, thrusting out his hand once more. 'Pleased to meet you indeed, Meredith Stratton!'

She took his hand and shook it for a second time.

He did not let go of it. Then he smiled at her, a wide warm smile that showed his beautiful teeth. They were very white in his tanned face.

She smiled back at him, liking him.

He started to laugh, for no apparent reason.

She laughed with him, instantly captivated by this man whom she had never seen before.

Still holding onto her hand, he led her and the bike she was clinging to over to the front steps where he had been sitting. 'Come inside. But I do think you'll have to leave your transportation out here,' he said, and grinned.

Meredith nodded, her eyes dancing, and then she removed her hand from his and propped her bike against the porch railings.

'Nice bike you have.'

'It's not mine. I borrowed it. That was the only way I could get here.'

'Where did you come from?'

'New Preston. We've been living up above Lake Waramaug.' She glanced away, her eyes on the lake at the bottom of the rolling lawns and flower gardens. 'You've got a nice lake,' she murmured.

'Silver Lake,' he told her. 'It used to have a Native American name a few years ago, a few *hundred* years ago that is. Lake Wappaconaca. But an ancestor of mine bought this land and the local folk got into the habit of calling it Silver Lake, after him, and that name stuck. And this, of course, is Silver Lake Inn, built in 1832 by that same ancestor . . . 137 years ago this year.'

Meredith stood looking up at the inn. 'It's a lovely old building.'

'Come on, let's go inside. I want you to meet Amelia.'

The moment she stepped through the doorway of the inn Meredith knew that it was a very special place. The walls were painted a cloudy mottled pink and they gave the entrance the warmest of rosy feelings. The floor was so highly polished it gleamed like a dark mirror; an old carved chest, two high-backed chairs and a small desk were obviously vintage antiques, and looked valuable even to her untrained eye.

Everywhere there were fresh flowers in tall crystal vases and bulbs growing in Chinese porcelain bowls; their mixed fragrances assailed her ... the scent of mimosa, hyacinth, narcissi mingled with the smell of beeswax, lemons and dried roses, ripe apples cooking on a stove somewhere.

As she took all of this in, looking around her wide-eyed, Meredith was awed. Yet she was filled with a curious kind of excitement and pleasure, such as she had never known before. She crossed her fingers, praying she would get the job. Glancing at the small antique desk, with its silk-shaded porcelain lamp and telephone, she could not help thinking how nice it would be to sit in this entrance hall, being a receptionist, greeting guests. It was certainly more appealing to her than working as an *au pair*, looking after children all day long, even though she loved children.

Jack ushered her down a short corridor and opened the door at the end. A woman sat behind a desk with her back to the door; she was gazing out of the window.

'Amelia,' Jack said. 'We have an applicant at last. For the job of receptionist.'

The woman slowly turned, and Meredith realized immediately that she was sitting in a wheelchair. Her breath caught in her throat as she returned the woman's steady gaze. Meredith was startled by her beauty. Dark hair, parted in the middle, tumbled around a pale heart-shaped face. Wonderful high cheekbones, a dimpled chin and a sensual mouth were nothing in comparison to the amazing vivid green eyes below perfectly arched black brows. It's the woman from *Gone with the Wind*, she thought.

Amelia said, 'You're looking rather strange. Are you feeling all right?'

Meredith realized she was staring and exclaimed, 'Oh yes, I'm fine. *Sorry*. I'm so sorry to stare at you, it's very rude.' The words tumbled out, and then, because of her youth and ingenuousness, she rushed on unthinkingly, 'You're so beautiful. You look like Vivien Leigh in *Gone with the Wind*. Doesn't everybody tell you that?'

'Not everyone. But thank you for your lovely compliment,' Amelia answered with a smile and exchanged an amused look with Jack.

Jack cleared his throat and took charge. 'Amelia, darling, may I introduce Miss Meredith Stratton. Miss Stratton, this is my wife, Mrs Amelia Silver.'

Meredith walked across the polished wood floor and took the woman's slender hand in hers, then stepped back, still moved by such perfect beauty.

'Please, do sit down, Miss Stratton,' Amelia murmured. 'Make yourself comfortable.'

'Thank you.' Meredith lowered herself into a chair, straightening her cotton skirt as she did. 'I'd feel better if you called me Meredith, Mrs Silver. I'm not used to *Miss Stratton.*'

Again a small smile fluttered briefly on Amelia's pretty mouth. 'I'd be happy to call you by your first name.'

Jack, who was now sitting on the window seat to the right of his wife, remarked, 'Meredith comes from New Preston. At least, that's where she bicycled from this afternoon.' He now directed his words to Meredith and went on, 'But you originally hail from Australia, don't you?'

She nodded. 'Sydney. But how did you know? Oh, my awful voice, that's how, isn't it?'

'It's not awful,' Amelia said. 'But you do have a slight twang, one that's distinctly Australian. Tell me, when did you come to live in Connecticut?'

'Last year. I'll have been living here just a year this July. I came with the Paulsons. They're an American family I met when they were living in Sydney. Mr Paulson's with an advertising agency. I worked for them in Sydney as an *au pair*.'

'And now you wish to leave them. May we inquire why?' Jack probed.

'I want to change jobs, Mr Silver. But it's a bit more complicated than that. Mr Paulson has been transferred again, this time to South Africa. The family are about to leave for Johannesburg. They asked me to go too, but I don't want to. I want to live in America. I never want to leave Connecticut. It's the most beautiful place I've ever seen.'

'But what about your family? Your parents back in Australia? How do they feel about this?' Amelia seemed slightly puzzled. 'Surely they want you to go home?'

'Oh no, they don't . . . what I mean is . . . well, you see . . . they're . . . dead. They died, yes, they did. In a . . . car crash. When I was ten.' Meredith nodded to herself. 'When I was ten,' she repeated.

'Oh you poor girl,' Amelia exclaimed, her face filling with sympathy. 'How terribly sad, heartbreaking for you. And do you not have other family out there? Relatives?'

'No, I don't. There's no one.'

'But how awful for you to be so alone in this world.' Amelia turned her chair to face Jack. 'Isn't it sad, darling?'

'Yes, it is.'

'How old are you?' Amelia asked, giving her a warm encouraging smile.

'Eighteen. I was just eighteen at the beginning of May.'

Jack said, 'Have you ever worked as a receptionist? Had any experience in a hotel?'

'No, but I'm good with people. At least, Mrs Paulson says so, and I've been helping her with her paperwork for two years. You know, her chequebook, household accounts, things like that. She's even taught me a bit about bookkeeping. She says I have the right skills for this job, Mr Silver. And you can phone her any time. She's also going to give me a written reference. It'll be ready later this afternoon. I can bring it back to you tonight if you want.'

'That won't be necessary,' Amelia said briskly, then addressed Jack. 'I think you should speak to Mrs

Paulson about Meredith right away. Now. You don't mind if we call her whilst you're still here, do you, Meredith?'

'Oh no. She's at home, packing. I think she's sort of expecting you to give her a ring.'

'What's the number, Meredith?' Jack asked, crossing to the desk, picking up the phone.

She gave it to him; he dialled. And a moment later he was engaged in a conversation with Mrs Paulson, or rather he was listening, saying very little, hardly able to get a word in edgewise.

Amelia sat quietly, waiting for the conversation to come to an end.

Meredith clasped her hands tightly in her lap, suddenly anxious and tense. Even though she knew Mrs Paulson would say all the right things, she couldn't help worrying a little. This job was important to her.

When Jack finally hung up he said to Meredith, 'She's full of praise for you, says you're a clever girl, diligent, honest and hardworking, and she told me you looked after her children very well.'

Meredith beamed, and relaxed, then looked at Amelia expectantly.

Amelia said, 'It's good to know that Mrs Paulson thinks so highly of you.'

'Yes. And she did say she'll come to see you,' Meredith volunteered. 'She'd like to meet you.'

Jack walked over to the window seat, sat down, then said to Amelia, 'To continue. Mrs Paulson's sorry to lose Meredith, but she understands her reasons for wanting to stay in Connecticut. In any case, she thinks Meredith's cut out for better things.' Then to Meredith, he remarked, 'She says you were very good with her children. Apparently they love you.'

'I love them,' Meredith replied. 'I'm going to miss them, Mr Silver, but I don't want to go to South Africa.'

'I can't say I blame you for wanting to stay on in Connecticut,' Amelia murmured. 'The Litchfield Hills, in particular, are very lovely. Now, when would you be able to start?'

'Next week.' Meredith sat up straighter and glanced from Amelia to Jack. 'Do I have the job then?'

'Yes,' Amelia said. 'Mrs Paulson's recommendation sounds wonderful, and it's good enough for us. I don't think we'll find anyone better than you, Meredith. Isn't that so, Jack?'

'Yes, I agree. However, there's a slight problem, you know.'

'What's that, Jack darling?'

'Where is Meredith going to live?'

Taken by surprise on hearing this, Meredith gaped at the Silvers. 'Here at the inn!' she cried. 'The advertisement said *food and lodging provided if required*. I wouldn't have applied otherwise. That was the thing that pleased Mrs Paulson . . . that I would be living here at the inn with you. That I wouldn't be out on my own.'

'We do have a room, but it's up in the attic,' Jack explained. 'And it's not very nice. The assistant housekeeper occupies the one good staff bedroom. We're a bit short of staff quarters, if truth be known.'

'I don't mind the attic,' Meredith said, suddenly afraid the job would slip through her fingers. 'Honest, I don't.'

'We were hoping we'd find a receptionist who lived nearby and could come in daily,' Amelia murmured. 'But no one applied, even though the advertisement's been in for a few weeks. Until you came today, of course.' Amelia gave Jack a long, searching look. 'Perhaps we could make the attic more presentable, get it painted and wallpapered. We could put in a few pieces of really nice furniture, spruce it up. And let's not forget that it is fairly spacious.'

'I don't know . . .' Jack began and stopped when he noticed the crestfallen look on Meredith's face. Making a sudden decision, he jumped up. 'Let me show you the room.' Turning to his wife, he explained, 'I think we should let Meredith be the judge of the room. Let's hear what she thinks of it.'

'You're quite right. Run along with Jack, Meredith. He'll take you to the top floor.'

A few minutes later Meredith and Jack were standing in the attic under the eaves. Meredith was relieved to see there were two dormer windows and that the room *was* quite large, as Amelia had indicated. She walked around, then said to Jack Silver, 'But I love it; it's quaint, cute. I'll soon make it look nice. Don't worry, I'll be fine up here.'

Jack merely nodded and they went back downstairs.

'Well, what do you think, my dear?' Amelia asked, raising a brow quizzically as they walked in.

'It's unusual, Mrs Silver, but it'll work nicely for me. I'll make it comfortable. Do you want me to start next week?'

'If you can. I'm really looking forward to your arrival, Meredith.'

'So am I. And I'll bring the written reference with me.'

'If you wish. Goodbye for now,' Amelia said, and wheeled herself behind the desk. 'I must get back to all this tedious paperwork which has recently landed in my lap.'

Jack and Meredith went out to the front porch and he walked with her down the steps. 'The inn's not busy at the moment,' he confided, 'but it will be in another week or so. What day do you think you can come?'

'Monday. That's only four days from now. Will that be all right, Mr Silver?'

'It certainly will. You're going to take a huge burden off me, and I'll be able to tackle some of the other chores that Pete O'Brien has been doing. He's the estate manager and he's badly overworked. Amelia will feel more at ease too, once you're installed. She gets so tired at times, but try though I have, I've not been able to find anyone to assist her.'

Meredith nodded her understanding, full of empathy for the Silvers. 'It must be difficult, but don't worry, Mr Silver, I'll help her with that paperwork. I'd really like to do so, in my spare time.' She glanced across at him, hesitated, and then said softly, 'What exactly happened to Mrs Silver? Why is she in a wheelchair?'

'Amelia had a riding accident eleven years ago. Her spine was damaged. She's been paralysed from the waist down ever since.'

'How dreadful, I'm so sorry . . . she's so beautiful.'

'Yes, she is . . . inside as well as out. She's a truly

good person, Meredith, the best I've ever known. So brave, so patient . . .'

There was a small silence, and then Meredith said, 'Thank you for giving me the job. I won't let you down. And I'll work very hard.'

'I'm sure you will.'

Meredith walked over to her bike, then suddenly, swinging around, she stood looking across at the lake. She could see it through the trees, glistening in the late-afternoon sunlight. 'Do you get much wildlife on the lake?' she asked at last in a strangely wistful voice.

'All year round, I'm happy to say. There're probably flocks of birds down there now. Ducks, Canada geese especially. Shall we walk over and have a look?'

Meredith nodded, reached for her bicycle and wheeled it along between them.

Jack said, 'Do you like biking?'

'Sometimes. Why?'

'I have a bike, and I often ride it around the property. I can't claim to have covered the whole hundred and fifty acres, but I've done my best to see as much as I can. And there's a lot to see, most of it interesting.'

'It's a big place, isn't it?'

'Yes, but not as big as some of the spreads in the outback, I bet.'

She laughed. 'The only part of Australia I know is Sydney.'

He shrugged. 'But it *is* a big country.'

'Yes, it is. And is this all your land, Mr Silver?'

'It is. My great-great-great grandfather, Adam Silver, and his wife Angharad, bought it in 1832, as I told you. They built the inn, the house next to it which is the one where Amelia and I now live, and various other small buildings on the property. And, of course, the family's been running the inn since those days.'

'An unbroken chain,' she said, the awe creeping into her voice again.

Jack simply nodded.

The two of them walked on, taking the wide path. This cut down through the green lawns and flower gardens, which were just starting to bloom; it stopped at the edge of the lake.

'I know it's called Silver Lake because of your name, but the lake *is* silver in colour. And it's so calm,' Meredith said.

She leaned against the handlebars of the bike and shaded her eyes with one hand. 'I've always liked being near water, for as long as I can remember. I don't know why, but it makes me feel . . .' She paused, unable to finish her sentence, at a loss for the right word to describe her emotions.

'*What* does it make you feel, Meredith?'

'I'm not sure . . . I can never really put my finger on the feeling.'

'Happy? Content? Secure? It's surely a *good* feeling you experience, or you wouldn't like being near the water at all.'

'That's true. I suppose it makes me feel . . . well, all of those things you've just mentioned. But sometimes I feel sad, as if I've lost something . . . something precious. The water reminds me of it.'

He made no response, merely looked at her closely before focusing on the lake. Suddenly he pointed and cried excitedly, 'Oh look! Over there! That's the blue heron that comes every spring. It flies away after a few days and rarely comes back to the lake until the next year. But it's marvellous and I'm certain it's the same bird.'

'How strange. I can't imagine why it does that. If I were a bird I would never want to leave Silver Lake. I would want to live here forever and ever, it's so beautiful.'

Jack Silver stared at her, taken by her words so softly spoken.

Meredith met his eyes. She was quite startled by their intensity. They did not leave her face and there was an expression in them she could not fathom. And she discovered that she could not look away . . .

It was Jack who broke the spell between them. He said suddenly, gruffly, 'I'm glad you're coming to work at Silver Lake Inn, Meredith. I have a feeling things will go well. Amelia likes you. I like you. I sincerely hope you like us.'

'I do, Mr Silver, and *I'm* glad I'm coming here, too.'

They walked back to the inn in silence, both lost for a few moments in their own thoughts.

'See you on Monday, Mr Silver,' Meredith said, climbing onto her bike, riding away.

'Call me Jack,' he shouted after her.

'All right, I will,' she answered, half turning, waving before disappearing down the long drive.

He stood watching her until she was out of sight, and he was amazed at himself when he suddenly realized he did not want her to leave. There was something most appealing about this girl; she was fresh and sweet and very beautiful, although he knew *she* did not realize just how beautiful she truly was. Nor did she understand the impact she made with her long legs, sun-streaked brown hair and smoky green eyes. He discovered he missed her already and he had only known her for a couple of hours; and he was further amazed at himself.

The insistent ringing of the telephone awakened Meredith with a sudden start. As she jumped up and went to answer it she realized she had fallen asleep on the sofa earlier.

'Hello?'

'Good morning, Mrs Stratton. This is your wake-up call. It's five o'clock,' the hotel operator informed her.

'Thank you,' she answered, putting the phone back in the cradle and turning on a lamp. Glancing at her watch she saw that it *was* five; it surprised her that she had spent the entire night on the sofa without waking up once. She must have been extremely tired. On the other hand, the big overstuffed sofa was as comfortable as the bed.

Patsy will soon be here, she thought, hurrying into the bedroom, slipping out of her dressing gown, then heading for the shower. She was filled with relief that she had packed the night before.

An hour later she was standing in the lobby of Claridge's waiting for her partner who was going to drive them to the North of England.

# Eight

It was a dull morning, grey and overcast, when Patsy and Meredith drove away from Claridge's. Leaden skies threatened rain and by the time Patsy was pulling onto the motorway, pointing the Aston Martin in the direction of the North, it was already pouring.

Meredith leaned back against the car seat, only half listening to the radio, her mind preoccupied with business. But at one moment she closed her eyes, and then, almost against her own volition, she began to doze, lulled by the warmth in the car and the music on the radio.

'Go to sleep if you feel like it,' Patsy said, glancing at her quickly, before focusing on the road ahead again. 'I don't mind, and we don't have to talk if you're tired.'

'I'm fine,' Meredith replied, opening her eyes, sitting up straighter. 'Even though I spent the night on the sofa I did in fact have a good rest.'

'Why did you sleep on the sofa?'

'I was still wide awake at one in the morning, too much on my mind, I guess. So I decided to get up, then I must have dozed off a bit later on.'

'I hope you weren't up in the middle of the night fretting about Reed Jamison.' Patsy frowned, throwing her a concerned look.

'No, of course not.'

'Good, because he's certainly not worth worrying about.'

'I agree, and I'm relieved I told him how I felt, Patsy.' Meredith laughed dryly. 'It's probably the only time I've had his full attention.'

'What do you mean?'

'I always thought Reed wasn't really listening to anything I had to say. It seemed to me that he was very busy formulating his reply, preoccupied with what he was going to say rather than with the meaning of my words.'

'A lot of people suffer from *that* particular ailment,' Patsy muttered. 'It's a kind of self-involvement, I suppose. Then again, nobody seems to *really* listen any more. Except you. You're the best listener I've ever known.'

'I learned that from Amelia. She taught me how important it is to listen. She was always saying that you didn't learn anything if you were the one doing all the talking. How right she was, but she was generally right about most things; she taught me such a lot.' There was a small pause, and then Meredith added, 'She was quite the most remarkable person I've ever known.'

'I'm sorry I never knew her,' Patsy said. 'And it's funny you should mention her this morning, because I was thinking about her only last night, thinking what an influence she's been on both our lives, although indirectly on mine, of course. Just think, if John Raphaelson hadn't been her lawyer and then yours, you would never have met his brother, who was one of my father's best friends, and therefore *we* would never have met, would we?'

Meredith smiled. 'That's true, and *I* wish you'd known Amelia. She was so special.' Meredith let out a little sigh. 'You know, if she'd lived she'd only be sixty-two this year. Not that old at all.'

'And Jack? How old would he have been?'

'He was four years younger than Amelia, so he would have been fifty-eight ... at the end of this month, actually.'

'How sad for you that they died so young.'

'Yes ... Amelia struggled to keep going after Jack's death, but the light had gone out for her. She just gave up in the end. I've always thought she died of a broken heart, if that's possible.'

'Oh *I* think it is, Meredith. I believe my mother did ... she went so quickly after my father passed away. I've always thought she just lost all interest in living once he was gone. In fact, I found out from my aunt, after Mummy had died, that she was always saying, "I want to go to Winston," and she stopped eating – well, she ate very little. It was as if she lost her appetite ... for everything, including life. I do think she'd made up her mind to die.'

'Amelia was a bit like that too, although she did live for a year after Jack's death. Not surprising really, when you think about it. People who have been together for a long time are so dependent on each other, and when one of them is suddenly alone it's traumatic.'

'They're lonely, and loneliness is a pretty unbearable state to be in.'

'Amelia once said the same thing. Actually, she said loneliness was another kind of death. She loved me and she loved Cat, but Jack was the light of her life. Without him she seemed to lose her purpose, her *raison d'être*. Did I ever tell you that they'd known each other since their childhood?'

'No, you never did. Did they grow up together?'

'Part of the time, yes. Her parents had a summer home in Cornwall Bridge, not far from Silver Lake, and they were friends of the Silvers. Jack and Amelia met when they were children. Amelia was fourteen and Jack ten. They became best friends. They were both only children, you see, only children of only children, so there were no brothers and sisters or cousins. "I'm going to marry you when I grow up," Jack was forever telling her, and she'd laugh and say she couldn't possibly marry a younger man. But they did marry when they were in their twenties. And then Amelia had the riding accident . . . how different their lives would have been if she hadn't been thrown by her horse. But that was her destiny . . . at least, that's what she used to say to me.'

'What did she mean?'

'Exactly that, Patsy. She said that none of us could tamper with fate. Or avert it. *Qué será será* she would say, *what will be will be*. She said it was fate that brought me to Silver Lake that day in May of 1969. She said I was simply living out my destiny, just as she was doing, and Jack too. "I'm meant to be in this chair, Meri, I don't know why, but I am," she would tell me over and over again.' Meredith paused, looked at Patsy through the corner of her eye. 'According to

Amelia, fate brought me to them. And as I've told you many times before, they changed my life, just as I changed theirs, in so many different ways. For the better . . . for all of us. They gave me love and warmth and understanding, and the only real home I'd ever known until then. And I gave them something they'd always wanted, always missed . . .'

'You were like a sister to them, the sister neither of them ever had.'

'Yes, I *was* a sibling, in a sense. But what I meant was that I gave them Cat. My baby was like their child as well as mine. And how much they loved her.'

'I know, and just think how happy they'd be if they could see her today. She's really grown up to be such a fine young woman. Do you think she *will* get engaged to Keith?'

'I do, and it'll be soon. Catherine has very good instincts, and she wouldn't have said anything to me the other night if she hadn't felt Keith was on the verge of proposing.'

'I hope I get an invitation to the wedding.'

'Don't be so silly, of course you will. Cat loves you, and she's never forgotten how marvellous you were to her the year she lived with you in London. And neither have I, for that matter. Because of you I was able to sleep every night. I didn't have to worry about my daughter being alone in a foreign country.'

'I was happy to look after her, be a big sister. Will you have the reception at Silver Lake?'

'Oh, yes, I'm sure of that. Cat wouldn't want it anywhere else. She loves that place the way I do. And it's the perfect setting for a wedding. Blanche is all excited, planning it already in her mind. The other evening she was talking about marquees and the menu and no doubt she's got everything planned by now, from the flowers to the parking arrangements. Anyway, you're going to come, and you'll stay with me at the house.'

'How lovely, thank you. Oh gosh, Meredith, being in love is wonderful! I'm thrilled for Cat, thrilled that she's found the right man. I wish I could.'

'When you're looking there's never one around.' Meredith leaned her head against the back of the seat, closed her eyes. 'And a man isn't always the answer, you know.'

'Only too true!' Patsy peered ahead, cursing under her breath. The heavy rain was slashing against the windscreen, so that everything looked blurred despite the wipers. 'I hope this awful weather is going to let up soon. It's just miserable.'

'Do you want me to drive?'

'No, no, I'm okay. And I know this road like the back of my hand. Don't forget, it leads to the North of England.'

'Your favourite place.'

'One of them anyway,' Patsy said, smiling to herself.

Meredith fell silent, her thoughts taking over.

Patsy concentrated on her driving. There was a strong wind blowing, and she suspected it was bitterly cold outside; the road had recently grown slick, icy, suddenly slippery because of the freezing rain and sleet.

As she drove on, her eyes fixed ahead, she thought of Meredith and how she had gone to Silver Lake all those years ago, how her life had been transformed overnight. What an extraordinary story it was. She knew that Meredith had become indispensable to Amelia very quickly; the two women had developed a symbiotic relationship. Meredith had once told her how Jack had come to rely on her as well, teaching her so much about the management of the hotel, teaching her everything he knew about business. Yes, Meredith had confided a great deal about her years with the Silvers, but not much else about herself. She never talked about her earlier life in Australia. In fact, everything before the Silver Lake years seemed to be clouded in mystery. It was as if there were another part of her life, a secret part, which Meredith did not want anyone to know about. Patsy had no inclination to pry, ask questions; that was not her way. She respected Meredith's desire for privacy.

Meredith interrupted Patsy's thoughts when she turned to her and said, 'This may sound funny to you, but I have a feeling you prefer the inn in Ripon. Skell Garth is your favourite of the two, isn't it?'

Taken aback, Patsy exclaimed, 'Why do you say *that*?'

'I just know. I've put two and two together from the few things you've said. Anyway, you love Yorkshire so much, it's where you grew up.'

'As I've been telling you all along, I want you to be the judge, Meredith, I really do. I don't want to influence you, set you up in advance.'

'What's wrong with the one in the Lake District?'

'Nothing. You've seen the pictures.'

'Yes, and it does look gorgeous, and so do the gardens and the view. You've said it's luxurious, beautifully done, and yet there's a *but* in your mind; I know you.'

'Too many cushions,' Patsy muttered.

Meredith began to laugh. 'I'll never live that down, will I?' she said, remembering a comment she had made about another inn they had considered six months ago. 'So what you're saying really is that it's *overstuffed, over-decorated.*'

'Sort of . . . lots of luxury and comfort, and I think the place does make you feel terribly pampered. But despite all the lovely fabrics and rugs and nice antiques there's nothing unique or different about Heronside. There's nothing there that's gone awry. You've always told me that it's important for a room to be slightly askew, a bit "off". You said it makes a place interesting.'

'Oddities add character, and that's something we have always taken into consideration.' Meredith looked at her partner and friend, and nodded to herself. 'I *feel* you don't like Heronside.'

'I don't *dislike* it,' Patsy answered, speaking the truth.

'Look, why are we going there? Why not go directly to Ripon?'

'Because it is a wonderful inn, and I want you to see it for yourself. It doesn't need much money spent on it, since it was redone two years ago, and the views are magnificent. Also, I'm not sure I'm right about it. Truly, Meredith, I want *you* to make the decision.'

'All right, I will. But you're not often wrong, Patsy. We have very similar tastes.'

# Nine

The morning was clear, cold, the kind of crisp bright day that Meredith liked. The sky was a dazzling blue without cloud and the sun was shining; whilst this offered little warmth it added radiance to the day.

It was just turning nine o'clock on Tuesday morning. Meredith was bundled up in boots and a sheepskin coat, walking through Studley Park. The stately avenue of lime trees down which she hurried led to Studley Church, just visible on top of the hill at the end of the avenue. She knew, from Mrs Miller's directions, that within a few minutes she would be at the abbey.

Yesterday afternoon, when she and Patsy had arrived in Ripon, they had gone directly to Skell Garth House. It was situated between the tiny villages of Studley Royal and Aldfield, and stood on the banks of the little River Skell, as did Fountains Abbey on the opposite bank.

After the Millers had been introduced to her, Patsy had explained to the couple that they would like to stay the night at Skell Garth. Since it was midweek in winter, this had not presented a problem. There were plenty of available rooms and Claudia Miller had given them a choice.

'I think we'd like those two that adjoin each other on the top floor,' Patsy had said, as they followed the owners up the wide main staircase. 'You know, the two that face Fountains.'

The minute they had walked into the first of the rooms, Patsy had dragged Meredith to the window. 'Now isn't that the most spectacular sight!' she had cried. 'Behold Fountains Abbey! One of the two most beautiful ruined abbeys in the whole of England.'

Meredith had stared out across the sloping lawns and gardens of Skell Garth House, now obliterated by a covering of snow, her eyes fastening on the abbey. It rose up out of glistening white fields, huge, dark, monolithic, silhouetted against the fading greenish sky like some ancient tribute to God. She caught her breath, struck by its beauty. She agreed that it *was* magnificent; that was the only word to describe it, she thought.

'It's one of the best-preserved abbeys in the country,' Bill Miller had pointed out. 'There are stone masons working on it all the time, trying to keep it from crumbling away. It's a national treasure, you know.'

At that moment, and for a reason she could not fathom, Meredith had made up her mind to take a closer look, feeling oddly drawn to those ruins.

After they had taken tea with the Millers, the rest of the afternoon had been devoted to a complete guided tour of Skell Garth House, which dated back to the nineteenth century. By the time they had finished talking with the owners, going over all aspects of the inn and the pros and cons, it had grown dark outside. I'll go tomorrow, before we leave, Meredith had resolved, filled with determination to visit the ruins, a determination she did not quite understand.

This morning, when she was finishing her breakfast, Claudia Miller had come into the dining room to see if she needed anything else. Meredith had seized the moment and had asked her how to get to the abbey from the inn.

'You'll have to approach it on foot, that's the best way. Wear a pair of wellies, if you've got them with you, or boots. There's still a bit of snow out there by Studley way.' Claudia had then given her directions.

And I'm almost there, Meredith told herself, as she finally reached the top of the hill at the end of the avenue of limes. She glanced over at Studley Church, so picturesque in the snow, and at the obelisk nearby; she then directed her gaze to the lake below, glittering in the sunlight. The River Skell flowed beyond it, and there, just a short distance upstream, was the abbey.

Meredith stood for a moment longer on top of the hill, shading her eyes against the sun with one hand, thinking that Fountains looked more imposing than it had yesterday afternoon. But of course it would, she told herself. She was, after all, much closer to it now, viewing it with the naked eye, not through a glass window from a distant house.

Unexpectedly Meredith shivered. She felt as though a cold wind had blown around her, through her. But there was no wind this morning. Someone walked over my grave, she muttered under her breath, and then wondered why she had thought this, wondered how she knew such an odd phrase. She had never used it in her life before.

A strange sensation came over her. She stood very still, all of her senses alert. Instantly, she knew what it was . . . a curious feeling that she had been here before, that she had stood on this very spot, on this very hill, gazing down at those medieval ruins. It seemed to her that the landscape below her was familiar, known to her. She shivered again. *Déjà vu,* the French call it, *already seen,* she reminded herself. But she had not been here before; she had never even been to Yorkshire.

Yet this ancient place stirred something in her. The ruins beckoned, seemed to pull her forward urgently; she set off, began to hurry down the hill, her boots crunching on the frozen snow. She was almost running, slipping and sliding in her haste to get there. Several times she almost fell but managed to recover her balance and go on running.

At last, somewhat out of breath, she was hurrying into the centre of the ruined Cistercian monastery.

It was roofless, open to the vast arc of sky floating above it like a great canopy of blue, and the glassless windows were giant arches flung against that empty sky. Meredith stood there, turning slowly, her head thrown back as she gazed up at the soaring stone walls, jagged and broken off at the top . . . the immense columns only partially intact . . . the cracked flagstones covered today in pure white snow. A sense of timelessness enveloped her.

As she looked around, absorbing everything, her heart clenched, and she felt a strange sense of loss. So acute, so strong, so overwhelming was this feeling, that tears came into her eyes. Her throat closed with such a rush of emotion she was further startled at herself.

Something was taken from me here . . . something of immense value to me. *I have been here before.* I know this ancient place . . . somehow it's part of me. What was it I lost here? Oh God, what was it? Something dearer than life. Part of my soul . . . part of my heart. Why do I feel this way? What do these ruins mean to me?

Meredith stood perfectly still in the middle of the ruined abbey. Unexpected tears ran down her face, warm against her cold cheeks. She closed her eyes, not understanding what was happening to her; it was as though her heart were breaking. Something had been taken from her. *Or someone.* Someone she loved. Was that it? She was not sure. The only thing she really knew at this moment was that she was experiencing an immense sense of deprivation.

Opening her eyes, moving slowly, she went and stood near one of the walls of the monastery, resting her head against its time-worn stones. There was a stillness here, a quietness that was infinite; it calmed her.

Far away, in the distance, she heard the call of a lone bird high on the wing. There was a sudden rush of wind through the ruins, a moaning, sighing wind, and then everything was still, silent again.

She began to walk towards the cloisters, moving like a somnambulist. She knew the way. Once inside she was protected from the wind. And there was no sound here at all. Just perfect silence in these great vaulted halls of the cloisters.

Pain, she thought. Why do I feel pain and hurt and despair? What is it about this place that makes me feel like this? What does Fountains mean to me? She did not know. It was a mystery.

When Meredith returned to Skell Garth House an hour later, Patsy was waiting for her in the sitting room.

'My God, you look frozen to death!' her partner cried as she walked in. 'Come and sit by the fire and have a hot drink before we leave for the airport.'

'I'm all right.' Meredith took off her coat and walked across to the fireplace, warming her hands in front of the flames for a moment.

'I couldn't believe it when Claudia told me you'd gone to Fountains Abbey. And in this weather. If you'd waited for me to come down for breakfast I would have driven you there. At least, I would have driven you as close to the abbey as I could get.'

'I enjoyed the walk.' Meredith sat down on a chair, turned her head, gazed into the flames burning so fiercely.

'I'll go and order a pot of tea,' Patsy said, jumping up. 'Would you like something to eat? Pikelets, maybe? I know you enjoy them as much as I do.'

'No thanks, not now. The tea would be nice, though.'

When Patsy came back she threw Meredith a curious glance. 'This may be a strange thing to say, but you look quite white, as if you've seen a ghost.' Then she grinned and added, 'A couple of Cistercian monks perhaps, walking around the abbey's ruins with you?'

When Meredith did not respond with a gale of laughter, as she usually did, but looked at her oddly and remained silent, Patsy stared at her harder.

'*Is* there something the matter, Meredith?' she probed.

At first Meredith was silent, then said, 'No, there's nothing wrong. But I did have a funny experience at Fountains.'

'What happened?'

'I was drawn to the ruins. It was as though a *magnet* was pulling me forward. I practically ran there from Studley Church. I almost fell a couple of times. The thing was, Patsy, I couldn't wait to get there, to be in the middle of those ruins. And once I was standing in the centre of them I felt as if I knew that place so well. It was curiously familiar. And then something happened to me . . . I had this immense sense of loss. It was so overwhelming, I was shaken. I can't explain it, I really can't.' Meredith stared at Patsy. 'You probably think I'm crazy . . . Anyway, Fountains Abbey *does* mean something to me, of that I'm sure. Something special. And yet I can't tell you why that is so. I'd never heard of it until the other day. And I've never been there in my life.'

For a moment there was no response from Patsy, then she said, 'No, you never have. Not in this life, at any rate. However, maybe you were there in another. In the past . . . in a past life. Do you believe in reincarnation?'

'I don't know.' Meredith shook her head. 'To say I don't believe sounds so arrogant . . .' She shrugged, looking suddenly baffled. 'Who knows anything really about this strange world we live in?'

'Perhaps you saw a movie – a documentary about Yorkshire that featured the abbey. Perhaps that's why it's so familiar to you,' Patsy suggested.

'I don't think so. And how do you explain that peculiar sense of loss I experienced?'

Patsy said, 'I can't.'

A young waitress came in with the tray of tea; the two women fell silent.

Once they were alone again, Patsy remarked quietly, staring closely at Meredith, 'You were pretty excited last night . . . I mean about buying Skell Garth House. I hope your odd experience this morning hasn't made you change your mind.'

'No, it hasn't, Patsy. Quite the contrary. It's obvious that Fountains Abbey means something, although I don't quite understand what. Still, I see that as a good omen for the future. Anyway, I like the inn. You were right about it.' She gave her partner a warm smile. 'It's a little gem in its own way, and certainly it's got a lot more going for it than Heronside. Too many cushions *indeed*. Skell Garth is charming, and it has a great atmosphere, is loaded with comfort. Of course, it's a bit shabby, but it doesn't need any big money spent on it.'

'All Skell Garth House needs, in my opinion, is a good decorating job. And you're the best person to do it, Meredith.'

Meredith nodded, but made no comment.

Patsy lifted her cup of tea. 'Here's to our new inn, then. May it be ever prosperous.'

'To Skell Garth House.'

# Ten

Luc de Montboucher looked from Agnes D'Auberville to Meredith and said, 'You must allow six months at least for the remodelling. To cut the time down to four months will only mean disaster.'

Agnes said, 'We'd hoped to have the inn open by the summer –'

'That is not possible!' he exclaimed, cutting in swiftly. 'There's too much to do, and some of the work is major, such as the architectural changes you want. And which are necessary, I might add. Then there's new wiring, plumbing, windows, and floors. Most of the walls have to be re-plastered and sanded.' He lifted his hands in a typically Gallic gesture, and finished, 'To be honest, Agnes ... Meredith ... six months is going to be a tough schedule for the contractor, please let me alert you to that fact right now. I sincerely hope he can keep to it.'

'But the Manoir de la Closière is not such a large house,' Agnes remarked, and turned to Meredith. 'You've now been there twice this week. What's your opinion?'

It was Friday. The three of them were having lunch in the Relais Plaza of the Plaza Athénée Hotel in Paris, having spent the morning going over ideas for the transformation of the old house.

Now Meredith put down her fork and returned her French partner's look. 'You're right, Agnes, inasmuch as it's not a huge house, but it *is* in terrible disrepair, in much worse shape than the château was. I happen to think Luc is correct. And I doubt very much that we can get the remodelling finished in less time than he suggests. In fact, I believe it's a bit foolhardy to allow only six months.' Glancing at Luc, she asked, 'Don't you think it would be wiser to settle for eight?'

Before he had a chance to answer, Agnes exclaimed, somewhat heatedly, 'But we remodelled and redecorated Château de Cormeron in a year! And that's a much bigger place.'

'I know. However, the manor house at Montfort-L'Amaury hasn't been so well cared for,' Meredith pointed out. 'I think it's unfair of us to expect Luc to work with unrealistic time schedules. He's right, we're only going to end up with a disaster.'

Agnes was silent.

Luc nodded, gave Meredith the benefit of a warm smile. 'Thank you for understanding my problems.'

Meredith liked him. He was an attractive man, with a great deal of continental charm, yet sincere.

'When *would* we open the inn then?' Agnes asked.

'I think it will have to be next spring . . . the spring of 1996. I don't believe we have any other alternative. Luc's pretty clear in his mind about what we want, and he will soon know what's feasible. I suppose he could start the work in a month from now. Am I correct, Luc?'

'You are. I will complete my plans for your approval as quickly as possible. If you like them and give me the go ahead, I can have the contractor in there by the end of the month. He can start demolition of some of the interiors. And if there are no unforeseen problems we should be able to finish by June. I will try to complete the job in six months, not eight, as you suggested. Thank you for offering those extra two months; however, I don't think we'll be needing them.'

Meredith said, 'That's good to know.' Addressing Agnes, she continued, 'As soon as the contractor is finished we can bring in the other trades . . . the painters, paperhangers, etcetera, and they will be finished in four months quite easily. Starting next week, you and I can begin to create the decorative schemes.'

'Well, all right,' Agnes murmured. 'If you think it's going to take a whole year then it will.' She laughed, suddenly relaxing, and shrugged. 'I must admit, you're rarely wrong when it comes to a remodelling job.' Digging her fork into a piece of fish, she finished, 'The problem with me is that I'm over-anxious. I can't wait to get the new inn running properly and open to the public.'

'There's nothing wrong with that,' Meredith responded. 'But if we try to do it at breakneck speed it's asking for trouble.'

'I'm glad we're all agreed,' Luc said. 'And let me just add that the manor is charming, and has endless possibilities, especially since the grounds are also so pleasant. I think you've made a good choice.'

'Thanks to you, Agnes,' Meredith said. 'You spotted the house.'

Looking pleased, her nervousness about the schedule now abating, Agnes took a long swallow of white wine. 'Then it's settled. Luc will get the plans done quickly and once they're ready he can send them on an overnight to New York. Now . . .' She paused, reached out and squeezed Meredith's arm. 'What are *your* plans for the weekend?'

'Nothing special, really. I thought I'd take it easy, do a little shopping, and maybe go to the *Marché aux Puces* on Sunday. But please don't worry about me, Agnes, I know you've got your hands full.'

Agnes grimaced. 'I'm afraid I do, with Alain and Chloe both down with the flu. Thank God I haven't caught it from them.'

'I'm sorry they're not well, and you mustn't fuss about me, I'll be all right on my own this weekend.'

Luc lifted his glass, drank a little of his wine, and sat back in his chair, scrutinizing Meredith across the luncheon table. Eventually he said, 'If you really don't have anything special to do this weekend, I would like to invite you to my house in the country. I'm leaving tomorrow morning; we could drive there together, and I would bring you back to Paris early on Monday.'

'That's so nice of you, Luc,' Meredith murmured and hesitated. 'I don't know . . . I don't want to impose . . .'

'But you're not imposing, I invited you. And I would *like* you to come. It's not going to be a very fancy weekend with lots of guests, if that's what is worrying you. In fact, I must warn you, we will be there alone and you might find that boring. Although the countryside is beautiful, and perhaps you would enjoy it.'

'Well, thank you . . .' Meredith began and stopped, still uncertain.

Agnes looked from one to the other and jumped in, saying swiftly, 'Luc has the most charming old house. In the Loire. It's really unique, Meredith, you'll love it. You *must* go for the weekend.'

'Yes, do please come, Meredith,' Luc insisted.

'All right then, I will,' Meredith said, suddenly making up her mind. 'And again, thank you very much for inviting me.'

After lunch Agnes and Meredith walked back to the Havens offices, which were located in a narrow street off the Rue de Rivoli.

'I've been collecting fabrics and wallpapers for the past few weeks,' Agnes explained, once they were ensconced in her cluttered private domain.

Flopping down onto a sofa, she dragged two large shopping bags towards her and said, 'Come on, Meredith, sit here next to me and we'll go through some of these. I thought it would be a good idea to have something on hand, so we can start formulating our decorative schemes well in advance.'

'You must have scoured the whole of Paris,' Meredith laughed, joining her, plunging her hands into one of the shopping bags. 'I've never seen so many samples.' She took out a blue-and-red fabric and stared at it. 'I like this . . . it looks like a Manuel Canovas . . . oh yes, so it is.'

'He's very eligible, you know,' Agnes said, also delving into one of the bags.

'Who? Manuel Canovas? I thought he was married.'

'No, not Manuel Canovas. *Luc de Montboucher*. That's who I'm talking about.'

'Oh.'

'Why do you say *oh* like that? In that surprised tone?'

'Are you trying to be a matchmaker, Agnes?'

'Not really,' Agnes laughed. 'It hadn't really crossed my mind until he invited you for the weekend. Then it suddenly hit me . . . he's attractive, successful and, most important, single.'

'Divorced?'

'No, I don't think he's been married.' Agnes frowned and bit her lip. 'No, wait a moment . . . perhaps he *was* married and she died. I can't remember. He's a friend of Alain's, I'll have to double check that.'

'How old do you think he is? About forty?'

'I think he's a bit older than that, if I remember correctly. About forty-three perhaps. I'll ask Alain when I get home tonight and I'll call you at the hotel.'

Meredith laughed, shook her head. 'He's only asked me to go to his house for the weekend, he hasn't proposed marriage.'

'I know. On the other hand, my dear Meredith, I believe he's rather taken with you. I've noticed him looking at you over the past few days, and looking at you with great interest, I might add. In that certain way.'

'What do you mean by *certain way*?'

'With curiosity. It's perfectly obvious he wants to get to know you better. Do you like him?'

'Of course, otherwise I wouldn't have accepted his invitation to go to the Loire with him.'

'He's a very talented architect. But you know that from the examples of his work he showed you at his office yesterday. We've been lucky to get him for this job. And as I said, he's very eligible, which is most important.'

'The way you spoke, you must know his house,' Meredith murmured, changing the subject.

'Yes, Alain and I have been there a couple of times. In the summer . . . never at this time of year. But it's a lovely old place. Between Talcy and Menars.'

'Where's that in relation to our inn?'

'It's higher up, just up beyond Blois, closer to Orléans than Cormeron. Do you remember that time Alain and I took you to Chambord?'

Meredith nodded.

'Well Chambord is in a direct line to Talcy across the River Loire.'

'I think I know where you mean. What kind of house is it?'

'Big . . . Clos-Talcy has been in his family for hundreds of years. It's been well looked after, kept in good repair. I think Luc goes there most weekends; it's only a few hours' drive, closer to Paris than Cormeron.'

'I'm glad I brought some country clothes,' Meredith said, now suddenly wondering what she had let herself in for this weekend.

'Oh, you don't have to worry, I think he lives quite casually,' Agnes remarked and handed her a swatch of fabric. 'Do you like this?'

Meredith examined it and nodded. 'You know I love

red *toile de Jouy*. It would work well with black furniture or black accessories.'

'Luc really was looking at you in that certain way, *chérie*,' Agnes remarked, eyeing Meredith. 'I'm not inventing that.'

'I believe you,' Meredith answered, and began to laugh, amused by Agnes and her romantic notions.

# Eleven

Her first sight of Clos-Talcy was of a double image – the house itself and its reflection in the large ornamental lake in front of it.

'Oh how beautiful!' Meredith cried when Luc de Montboucher walked her around the bend in the driveway and directed her attention across the lake, pointing out the house in the distance.

'I wanted you to see it from here, not from the car,' he said. 'This view surprises everyone, and I must explain to you that it's one of my own special favourites . . . it's the reflection, of course, that intrigues me.'

'What a perfect house in a perfect setting,' Meredith murmured, almost to herself. She stood next to Luc surveying the great château with interest. It was built of pink brick and pale stone, topped with a roof of dark grey slate. There were a number of tall, slender chimneys rising up from the roof and she counted thirty-eight windows and five dormers.

The many tall trees surrounding the château were reflected in the lake, along with the façade of the house itself, and to Meredith there was a marvellous symmetry to the two in combination. Certainly it was the loveliest initial view of any house she had ever seen.

Turning to Luc, she asked, 'How old is the château?'

'It was built in the early seventeenth century, and the gardens were designed about fifty years later by Le Nôtre, the famous landscape artist.'

Taking hold of her arm, he continued, 'But come, let us go back to the car. Later, after lunch, I'll drive you around the park, and we can go for a walk in the gardens, if you would like. I must warn you, though, they are rather bereft-looking at this time of year.'

'Oh I don't mind that; in fact, I like gardens in winter. Very often they're interesting, different naturally, but still eye-catching.' She gave a wry little laugh. 'Well, some of them, anyway.'

'I happen to like winter gardens myself,' Luc remarked, opening the car door, helping her in, then going around to the other side.

Starting the car, he drove up the majestic avenue lined with plane trees, continuing, 'Fortunately, we haven't had much snow here this year, so we'll be able to have a pleasant stroll later in the day.'

Meredith nodded and turned her head, glancing out of the car window. She saw another lake, this one smaller than the first, and it prompted her suddenly to confide, 'I've always been drawn to houses that are on water, or very near it, although I've no idea why.'

'Oh, I understand that feeling well,' Luc replied, giving her a swift look, then immediately swinging his eyes back to the road. 'I have the same attraction myself. There's something truly wonderful about water in the middle of a land mass; it enhances natural surroundings as well as any buildings that might be nearby. We have a lot of water here in Talcy. Apart from the ornamental lake, there's the smaller one you just noticed, plus a fish pond near the orchard, a stream that runs through the woods, a waterfall, and innumerable fountains.' He began to chuckle. 'I had an ancestor who was obviously extremely fond of those . . . we've got over a dozen of them in the park, and some are quite magnificent, even though I do say so myself. You'll find you're never very far from running water at Talcy.'

Meredith smiled. 'That's nice . . . You know, Luc, all of my inns are near water too, except for Montfort-L'Amaury. That's the only thing I wasn't happy about when I first saw the manor earlier this week.'

'If you wish, I could create a lake or a pond at the new inn,' Luc volunteered. 'It's not so difficult to do, and there is a fair amount of land attached to the manor house. What do you think?'

'That might be rather nice. I'll talk to Agnes, and perhaps you could give me some idea of the cost.'

*'Mais certainement* . . . of course. Ah, here we are, Meredith, we've arrived at the house at last.'

Luc had driven into a large cobbled courtyard and parked; it was apparently the front entrance to the château. Wide steps led up to a huge double door made of dark wood embellished with iron ornamentation. Before they had even alighted, a middle-aged man in his shirt sleeves, wearing a black waistcoat and a green-striped apron, had come out of the house. He ran down the steps, a broad smile creasing his cheerful face.

*'Bonjour,* Vincent!' Luc called as he climbed out of the car and hurried to assist Meredith.

*'Bonjour, Monsieur,'* the man responded.

Luc and Meredith walked towards him. He shook Luc's hand.

Luc said, 'Meredith, this is Vincent Marchand, who, with his good lady Mathilde, runs this place. Vincent, this is Mrs Stratton.'

*'Madame,'* the man said, inclining his head reverentially.

Meredith smiled at him. 'I'm pleased to meet you, Vincent,' she said, stretching out her hand.

Shaking it vigorously, he responded, *'Grand plaisir, Madame.'* With a nod he hurried to the boot of the car and took out the luggage. Grasping several bags, he followed them up the front steps.

Luc led her into a vast entrance hall which was almost cavernous, with soaring stone walls and a stone-flagged floor. The pale-coloured limestone walls were hung with two Gobelin tapestries and a bronze-and-crystal chandelier floated down on chains from the high ceiling. The only piece of furniture was a long ornately carved and gilded console upon which stood two large stone urns filled with dried flowers; a huge gilded mirror hung above the console and there was a stone statue of a knight in armour in one corner.

Luc said, 'Let me take your coat,' and after she had shrugged out of it he carried the sheepskin over to a cupboard built into one of the walls.

A split second later, a door at the end of the hall flew open and a tall, plumpish woman came hurrying towards them on fast-moving, nimble feet.

*'Monsieur!'* she exclaimed, beaming at Luc before

flashing Meredith a glance filled with undisguised curiosity.

Luc kissed her on both cheeks. '*Bonjour, Mathilde.* I would like to introduce Mrs Stratton. As I told you on the phone, she's my guest for the weekend.'

Nodding, smiling, Mathilde stepped forward. The two women shook hands, and Mathilde said, 'I will show you to your room, *Madame*.' Glancing at Luc, she continued quickly, 'As you suggested, *Monsieur*, I have given Mrs Stratton the room of your grandmother.'

Luc guided Meredith towards the staircase, saying, 'I do hope you like your room, it was my grandmother's favourite. I'm sure you will . . . it overlooks water . . . the ornamental lake, actually, which was your first glimpse of Talcy. It was a lucky choice on my part, I think.'

'Yes, it was, and I'm sure I'll love it.'

Mathilde led the way upstairs, followed by Meredith and Luc, with Vincent bringing up the rear, carrying Meredith's two suitcases.

Mathilde marched them down a long corridor, thickly carpeted and lined with windows; the walls were hung with many paintings. Meredith sneaked a look at them as they hurried by, realized they were family portraits, probably of minor members of the family, since they were relegated to this corridor.

'*Voilà!*' Mathilde suddenly cried, flinging open a door. 'Here is the room of *Grand-mère* Rose de Montboucher. Whom everybody loved.'

'And feared,' Luc added, winking at Meredith. 'She

was quite a terror at times. But also very, very beautiful.'

Noticing her glancing around, Luc explained: 'This is the sitting room, the bedroom and bathroom are through that door over there. But to continue, my grandmother fell in love with this suite of rooms when my grandfather brought her to Talcy for the first time. And she made them hers. That's a portrait of her, by the way. The one hanging over the mantelpiece.'

Meredith followed his gaze.

Her eyes settled on the painting of an extraordinarily lovely young woman. Red-gold curls framed a piquant face set on a long white neck. Her eyes were bright blue under arched auburn eyebrows and her wide mouth had a generosity about it.

Walking over to the fire, Meredith gazed up at the portrait with great interest. The artist had captured something of the woman's personality . . . there was an inherent warmth in the smile, and happiness dwelt in that face as well. Rose de Montboucher wore a dress of palest pink chiffon with a softly draped collar and a string of pearls. Meredith decided the portrait had been painted in the 1920s.

'Your grandmother was absolutely gorgeous, no two ways about it,' she said, looking over her shoulder at him. 'I think she was probably a bit mischievous: there's a certain glint in those rather remarkable eyes and in her smile.'

Luc nodded. 'Quite an accurate assessment of her. *I* believe she had a lot of mischief in her, as well as a special kind of *joie de vivre*. It was a true gaiety that people found irresistible. I knew her as a much older woman than she is in that portrait. But even then I felt she was up to something all the time. Up to no good, my father always said. He was her firstborn and the favourite of her four children. I recall that she had a good sense of humour and was a marvellous ranconteur. I think she must have kissed the Blarney Stone.'

'Was she Irish?'

'She was. My grandfather met her in Dublin. At a ball. He had gone there to shoot.'

Mathilde bustled in from the bedroom with Vincent in her wake. 'Would you like to have help with your unpacking, *Madame*? I will send Jasmine to assist you.'

Meredith shook her head. 'Thank you, Mathilde, but I can manage.'

The housekeeper nodded, gave her a quick smile, then flew out of the room. Vincent hurried after her, endeavouring to keep pace.

'He's her shadow,' Luc murmured in a low voice, once they were alone. 'They're both the salt of the earth, and have worked at Talcy all of their lives, and their parents before them. They have two daughters, Jasmine and Philippine, and a son Jean-Pierre, who all work here at the château. I'll leave you now, Meredith, so that you can freshen up. Are you quite sure you wouldn't like Jasmine to come upstairs and help you with your clothes?'

'No, really, I'm fine, thanks.'

Luc looked at his watch. 'Ah, it's only just a little after twelve. Let us meet, then, in the library, in an hour, shall we say? Does that give you enough time?'

'Of course.'

He half smiled, turned on his heel and headed towards the door.

Meredith said, 'Luc, where *is* the library?'

He swung around, grinning, and answered apologetically, 'So sorry, I forgot you don't know the house. The library is the middle room of the *enfilade* . . . that's the series of rooms which adjoin each other, off the entrance hall on the right-hand side. We'll have a drink in there before lunch.'

'Yes, that'll be nice.'

The door closed softly behind him. Meredith turned back to the portrait of his grandmother; she studied it again for a moment or two.

'Irish eyes are smiling,' Meredith murmured aloud, thinking of the famous old ballad. And indeed Rose de Montboucher's eyes *were* full of laughter; and it was very much an Irish face, of course. It couldn't be anything else. Stepping back, Meredith stared at the portrait for a second longer, her head held on one side. Her eyes narrowed slightly; Rose de Montboucher reminds me of someone, she thought, but she had no idea who that was. Rose's grandson perhaps. No, not Luc. He was dark-haired with dark brown eyes. A woman with a red-gold hair and clear blue eyes . . . this image and a tiny fragment of a memory leapt into her mind. But it was fleeting, disappearing before she could grasp it properly. Shaking her head, she gave the portrait a last glance and went through into the adjoining bedroom.

The minute she entered it a smile settled on Meredith's face. It was charming, welcoming, with a fire burning brightly in the grate and the silk-shaded lamps turned on. The room was decorated in a mélange of greys and soft greyish blues. The walls were covered with silver-grey moire silk, the flowing, bouffant draperies at the three tall windows were of silver-grey taffeta, and the large four-poster bed was hung with the same taffeta that looked as if it had been hand-embroidered. On closer inspection, Meredith realized that the pink, red and yellow roses and trailing green vines had been hand-painted on the grey silk. There were several chairs and a loveseat covered in pearl-grey cut velvet arranged around the fire, and in a corner stood an unusual antique dressing table made entirely of Venetian mirror.

Fascinated, Meredith walked slowly around the bedroom, looking at everything closely, admiring its style and elegance, nodding to herself as her glance lighted on a particular painting or an *objet d'art*. Certain things in the room were worn, even a little shabby, but the overall ambience was one of old-world elegance, luxury and a bygone age. It also had a restful feeling, as did the adjoining sitting room which was decorated in a mixture of greyish pinks, smoky blues and greens, all taken from the colours of the Aubusson rug on the floor.

Moving across the bedroom, Meredith finally came to a standstill in front of the Venetian dressing table. Silver brushes with Rose de Montboucher's initials were lined up on the mirrored surface, and there was a collection of crystal perfume bottles, silver-topped powder bowls and rouge pots grouped together.

To one side of them stood a silver-framed photograph of a darkly handsome man in evening dress.

Meredith bent down, stared at it, and for a split second she thought it was a picture of Luc. Then she realized it was not he; the evening suit bespoke the 1920s. It was obviously his grandfather, Rose's husband. That's who Luc must resemble, she decided. His grandfather . . . he's the spitting image of him.

After unpacking her two suitcases, Meredith picked up her toilet bag and went through into the bathroom. Immediately she came to standstill, taken aback by its size and by the fire burning merrily in the white-marble hearth.

The bathroom was enormous, with a soaring window draped with white lace curtains, an old-fashioned tub on feet and bell pulls dangling over it to ring for the maids. She wondered whether they still worked but refrained from pulling one, just in case they did.

# Twelve

Downstairs in his office at the rear of the château, Luc de Montboucher sat at his drawing table, a series of blueprints spread out in front of him.

The plans had been done by a colleague in his architectural firm, and Luc had fully intended to go over them before lunch, hoping to give his approval. But so far he had paid scant attention to the blueprints.

His mind was not on work. It was on Meredith Stratton.

From the moment he had met her on Wednesday morning, out at the manor house in Montfort-L'Amaury, he had been intrigued by her; he was very taken with her, in point of fact. Being an architect and a designer he was an extremely visual man, and so it was her looks which had initially attracted him to her. He liked her height, her blondeness and fair skin, those smoky green eyes which told him so much about her.

She was a good-looking woman with a great deal of personal style, and he experienced a jolt of genuine pleasure whenever his eyes rested on her. He also appreciated her self-confidence and composure, found them reassuring. Skittishness in women invariably made him nervous.

Luc had realized within the first couple of hours of being in her company that she was businesslike, practical, professional, organized, and decisive, and, not unnaturally, these traits appealed to his love of order.

He couldn't abide chaotic women who dragged trouble in their wake, who lived in perpetual mess and created mess in other lives. Also, he found Meredith's energy and effervescent personality most appealing; they buoyed him up, gave him a sense of *élan*, the like of which he had not experienced in a long time.

What a pity she lives so far away in New York, he thought, tapping his pencil on the drawing table. But it was not so far away that it made a relationship impossible. There was, after all, a supersonic flight. He could be in Manhattan in three and a half hours, four at the most, on Concorde. He had made the trip from Paris to New York only three weeks ago, to visit a client. It had been easy.

Luc wanted, had the *need,* to know Meredith Stratton better. Much better. *Intimately*. He found her sexually attractive, more so than any woman he had met in some years. He realized on Wednesday night, after their first business meeting, that he desired her. If a man didn't know that after the first encounter, then when would he ever know? Luc suddenly wondered. And he felt certain it was the same way for a woman.

Almost against his own volition, he had confided in Agnes, but only to a degree. He had merely told her of his interest in Meredith, his wish to know her better. These confidences had been passed on

Thursday evening, when he had called her at home. He had not been able to help himself. Then he had invited the D'Aubervilles and Meredith to Talcy for the weekend, but Agnes had been obliged to decline because Alain and Chloe were ill with the flu.

Agnes had said he should issue the invitation to Meredith anyway. 'Don't worry,' Agnes had promised, 'I'll suggest we all have lunch after our Friday-morning meeting, and you'll find a way to invite her to the château. I'll lead you into it quite naturally.'

When he had demurred, Agnes had exclaimed, with a laugh, 'Don't be so faint-hearted, such a coward, Luc. Meredith has absolutely nothing to do this week-end, and she has no friends in Paris, other than us. I happen to know she likes you, so she'll accept the invitation. And you're going to enjoy being with her. She's wonderful. Everyone loves her.'

*Love,* he murmured to himself. Will I ever find love again? He wanted to, very seriously. He liked women, admired and respected them, and he wanted a wife. Certainly he did not relish the idea of living alone for the rest of his life.

So far love had proved elusive. After Annick his life had stopped. He had been numb. But eventually he had tried to start over, God knows he had, to start life anew, to have a worthwhile relationship. But there had been no success. Only abundant failure.

It was true he had known a couple of women in the last few years, and they had been perfectly nice human beings, but neither of them had ignited a spark in him. He had begun to wonder if the spark had left him forever, had quite recently decided that it had, convinced himself of it, really. Until Meredith. But she had so enthralled him, without even trying, that he had actually been startled at himself. So rare was this feeling, so strong this desire, this need to become part of another person, part of her life, that he felt bound to pursue her.

How often did a man feel like that? Once in a lifetime perhaps. Instantly he corrected himself. It was twice in his case; he had felt the same way about Annick.

Meredith Stratton, he said under his breath, and wrote her name on the notepad in front of him, stared down at it.

Who are you, Meredith Stratton? And why are you so troubled? Where does that deep well of sadness inside you spring from? Who was it that hurt you so badly they've scarred your soul? Who broke your heart? Instinctively, Luc knew Meredith had experienced great unhappiness. He saw pain mirrored in those smoky eyes, saw infinite sadness dwelling there. He wanted to ease the pain, chase away the sadness, if he could; he was sure he could, given the chance.

Luc had not wished to ask Agnes questions about Meredith, although he longed to do so. He had felt awkward about prying, which went against the grain. In certain ways, he felt that he did *know* Meredith, knew what she was truly like, the kind of person she was inside. A good woman.

What was that phrase his lovely Irish grandmother had always used? 'True blue,' Rosie de Montboucher would say to him, 'your grandfather is true blue, Luc.'

And so was Meredith.

The small black clock on the drawing table told him it was almost twelve-thirty. Throwing down the pencil, suddenly impatient, he stood up, stretching his long legs. He was tired of sitting, and he felt cramped after the drive from Paris this morning.

Leaving the office, he ran up the back staircase and down the corridor to his bedroom. Shrugging out of his blazer, he went through into the bathroom, where he splashed his face with cold water, dried it, and combed his hair.

Luc peered at himself in the mirror. There were a few silver strands in his black hair these days; he stared harder, thinking he seemed drawn, fatigued. There were lines around his eyes. He decided he looked older than forty-three.

Meredith was also in her early forties, he was certain of that. It was something Agnes had said about her age, before Meredith had arrived from London. He wondered if that was too old to have a child, then supposed it depended on the woman. He had always wanted a child. To carry on the line. But if he didn't have one, it wouldn't matter in the long run. Life was such a struggle, and Luc suddenly understood that he wanted to reach out, grab life, grab happiness. Loving someone was not about progeny.

*Meredith*. She could make me happy. I know it in my bones. Bones don't lie, Luc, Grandma Rosie used to tell him when he was a boy growing up. You can tell a lot by the bones, child, she would add. Breeding's in the bone, Luc. Look at horses. Even when the stamina's there, it's not enough. Got to have breeding in a racehorse. I know my horseflesh, Luc, I'm a good judge. *Oui, Grand-mère,* he'd answer dutifully. Luc, please speak English today. Yes, Grandmother. Always trust your bones, she would repeat. They never lie, Luc, never. Oh Grandma Rosie, he thought, smiling inwardly at this lovely memory of her, you were a genuine original.

Turning away from the mirror, Luc hurried into his bedroom, took a grey tweed jacket out of the armoire, put it on over his black sweater and dark grey slacks, and left the room.

He ran down the front stairs at a rapid pace, crossed the front entrance hall and strode into the library, glancing around as he did.

The fire crackled in the hearth, the drinks tray was well stocked and there was a bottle of Dom in the silver ice bucket, just as he had instructed Vincent. There was nothing to do but wait for Meredith to appear.

Walking over to one of the French windows, he stood looking out at the garden, thinking how arresting the parterres looked: the clipped, dark green hedges were covered with a light frosting of snow that highlighted their intricate geometric shapes. His thoughts moved on, turned to his sisters. How lucky it was they had decided not to come to Talcy this weekend. He loved them dearly and liked their husbands, but he was relieved, and glad to have the house to himself. He had no great seduction plans, that was not his style; he liked everything to happen naturally. But he did want Meredith to feel relaxed, at ease, not on display for his family.

There was a slight noise, the sound of a step.

Swinging away from the window, he looked towards the adjoining living room expectantly. Meredith was walking towards him and he felt that same jolt of pleasure at the sight of her, the rush of excitement inside.

Moving forward, he exclaimed, 'There you are! Come in, Meredith, come to the fire where it's warmer. Now, would you care for a glass of champagne?'

'That would be lovely, Luc,' she answered, gliding across the floor.

He went to open the bottle of Dom Pérignon, but could not resist looking at her surreptitiously out of the corner of his eye. She was wearing a beige check jacket over a cream cashmere sweater and trousers, and he thought she looked stunning. He bit back a smile. Of course she did. There was no question in his mind that he was quite prejudiced when it came to Meredith Stratton.

After bringing their flutes of champagne to the fire-side, Luc sat down on the sofa opposite Meredith and said, 'I hope you have everything you need, that you're comfortable in Grandma Rosie's rooms?'

'Oh yes, I am, thank you very much. I love them, and that bathroom. My goodness, a fireplace, no less.' She laughed and added, 'What a luxury. I feel thoroughly spoiled.'

He laughed with her. 'All of the bedroom suites on that floor have fireplaces in the bathrooms, but we don't often use them, only for guests really, and only when it's cold weather. It's such a lot of work, keeping all the fires going. In my great-grandfather's day, even

Grandfather's, they had armies of servants to do that, to look after everything. Nowadays it's hard to get staff, and expensive, so I keep such things as fires down to a minimum.'

'I can't say I blame you.' She looked across at him, smiled warmly. She liked him a lot, wanted to know more about him. 'Did you grow up here?' she asked, filled with curiosity.

'Yes, I did. With my sisters Isabelle and Natalie. They're younger than I, but we had great times together, and an estate such as this is a wonderful place for young children.'

'It must have been an idyllic childhood.'

'I suppose it was, although it didn't always seem so at the time. My father was rather strict. And rightly so.'

He observed her over the rim of the flute for a brief moment. 'You're looking rather wistful. Is something wrong?'

'Oh no, not at all,' she replied swiftly. 'I was just thinking how different my childhood was – ' Meredith stopped abruptly, wondering what had induced her to say this. She rarely confided details about her childhood to anyone.

Although he had no way of knowing her thoughts, Luc suspected that Meredith had said more than she had intended. He could tell from the startled expression on her face. Quickly he said, 'But you grew up in the country, too, didn't you? In Connecticut?'

She shook her head. 'No, I didn't. I suppose Agnes told you I come from Connecticut, that I have a family home there and an inn, and that's true, I do. But I grew up in Australia. My childhood was spent in Sydney.'

'You're an Australian?'

'Yes. At least, I was born there, and that's my original nationality, but I became an American citizen when I was twenty-two.' Leaning back against the tapestry cushions, she gave him a direct look and finished, 'That was exactly twenty-three years ago.'

'You're forty-five? But that doesn't seem possible. You certainly don't look it.' Luc was genuinely surprised.

'Thank you, I'm still forty-four, actually, Luc. I'll be forty-five at the beginning of May.'

'And I'm forty-three . . . I'll be forty-four on June third.' There was a small pause, and then he said carefully, not wanting to stir up bad memories, 'From the tone of your voice, I rather got the impression you didn't have a very good childhood.'

'I didn't. It was terrible. Horrible, really. No child should have to go through that,' she blurted out, and then bit her lip, averted her face, stared into the fire.

So that's the source of the pain, he thought, at least some of it. There's much more that she is concealing. He remained silent for a few moments, allowing her the space and time to compose herself.

Eventually, Luc said, 'I'm sorry to hear that you were unhappy, Meredith. What happened to you?'

'I was orphaned when I was young. Ten years old. My parents were killed in a car crash. I got pushed around a lot after that . . . it was rough, hard –' She cut herself off again, forced a smile, met his direct gaze. Hers was equally as candid, as she finished. 'But that's such a long time ago. I've forgotten about it really.'

Not true, he thought to himself, and asked, 'When did you go to America?'

'When I was seventeen. I went to Connecticut as an *au pair* with an American family who'd been living in Sydney. Later I worked for Jack and Amelia Silver. They sort of . . . turned my life around.' A lovely smile spread across her face. 'What I mean is, I was like a younger sister to them. You see, Luc, they weren't much older than me, in their early thirties. Anyway, they treated me like a member of the family. Amelia and Jack made up for . . . well, for all those bad years.'

Luc nodded, refrained from commenting. He sat staring into her smoky green eyes. The sadness of a moment ago had lifted, but he knew it still lurked at the core of her. He wondered if he could make it go away entirely; he was not sure. All he knew was that he wanted to try.

Meredith said, 'You're staring at me, Luc. Do I have a smudge on my nose or something?'

'No, you don't.' His dark brown eyes suddenly twinkled. 'I was just admiring you, if you want the truth. You're a beautiful woman, Meredith.'

She felt the colour rising up from her neck to flood her face and was mortified at herself. Men had paid her compliments before; why was she blushing because Luc had? 'Th-thank you,' she managed to stammer, and was relieved when the telephone began to shrill.

Luc rose, went to answer it. 'Clos-Talcy. *Bonjour.*'

After listening for a second, he said: 'Hold on for a moment, please,' and looked across at her. 'It's your daughter Catherine.'

Meredith's face lit up and she jumped to her feet. She stepped over to the desk, took the receiver from him, thanking him as she did.

Luc merely nodded, walked over to the window, stood gazing out, his head full of this woman. He felt he knew her intuitively, and yet she baffled him. There was an air of mystery about her. He found her irresistible.

'Hello, Catherine, how are you, darling?' Meredith asked, then listened attentively as her daughter's voice floated to her across the transatlantic wire from New York. Her smile widened. 'Yes, I'm happy for you, darling, I'm thrilled, actually.' She clutched the phone tightly, continued to listen, then said into the mouthpiece, 'Yes, I'll be back in Paris on Monday, and no, I won't be home for at least another week.' There was a pause at Meredith's end, before she answered, 'Yes, all right, I'll call you on Wednesday. Give Keith my love. Don't forget to tell Jon. Have a great weekend. I love you, Cat. 'Bye now.'

She replaced the receiver and smiled at Luc when he turned around to face her, an expectant look in his eyes.

'My daughter just got engaged. Last night. She's floating on cloud nine.' Meredith blinked and looked away, pushing back sudden tears. She was so happy for Catherine that her emotions got the better of her for a moment.

'What wonderful news! It calls for a toast and

another glass of bubbly, as Grandma Rosie used to call it.'

After filling their crystal flutes, Luc raised his and clinked it against hers. 'Here's to love . . . and happy endings,' he murmured, staring at her closely, his dark eyes on hers.

Meredith stared back, felt the warmth rising to fill her face again. 'Love and happy endings, Luc,' she repeated and took a sip of champagne. Then she went over to the sofa, where she sat down. She was very conscious of Luc de Montboucher all of a sudden.

Luc followed her, but remained standing, his back against the fire. 'How old is your daughter?' he asked.

'Twenty-five. And I have a son, Jonathan, who's twenty-one. He's studying law at Yale.'

A smile flashed across his face, and he exclaimed, 'I studied architecture there. Graduate school after the Sorbonne. What a coincidence! Does he like it?'

'Yes, he does.'

'I'm glad. I did, too. Best years of my life.' He chuckled.

'Were they really?'

'Up to a point. I had some other good years. Before. After.' He took a swallow of his drink, a reflective look washing over his face.

'Luc?'

'Yes?'

'Have you ever been married?'

'Oh yes. Didn't Agnes tell you about me?' He raised a brow questioningly.

'No.' She frowned. 'What makes you think she would?'

'Oh no special reason,' he answered and shrugged. 'I thought she might have, that's all. And yes, I was married. My wife died six years ago. Annick was in good health one day, dying of cancer the next. It was virulent; she went very quickly. Just six months after being diagnosed. She was only thirty-seven.' He paused, cleared his throat. 'We were married eight years.'

'Luc, I'm so sorry. How tragic. What a terrible loss for you.' Meredith looked up at him worriedly, hoping she had not upset him. How stupid she had been, thoughtless, to bring up his wife.

'We didn't have children,' Luc volunteered.

Meredith said nothing, gazed across the room, lost in thought.

Luc put down his drink on the coffee table between the two sofas; he threw a couple of logs onto the fire, straightened up. Lifting his drink, he took a sip.

The room had gone very quiet. The only sounds were the crackling logs, the ticking clock.

At last Meredith said, 'Nobody's life is ever easy, whatever we might think. There's always pain and heartache, trouble, problems, ill health. Loss . . . of one kind or another.'

'That is so . . . yes, it's very true what you say. My Irish grandmother was not only beautiful but also very wise. She was forever telling us, when we were growing up, that life had always been hard, was meant to be hard, and that it would never be anything else but hard. That is the earthly lot of us poor mortals, she would say, and therefore we should grab what bit of happiness we could whenever we could. And if we found the right person we must hang onto them for dear life. Forever. That's what she said, and I strongly suspect that Grandma Rosie spoke the truth.'

'I've never met the right person,' Meredith said, surprising herself, instantly regretting these words.

'I did. But she died.' Luc stared off into the distance for a moment, as if he could see something visible only to himself. Then he said, 'I've never met anyone else. But I haven't given up hope . . .' He looked at her pointedly, but Meredith did not appear to notice.

'Catherine's father died,' she suddenly said, 'but he was a married man anyway . . . I would never have been able to marry him. I divorced Jon's father . . . that was all wrong . . . we weren't right for each other at all . . .' She let her sentence float in mid-air, unfinished.

'Was that a long time ago? Your divorce?'

'Sixteen years.' Confessions, she thought. And more confessions. What's suddenly got into me? Why am I telling him all these private things about myself? This man is a stranger.

Luc said, 'You will meet the right person, Meredith. I know you will.' He wanted to add that perhaps she already had, but he refrained.

Mathilde appeared in the doorway at the far end of the library. She cleared her throat.

Luc glanced at her. 'Ah, Mathilde. Is lunch ready?'

'*Oui, Monsieur.*'

'*Merci.*' Turning to Meredith, he said, 'I don't know about you, but I'm ravenous.'

'Yes, I am too.'

As he led her across the library in the direction of the dining room, Luc explained, 'I asked Mathilde to make a fairly simple lunch. Vegetable soup, plain omelette, green salad, cheese and fruit. I hope that's to your taste.'

'It sounds perfect,' Meredith answered, looking at him.

Luc smiled at her warmly, and took hold of her arm, led her into the dining room where Mathilde was waiting to serve lunch.

Suddenly Meredith did not care what she had told him about herself. She knew he would not judge her; she trusted him.

She felt safe with Luc de Montboucher.

# Thirteen

After lunch Luc took Meredith on a tour of the park in which Clos-Talcy stood. As they walked they talked about a variety of things, but eventually the conversation came back to his grandmother. Luc told her several amusing stories about Rose de Montboucher, keeping her thoroughly entertained.

At one moment, she said, 'The way in which you speak about *Grand-mère* Rose really brings her to life for me. I wish I'd known her.'

'You would have enjoyed her,' Luc answered, glancing at Meredith. 'She was a true original. Strong of character, spirited and courageous, and she truly ran our family. Ruled it with an iron hand. In a velvet glove, of course.' He chuckled, continued, 'My father loved to tease her, and when her birthday came around he always used to lift his glass and say, "Here's to that great man whose name is Rosie," borrowing the line from Voltaire.'

'Who said those very words to Catherine the Great, when he met her in Russia for the first time,' Meredith remarked. 'She's one of my favourite characters in history. I've read a number of biographies about her. *She* was strong and courageous, too. And she made her own rules.'

'That's true, she did, but then most strong women do that, don't you think?'

'Yes, they do . . . sometimes they have to, because they have no other choice.'

Luc took hold of her arm and led her down a side path, heading for the orchard ahead of them. 'In 1871, when my great-great-grandfather acquired Talcy from the Delorme family, he built the fish pond over there. It's actually fed by the stream that flows through the wood. It was a marvellous bit of engineering on his part.'

They came to a stop by the edge of the pond, and Meredith peered down into its murky depths. 'There really are fish in it,' she said, sounding surprised.

'Of course. When I was a little boy, I used to fish here. My sisters and I all had rods and lines, and sometimes Grandma Rosie joined us. She was rather good at fishing.'

'I can just imagine.' There was a silence between them as they walked around the pond, turned, and headed towards the woods. After a moment, Meredith murmured, 'Your grandmother was a great influence on you, wasn't she?'

'Oh yes. She brought us up, you see. My mother died in childbirth, giving birth to our little brother Albert, who was premature. He also died that same week. It will be thirty-three years ago this summer, to be exact.'

'How sad for you and your sisters . . . for your whole family.'

'Everyone took it very hard, especially my father.

He never remarried, and I believe he mourned my mother until the day he died.'

'When was that, Luc?'

'Almost two years ago. He wasn't very old, only seventy-one, which is no age at all these days. He dropped dead suddenly of a stroke. He was in the stables, didn't know what hit him, thankfully. It would have been terrible if he had been an invalid; he was a very active man, a great sportsman.'

'And your grandmother? When did she die?'

'In 1990 at the age of ninety. She was wonderful right to the end, not a bit senile or decrepit, and she was very active, had all of her faculties. Oh yes, *she* was still the boss around here. One night she went to bed and never awakened, just died in her sleep, very peacefully. I was glad of that, glad she didn't suffer. Neither did my father, for that matter.'

'I think that's the best way to go, with your boots on, so to speak,' Meredith said, thinking out loud. 'Or when you're asleep, as your grandmother was. Dying of old age is the most natural thing.' Meredith turned to Luc, smiled at him. 'That painting of her in my sitting room is very lovely, isn't it? I was trying to figure out how old she was when it was painted.'

Luc's brow furrowed as he said, 'I'm not exactly sure. However, she'd just married Arnaud de Montboucher, my grandfather, and come to live at Talcy when she sat for the portrait. So she must have been in her early twenties.'

'That's what I thought. She reminds me of somebody, I'm not sure who.'

'My sister Natalie favours her, but you've never met Natalie. Or have you?'

Meredith laughed, shook her head. 'No, I haven't.'

'Natalie resembles Grandmother physically, she's really rather beautiful, but she's not like her in character. Neither is Isabelle. I'm the one who inherited Rose's basic character,' Luc confided.

'She really put her imprint on you, didn't she?'

'*Absolutely*. I have come to realize that I think like her, and I have a tendency to do things the way she did. When someone really influences you in childhood, you carry their imprint. Always, I think. It's like an indelible stamp. And who was it who put their imprint on you, Meredith?'

'No one did,' she answered almost fiercely, and bit her lip, suddenly aware that she had sounded angry. Speaking in a softer tone, she went on, 'I just muddled through on my own, doing the best I could, teaching myself. Nobody influenced me. There was no one in my life to do that, no one at all, I was completely alone.'

They had stopped walking a few seconds before, had paused near one of the fountains, now stood face to face as they spoke. The sadness invading her face touched Luc; he wanted to reach out, pull her into his arms. But he did not dare. He was about to say something comforting to her when she suddenly smiled. The bereftness vanished instantly.

Meredith said, 'But there was someone later, when I was a bit older . . . eighteen. Amelia Silver. She showed me how to do certain things, taught me about antiques and art. She had wonderful taste and was very artistic. Her husband Jack influenced me in certain ways, too.'

'Are the Silvers still living in Connecticut?'

'Oh no, they're both dead. They died years ago, over twenty years ago. Sadly, neither of them was very old.'

'I'm sorry. They were like family, weren't they?'

She nodded, half turned away from him. 'I was twenty-two when Jack died, twenty-three when Amelia followed him to the grave. I only had them in my life for a few years.'

Aware that the sadness had surfaced again, Luc took hold of her hand. 'Come on, let's walk down to the ornamental lake. It's so picturesque, one of the prettiest parts of the park.'

By the time they reached the lake, at the far side of the house, Meredith was beginning to feel unwell. A wave of nausea passed through her and a peculiar kind of exhaustion seemed to settle in her bones. Unexpectedly, she thought she was going to collapse, and she grabbed hold of Luc's arm, said in a faint voice, 'I don't know what's wrong with me, but I feel awful. Nauseous, and suddenly very tired.'

Luc looked at her in concern. 'I do hope you're not getting the flu, that Agnes hasn't passed on any germs.'

'I doubt it, and Agnes wasn't ill.'

'No, but her family were. Do you think it was the wine at lunch? Could that have upset you?'

She shook her head. 'I didn't drink very much. Anyway, I remember now that I felt a bit queasy when I arrived in Paris on Tuesday night. I'd spent the morning wandering around an old ruined abbey in

Yorkshire, and it was bitterly cold. That night I thought that I'd probably caught a chill. But I was all right the next morning, so perhaps I'm just tired in general, run down.'

'Perhaps. Let us return to the house. You must rest for the remainder of the afternoon.' So saying, he put his arm around her and together they walked back to the château.

Luc accompanied her upstairs to her rooms and fussed around her. He made her take off her boots and forced her to lie down on the sofa. After adding more logs to the fire, he brought her a thick cashmere wrap and laid it over her.

'Don't go away,' he said, smiling down at her. 'I'll be back in a few minutes with a pot of hot lemon tea laced with honey. It'll do you the world of good . . . one of Grandma Rosie's cures.' He left the room, closing the door quietly behind him.

Meredith leaned her head back against the pile of soft velvet cushions and closed her eyes; she was so sleepy she could barely keep her eyes open.

She must have dozed off, for she awakened with a start when Luc bent over her and moved a strand of hair away from her face. This intimate gesture on his part startled her for a moment, and then she realized that she did not mind. It suddenly seemed perfectly natural to her.

'I put the tea here on the ottoman,' he said, his voice low, concerned still. 'Drink some of it whilst it's hot. Now I shall go and let you rest.' He squeezed her shoulder.

'Thank you, Luc, you're so kind. I'm sorry I cut short our walk, but I –'

'Think nothing of it,' he said swiftly. 'It's not important.'

'Would you turn off the lamp, please?'

'Of course. Now rest.' He left the room.

Meredith turned on her side, lay curled in a ball under the cashmere wrap, staring into the fire's bright flames. The logs hissed and crackled and sparks flew up the chimney. She raised her eyes at one moment and gazed for a long time at the portrait of Rose de Montboucher.

The afternoon light was fading rapidly, the room filling with shadows, but the roaring fire and its dancing flames introduced a rosy glow. In the soft incandescent light it seemed to Meredith that the painting of Rose came alive. Her face was full of life, her delphinium-blue eyes brilliant, sparkling with joy, and the red-gold curls framed the sublime face like a halo of burnished copper. How beautiful she was ... so radiant.

Meredith's eyelids drooped. She drifted on a wave of warmth. Her mind was filled with that face ... memories jostled for prominence ... fragmented into infinitesimal pieces. She fell into a deep sleep. And she dreamed.

The landscape was vast and it stretched away endlessly, as far as the eye could see, miles and miles of desolation. There was something oddly sinister about this place where there were no trees and nothing bloomed on the parched, cracked earth.

She had been walking and walking for as long as she could remember. It seemed like forever. She felt tired. But some inner determination pushed her forward. She knew they were here somewhere. The children. She had followed them here. But where could they be? Her eyes darted around. The land was empty; there was nowhere for them to hide.

Help me to find them, please. Oh God, help me to find them, she pleaded. And immediately she understood that her prayers fell on arid ground. There was no God here. Not in this empty void. It was Godless, this netherworld.

And then unexpectedly she saw something moving near the pale rim of the far horizon. She began to run. The cracked dry earth suddenly gave way to mud flats and her shoes squelched and sank into the mud and sometimes stuck and her progress was slowed. She persisted. Soon the land was dry again. She ran and ran.

The specks on the horizon grew closer and closer, loomed up in front of her as if they had jumped backwards. She saw a young boy holding a girl's hand. Just as they had drawn closer to her, now they withdrew, moved forwards again, rapidly. She ran, almost caught up to them once more. They walked on slowly, the two of them, still hand in hand, perfectly in step. She called out to them, called for them to wait for her. But they did not. They went on walking as if they had not heard her. The sky changed, turned a strange greyish-green and a high wind began to blow, buffeting her forwards. Suddenly the boy flew up in the air, as if blown upward by a gust of wind. He disappeared into the sky.

The little girl was alone now. She suddenly turned around and began to walk towards her. Meredith hurried forwards to greet the girl, so wan, so pathetic, with her pale pinched face and big sad eyes. She wore black stockings and shoes, and a heavy winter coat. There was a small black beret on her head and a long striped scarf was wrapped around her neck. The label pinned to the lapel of her coat was huge. The girl pointed to it. Meredith peered at it, trying to decipher the girl's name written there, but she could not.

Suddenly, taking her by surprise, the girl began to run away. Meredith tried to run after her but her feet were stuck, encased in the mud. She cried to the girl to come back but she did not stop, just went on running and running and running until she was gone out of the landscape.

There was a cracking sound and then a terrible noise like shell fire and everything exploded around her . . .

Meredith sat up with a jolt. Her face and neck were bathed in sweat. She was disoriented, and it took her a moment to get her bearings. Then she realized she was in Grandma Rosie's sitting room at Talcy.

Outside a storm was raging, lightning streaking through the darkening sky, thunderbolts rattling the windows. She shivered and huddled under the wrap that Luc had put around her earlier, stared at the fire, grown low in the grate. And the fear was there inside, ravaging her.

Closing her eyes, she tried to push the fear away, not understanding why she was so frightened. She was here at the château, perfectly safe from the violent storm raging outside.

And then it came to her. She knew why she was so fearful. It was the dream. The dream that had recurred so many times in her life. She had not dreamed it for years now. Suddenly, the old, familiar dream had come back to haunt her, to frighten her again, as it always had in the past.

# Fourteen

Once she had returned to Paris, Meredith's thoughts frequently focused on her weekend at Clos-Talcy. And most particularly, Luc de Montboucher was at the centre of her reflections.

She liked him, more than liked him, in fact, and his kindness to her had left a lasting impression.

Kindness had always been important to Meredith, perhaps because she had experienced so little of it in her life. None at all when she had been a child, and growing up without kindness had made her acquire a carapace of iron. Only Mrs Paulson had been able to break through this tough protective shell; and then, of course, the Silvers, when she had gone to work for them at Silver Lake.

And just as kindness was important to a child, so it was to a grown woman, and especially a woman over forty. But this characteristic aside, she found him extremely attractive as a man.

Luc was very good-looking, darkly handsome and fine of feature, but that was not his most important asset, as far as she was concerned. Just a pretty face had long ago ceased to hold her interest.

She admired his intelligence and talent, and his integrity, which instinctively she knew was unassailable. He also had a good sense of humour, and she discovered they liked so many of the same things – good books, classical music, a glass of icy champagne in front of a blazing fire on a wintry night, not to mention houses built on water, stained-glass windows and the delicate paintings of Marie Laurencin. All in all, Luc was an impressive man and she was glad she had met him, glad she had accepted his invitation to go to the château in the Loire.

They had driven back to Paris early on Monday morning, and she had spent most of the afternoon with him and Agnes out at the Manoir de la Closière in Montfort-L'Amaury, going over the changes they wanted to make. That evening Luc had taken her to dinner at the Relais Plaza, and last night they had eaten at Grand Vefour.

They had laughed a lot over the past few days, and she had begun to realize what an enormous impression he was making on her, and just how much she really did care about him.

Meredith had known Luc only a week, but he was already under her skin, and she knew she was going to miss him when she returned to New York. In her mind she was already planning her next trip to Paris. There was business to attend to in Manhattan; also, she had to sign the initial documents for the sale of Hilltops Inn to the Morrisons. And she couldn't wait to see Cat, to hug her, fuss over her, and celebrate her engagement to Keith.

But all of this would take only ten days at the most, she had calculated, and then she would fly back on Concorde. In any case, she was needed in Paris because of the remodelling and renovation of the old manor house. The three of them had agreed on Monday that it must be modern and up-to-date in every way, whilst still retaining its basic character and charm. And of course it required her decorative imprint, the look and the stylishness which proclaimed it to be a creation of Havens Incorporated.

In the quietness of her hotel suite last night she had wondered what would happen after the inn was finished; she had an immediate answer for herself. The inn would take a whole year to complete, therefore she would be spending a great deal of time in this city. Paris. The City of Light. And of lovers.

Things will work themselves out, she had reassured herself in the early hours of the morning. A long time ago Meredith had come to understand that life had a way of taking care of itself.

Day by day, step by step, she had decided, as she had prepared for bed. It's the only thing I can do, and we'll see what happens. Everything must take its normal course.

Meredith knew only too well that a relationship which looked promising could quite easily come to nought, fizzle out in a flurry of recriminations and bad feeling. After all, that had happened with Reed Jamison. Her face had changed at the thought of him. What an unpleasant encounter that had turned out to be in the end. But then Reed and Luc were as different as any two men could be, poles apart.

Luc was so straightforward, so honest, she believed she would always know exactly where she stood with him. No game-playing there. He was a thoughtful, responsible, mature man whom she knew respected her; certainly she respected him.

Meredith had spent most of Tuesday with Agnes, and had been surprised that her French partner had not probed too deeply about the weekend; Agnes had asked only a few cursory questions. But then again, they had been very preoccupied with their plans for the inn and busy rushing around Paris. They had visited innumerable antique shops and fabric houses, taking polaroids of furniture and collecting samples of fabric and wallpaper. Since they had similar tastes and the same ideas about the decoration and furnishing of the inn, there were no problems in this respect.

It was on Wednesday afternoon, when they were sitting in Agnes's office at Havens, that Meredith mentioned Luc. The two of them were selecting fabric swatches and lining them up on a flat board, trying to create viable colour schemes.

Quite suddenly, Meredith said, 'Last night Luc invited me to the château again. For a long weekend.'

Agnes glanced up. 'I'm not surprised, he likes you a lot.'

'And I like him.'

Agnes laughed. 'Most women do. He's irresistible. I've always wondered why he's never remarried.'

'Perhaps it's taking him a long time to get over his grief for his wife.'

'Oh, so he told you about her?'

'Yes, which is more than you did, after you'd promised. I sort of blundered in on that one, and I was afraid I'd upset him.'

'I'm sorry I didn't phone you, as I promised, but Chloe was so sick I had my hands full. Anyway, Alain and I only had a chance to talk on Sunday afternoon, and I certainly didn't want to call you at Talcy to gossip about your host.'

'No, I understand that, and I'm glad you didn't. I would have been embarrassed.'

'Alain has known Luc off and on for many years, Meredith, but not really well. We only became a bit closer to him in the last year, mainly because he was designing a house for Alain's sister. And even so, he never discussed Annick . . . his past was sort of . . . well . . . *vague* to us, and we're not the kind to pry . . .' She did not finish her sentence, merely looked across at Meredith and shrugged.

Meredith said, 'I understand. You can know people, be very friendly, and yet not know too much about their private life at all.' She leaned back in the chair and crossed her long legs. 'There's so much I like about Luc, Agnes. He's very straight, honest. Also, he really listens, pays attention. That's a rarity these days.'

'I believe him to be the kind of man who's worth taking seriously. I know for a fact he's not a playboy. Not at all, not one bit the philanderer.' Agnes eyed Meredith, and probed, 'Could you become involved with him? On a serious level?'

There was a brief hesitation on Meredith's part and then she said, 'Yes, I could, Agnes. He's the type of man I like, the kind I thought I'd never meet again. Men like Luc are usually well and truly spoken for.'

'You are indeed correct, *ma chérie*, but I think Luc has chosen not to be spoken for. Until now. He did tell me he liked you, wanted to get to know you better.'

Meredith stared at Agnes. '*Oh*. And when was that?'

'Last week, just after he met you.'

'And you never told me. Thanks a lot, friend!'

Agnes burst out laughing. Shaking her head, her grey eyes full of merriment, she said, 'He didn't tell me not to say anything, but I thought discretion was the better part of valour, and all that. In any case, I didn't want to frighten you off him. I thought you'd probably bite my head off and tell me I was a romantic fool. Consider them, Meredith, the various men I've introduced you to in the past eight years. They were attractive, eligible, but you never seemed interested in them. Not one little bit.'

'I wasn't.'

'But you *are* interested in Luc?'

Meredith nodded.

'*Mmmm*, I can't say I blame you. He is very sexy-looking. Sensual, I think, no?'

# Fifteen

They worked together in Luc's office from the moment they arrived at Talcy until seven on Thursday night. And then they started again at nine the next morning.

Once more it was a long day, broken only by lunch. Late on Friday afternoon Luc put his pencil down and looked across the room at Meredith. She was seated at a small desk, pasting fabric, carpet and paint samples onto boards, creating her first schemes for the inn.

'I shouldn't have done this to you,' he said, leaning back in his chair, his eyes lingering on her.

'What do you mean?' she asked, looking up.

'I've kept you cooped up in this office since yesterday morning, and all because I wanted to work and wanted you near me whilst I did so.'

She said nothing, merely stared back at him.

He went on, 'I've been rushing, trying so hard to finish the plans for the pond, and complete this drawing of it. I feel guilty though, about you. I should have sent you walking or riding, or at least let you rest –'

'Luc, I enjoyed being here with you,' she interrupted, 'working alongside you. And I would have been doing the same thing in Paris anyway, sorting through the swatches, making my boards. Truly, it's been wonderful sharing this time here with you.'

'Has it?'

'Oh yes.'

'Meredith?'

'Yes, Luc?'

He opened his mouth to say something, changed his mind, and stood up, walked over to her. He placed the sheet of paper he was carrying in front of her on the desk. 'This is the drawing of the pond, as it will look when it's finished.'

'Oh Luc, how marvellous! It's like the fish pond here!'

'I positioned the pond near the small wood behind the manor in Montfort-L'Amaury, in the same way the pond is next to the orchard at Talcy. I think it is picturesque, don't you?' As he spoke he bent over her, his finger tracing the drawing of the pond, the copse, and the manor house in the background.

She could feel his warm breath against her neck and she held herself perfectly still, hardly daring to breathe. Her cheeks flamed and she felt an unexpected warmth spreading through her, desire flooding her.

He said, 'I wanted to please you, Meredith.'

Meredith half turned to look at him, tilted her face up to his. 'I love it, Luc, it's perfect.'

She smiled.

He was dazzled.

He said nothing. He was unable to speak. *I want you*. Those were the words on the tip of his tongue. It was the only thing he could think of at this moment. He had been thinking of it for days. He was about to tell her so, but instead he leaned closer to her and before he could stop himself he kissed her on the lips, lightly at first, and then as she responded ardently his kisses became more intense.

He paused after a moment, but only briefly, in order to pull her to her feet. She was in his arms instantly. He held her close; her arms went around his neck. They were clinging to each other, their passions rising.

Meredith thought: Oh Luc, my darling, I've longed for this, longed to hold you in my arms. But her thoughts were unspoken; his hungry kisses stopped her words.

And then he stopped abruptly and said, in a voice thickened by emotion, 'I want you, Meredith, I've desired you since the day we met.'

'Oh Luc –'

He was kissing her again, greedily, as if he were about to leave her forever. He pulled her closer to him, fitting himself to her body, and he thought how perfectly they blended together.

She knew this was how it should always be between a man and a woman. He was kissing her cheeks, her eyes, her brow, her neck, her ears. His mouth went back to her mouth, and then he whispered against her neck, 'I've thought about you so much, I feel as if we've already made love. Do you understand what I mean, how I feel?'

'Yes.'

'I'm serious about you, Meredith. Say no to me now if you don't feel the same way. Because once we start this, there's no going back. Not for me.'

'I want *you*, Luc, I feel as you do.

He held her away from him, his hands firm on her shoulders, and looked deeply into her eyes. Smoky green eyes, always mirroring her thoughts, her feelings, mirroring her soul. He had seen intelligence shining there, and reflectiveness and merriment, but also a deep-rooted sadness. Now he saw only desire and longing, and it was for him.

He took hold of her hand, and led her across the room, and still gripping her tightly he hurried her up the back stairs and down the corridor.

Once inside his bedroom, he locked the door with one hand, drew her into his arms, kissing her over and over as he walked her in the direction of the bed. Releasing her at last, he pulled down the quilt, threw his jacket on a chair, struggled out of his sweater and jeans. Slowly she undressed.

Luc reached for her, pulled her to him, repeating her name as they fell onto the bed. They lay together, still half dressed, their bodies entwined. He ran his hands up into her thick golden hair, caught hold of it, wrapped his fingers around it, brought his face down to hers, his mouth, his tongue grazing her lips, touching her tongue lightly, tantalizingly.

Meredith responded to him eagerly; she knew this was right, that it was meant to be. She harboured no qualms about this man. The desire in his voice, the yearning in his dark eyes had told her everything she needed to know.

Her heart lifted. She wanted him, wanted to feel his hands all over her like this, taste his kisses, savour his passion. She wanted to be with him, joined to him.

Luc was fully aware of her desire for him, her growing ardour, and this further inflamed him. The most sensual sensations rolled over him; he wanted to give himself up to them entirely.

Somehow they hastily shed the rest of their clothes, came back into each other's arms. He looked down into her face for a long moment, took pleasure from seeing her pleasure reflected there, now just visible in the fading afternoon light. He brought his hand to her face, traced a line down her cheek and across her mouth and he did so with tenderness.

Arms entwined, legs entwined, mouth on mouth, hands smoothing and stroking, caressing and exploring, each of them hungry for the other. It had been too long for them both.

Luc gave himself up to the pure joy of her touch, of her kisses falling on him. On his mouth, his face, his eyelids. He rolled on top of her, aligning his body to hers.

Silken arms, silken legs wove themselves around him, bound him to her, the most welcome and softest of ropes. He moved into her deeper, harder, heard the soft moans escaping her throat. Deeper and deeper he sank, revelling in the sheer pleasure of her, knowing he had found the right woman. At last. The woman he had known would one day come to him ... to fill the darkness, fill the void in him, and as he buried himself yet deeper in her there was, miraculously, the total cessation of pain. She had liberated him, set him free. He soared. Higher and higher.

Meredith was moving against him, matching his

rhythm; they were joined, became one entity. A perfect mating, he thought, and it was exactly as he had imagined, had known it would be.

And as she had known, too. Luc was touching the core of her, reaching to her heart, filling her as she had never been filled, not since she was a young girl . . . so long ago . . . time past. He slipped his hands under her buttocks, brought her closer to him. I want you closer still, she cried out silently, all of you, Luc, I want all of you. And she willingly abandoned herself to him.

Luc could feel his heart pounding as he moved against her, almost violently now, caught up in the rhythm of their moving bodies; their joy was mounting.

Oh God, he thought, there is only this. Only this woman. Only me and her and this joining. She is all I will ever want. For the rest of my life, until the day I die. With her I am made whole again. And then he stopped thinking as they moved together in a sudden frenzy, flying higher and higher until they reached that peak of pure sensation. He wanted it to last forever, this ecstasy.

And Meredith understood that she had found her true mate at last, after all these years. He carried her upwards with him.

He was shuddering, wracked by spasms, shouting her name as he lost himself in her. And she answered him, calling out, 'Luc, oh Luc.'

Later, when their frenzy had ceased, he held her in his arms, stroking her hair. She moved closer to him, draping her leg over his, and he tightened his hold on her.

Her face was against his chest. She kissed it, then he felt her smile.

'What is it?' he asked.

'What do you mean?'

'Why are you smiling?'

'Because I'm happy, Luc.'

'This is only the beginning,' he answered and bent over her, kissed the top of her head. 'I thought I would never find you.'

'Were you looking for me?' Her voice was light, filled with happiness.

'Oh yes, *ma chérie*, ever since . . . for a long time.'

'And I've been looking for you, although perhaps I didn't realize it. I was beginning to think I'd never find the right man.'

'Am I?'

'Are you what?' she teased, knowing what he meant.

'The right man, Meredith?'

'Oh yes, Luc, very much so, in every way.'

'We're good together, Meredith, very good. I enjoy every minute we are together, and just now, well, you gave me such pleasure I'm still reeling. And you? Did I please you?'

'Of course. You must know that.'

'Yes, I suppose I do, but it's nice to hear it from your lips, Meri.'

He felt her stiffen against him. 'What's wrong? Don't you like me to call you Meri?'

'I don't mind,' she replied quickly, catching the note

of concern in his voice. 'It's just that few people do.'

Pulling her around and up into his arms, he touched her face lightly, gazed into her bright eyes, and said in the softest of voices, 'I don't want to see that terrible sadness in your eyes ever again. There's been too much hurt and pain in your life, too much sorrow.'

She did not respond.

'I'm here for you, Meri, if ever you want to talk about it. Sometimes it is helpful to unburden oneself.'

'One day, perhaps.'

He nodded, leaned forward and kissed her on the lips. 'I've fallen in love with you, Meri.'

Meredith stared at him. Unexpectedly, tears welled up in her eyes. She swallowed hard, trying to push them back, but she could not. Slowly they rolled down her cheeks.

'Oh, *ma chérie,* don't weep, there's nothing to weep about.' Luc lifted his hand, wiped away her tears with his fingertips. 'Do you think you could fall in love with me?'

'I already have,' she whispered and began to cry again.

'Thank God!' Luc exclaimed, and kissed her on the lips. And as he kissed her cheeks and her eyes he tasted the salt of her tears. 'No more sorrow. I'm going to make sure of that,' he said against her damp face. 'Only happiness from now on, Meri.'

But he was wrong.

# PART TWO

## *Time Present, Time Past*

# Sixteen

Meredith stood at the far end of the drawing room, leaning against a Sheraton cabinet. The interior of the antique piece was illuminated, its shelves filled with priceless Meissen figurines.

A few minutes before she had wandered over to look at this unique collection and had suddenly felt weak. Reluctant to manoeuvre through the crowded room looking for somewhere to sit down, she had stayed where she was, nursing a glass of champagne.

She took a deep breath, hoping she was not going to have one of her attacks, which was what she had begun to call them. There had been two in January when she was in France, then three last month; she wondered how many she would have in April.

They passed as quickly as they occurred, and she was never the worse afterwards; nonetheless, they made her nervous. She never knew when one would strike her.

The other day, in the office, she had told Amy about them, had explained how they had started in Paris and had continued off and on.

Amy had said at once, 'They're becoming too frequent. I think you should get medical advice. Let me make an appointment for you with Jennifer Pollard.'

Meredith had shaken her head, told Amy not to call the doctor. Now she asked herself if she had been foolish. Perhaps she should have listened to her assistant. At this moment her legs were weak, she could feel the fatigue slowly creeping through her entire body, and she could not help wondering whether she would be able to last through the evening.

She must do that, no matter how she felt. Tonight was a very special occasion in her daughter's life, and in hers. It was Cat's engagement party and she had been looking forward to it.

Meredith believed that by rights *she* should have been giving the party, but Keith's sister Margery, and her husband Eric, had insisted on hosting it at their Park Avenue penthouse; she had had no alternative but to acquiesce.

But she fully intended to plan a celebration dinner for Cat and Keith, which she would give in the next few weeks, and she hoped Luc would be able to attend. He had spent the past week in New York with her, and had planned to stay on for the engagement party tonight. Then at the last minute he had been called back to France. A problem had developed with one of his larger architectural jobs, a shopping complex in Lyons, and his presence on the site had been imperative.

They were both disappointed he had been forced to leave. But he was coming back to New York in ten days, to spend a long weekend with her at Silver Lake; she could hardly wait for his return. They were very much in love, and in the past two months had grown extremely close. They were rarely apart when they were in the same city, and when separated by the Atlantic they spoke every day by phone. He's everything I want in a man, she thought now, missing him. How she wished he were here with her tonight.

Meredith constantly marvelled at her luck in meeting Luc, and at their extraordinary compatibility. Her children knew him now and liked him, and he was very taken by them. He and Jon got on extremely well; apart from having Yale in common, they were both sports fans and especially addicted to football. And Cat was equally at ease with Luc, since they both had artistic natures. He was impressed with Cat's talent as an illustrator, thought her an accomplished artist. She had been very proud when he had congratulated her on her fine children, noting the admiration in his voice.

Meredith now peered into the milling crowd filling the drawing room, wishing Cat or Jon would reappear. There were about sixty people present and she hardly knew any of them, only the immediate members of the Pearson family: Anne and Paul, Keith's parents, his sisters Margery, Susan, Rosemarie, Jill and Wendy, and his two brothers Will and Dominick. And Eric Clarke, Margery's husband, one of her hosts this evening.

The Pearson family was a large and boisterous American-Irish clan. As big as the Kennedy tribe, Cat had told her recently. However, the Pearsons did not hail from Boston; they were dyed-in-the-wool Yankees from the heart of Connecticut. It struck Meredith that the Pearsons were out in full force this evening, since there were innumerable aunts, uncles, cousins and their offspring present.

And we are only three, such a small family, she thought. Not much of a match for a crew like the Pearsons. Meredith felt unexpectedly overwhelmed, and then she experienced such a sudden sense of loss that she was startled. It was a feeling she could not rightly explain to herself.

Blanche and Pete O'Brien had come in from Silver Lake to attend the party, and they were extended family. But even so ... Meredith snapped her eyes shut, endeavouring to shake off that awful feeling.

Opening her eyes a moment later, she scanned the room wondering where Blanche and Pete were. Somehow she had lost track of them in the last hour. Perhaps they were in the crowded dining room, where a buffet table groaned with all manner of fancy hors-d'oeuvre.

Meredith felt strangely isolated, standing there alone, propped up against the cabinet. I must sit down, she thought, and decided to head for a chair near the fireplace. It was then that she spotted her daughter.

Catherine was glancing around, obviously looking for her.

Meredith raised her hand, waved.

Instantly Cat saw her, smiled, waved back and hurried across the drawing room.

'Mom, there you are, I've been looking all over for you,' Catherine said, rushing up to Meredith. 'Isn't this a wonderful party? I'm so excited tonight. I can't stand it.' She looked down at her left hand, gazed at her sapphire ring admiringly, then flashed it at Meredith. 'It's gorgeous, isn't it, Mom?'

'Beautiful, darling,' Meredith answered, and caught hold of Cat's arm to steady herself.

Catherine gave her a quick look, and exclaimed, 'Mom, are you all right?'

'Yes.'

'But you're very pale. Not only that, you look taut, tense. Are you sure nothing's wrong? Look, if you're not ill, is there something else the matter? You're not angry are you? I mean because Margery and Eric insisted on throwing the party?'

'Don't be silly, you know I'm not like that. I feel a bit tired, that's all. I've probably been overdoing it at the office.'

'Let's go and sit on the sofa over there, Mother. My feet are killing me anyway. These shoes are fab, but gosh, they're agony.'

Meredith allowed her daughter to guide her to a sofa near the fireplace, and she sat down gratefully. A moment ago she felt as though all of her strength was ebbing away. The last thing she wanted was to pass out here. She would be humiliated in front of all these people.

Turning to Catherine she said, 'Perhaps a glass of water would help. Could you get me one, please?'

'Of course, Mom. I won't be a minute.' Catherine threw her mother a reassuring smile and glided across the floor towards the large entrance foyer, where a bar had been set up.

No one would know her feet are killing her,

Meredith thought, watching her daughter float through the room as if she were walking on air.

How beautiful Catherine looked tonight, so elegant in her short, midnight-blue taffeta cocktail suit and Amelia's pearls. Her brown hair was cut in a sleek shape and her lovely, open face looked so young and fresh, her wide-set eyes very blue. Cat was tall, like she was, with long shapely legs. I can't imagine why she wants to wear five-inch heels, Meredith thought in bafflement, then leaned back against the sofa, trying to relax.

Suddenly, there was her son, pushing forward through the throng. She watched him walking rapidly towards her, tall, slender, as blond as she, with her green eyes. Cat resembled her father, whilst Jon took after her.

As he drew closer, she saw that he wore a worried expression on his lean face. 'Mom, what's the matter?' he asked, drawing to a standstill by her side. 'I just saw Cat getting you a glass of water, and she thinks you're not well. Are you ill?'

'No, Jon, I'm not,' she answered evenly, in a firm voice. 'Truly, darling. I felt a bit queasy earlier. Perhaps I'm tired.'

'You work too hard,' he said, bending his lanky frame over her, resting his hand on the sofa's arm. Bringing his face closer to hers, he dropped his voice. 'If you want to leave, I'll go with you. I wouldn't mind splitting this scene myself.'

'I'm fine,' she replied swiftly. 'And I don't think we can leave. It wouldn't be polite, and anyway we can't abandon Cat to all these Pearsons.'

'She's got Keith to protect her, and anyway she'll be a Pearson herself soon.'

Meredith frowned, searched his face. 'Aren't you having a good time, Jon?'

'Sure, it's okay, but . . .' He shrugged. 'I'm just here for Cat and you, Mom. I don't have a lot in common with this group.'

'*Oh.*' She drew back, looked at him closely. 'Are you trying to tell me something?'

Jonathan shook his head and grinned. 'No, not at all. And don't get me wrong, I like Keith. I think he's a pretty nifty guy, and he's great for Cat. But I'm not particularly close to their friends, my group's different, that's all.' He looked directly at his mother, grimaced, and finished, 'The Pearsons are a nice family, just a bit too social for me.'

'I know,' Meredith murmured. 'And I'm glad you came . . . for my sake and Cat's.'

'You can always depend on me, Mom. I wish Luc were here, he'd liven things up a bit.'

Meredith laughed. 'Here's Cat now.'

'With Keith hot on her heels,' Jon said, straightening up, glancing over his shoulder at his sister, who was heading their way.

'Here's your water, Mom.' Cat handed her the glass and sat down on the sofa next to her.

'Thanks, darling.'

'I'm sorry you're under the weather, Meredith,' Keith said, bending over her as Jon had done a moment before. 'Is there anything else I can get you?'

Meredith looked up into his freckled face, as always thinking how honest his light grey eyes were, and shook her head. 'Thank you Keith dear, but I'm feeling much better.' She smiled at him warmly, liking him, knowing he would make her daughter a good husband, just as Jon knew. Cat would be safe with Keith Pearson; he was devoted, loyal and loving.

Clearing her throat, Meredith said, 'The three of you are beginning to make me feel like an invalid.'

Keith grinned at her. 'We don't mean to, we just care about you, that's all.'

'You're very sweet, Keith,' she answered.

'You *will* come to dinner later, as planned, won't you?' Keith went on, fixing her with his serious grey eyes. 'I don't want to pressure you, but we'll all be disappointed if you don't. It won't be the same without you.'

Meredith answered, 'I wouldn't miss it,' and patted his hand reassuringly. 'Jon is my escort, he'll look after me.'

'Keith's right, Mother, the evening would certainly fizzle out for me without *you* at the engagement dinner,' Catherine said.

'I'll be there.' Meredith smiled at her daughter, loving her.

Catherine smiled back, lifted her left hand, tightened a loose pearl earring. The sapphire engagement ring flashed in the bright lamplight.

It's the colour of her eyes, Meredith thought. Jack's eyes.

'You're a good sport, Mother,' Jonathan said several hours later, as he helped Meredith out of her coat and hung it in the hall closet.

'It was a lovely dinner in many respects, and generous of the Pearsons to have it in the private room at La Grenouille. But they're a bit – '

'Overwhelming,' Jonathan interrupted and shook his head. 'My God, all those Pearsons, Mom! My sister's pretty brave, taking on that clan. I wouldn't want to, I can tell you that.'

'I know what you mean, but individually they're very nice really, and Keith's parents are lovely, Jon.'

'True, but Keith's sisters are a pretty rowdy bunch.'

'The problem is, darling, we're used to a whole different kind of family life, so much quieter. After all, there's only been the three of us all these years.'

'And thank God for that,' he answered, hanging up his overcoat. 'In my opinion you deserve a medal, sitting through the dinner the way you did, all those toasts. *Mind-boggling*.'

Meredith laughed. 'Yes, it was a bit much. But I began to feel better once we left the apartment, and I got some fresh air. And I do like the food at La Grenouille.'

'You didn't eat very much.'

She smiled at her son. 'I'd like a cup of tea, Jon, how about you?'

'Great idea.'

He followed his mother into the kitchen and glanced out of the window. The lights of the Fifty-Ninth Street Bridge twinkled brightly against the dark night sky; beyond he could see another bridge glowing in the distance. Beautiful glittering city. He had always loved Manhattan. Jonathan stared down at the East River flowing far below and then across at Roosevelt Island. Funny how his mother always wanted to live near water, needed to, really. This was the second apartment she had owned on Sutton Place. He liked this one the best; they lived in the penthouse and the views of Manhattan were spectacular.

Meredith said, 'When are you going back to New Haven?' and put two cups and saucers on a tray as she spoke.

'Tomorrow morning. Early. I'll do it in under two hours. It's not that bad a drive. By the way, has Cat indicated when she wants to get married?'

Meredith nodded. 'This year, certainly. They don't want to wait too long, she told me. I've suggested September. It's very lovely at Silver Lake at that time of year.'

'Early October's better, Mom, when the leaves are turning. I think an autumn wedding would be picturesque.'

'You're right, and I did suggest that only the other day. Cat's going to let me know sometime next week, so we can get the invitations engraved and sent out, make proper plans.'

'Aunt Blanche is all worked up about the reception,' Jon said, laughing. 'She's been planning it for weeks. In her head that is . . . she told me tonight that she wants to top your wedding reception, which she was apparently involved in.'

'Very much so. In fact, she really designed and planned the entire thing by herself. She has such a talent for that kind of occasion. Make the tea, Jon, the kettle's screeching its head off.'

'Okay. Why don't you go and sit in the library. I'll bring the tea.'

'Thanks, darling,' she said, and did as he suggested, walking out of the kitchen, across the entrance foyer and into the library, which overlooked the water. She went to one of the windows, stood staring out. A great barge was floating down, loaded with cargo, heading for the docks, no doubt.

Meredith never got tired of looking at the East River. There was a great deal of traffic on this waterway and something was always moving on it, going up or down.

Her thoughts turned to Catherine as she swung away from the window and went and sat down near the fireplace. She was going to give her the best wedding any girl had ever had, make sure that she –

Jon interrupted her thoughts when he said, 'Where do you want the tray, Mom? Over there by you, I guess.'

'Yes, that's fine, put it here on this coffee table.' Meredith moved a pile of large art books to make a space.

Meredith poured, and they sipped their tea in silence for a few minutes, and then Jon suddenly said, 'Are you going to make it permanent with Luc?'

Startled, Meredith gaped at him.

Jon said, 'What I mean is, are you going to marry him, Mom?'

'He hasn't asked me,' Meredith replied.

'But would you, if he did?' Jon pressed.

'I honestly don't know.'

*'Why?'*

'Why don't I know? Is that what you mean?'

'Yes.'

Meredith lifted her shoulders in a small shrug. 'I just don't, that's all. It would be a big step for me to take, it would mean rearranging my life completely.'

'So what? I think you *should* marry him.'

'You do, do you?'

'Sure. You're in love with him, he's in love with you. I bet if you gave him half a chance, he'd ask you.'

Meredith said nothing.

'You've been used to having *us* with you always, Mother. The Three Musketeers, remember? That's what you used to call us. Cat's getting married, starting a whole new life soon, her own family. And I expect I'll get married when I meet the right woman. I just don't want you to be all alone one day.'

Meredith stared at her son, touched by his words, then her brows drew together in a furrow. 'You're worrying about my old age, is that it, Jon?'

Laughing, he shook his head. 'You'll never be old, Mother. You'll be beautiful forever. You're the greatest-looking forty-four-year-old I've ever seen.'

'And you've lived such a long time,' she shot back, laughing with him. 'Known so many women.'

Jonathan's face sobered when he continued, 'I just don't want you to be by yourself, lonely later in your life.' He cleared his throat, and gave her a piercing look. 'When I was little I used to hear you . . . *crying*, Mother. Sobbing as if your heart were breaking, at night in your bedroom. I used to stand outside the door and listen, hurting for you inside. But I didn't dare come in, even though I wanted to comfort you.'

'You could have,' she said softly, touched by his words.

'I was afraid. You could be very fierce you know in those days. Do you remember, I once asked you why you cried at night, when I was a bit older?'

'Yes, vaguely.'

'Do you recall what you said?'

Meredith shook her head.

'You told me you cried because you'd lost someone when you were a child. When I asked you who, you wouldn't answer me, you just turned away.'

Meredith stared at her son, speechlessly.

'Mom, who was it that you lost? I've always wondered.'

'I don't know,' she replied after a long and thoughtful pause. 'If I did I would tell you, Jon. Truly, I would.'

Her son rose and came and sat next to her. He took hold of her hand, looked into her face. His own had a loving expression on it. Slowly, he said, 'It broke my heart to hear you crying. I wanted to help you and I didn't know how. It's always worried me that you cried in that way.'

'Oh Jon.'

'That's why Luc is so important to me . . . I want him for you, Mom, he's such a great guy, and he loves you. Maybe he can make up for . . . everyone that hurt you.'

During the night Meredith awakened.

Immediately she slipped out of bed, put on a dressing gown and went into the library. There was a tray of drinks on a console table and she poured herself a small brandy in a tall glass, added soda water, then carried it over to a chair. She sat down, made herself comfortable, took a sip of the drink.

Lately she had discovered that it was far better to get up when she awakened in this way. It was easier to think through what was troubling her when she was sitting in a chair, rather than lying down in bed.

Now placing the glass on the coffee table, she sat back, relaxing, thinking of her son's words of earlier.

Jon had taken her by surprise, but she had also been moved by his words, his loving concern. Although she did not want him to worry about her, it was gratifying, in some ways, that he did. Her son cared about her wellbeing, and that was important to her.

She had tried to bring her children up properly, had always striven to do the right thing for them, and she believed she had succeeded. Catherine and Jonathan had turned out to be good human beings, with all of the right values. They functioned, were well adjusted, very normal young people, and thank God they had never been tempted by their peers to experiment with drugs, nor did they drink much. She had been lucky with her children.

It was startling to her that Jonathan remembered how she used to weep at night, when she thought her children were fast asleep. The odd thing was, she had no recollection of ever telling him she cried for someone she had lost when she was a child. Yet she knew he was not lying. Why would he? She must have forgotten what she had said to him, all those years ago.

And who had she meant? She had no idea; she was truly baffled.

Sighing to herself, finishing the drink, Meredith got up, walked back to her bedroom. Perhaps now she would be able to fall asleep. Certainly she must try. She had a busy day ahead of her. She took off her dressing gown and got into bed. Almost immediately she began to doze, drifting off into a deep sleep.

There were many children. Boys and girls. Some of them were very young. Three and four years old. Others were older, perhaps seven and eight. They were all walking across the vast landscape. Some were hand in hand, boys and girls, and girls together. Many walked alone. Too many children, she thought, filling with fear. I'll never find that little girl again. Or the boy. They are lost to me. Where are they? They must be among these children. I must find them.

She was frantic, running in amongst the children as they walked, perfectly in step, towards the distant horizon. She peered into their faces. She did not know them. They marched across the parched, cracked mud flats like automatons, staring straight ahead, paying no attention to her. Their faces were glazed, empty of expression, their eyes dull, lifeless.

Where are you going? she cried. Where are you heading? None of them answered her. Have you seen them? she cried. The girl with the long striped scarf? The boy with the cap? Please tell me if you've seen them.

The children turned en masse, veered to the right, began to walk towards the sea. She had never seen the sea before. The water was black, the colour of oil. She shuddered and called to the children to come back.

They did not heed her. She was afraid, shivering with fright. The children marched on. No! she cried. Stop! Still they paid no attention. They marched on and on, marched right into the sea. Slowly they sank, disappeared from sight. Oh God, no! she cried. Nobody heard her.

The landscape was empty. She was the only one left. And then she saw them. They were skipping towards her holding hands. The little girl with the scarf and the boy in his school cap. She waved. They waved back. She began to run. She was getting closer and closer. The labels pinned to their coats were huge, bigger than before. They fluttered in the wind, blew against their necks, obscuring their faces. Suddenly they turned around, veered to the right and began to walk towards the sea. No! she shouted. No! Stop! Don't go there! They did not listen. She ran and ran. Parts of the arid landscape opened up, cracking in half. She jumped over the cracks. Went on running. Her breathing was laboured. Finally she caught up with the children. She reached out, grabbed the boy's shoulder. He resisted. Then slowly he swung around. She screamed. He had no face. She grabbed the girl's arm. The girl turned. Meredith screamed again.

'Mother, what's wrong, what is it?' Jon exclaimed, bursting into her room, snapping on the light as he did. He hurried over to the bed.

Meredith was sitting up, her eyes wide with fright, her face and neck damp with perspiration. She shook her head.

Her son sat down on the bed. He stared at her closely, took hold of her hand, wanting to comfort her. Again he asked, 'What is it, Mom?'

Meredith took a deep breath. 'I had a strange dream, a nightmare.'

'It must've frightened you. I heard you screaming.'

'Yes, it must have. I'm sorry I woke you, Jon.'

'That's okay.' He frowned. 'What was the nightmare about?'

'It doesn't make sense, it was very muddled.' She forced a smile onto her face, hoped it reassured him. 'Let's forget it. I'm all right, really. Go back to bed, honey.'

Jonathan leaned forward, kissed her lightly on the cheek. 'I'm just across the hall if you need me.'

'I'm fine,' she replied.

Long after Jonathan had returned to his own room, Meredith lay awake, remembering every detail of the dream, pondering on it.

It was a dream she had first dreamed many years ago, when she was young and still lived in Sydney. It had recurred off and on over the years; and then it had stopped all of a sudden when she was in her thirties. Unexpectedly, she was having the dream again – twice in the space of two months.

The details were always the same. The barren landscape, sinister and Godforsaken. The children marching to their doom in the sea. Her desperation as she tried to find the little girl and boy.

She always woke up in a cold sweat. And she was always fearful when she awakened. Why? What did the dream mean?

# Seventeen

'How many of these attacks have you had?' Dr Jennifer Pollard asked, scrutinizing Meredith across her desk.

'I had two in January, two in February, three in March, and two this month . . . last Thursday at Catherine's engagement party and again on Sunday. The last was the worst one yet. It lasted most of the day, and I felt more debilitated than usual. So much so, I didn't go to the office yesterday. When I went to work this morning I was still feeling very tired. I thought I'd better come and see you.'

'I'm glad you did,' the doctor answered. 'Earlier, on the phone, you told me the symptoms are always the same – nausea and a feeling of total exhaustion. Are there no other symptoms, Meredith?'

'None at all.'

'No vomiting, fever, pains in your stomach, diarrhoea, high temperatures, headaches, migraines?'

Meredith shook her head. 'No, nothing like that. I just feel sort of queasy, but mostly very tired, exhausted really.'

'I see.' Jennifer brought her hand up to her chin, looking thoughtful.

Meredith leaned forward intently. 'Jennifer, what do you think is wrong with me?'

'Frankly, I'm not sure. First we must give you a very thorough examination, then I'll be able to make a proper diagnosis.' As she was speaking the doctor opened the folder in front of her and scanned the top page. 'I looked at your records just before you arrived, and you had a check-up three months ago, at the end of December. You were in perfect health then, Meredith.'

'Yes, I know, that's why I'm so baffled.'

'We'll get to the bottom of it, don't worry.' Closing the folder, the doctor went on briskly, 'All right then, let's start by getting the tests done.'

She stood up, walked around the desk.

Meredith also rose.

Jennifer Pollard put her arm around Meredith's shoulder. 'Don't look so apprehensive. We'll get to the bottom of the problem.'

'What do you think it *could* be?'

Jennifer hesitated, then said, 'Any number of things, but I don't want to make guesses. Also, I'm not going to pretend it's nothing, Meredith, I've too much respect for your intelligence, and in any case, you know that's not my way. I believe in being very honest with my patients. The kind of exhaustion you've described can mean any number of things. It could be caused by anaemia, a hormonal disorder or a chronic infection of some kind. Then again, it might be tiredness due to burn-out.'

'Not burn-out, no!' Meredith exclaimed. 'Most of the time I'm full of energy and vitality.'

'Let's go through to Angela,' Jennifer said, leading the way out of her office and down the corridor. 'You know the routine after all these years. Angela will take blood samples, do the EKG and a chest X-ray. We'll also need a urine sample from you. Once these tests are completed, I'll give you a thorough physical examination.'

Opening the door of the small examination room, Jennifer said, 'I'll send Angela in with a gown, so you can get undressed.'

'Thank you,' Meredith murmured.

Exactly one hour later Meredith was dressed again and sitting in her doctor's office, once more staring at Jennifer Pollard. Her expression was worried and there was a questioning look in her eyes. 'What did you find?'

'Nothing.' Jennifer smiled at her confidently. 'As far as I can tell, there's nothing physically wrong with you. No lumps, no swelling anywhere, and you didn't flinch when I put pressure on your abdomen. And your reflexes and blood pressure are normal. Of course, I don't know what the blood and urine tests are going to reveal, and I won't have the results for a couple of days. But frankly I'm pretty sure they're going to be normal, too. It seems to me that you're as physically fit as you were three months ago.'

'Then how do you explain the attacks?'

'Not sure.' Jennifer leaned back in her chair, focused her eyes on Meredith. 'Nerves, maybe? Stress? You push yourself very hard. For as long as I've known you, which is a good ten years now, you've been a workaholic, to use a nasty word. And stress can play havoc with a person's nervous system.'

'I realize that, but I don't feel stressed out, not at all. Honestly, Jennifer, I've been taking it a lot easier lately, especially when I'm in France. I'm remodelling an inn there, but I have a very good French partner, who takes a load off my shoulders. And I spend long weekends with my boyfriend in the Loire. He has a country house there.' Meredith leaned forward and finished, 'I've never been happier on a personal level. Business is good, the kids are great.'

'I'm glad to hear it,' Jennifer answered. A reflective expression flickered in her eyes, and after a moment she asked, 'Is there anything at all worrying you?'

'No. As I just said, my life has never been better.'

Jennifer nodded. 'Let's see what the blood tests tell us. I'll call you as soon as they come in. Probably by Thursday, Friday at the latest.'

Meredith was signing a batch of letters late on Thursday afternoon when the private line in her office rang. Picking up the phone, she said, 'Hello?'

'*C'est moi, chérie*.'

'Luc!' she exclaimed. 'How are you, darling?'

'Not so good, I am afraid.'

'What's wrong?' she asked, her voice rising slightly, her concern apparent.

Luc sighed over the transatlantic line and explained, 'I am so terribly sorry about this, Meredith, but I cannot now come to New York this weekend. I am afraid I am stuck here in Lyons. Because of the job, I am needed here.'

'Oh Luc, what a shame, I was so looking forward to it,' Meredith said. 'I'm very disappointed, darling, but I understand. Work has to come first.' She too sighed resignedly.

'I have to be on the spot,' he continued. 'There is an unanticipated condition in the foundation that is going to require major redesign. I can't just delegate this particular part of the job. We have run into subsurface ledgerock which requires redesigning the foundation in the first of the buildings. It is vital that I am here. I'm meeting with the contractor and structural engineer tomorrow. We'll complete the design on Saturday and bring in the crew next week.' There was a fractional pause before he laughed quietly and said, 'I don't suppose you could come to Lyons, could you?'

'I'd love to but I can't. I told you, I have the closing on the inn tomorrow. And I have to be in New York on Tuesday for a meeting with the bank. Henry Raphaelson is going to the Far East the following day, so I can't change that appointment. Next week is a bit tough for me, Luc. I'm due in Paris soon, in case you've forgotten.'

'I hadn't, *ma chérie*, I was just hoping to see you before.'

Meredith glanced at the calendar on her desk. 'I was planning on being there at the end of April, and I will be staying the whole month of May, you know.'

'Well, that is wonderful! I am happy. But I shall miss you, Meri.'

'And I will miss you too,' she said. They went on talking for another ten minutes. At one moment, Meredith almost confided in him, almost told him about her visit to the doctor, and then changed her mind.

She did not want to worry him. He had enough problems with the shopping centre in Lyons.

'There's absolutely nothing physically wrong with you, Meredith,' Jennifer Pollard said, reclining in her chair, smiling at her. 'I'm happy to tell you the blood and urine tests are normal.'

Meredith smiled back, filled with relief, and then she frowned and asked, 'But this morning when you called the office you told Amy you wanted to see me, talk to me.'

The doctor nodded. 'I do.' Jennifer cleared her throat, and went on, 'There's still something wrong. Those attacks. Now, in my experience, people who suffer from the kind of exhaustion you described to me earlier this week usually do so all the time. In other words, it's chronic. And permanent. It doesn't come and go, the way you have described *your* attacks.'

'Meaning what?'

'Meaning that your attacks could easily become increasingly frequent, until, in the end, you too have the exhaustion on a permanent basis, rather than only occasionally.'

Meredith was silent; she sat staring at the doctor.

'Let me explain something to you, Meredith,' Jennifer said. 'Very often this kind of exhaustion is due to psychological causes.'

'Do you think that's the case with me?'

'Possibly. You could be suffering from psychogenic fatigue.'

'What does that mean?'

'That the cause of your tiredness is an emotional

problem. Or alternatively, you could be depressed, without knowing it.'

'I'm definitely not depressed!' Meredith answered with a dry laugh. 'When I was here on Tuesday, I told you my life was on an even keel, and rather wonderful these days. I'm in love with a fabulous man, he with me.'

'I believe you, and I'm happy for you. However, let's not dismiss the idea of psychogenic fatigue due to an emotional problem, or an upset mental state. What's causing it, the thing that's bothering you, doesn't necessarily have to be of this moment. It could go back in time.'

'How do you treat something like that?' Meredith asked nervously, eyeing her doctor warily.

'We have to determine the nature of the actual problem, get to the root of it, then treat it.'

'*Psychiatry*. Is that what you're getting at, Jennifer?'

'Yes, it is. If you are suffering from psychogenic fatigue, I recommend that you see someone immediately. The illness, and it *is* an illness, is not going to go away on its own. Furthermore, it could become chronic.'

'Who . . . who would you recommend?' Meredith asked quietly.

'Dr Hilary Benson. She's very sympathetic, you'll like her. And she's a brilliant psychiatrist. Her office is just around the corner from me on Park and Sixty-Ninth.'

Meredith leaned back in the chair, looking worried.

'There's nobody saner than you, Meredith,' Jennifer said swiftly, responding to the look in Meredith's eyes.

'I can testify to that. Listen to me, you might not have psychogenic fatigue at all. It could be stress . . . I said that to you earlier in the week.'

'I don't think so.'

'Then you will go and see Hilary Benson?'

Meredith nodded.

# Eighteen

Meredith was nothing if not decisive, and once she had agreed to see the psychiatrist she told Amy to make an appointment for the following week.

After that she tried to put the matter out of her mind; she had always had the ability to pigeon-hole problems until it was the appropriate time to deal with them. And so she managed to get through the next few days without dwelling too much on her health or mental state, and fortunately there were no more attacks.

On Tuesday afternoon, when she walked into Dr Hilary Benson's private office, her first impression was of a good-looking but stern woman. The doctor had a rather lovely face with high cheekbones, and the palest blue eyes that appeared almost transparent. But her mouth had a severe set to it and her dark brown hair was pulled back in a plain chignon that was singularly schoolmarmish.

There was a no-nonsense, businesslike air about her, and for a split second Meredith was put off, thinking that she might be a cold fish. Then she recalled her physician's words. Jennifer had told her that Hilary Benson was a sympathetic person as well as a brilliant psychiatrist.

I must give her a chance, give this a chance, Meredith decided. She needed to understand what was wrong, why she was having these attacks. According to Jennifer, only a psychiatrist could help her get to the root of the problem.

After greeting Meredith pleasantly, and shaking hands, Dr Benson said, 'Come and sit down, Mrs Stratton.'

'Thank you,' Meredith answered and followed the doctor over to the desk, where they sat facing each other.

Meredith, studying the doctor, decided that she was probably the same age as Jennifer and herself: in her early forties.

The psychiatrist said, 'Dr Pollard and I have spoken at length. She has filled me in, given me your medical history in general. Apparently you're a very healthy woman.'

'Yes, I am, thank goodness,' Meredith replied, smiling faintly.

Dr Benson nodded, and sat back in her chair, taking stock of Meredith for a moment. Beautiful woman. Puts up a good front, she thought. But there's pain in her, hurt. I can see it in her eyes. Getting straight to the point, she said, 'Jennifer believes you could be suffering from psychogenic fatigue.'

'So she told me.'

'Let's talk about that fatigue, the attacks you've been having. When did the first one occur, Mrs Stratton?'

'Early in January. I was in Paris on business. I'd been travelling part of the day, and that night, after

I'd checked in to my hotel, I felt quite ill. Exhausted, a bit queasy . . . nauseous.'

'Where had you travelled from?'

'England. Not a long trip by any means, and travelling doesn't affect me usually. I have a lot of stamina and tremendous energy, Dr Benson.'

'So, feeling ill was unusual for you. I understand.' There was a moment's pause, then Hilary went on, 'Had anything happened to upset you that day?' She put her elbows on the desk, steepled her fingers, and looked over them at Meredith.

'No, it hadn't. To tell you the truth, I thought I was probably coming down with the flu. That morning I'd been outside for a long time in the cold, in the snow. I'd been wandering around a ruined abbey. I thought that –' Meredith stopped short, abruptly cutting herself off.

'You thought what, Mrs Stratton?' Dr Benson asked, giving Meredith a quiet, encouraging smile.

'I was going to say that I thought I'd caught a chill when I was lingering at the abbey. But come to think of it, something odd *did* occur that morning, something quite strange, really.'

'And what was that?'

'I had a peculiar sense that I'd been there before. It was a feeling of *déjà vu*.'

'But you had *not* been there before. Is that what you're saying?'

'Yes, it is.'

'Can you recall how you actually felt?'

Meredith nodded.

'Will you tell me about it, Mrs Stratton?'

'Yes. But let me explain something, Dr Benson. I saw the abbey for the first time the day before . . . I was looking at it from the window of an inn, viewing it across snow-covered fields. It was beautiful. And I realized I was curiously drawn to it. The next morning I had a little time to spare, I was waiting for my English partner to get up, come down to breakfast. Well, anyway, not to digress . . . I had a little free time, so I went to look at the abbey close up. As I approached the ruins I felt that I was literally being pulled towards them, and that even if I'd wanted to, I couldn't have turned back. A short while later, when I finally walked into the actual ruins, I had the queerest feeling that I'd been there before. It was strong, rather overwhelming.'

'And you *are* positive you didn't know this place?'

'Oh yes. I had never been to Fountains Abbey before; I was visiting Yorkshire for the first time in my life.'

'I see. Did you experience anything else? Did you have any other emotions that morning?'

'Yes, I did, as a matter of fact. I felt a great sense of loss. And sadness . . .' Meredith paused. There was a reflective look on her face when she added quietly, 'I experienced a feeling of true sorrow.'

'Have you any idea why?'

'Not really, although I do recall that I had a sudden flash of clarity at that moment. I was sure that I had lost someone there, someone very dear to me. Or rather, that someone had been *taken* from me. It seemed to me that I *knew* those ruins, and I sensed a tragic thing had happened there. Yet it didn't feel like a bad place. Quite the opposite. I had a sense of belonging, and I was at ease.'

'Do you know England well, Mrs Stratton?'

'Not really, although I've been going there for over twenty years. However, as I just said, I had never been to Yorkshire.' Meredith leaned forward, gave the psychiatrist a piercing look. 'How do you explain what happened to me that morning?'

'I don't think I can. At least, not at this moment.'

'Do you think my experience at Fountains Abbey triggered the first attack?'

'I don't know.' Hilary Benson shook her head. 'The human mind is a strange and complex piece of machinery. It takes a lot of understanding. Let's leave your experience at the abbey alone for the moment, and go in another direction. I understand from Dr Pollard that you're an Australian. Please tell me a little about yourself, about your background.'

'I'm from Sydney. I grew up there. My parents were killed. In a car crash. When I was ten years old. Relatives brought me up.' Meredith sat back in the chair, crossed her legs and gave the psychiatrist a cool, very direct look.

Hilary Benson returned this glance and thought: Her expression is candid but she's lying. I know it. What she's just said has been well learned. She's repeating it by rote to me, just as she's done before, to countless others.

After a short pause, Hilary said, 'How sad for you to be orphaned so very young. Who was it that brought you up?'

'Relatives. I just told you.'

'But *who* exactly?'

'An aunt.'

'I see. Did you have any siblings?'

'No, I didn't. There was just me. I was always on my own.'

'Is that actually how you felt, that you were on your own, even though you had an aunt?'

'Oh yes, I always felt that way.'

'Tell me how you came to this country, Mrs Stratton.'

'I'll be happy to,' Meredith replied, and then added, 'I'd like you to call me Meredith, Dr Benson.'

The doctor nodded. 'Of course. Please give me a little background about your arrival in America.'

'I came with an American family who'd been living in Sydney. The Paulsons. I'd been working as an *au pair* for them since I was fifteen. Mr Paulson was transferred back to the States two years later, when I was seventeen, and they asked me to go with them. So I did.'

'And your aunt didn't object?'

'Oh no. She didn't care. She had four daughters of her own. She wasn't interested in me.'

'And so she gave her permission for you to travel to America with the Paulson family? Am I understanding this correctly?'

Meredith nodded. 'She helped me get my passport.' Meredith made a small grimace. 'She was glad to be rid of me.'

Hilary Benson frowned. 'You were not very close then?'

'Not at all.'

'And what about your parents? Were you close to them?'

'Not really.'

'But you were an only child. Only children are usually very close to their parents.'

'*I* wasn't, Dr Benson.'

The psychiatrist was silent. She looked down at the pad in front of her, made a few notes on it. She was more convinced than ever that Meredith was lying about her background. It seemed to her that everything was too well rehearsed, and Meredith spoke in monosyllables, as if she was afraid to elaborate in case she made a mistake. Or revealed something she was trying to hide.

Hilary put down her pen, and looked up, smiling at Meredith. 'You came to New York with the Paulson family. Did you ever go back to Australia?'

'No, I didn't. I stayed here. In Connecticut. That's where we lived, near New Preston. Up above Lake Waramaug. I was with the Paulsons for another year, and then Mr Paulson was transferred to South Africa. He was a trouble-shooter for an international advertising agency, and he was always moving around.'

'And did you go there with them?'

'No, I didn't want to go to Johannesburg. I stayed in Connecticut.'

'*Alone?* You were only eighteen.'

'Well, Mrs Paulson agreed I could stay on, because I had found myself a job. At the Silver Lake Inn. She came to meet the Silvers and liked them. They were providing room and board, as well as a wage, and she approved. The Silvers were from an old family and well known, very respected in the area.'

'So at the age of eighteen you were on your own, working at an inn. How did you feel about this? About being so . . . so independent.'

'I was pleased, but I wasn't really on my own, Dr Benson. The Silvers treated me like family right from the beginning, and they made me extremely welcome. I felt at home, as I'd never felt before in my life, actually.'

'If I am understanding you correctly, they treated you like a daughter. Am I right, Meredith?'

'Not a daughter, no, they weren't that much older than I was. More like a sibling, a younger sister.'

'How old were the Silvers?'

'Amelia was thirty-six when I went to work there, and Jack was thirty-two.'

Hilary Benson nodded. 'And what was your job at the inn?'

'I started as a receptionist, but it was always understood, right from the beginning, that I would help Amelia with the office work. She was very overloaded, and since she was paralysed, things weren't easy for her. I became her assistant, as well as the receptionist. And I helped Jack a lot with the management of the inn.'

'What had happened to Amelia Silver? Why was she paralysed?'

'She'd had a riding accident when she was twenty-five, just after they were married. She injured her spine and she lost the baby she was carrying. It was a great tragedy. But she coped very well.'

'Tell me more about her. She was obviously someone you cared about.'

'Oh yes, I did. She was remarkable, and she taught me so much. Not only that, Amelia was the most beautiful woman I've ever known, ever seen. She was like Vivien Leigh in *Gone with the Wind*. That was the first thing I said to Amelia ... that she resembled Vivien Leigh.'

'Then she must have indeed been beautiful. You say she taught you many things. Would you explain this to me, please?'

'She loved art, antiques, and decorating, and I learned about those things from her. But I also learned about courage . . . she was so courageous herself. And I learned about dignity and decency from Amelia Silver. Those were some of her other qualities.'

'What you're saying is that she gave you certain values.'

'Yes. And so did Jack. I learned about true kindness from him, and he encouraged me, helped me to understand business. He taught me a great deal about running an inn, almost everything I know, in fact. He was a very smart man.'

'Was it a busy hotel?'

'Only at weekends. It was quiet during the week. Silver Lake Inn was and is very much a weekend retreat, all the year round. But more people came in the good weather, in the spring and summer, than they did in winter. And we were always full in the autumn, of course, when the leaves changed colour. People loved to come and see the foliage. They still do.'

'You describe the inn in a very loving voice, Meredith.'

'I do love Silver Lake. I always have, from the very first moment I saw it. And it was the first real home I ever knew. My first safe haven – ' Meredith stopped. She had said too much. She shifted slightly in the chair and focused her eyes on the painting above Hilary Benson's head.

Hilary said, '*Safe* haven . . . had you not felt safe before then, Meredith?'

'It's just an expression,' Meredith hedged.

'You speak so beautifully about the Silvers, I know you must have loved them, obviously still do. How are they – '

'They're both dead!' Meredith exclaimed, interrupting the psychiatrist.

'I'm sorry to hear that. Their passing must have been a great loss to you.'

'It was. I was heartbroken.'

'When did they die?'

'Jack died in 1973. He was only thirty-six. And Amelia about a year later, just a bit longer than a year, actually, late in 1974. She was young too, only forty-one.'

'How truly sad for you to lose two people you cared about so close together. They must have loved you very much.'

'Oh, yes, they did,' Meredith said softly, remembering them, cherishing them inside. 'That's why it was so hard for me when they died. Jack was the first person to ever show me any affection in my life, put his arms around me, comfort me.'

There was a brief silence before Hilary Benson asked softly, 'Are you saying that there was a sexual relationship between you and Jack Silver?'

'I'm not suggesting anything of the sort!' Meredith shot back, her voice rising. 'Amelia also loved me as much as Jack did. She showed me a great deal of affection too, but it was verbal. The poor woman was in a wheelchair. *She* couldn't very well put *her* arms around me.'

'I understand,' the psychiatrist replied quietly, noting Meredith's anger, her over-reaction, realizing that there had indeed been a sexual relationship between Meredith and Jack. But it was far too early to probe this. Meredith Stratton was not ready.

Meredith looked at her watch; it was four o'clock. She had been here almost an hour. 'I have an appointment at my office at four-thirty, Dr Benson, and in any case I think our first session is finished, is it not?'

'Yes, you are correct,' Hilary answered, glancing at the clock on her desk. 'I believe we have another appointment on Thursday of this week.'

'Yes, we do,' Meredith replied, standing up. As she shook the doctor's hand and then left the private office she wondered if she would keep it.

# Nineteen

Despite her misgivings, Meredith did keep her Thursday appointment with Dr Hilary Benson. And she agreed to three more sessions the following week. So far, the psychiatrist had not pinpointed the cause of her attacks of fatigue.

It was at her fifth appointment, at the end of the second week, that Meredith finally decided to make it their last meeting.

'I don't think we're getting anywhere at all, Dr Benson,' she said slowly. 'I've talked endlessly and you've listened, and we've not really progressed, or come up with anything of real value. We don't even know if I'm suffering from psychogenic fatigue.'

'*I* think you are,' the psychiatrist said firmly.

'But I haven't had any more attacks.'

'I know. But that doesn't mean very much.'

'Let's make this our last session.'

'I think that would be foolish of you,' Hilary answered quietly, observing her closely. 'Something is troubling you. I am certain of that. We just haven't uncovered it yet.'

'I can't come again for several weeks. I'm going to London and Paris for a month.'

'When are you leaving?'

'On Wednesday or Thursday of next week.'

'Shall we see how we do today, Meredith?'

'All right,' she agreed. She did so because she had grown to like Hilary Benson, felt at ease with her and she trusted her. Even though they had not discovered the root of her problem, she knew that she was at fault. For years she had lived with half-truths, had hidden so much, that it was difficult to unearth it all now.

Hilary said, 'I'm not going to mince my words today, Meredith, I'm going to be brutally honest with you. I know you are lying to me. I know you had a sexual relationship with Jack Silver. I want you to tell me about it.'

Meredith was so taken aback, she blurted out, 'It wasn't just sexual. We loved each other – ' Breaking off, she swiftly averted her face, regretting the words.

'You mustn't be embarrassed,' Hilary murmured in an understanding tone. 'I'm not here to judge you, I'm only trying to help you . . . Talk to me, tell me about Jack, tell me what happened all those years ago at Silver Lake Inn. I *know* you'll feel better if you do, and having more information about your past will help me to trace the cause of your illness.'

There was a very long silence. Meredith did not answer. Instead she rose, walked over to the window, stood looking down onto Park Avenue, thinking about Jack and Amelia and herself, and all that had happened between them so long ago. It had shaped her life, changed her life. She had had so much from them. She did not want Hilary to think badly of Jack. Or of her.

Turning around, she walked back to the chair and sat down opposite Hilary, who was behind the desk. 'Yes, it's true. We did have a sexual relationship, but we also loved each other very much. I haven't wanted to talk about it to you because I don't want you to misunderstand. Words can sound so cold when they're said. Perhaps you could never understand the love, the emotions, the feelings there were between us, because you were not a witness to them. No one could understand.' Meredith gave her a long hard stare.

Hilary nodded. 'I appreciate everything you're saying. I know exactly what you mean. But as I just told you a moment ago, I'm not a judge or juror, just your doctor. And if I am to help you I must understand your past.'

'Do you think that's troubling me? Our love affair? Jack's and mine?'

'I'm not sure, Meredith. I have to hear everything first before I can make an assessment.'

'Because *I'm* sure it isn't. However, I will tell you about Jack, and what happened between us when I went to work at the inn in 1969.'

'Are you comfortable? Would you prefer to sit over there on the sofa?'

Meredith shook her head. 'No, I'm fine here. I just want to preface what I have to say about Jack with something else. A couple of weeks ago, my son Jon told me he used to listen to me crying at night when he was very young. And I did, I wept endless tears until I thought I had none left in me, but I always had. I cried for a lot of things in those days, but especially for Amelia and Jack. I missed them so much.'

Meredith paused, cleared her throat, then she went on softly, 'Jack Silver was my true love. I loved him from the first day I met him. He had fallen in love with me too that day. He called it a *coup de foudre*. I'd never heard that phrase before. He told me what it meant . . . struck by lightning. But we kept our love at bay for weeks, never disclosed our feelings for each other. Then Amelia had to go away. She had to visit her mother in Manhattan. The old lady was very ill, probably dying, and Jack drove Amelia into the city. When he returned on that July night he came looking for me. He found me down by Silver Lake, lying in the grass, trying to cool off. It was extremely hot that month, blistering. He said he needed to talk to me about Amelia; he was worried because he had left her alone with her sick mother, and with only two young maids in attendance. He wondered out loud if he ought to drive me into the city the next day, so that I could stay with Amelia, look after her. I told him I would be happy to go, that I'd do anything for him.

'And then suddenly, without either of us understanding exactly how it happened, we were in each other's arms, kissing each other. I'd never experienced anything like it before, the surging passion, the desire, and the love I felt for him. I hadn't had any previous sexual encounters, Dr Benson, and Jack was upset when he discovered I was a virgin, scolded me for not telling him. But by then it was too late. We had already made love.'

Meredith fell silent for a second.

Hilary Benson said nothing; she knew it was wiser

to wait until Meredith was ready to continue her story.

After a few moments, Meredith said softly, 'And we went on making love to each other even after Amelia returned to Silver Lake. We just couldn't help ourselves, we were so crazily in love. Jack had been terribly deprived for years, before my advent on the scene. He told me that he had once gone to a call girl in New York, but that it had been a failure, a waste of time because he had no feelings for her. But Jack loved me, and he loved Amelia, and we were scrupulous. We never displayed our intense feelings for each other in front of her. Jack always said that Amelia must never know about us, that we must not hurt her in any way whatsoever, and we never did.'

'She never knew?' Hilary asked.

Meredith did not answer. Instead, she went on, 'Then one day I missed my period. I knew I must be pregnant. I was terrified, convinced Amelia would guess the baby was Jack's child. But he reassured me, told me Amelia would never suspect. I believed him, why wouldn't I? I loved him beyond all reason. When I asked him what I would say to Amelia, how I would explain my pregnancy, he said I must invent a boyfriend, say that my new young man was the father. Later I could explain to her that my boyfriend had let me down, gone away and left me in the lurch, left me to fend for myself. And this is what I did tell Amelia, and she believed me.

'Actually, Dr Benson, Amelia was so thrilled I was pregnant she was in seventh heaven. When I became really heavy, six months into my pregnancy, she insisted I move into the apartment over the garage adjoining their house. I had been living in the attic of the inn, and Amelia just decided one day that the stairs were too much for me, and this was true. And so we all settled down in the house together. Naturally, Jack and I were as careful as we'd always been in front of Amelia.

'One afternoon, when I was eight months into my pregnancy, Amelia asked me if I intended to go away once the baby was born. I told her I didn't want to leave, that I hoped I could stay at Silver Lake, continue working for them. She was very happy to hear this, and I remember how she placed her small hand on my stomach and smiled and said, "Our baby, Meri. It'll be our baby. We'll all bring it up, and we're going to be so happy here together." And we were, that's the truth. Sometimes, I wondered out loud to Jack whether Amelia suspected the baby was his and he assured me she did not.

'Finally, our daughter Catherine was born. The most perfect baby any of us had ever seen. Beautiful, with Jack's bright blue eyes. And then three years later tragedy came to Silver Lake. Jack died, just like that, in the flick of an eyelash. He had a heart attack when he was talking to Pete O'Brien on the front lawn. And he never knew he had a heart problem, none of us did.' Meredith sat back in her chair, stared off into space, lost again in that faraway time.

'And then what happened?' Hilary asked after a few seconds had elapsed. 'Please continue.'

'What happened? We *grieved*, Amelia and I. We were so sorrowful. But I had the baby to look after and the inn to run for Amelia . . . so much work in those days, but I was young, strong . . . I had my hands full but I coped. And poor Amelia was in such a bad way, I had to take care of her as well. You see, she did not really want to live after Jack's death, and by the following spring she was fading. I knew she was not long for this world. At least, I felt that, felt that she was literally willing herself to die. My heart grew heavier and heavier as the months passed. I couldn't bear the thought of losing her so soon after Jack . . . the very idea of it filled me with dread.

'One day, a Friday it was, Amelia and I were sitting together in the flower room of the hotel, arranging daffodils for the restaurant tables. Cat was playing on the steps in the spring sunshine. Suddenly Amelia looked at me in the most peculiar way, and she told me she had made a will. "It's all for you and Cat, Meri. I've no one else to leave all this to, and besides, Catherine is a Silver. The last of the Silvers, until she grows up and has a Silver of her own. So all this belongs to the child, Jack's child. *You* must keep it safe for her. I trust you to do the right thing; you're smart, Meri. If you ever have to sell the inn for any reason, then do so. Or rent it out, if running it gets to be too much for you. But keep the land, keep the Silver Lake property, no matter what. It is already worth millions, and can only increase in value. That's what Jack would want you to do, Meri, he'd want you to keep the land. It's belonged to the Silvers for almost two hundred years." As you can probably imagine, I was stunned, Dr Benson. Aghast that she knew Catherine was Jack's child.

'Once I'd recovered from my surprise, I asked

Amelia how she had guessed about the baby, and she gave me that weird look again and said, "But I've always known, Meri, since the day you became pregnant." I suppose I must have looked extremely baffled, and so she went on to explain. "Jack told me, Meri dear," she said, and then took hold of my hand, held it tightly in hers. "He loved me from childhood, but he loved you, too, and he needed you desperately, Meri. He was a virile young man, full of passion. I was of no use to him as a woman any more, not after my accident. He never looked at another woman and for years he was celibate, until you came here. He fell for you, Meri. And once you were pregnant he wanted the child, oh how he wanted it, my darling. And I've never begrudged the relationship he had with you. I knew he would never hurt me or leave me. And I also knew you would always be loyal to me. I loved Jack so much, Meri, and I love you and the baby, too. She's like my child." And she meant every word, Dr Benson, Amelia always spoke the truth.'

Meredith fell silent again. Remembering that particular day with Amelia, so long ago now, still affected her deeply. Her eyes were bright with tears when she eventually focused her gaze on the psychiatrist. 'Amelia died later that year – 1974 – and she made me a wealthy woman and Cat an heiress. She did leave us everything, and there was so much more than the Silver Lake Inn and the land. There was her own estate, which she had inherited from her mother. She made a few bequests – to Pete O'Brien, who had run the property for years, and his wife Blanche, and other people who worked at the inn. But the bulk of the

Silver estate and her own inheritance came to us. And yet I would have given it all up just to have Amelia back. I longed for her, grieved for her for years. And I also grieved for Jack.'

'It's a most unusual story, very moving,' Hilary said, her voice low, compassionate. She had noted Meredith's emotions a moment before, and she fully understood how much Meredith had cared for the couple. It was on the tip of her tongue to ask Meredith if she thought the Silvers had used her as a surrogate, and then she instantly changed her mind. In her heart of hearts, Hilary knew this was not the case. She believed that Meredith had told her the story of her life with the Silvers exactly the way it had happened. Her words had the ring of truth to them. She might well be lying about other parts of her life, but not about these particular years.

There was a carafe of water on a console table nearby, and Meredith rose, went to pour herself a glass. Turning to look at Hilary, she murmured, 'I am convinced my attacks of fatigue have nothing to do with my early years in Connecticut. I was very happy with the Silvers, they were very good to me.'

'I know,' Hilary replied. 'And I think you are right. The attacks are not related to that time at all. So we must dig deeper, go further back. But I don't know when we can do this. Unless you come in for another session before you leave for London and Paris. That would give us a start, at least.'

Meredith hesitated momentarily, and then she made a decision. 'All right,' she said, 'I'll come tomorrow afternoon, if you can fit me in.'

'Let me check my other appointments with my secretary,' Hilary responded, pressing the button of the intercom.

That night Meredith dreamed the dream of her childhood again.

After a light supper she had gone to bed early.

She had a number of important appointments the next morning, and she also wanted to clear her desk before her afternoon session with Hilary Benson.

Almost immediately she fell into a sound sleep, and it was a dreamless sleep for most of the night. Then just as dawn was breaking she awakened with a start and sat bolt-upright in bed. Her face, neck and chest were covered with beads of sweat and she was filled with apprehension.

Snapping on the light, she glanced around the room, and then she lay back against the pillows. After a moment, she reached for a tissue on the bedside table, wiped her neck and face, and then crumpled the damp tissue in a ball in her hand.

She had just had that awful dream again, and as always it alarmed her. She focused on it, remembering.

She was alone in the vast, parched landscape. She was looking for the little girl and boy. But she could not find them. They had disappeared, had fallen through a giant crack in the earth's surface. She had seen them dropping away, and she was afraid for them. Now she must find them again. They knew. They knew the answer to the secret.

She walked and walked, her eyes scanning the landscape. Just as she gave up hope of ever finding them again they appeared at the edge of the dried mud flats. She was so happy she had found them. The boy took off his school cap and waved it in the air. Suddenly they were all together, the three of them holding hands, walking across the vast and arid landscape towards the far horizon. Now she was dressed like the little girl. She wore a dark coat, a long striped scarf around her neck and a beret on her head. They all had giant labels on their coats. Luggage labels. She peered at the little girl's label. The writing was smudged from the rain. She could not read the name. Or the name of the boy. She looked down at her own luggage label. This too was indistinct. What was her name? She did not know.

Ahead of them was the great ship. It was so huge it loomed up high on the docks. The little girl was afraid. She did not want to go on the ship. She began to cry. The boy cried and so did she. None of them wanted to go on board. Tears rolled down their cheeks. It was so cold the tears froze on their skin. It began to snow.

The sea was like black oil. They were afraid, terrified. They clung to each other, weeping. They were led off the ship. They had reached their destination. It was the grey cracked landscape where nothing grew. The sky was very blue; the sun blistering. They walked and walked. There were many, many children, all walking until they came to the black sea once more. And they all walked into the sea. She pulled back; she would not move. She tried to stop the little girl from walking into the sea, walking to her doom. But she could not. The girl moved away from her, and so did the boy. Together the two of them walked into the sea. She tried to shout at them to stop. But no words came out of her mouth. She was alone again on the mud flats. And she was afraid. They knew the answer to the secret. She did not. Now they had gone. Forever. She would never know.

This time the dream had been different, Meredith realized that as she examined every detail of it. She wondered what it meant; she had no idea. But she now resolved to tell Hilary Benson about it. Perhaps the psychiatrist would have an explanation for her.

'There's something I haven't told you,' Meredith said to Dr Benson later that afternoon.

Hilary looked at her alertly. 'Oh, and what is that, Meredith?'

'It's something to do with my attacks. At least, I think that's so. Certainly it started again after my second attack.'

'What started again?'

'The dream. A nightmare, in fact. I've had it on and off for years.'

'How many years?' Hilary asked, leaning forward over the desk, scrutinizing her patient intently.

'For as long as I can remember. Since I was about twelve, thirteen, perhaps even a few years younger. The dream stopped when I first came to Connecticut. In fact, I only had it once in the early years there, when I first started working for Jack and Amelia at the inn. Then it occurred a couple of times in my twenties, again in my thirties. But I hadn't had it since then until January of this year.'

'And the dream occurred after you had an attack of fatigue?'

'Yes. I was in the Loire Valley, staying with a friend. I suddenly felt ill that afternoon and I went upstairs to rest in my room. I fell asleep, I was so tired. And I had the dream. When I awakened I was startled that it had come back after so many years, and also that I felt the same way.'

'How did you feel?'

'Frightened, alarmed.'

'Try to recount the dream for me, please, Meredith.'

Meredith nodded and did as the psychiatrist asked. Then she explained that the dream had differed slightly each time she had had it in the last few months.

'So last night in the dream you were finally reunited with the boy and the girl in the arid landscape,' Hilary said. 'Was there anything else? Anything different?'

'Yes. There was the ship in the dream . . .' Meredith left her sentence unfinished, snapped her eyes shut.

'Are you all right?' Hilary asked.

'Yes, I'm fine,' she answered, instantly opening her eyes. 'Dr Benson?'

'Yes?'

'What do dreams mean?'

'I think they are usually manifestations of impressions we store in our subconscious. Then again, sometimes what truly frightens a person can come to the fore in sleep, when the unconscious rises. I personally think that we dream our memories, and also dream our terrors, Meredith.'

'So what do you think my recurring nightmare means?'

'I'm not certain. Only by talking, exploring a little more can we eventually come to some interpretation of it.'

Meredith took a deep breath. Unexpectedly and inexplicably she felt as if she were choking. Agitation took hold of her. She had to get out of here; she needed air. She stood up, then sat down again abruptly. She thought she was going to open her mouth and start screaming. She compressed her lips, striving for control.

Hilary Benson frowned, stared at her. She realized that Meredith, who had always appeared the calmest of women, was suffering from acute agitation. She was twisting her hands together anxiously, and her eyes had opened wide.

'You're suddenly extremely upset. What is it, Meredith?'

Meredith said nothing; she began to shake visibly, and she wrapped her arms around her body, hugged herself.

Hilary Benson jumped up, went to her, put a hand on her shoulder comfortingly.

Meredith gaped at Hilary. Her eyes filled with tears. 'I've not told you the truth . . . not told anyone . . . not ever . . .'

Hilary hurried to her desk, picked up the phone and spoke to her secretary. 'I can't see any other patients at the moment, Janice. Please reschedule them for another day. I have an emergency with Mrs Stratton.'

Walking back to Meredith, who was bent double in

the chair, rocking back and forth, the psychiatrist took hold of her arm, forced her upright.

'Come to the sofa, Meredith, sit with me. You're going to tell me everything. Slowly, in your own time. There's no hurry.' She had spoken softly, sympathetically, and Meredith allowed herself to be led to the sofa.

The two women sat down.

There was a long silence.

Finally, Meredith began to speak in a low voice. 'I don't know who I am. Or where I come from. I don't know who my parents were. Or my real name. I have no identity. I invented myself. I made my own rules and I lived by them. I had no one to teach me. No one to love me. I was completely alone. Until I met the Silvers. For seventeen years I was a lost soul. I'm still a lost soul in some ways. Help me . . . Oh God. *Who am I?* Where do I come from? Who gave birth to me?'

Meredith was weeping, the tears gushing out of her eyes and falling down onto her hands. She was in an agony of despair, and she started to rock back and forth again.

Hilary Benson let Meredith weep. She said nothing, did nothing, and presently the tears stopped. She handed Meredith a box of tissues in silence. Then she walked over to the console, poured a glass of water and brought it to her patient.

Meredith took it from her, sipped the water, and said, after a moment, 'I'm sorry for my outburst.'

'I'm not, and you shouldn't be either. You should be glad. It's done you good, I'm sure of that. And it is the first step towards your recovery. Whenever you are ready to start talking again, I am here to listen. Don't rush ... the rest of the day is for you. The evening too, if that is necessary, Meredith.'

'Thank you. Yes ... yes ... I must tell you ...' Meredith now took a deep breath and began:

'I grew up in an orphanage in Sydney. I was eight years old when Gerald and Merle Stratton adopted me. She didn't like my name, so she called me Meredith. They weren't very nice. Cold, hard-hearted people. They treated me like a maid. I did all the housework early in the morning and after school at night. I was only eight. They didn't really mistreat me, but he thought nothing of hitting me. She was mean, too, and stingy – with food especially. I grew to hate them. I wanted to go back to the orphanage. Then they were killed in a car crash when I was ten. His sister Mercedes didn't want me. She sent me back to the orphanage. I was there until I was fifteen. I only saw Mercedes once again, when she helped me get my passport. She was glad I was leaving with the Paulsons.'

Meredith stopped, leaned against the sofa cushions and closed her eyes. She took several deep breaths to steady herself. After a short time she opened her eyes and looked directly at Hilary. She began to tremble.

The psychiatrist took hold of her hand, asked softly in a gentle voice, 'Was there any sexual abuse when you were living with the Strattons? Did either of them abuse you?'

'No, there was never anything like that. They didn't sexually molest me. There was just this awful coldness and indifference, as if I wasn't there. I was only there to be their maid, that's what I thought then. I still think it. I was relieved when they were killed. They never showed me one iota of affection. I had always thought that when I got adopted somebody was going to love me at last. But no one did.'

A bleak look crossed her face, hurt shadowed her eyes, and when she spoke pain echoed in her voice. 'I can never begin to explain to you the horror of being in an orphanage. Nobody cares a thing about you . . . never to be touched, or held, or shown any love. I never knew why I was there. I worried a lot about that. I thought I'd been put there by my parents because I'd been bad. I didn't understand. All I wanted was to find out who my parents were. I never did. Nobody told me anything, they never answered my questions . . .'

'What is your earliest memory, Meredith? Close your eyes, relax, try to go back in time, try to focus on your youngest years. What do you see? What do you remember?'

After a while Meredith spoke. She said in a quiet voice, 'I see a river. But that's all.' She opened her eyes. 'Perhaps that's why I like living near water.'

'How old were you when you went to the orphanage?'

'I don't know, Dr Benson, I was always there.'

'From being a baby?'

'Yes. No. No, I don't think so. In my nightmare last night there was the ship. When I was a very little girl I used to remember being on a ship.'

'Do you mean a ship or a boat? There's a difference.'

Meredith closed her eyes again, pushing her

memory back to her childhood. She saw herself in her mind's eye; she saw boys and girls going up a gangplank. She was one of them. She saw sailors, seamen, docks. She saw a flagpole. The Union Jack flying atop it.

Meredith sat up straighter, opened her eyes and looked at Hilary intently. 'I do mean a ship and not a boat. And an ocean-going ship, too. A British ship, flying a British flag. I *must* have been on a ship, perhaps with other children. Maybe that explains the children who are always in the dream.'

'It's possible. Please try and think harder, think back. Could you have been born in England and taken to Australia when very young?'

'Maybe I was. But why don't I remember anything about it? Why don't I remember those years?'

'It's called repressed memory, Meredith. I believe something terrible happened to you when you were a small child, causing deep trauma which resulted in repressed memory. In fact, I'm pretty positive that's what you're suffering from, and I believe it's the reason for your attacks of fatigue. Psychogenic fatigue.'

'But why now? Why haven't I had the attacks in the past? Why not years ago?'

'Because the memory stayed deeply buried. That was the way you wanted it. So that you could function. Now something has triggered it. The repressed memory is trying to surface.'

'What do you think triggered it?'

'I can't be absolutely certain, but I believe it was your visit to Fountains Abbey.'

'You *do* think I was there before?'

'Possibly. Most probably. It would certainly explain a great deal.'

'Is there any other way you can trigger my repressed memory, Dr Benson?'

'Only you can do it really, by endeavouring to go back in time to your earliest childhood years. You're going to England next week. Something else might give your memory a good jolt whilst you are there. In the meantime, let us talk a little longer about your years in the orphanage.'

Meredith shivered violently and threw Hilary a look of horror. 'No child should ever have to live like that,' she exclaimed, anger surfacing. 'But I'll tell you more about it if you want me to.'

'I do. I realize how painful it is for you, but it may well give me more clues, something else to go on, Meredith.'

Later that night she rang Luc. She could no longer bear to keep the secret of her past from him. Also, she felt the need to confide, share, and in turn receive comfort from him.

# Twenty

Catherine Stratton sat back and studied the illustration on her drawing board, her head held on one side, her eyes narrowed slightly as she assessed her work.

The watercolour in front of her was of a small boy curled up in a crib sleeping, with one hand tucked under his cheek. She smiled to herself, liking its innocence, its charm. It was perfect for the last poem in the children's book of verse she had been illustrating for the past few weeks. Now, at last, it was finished and ready to go to the publishers.

Work well done, she thought, taking up a fine-nibbed pen, signing *Cat* with a flourish. She had always used her diminutive on her work, and it was a signature that was becoming well-known these days.

Sliding down off the tall stool, she lifted her arms above her head, did a few stretching exercises, and then walked across her studio and out into the main loft space, heading for the kitchen.

This was a good size, decorated in a crisp blue-and-white colour scheme, and it was equipped with all the latest appliances. It was the perfect kitchen for a dedicated chef, which Catherine was. She had loved cooking since childhood, had been encouraged and taught by her mother and Blanche O'Brien, at Silver Lake, who had always been like a favourite cuddly aunt.

Catherine stood washing her hands at the sink under the window which looked uptown. It offered a unique view of the Chrysler and Empire State buildings. This afternoon those towering skyscrapers sparkled against the blue April sky, and she thought they had never looked better than on this lovely spring day. Except perhaps at night when they were fully illuminated, their glittering spires etched against the dark sky. To Catherine they would always typify Manhattan.

Reaching for the kettle, she filled it and put it on to boil. Then she busied herself with cups and saucers, took out various items from the refrigerator, and started to make a selection of small tea sandwiches.

Catherine and her mother had designed her SoHo loft. Her studio was at one end, with big windows and a skylight in the sloping roof; the dining area flowed off the kitchen, and beyond there was a large living room decorated like a library. Two bedrooms were situated to the right of the living room, and each had its own bathroom.

It was a vast loft, cleverly divided to maximize the space and the light and it had a pristine, airy feeling. This was not only due to its grand size and many windows, but the pale colour schemes used throughout.

The loft had been Catherine's twenty-first-birthday present four years ago. 'But it's not from me, you know,' her mother had told her. 'It's from Jack and

Amelia in a sense, even though they're dead. I bought it for you with money from their estate.'

It was then that Meredith had fully explained about Amelia's will, the vast inheritance that was now hers along with Silver Lake Inn, the house she had grown up in, and all of the Silver land: 150 acres. All of this had been held in trust for her by her mother ever since Amelia's death; Meredith had effectively increased its value through clever investing of the money Amelia had left. Catherine had suddenly understood that day four years ago that she was an heiress, and a very lucky young woman.

Catherine had always known that Jack Silver was her father. Her mother had told her the truth when she was old enough to understand. She barely remembered him and even Amelia was a shadowy figure in her mind. Her mother had always been the dominant person in her life, and she adored Meredith.

Catherine had never judged Meredith and Jack. She was far too intelligent to do that, and mature enough to realize that no one else ever knew exactly what went on between two people. Three in this case, for obviously Amelia had acquiesced, or had perhaps turned a blind eye to their relationship.

Once, when she had questioned Blanche O'Brien, Blanche had said that she shouldn't waste time dwelling on that old situation. 'Nobody got hurt, everybody was happy, they all three loved each other, and you were the crowning point in their lives. They adored you, and Amelia behaved like a second mother to you.'

Sometimes she wondered about her mother's past; she understood many things about it, even though

Meredith had always been somewhat secretive about her early years in Australia. It seemed to her that her mother only started to live her life when she came to Connecticut.

From odd things her mother had said over the years, Catherine knew that her childhood had been terrible – bleak, without love, or even the merest hint of affection.

Meredith had loved Jon and her with a sort of terrible fury, single-mindedly, with total devotion, to the exclusion of anyone else.

Perhaps this was because of the deprivation Meredith had endured as a child. Certainly it had always seemed to Catherine that her mother had set out to give them all of the things she herself had never had, and much, much more.

Meredith had always been the most wonderful mother, probably to the detriment of her relationship with David Layton, Jon's father. She and her brother had always come first with Meredith, and perhaps he had grown tired and resentful of taking second place in her life and her affections.

That marriage had floundered after four years, and within no time at all, David, the country lawyer, had moved to the West Coast. Much to their amazement he had turned himself into a hot-shot show-business lawyer with a string of famous movie-star clients. They had never seen him again, heard only infrequently, and not at all after the first year or so. Not that her brother or she cared. Jon had always loved his mother the most, and anyway, David Layton had not been much of a father, or stepfather, for that matter.

Meredith was her best friend. She had not only given her a great deal of love and been supportive, she had encouraged her to chase her dreams and fulfil her ambitions. In fact, she had been instrumental in helping her to do this. And she had been exactly the same with Jon, always there for him, advising him when he asked, rooting for him, cheering him on. Meredith had been mother and father to them both.

She and her brother were delighted that their mother had met Luc de Montboucher. They had taken to him immediately, and had encouraged their mother in this relationship.

They thought he was the perfect man for her, and Jon was convinced they would get married. She hoped her brother was correct in this conviction. Nothing would please her more than to see Meredith in a happy relationship, especially now that she herself was getting married. She hated to think of her mother alone. It was about time she had some personal happiness in her life.

Luc had been to New York a number of times, and her mother was virtually commuting to Paris, and this seemed to bode well for the future. Also, she had put the Vermont inn up for sale, and had confided, only the other day, that she was not looking to make a big profit. 'I just want to get out unscathed financially,' Meredith had said. 'Fortunately, I've several potential buyers.'

When Catherine had told Jon about this conversation he had grinned and said, 'See, I told you so! Mom's going to marry Luc and move to France, or at least spend most of her time there. Just you wait and see, Cat.'

Her mother was leaving for Europe tonight, first stop London. She had business with Patsy, but she was planning to spend time in France.

Catherine covered the plate of tea sandwiches with a dampened linen napkin, the way Blanche had taught her as a child, and pushed the plate to a corner of the countertop; then she rinsed the strawberries and hulled them.

Her mind was still on her mother. She had been seeing a psychiatrist for the past few weeks, trying to discover why she had these peculiar attacks of fatigue. Over the weekend they had talked on the phone, and Meredith had said that Dr Benson was helping her to unearth repressed memories of her childhood. Finally she believed she was getting somewhere, making headway.

Catherine hoped so. All she wanted was for her mother to come to terms with her past, gain peace of mind, as well as a bit of happiness for once. After all, she was going to be forty-five years old next month.

'Everything looks beautiful, darling,' Meredith said an hour later, as she walked into the loft, glancing around. 'You've added a few things since I was here last. That painting over there, the lamp, the sculpture in the corner.' Meredith nodded approvingly. 'You've given it a wonderful look. It really works.'

'Thanks, Mom. Like mother like daughter, I guess. I take after you, you know, always fiddling with rooms, adding accessories and stuff. I'm a real "nester", just as you are.'

'Am I really?' Meredith said, sounding surprised, giving her daughter a quick glance. 'I hadn't realized.'

Bursting into laughter, Catherine exclaimed, 'Oh Mom, honestly, how can you say that! You can walk into the dreariest room, anywhere in the world, and transform it in a couple of hours, just by adding flowers, a bowl of fruit, a few cushions and photographs, magazines and books. Other bits and pieces. You've got a real talent that way. To coin a phrase, you make wonderful *havens*, Mom.'

Meredith had the good grace to laugh.

'Your company is aptly named, I've always thought.'

'I suppose it is.' Meredith sat down on the sofa, and continued, 'I'm glad I can spend a couple of hours with you before I catch the night flight to London; we don't see enough of each other these days. And perhaps we can talk about the wedding a little, come to a few decisions.'

'Yes, we can, Mom. Keith and I batted a few dates around this past weekend, and I think we'd like to have the wedding in the autumn, as you suggested.'

Meredith's face lit up. 'That's wonderful, Cat, the perfect time. I suppose you're thinking of early October, just as the leaves begin to turn?'

Catherine nodded. 'The second Saturday in October, that would be the fourteenth. Originally, Keith and I toyed with the first Saturday in the month, the seventh. But we weren't sure whether the foliage would have changed by then. What do you think?'

'Better go for the second Saturday, Catherine. The leaves will be in full colour, and they don't drop that quickly, remember. I'm assuming you're going to have the ceremony at Silver Lake?'

'Yes. Briefly, and only briefly, Keith and I had talked about the little church in Cornwall, but in the end we came to the conclusion that it's too small.' Catherine grinned at her mother. 'All those Pearsons, you know.'

Meredith smiled. 'From the sound of it, I'm going to be giving you a very big wedding.'

'Do you mind, Mom?'

'Oh darling, of course not! I'm thrilled. That's what I've always wanted for you, a big white wedding with all the trimmings. Anyway, getting back to the details, I think you'd better call the minister of the church in Cornwall, to make sure he will be able to officiate at the marriage, that he's available that day.'

'Yes, I'll do it tomorrow.' Catherine rose. 'Mom, I want to show you the sketches of my wedding gown. Let me get them, they're in the studio.'

A moment later she was back, sitting down next to Meredith on the sofa. The two of them pored over the series of drawings Cat had done; all were beautifully rendered and showed the gown from different angles.

'What do you think, Mom?' Catherine asked, eyeing her mother worriedly. 'You're not saying anything. Don't you like it?'

'It's absolutely beautiful, Cat. Very ... *medieval*, wouldn't you say?'

'In a way. But perhaps a bit more Tudor in feeling, Elizabethan. I've spent a lot of time on the design, Mother, and on the details in particular.'

'I can see it's quite elaborate.' Meredith stared at the sketch she was holding, which was a front view of the dress, and nodded her head. 'Yes, I see what you mean about it being Elizabethan . . . the squared-off neck, cut very near the edge of the shoulders, the long puffed-up sleeves, tight bodice and bouffant skirt. Very stylish, Cat; all you need is a white ruff.'

'Don't think I hadn't thought of it,' Cat laughed. 'Because I have, but I decided that might be going a bit too far. The veil will be held by a Tudor-style headdress, and this will fall into a train. I've yet to design the headdress. So, what do you think? Can I get away with it?'

'Of course you can, Cat, you will carry it off very well. I think you'll look stunning. Have you decided who's going to make it?'

'I thought I'd go to Edetta; she's created some lovely evening gowns for us in the past few years.'

'Yes, she has, and I'm sure she'll be able to find the right kind of white silk for you. Now, to move on to a few other details, do you know what time of day you want to have the marriage ceremony?'

'Keith and I thought it would be nice to have it at noon. Drinks first, then the ceremony, and a luncheon afterwards. With dancing.' Cat lifted a dark brow. 'Would that be all right?'

'Yes, I think that's a lovely idea, Cat. If I'm going to give you a big wedding we might as well do it in style. Do you know how many guests you'll be inviting?'

'I think the total will be around a hundred and thirty, or thereabouts. Keith and I counted about eighty, maybe ninety, from the Pearson side, and I figured around fifty from our side.'

Meredith laughed. 'I'm not sure that we can even rustle up that number, honey.'

'Oh we can, Mom, really we can. There are all my girlfriends and their husbands or boyfriends. Blanche and Pete. Some of the new friends I've made in the publishing world, the people from Havens, and Patsy will come from London, I'm certain of that.'

'She's already said she's coming. And there will be Agnes and Alain D'Auberville from Paris. Yes, I think you're right, we probably will be about fifty.'

'Luc will come, won't he, Mother?'

'I hope so.'

'Keith and I like him. So does Jon.'

'Oh I know. Your brother's made that only too clear.'

'Mom?'

'Yes, darling?'

'Luc loves you.'

'I know.'

'Do you love him?'

'Yes, Cat, I do.'

'So what's going to happen?'

'Are you and your brother in collusion?'

'What do you mean?'

'He was asking me the same thing, after your engagement party a few weeks ago. And to answer your question, I don't know what's going to happen. Being in love is one thing, getting married another. And there's so much to consider in my case.'

'I know, but you will work it out. You're both smart.' Catherine jumped up. 'I'm glad you came to see me at this time of day. I've made us a lovely tea ... like you used to do when we were little. A nursery tea you called it. I've prepared all sorts of tiny tea sandwiches, cakes, the works, actually. I'll just go and boil the water again. Be back in a jiffy ...' Cat winked at her mother, laughed, and added, 'Before you can say Jack Robinson,' and hurried off in the direction of the kitchen.

Meredith smiled and leaned back against the sofa, thinking about Luc. She would be seeing him soon, once she had completed her business in England. There were certain matters at the London office of Havens to attend to, and she and Patsy had to make a trip to Ripon. The refurbishing of Skell Garth House was almost finished, and they had various things to do before the inn reopened in May. She would then fly to Paris and base herself there, since she had much work to complete on the manor in Montfort-L'Amaury. Good progress was being made there, thanks to Luc and Agnes. Once she was in France she would spend weekends at Talcy with Luc, and they were both looking forward to this.

She wondered what she would do, if he did ask her to marry him. Jon and Cat thought it was all so simple, but in reality her life was rather complicated. She lived in America, he lived in France, and they both had businesses, commitments, responsibilities. She couldn't very well walk away from Havens Incorporated, and certainly Luc would never give up his architectural practice in Paris. Nor did she expect him to. So how could they ever work it out ...

'Mom, let's have tea in here,' Catherine called from

the archway leading into the dining area. 'It's so much easier.'

'I'll be right there,' Meredith said, pushed herself up off the sofa, and went to join her daughter. 'How nice it looks,' she said a moment later as she surveyed Catherine's handiwork.

'Thanks. Sit here, Mom.' Cat indicated a chair, took the one opposite, picked up the teapot, and poured. 'Now, here's this lovely cup of tea, Mother, just the way you like it, and help yourself to some sandwiches. There's cucumber, tomato, egg salad, and ham. Tiny ones but tasty.'

'I remember our nursery teas,' Meredith said, taking a minuscule cucumber sandwich. 'They *were* fun, weren't they?'

Catherine nodded as she munched on a sandwich. After a moment she said, 'I tried to get scones today, but no luck. My local bakery sometimes has them. I was hoping to give you warm scones with clotted cream and strawberry jam.'

'Thoughtful of you, darling, but this is fine. Not too fattening,' Meredith replied with a dry laugh.

Catherine eyed her mother. '*You* don't have to worry, Mom, you look wonderful.'

'Thank you.'

Catherine stood up. 'I won't be a minute, I've got to get something from the kitchen.'

When she returned to the table Catherine was carrying a glass bowl and a jug. She stood there, smiling at her mother, her bright blue eyes full of love.

'I have a treat for you, Mom. *Strawberries*. Your favourite.'

Meredith stared at Cat.

She felt herself go cold all over.

And then she heard a voice echoing in her head, faintly, as if it came from a very long distance. *'Mari . . . Mari.'*

A moment later the same voice was calling, once again echoing in Meredith's head. *'Mari . . . Come on. Come in.'*

A scene flashed.

In her mind's eye she saw a young woman with sparkling blue eyes and red-gold hair bending over a small child, her expression loving. *'Strawberries, Mari. A special treat.'* The child beamed at the mother. It was such a happy scene; there was such love on the mother's face. Then she heard the child crying. *'Mam, Mam, what's wrong?'*

The scene faded.

Meredith felt icy cold. She stared at Catherine. For a moment she was unable to say anything.

Catherine, who had been looking at her mother intently, now asked in a concerned voice, 'What's the matter? Don't you feel well? You've gone awfully white, Mom.'

'I'm fine,' Meredith managed to say. She shook her head. 'I think I've just had what Dr Benson would call a flashback. My first.'

'What exactly is it?'

'It's a memory, really, usually a repressed memory coming to the surface. I believe I just had one from my childhood. I saw a young woman of about your age, with bright blue eyes like you, and a small child. Maybe a five-year-old. At first the scene was happy, then suddenly the child was crying. It faded away.'

Meredith took several deep breaths. 'I think I had a memory of my mother and me. My biological mother, Cat.'

'Why do you think you had this flashback all of a sudden?' Catherine asked curiously, sitting down in the chair, her eyes pinned on Meredith's face.

'I believe you triggered it. It was the way you said *strawberries,* then mentioned *special treat*. And it was your eyes, Cat, so blue, so full of love.'

Meredith paused, shook her head. 'Jack had very blue eyes, and I always thought you had inherited yours from your father. But perhaps they're my mother's eyes.'

Catherine reached out, took hold of Meredith's hand resting on the table. 'Oh Mom, this is wonderful.' She felt her throat tighten, and she said in an emotional voice, 'Maybe you'll keep remembering more and more until you know everything about your past.'

'I hope so, darling.' Meredith bit her lip. 'Perhaps I ought to call Hilary Benson, tell her about this. She would want to know.' Glancing at her watch, she went on, 'It's just turned six o'clock. I'm sure she's still at the office.'

'Yes, call her,' Catherine exclaimed, getting up. 'The phone in the kitchen is the nearest.'

Meredith nodded and followed her daughter, then quickly dialled the psychiatrist's number from the wall phone. 'May I speak to Dr Benson please, Janice?' she said when the secretary came on the line.

'Who's calling?'

'It's Mrs Stratton.'

'Oh, hello, Mrs Stratton. I'll put you through right away.'

'Good evening, Meredith,' Hilary Benson greeted her a split second later. 'How are you?'

'I'm good. As you know, I'm going to London tonight. I stopped off to have tea with my daughter this afternoon, and she said something that triggered a memory. I think I've just had my first real flashback.'

'This is very good news, Meredith. Very good indeed. What exactly did you remember?'

Meredith recounted the flashback in every detail.

When she had finished, the psychiatrist exclaimed, 'This is your first significant memory, a true breakthrough, and I think it's just the beginning. You may find you have more in the next few days. That frequently happens. Try to focus on some of the details you've just mentioned to me, they might lead you into a whole series of significant memories.'

'I hope so. I'd really love to unearth the mystery of my early years.'

'You will, Meredith, I'm quite certain of that. If you have the need to call me, don't hesitate to do so. And I'll see you in a few weeks.'

'Yes, and thank you, Dr Benson. Goodbye.' Meredith hung up the receiver, turned around to face Catherine, who was standing in the doorway, an expectant look on her face.

'What did she say?' Catherine asked.

'That it was a significant memory, and that I'll probably have more now.'

'Oh Mom!' Catherine hurried into the kitchen, wrapped her arms around Meredith and held her close. 'I love you so much, Mother, I just want you to have peace of mind. And some happiness in your life finally.'

# Twenty-one

Patsy Canton had been listening attentively to Meredith for the past hour.

Now she said in a low, thoughtful voice, 'So what you're saying to me, in essence, is that you believe you were born in England and then taken to Australia as a child.'

Meredith nodded. 'Exactly. I think I must've been about six years old.'

'And you went alone? That can't be so. You must've been with your parents.'

'I'm pretty sure I went alone, Patsy. I'm convinced my mother was dead by then.'

'No father?'

'I don't remember him.'

'But why would you go *alone*? That seems awfully strange to me. And who sent you?'

'I don't know.' Meredith gave a light shrug of her shoulders. 'I truly don't have the slightest idea.'

'In your recurring dream, there are children ... could you have been sent with other children, perhaps? You know, the way evacuees were sent in groups to safe places during the Second World War.'

'Maybe. But *why*? There wasn't a war on in 1957,

when I was six years old, so why was I sent away? Exiled from England?'

Patsy shook her head. 'I haven't a clue, my darling. I want to help you, but I don't know how I possibly can. I'm as baffled as you.'

Meredith sighed and took a sip of water. She leaned back in the chair, glancing around the restaurant in Claridge's, and continued quietly, 'Last night on the plane, I couldn't sleep. I suppose I dozed off and on, but mostly my mind was racing, trying to remember things.'

'And did you?'

'A couple of things came back to me. The first has to do with my name. I was called Mary Anderson in the orphanage in Sydney. It was Merle Stratton who changed my name to Meredith. And of course I took their surname when they adopted me. But I was never Mary – what I mean is, that wasn't *my* name, even though they called me Mary at the orphanage. My real name is Mari, and my last name is Sanderson.'

'I see. So how did it get changed?' Patsy shook her head and exclaimed in a dismayed voice, 'Oh God, bureaucracy! Do save me from it. Your name probably got muddled up by some idiot at the orphanage.'

'That's exactly what happened, I think. I had this memory on the plane last night. It was of a woman, a rather stern one, who told me that my name wasn't Mari with an *i*, but Mary with a *y*. I kept telling her that I was called Marigold, but she wouldn't believe me. She scoffed and said that it wasn't a child's name, but the name of a flower.'

'There are some bloody awful people running these

institutions. It's just terrible what goes on in this world. Despicable.' Patsy sighed heavily, and gave Meredith a sympathetic look. 'So Marigold was your first name, and I suppose they also managed to get Anderson and Sanderson confused.'

'Yes,' Meredith replied. 'And this confusion about my name might well explain the luggage labels in the dream.'

'Absolutely,' Patsy cried. '*Brilliant*, darling.'

There was a small silence between them. Eventually, Meredith looked at Patsy earnestly, and said, 'My mother's name was Kate – I've remembered that. And I know she's dead, so there's no possibility of my meeting her. But now I've remembered her at last, after all these years, I need to do something. For myself. I need closure. And so I would like to visit her grave, at least. See it, take flowers, be with her there. That would truly help me. And perhaps I'll start feeling better, and maybe – hopefully – the attacks of psychogenic fatigue will go away.'

'I'm sure you *would* feel much better, Meredith. And I really understand your need . . . visiting her grave will give you solace, in a way.'

'At least I'd finally know she really did exist, and that she isn't a figment of my imagination. The only thing is, I don't know where she's buried. I've remembered her name, but I can't remember where we lived.'

'Yorkshire,' Patsy announced after only a moment's thought. 'I'm positive. And certainly it would explain the experience you had at Fountains Abbey. That's always seemed rather significant to me. I haven't forgotten the way you explained it that day: you had a very strong reaction to the abbey. You must have gone there as a child.'

'I agree. But I have a feeling I didn't grow up in that area. I remembered something else . . . being taken into a city. On a bus. It was a very big city, bustling, with lots of people milling around. There was a large square in the centre, with black statues. My mother used to take me to this city to go to a market. It was huge, covered with a domed glass roof.'

'And they sold everything at stalls. Am I correct?'

'Yes, you are.'

Patsy nodded. 'Vegetables and fruit stalls, fish, meat, cakes, bread, clothes, furniture, crystal and china stalls. Men calling out to passersby to come and look, sample their wares. All of them doing a very loud verbal selling job. Do you remember that?'

'Oh yes, I do, Patsy! We used to stand and listen to them. They all had . . . different pitches for their goods.'

Patsy nodded. 'Leeds Market. It's very famous, and in Leeds City Square there are black statues of nymphs holding torches. There is also a statue of Edward, the Black Prince, on a horse. Both are lifesized. Does that ring a bell?'

'It does. Let's assume I do come from Leeds . . . how can I find out where my mother is buried? Who would know anything about Kate Sanderson thirty-eight years later?'

'*Somerset House*. Actually, it's no longer called that, they changed its name. Now it's St Catherine's House, but it's the right place for us to begin. It's the general register office of births, marriages and deaths, for the whole of Great Britain. It's a place of records, a mine of information, in fact.'

'Where is it?'

'Here in London, in Kingsway. It's a quick cab ride from here.'

'I must go there this afternoon.'

'Yes, you must, and I'll come with you, Meredith.'

An hour later Meredith and Patsy were at St Catherine's House in Kingsway. They walked through the glass doors and found themselves immediately in the actual records office itself. On all sides were stacks and stacks of ledgers lined up on shelves.

'It looks like a library,' Meredith said as she and Patsy walked up to the security desk.

After the security officer had checked their handbags, Patsy said to him, 'How do we go about finding the record of a death?'

The officer directed them to an inquiry desk at the far end of one of the long aisles of ledgers on the left. Five clerks were standing behind the inquiry desk, ready to be of assistance. Patsy and Meredith approached one of them, and Patsy repeated her question.

The young woman clerk handed Patsy a pamphlet. 'This tells you how to use the Public Search Room. It's simple enough. Records of deaths are bound in the black ledgers, stacked on the left. Births are bound in red, and they are on the right. Look for the year of death. You'll find there are four books for the four quarters in each year. And there are three volumes per quarter. These are alphabetical. A to F, G to O, and P to Z.'

Patsy thanked her and she and Meredith retraced their steps. Once they were back in the Public Search Room they headed for the black ledgers and found the year they wanted. Meredith took hold of the handle on the spine of the first ledger inscribed March 1957, P to Z, pulled it off the shelf and placed it on the book stand which ran the length of the aisle in front of the shelves. Opening it, she saw that it covered January to March.

'To save time, why don't you look at the quarter that follows on,' Meredith suggested. 'That would be April May, June.'

'Good idea,' Patsy said, and went to look for the appropriate ledger.

Meredith ran her finger slowly down the lists of Sandersons deceased through the first quarter of the year 1957. The name of Katharine Sanderson was not amongst them. Glancing at Patsy, she said, 'She's not listed in this book. How about yours?'

'Give me a minute or two, I haven't quite finished.'

Meredith returned the ledger to its shelf, pulled out the one covering July, August and September of 1957. Once again her mother's death was not shown; nor was her death recorded in the two volumes Patsy perused in quick succession.

'We've covered the whole year,' Patsy murmured to Meredith. 'Are you absolutely certain your mother died in 1957?'

'Yes. Well, I think so.'

'But how do you know this, Meredith? You said you had so little information about yourself. Do you actually remember her dying?'

'Not really. But I do know I went to the orphanage in Sydney when I was six years old.'

'You remember that, do you? Are you really sure? How do you know?'

'Because Merle Stratton told me. She once said to me that I'd been at the orphanage since I was six but they hadn't taught me much in two years.'

'All right, so you went there when you were six years old in 1957. But that doesn't mean your mother died that year. Maybe it was 1956, when you were five.'

'I don't think so . . . I know I was six. But let's look at the ledgers for 1956.'

'Good idea.' Patsy agreed.

An hour later Meredith and Patsy had searched the entire set of ledgers for the year 1956 and turned up nothing. Meredith looked at her friend and said quietly, 'This is a wild goose chase. Her death is just not listed.'

'Do you want to try some other years?'

'No, there's no point,' Meredith answered. 'Maybe I have made a mistake about the date, but we can't stay here all day, searching through endless ledgers. Come on, let's go.'

'No, wait a minute,' Patsy said. 'What if she died abroad?'

'My mother was never abroad.'

'Humour me, let's go and talk to one of the clerks. Just for a minute. Please, Meredith.'

'All right.'

When they got back to the inquiry desk, Patsy zeroed in on the young woman who had helped them earlier. 'We're looking for the record of a death, and we haven't been able to find it. Now, what if the person died abroad, that would mean it isn't listed, correct?'

The young woman shook her head. 'No, it would be listed. Wherever a British subject dies, the death is eventually recorded here. The information comes through all of the British embassies and consulates around the world.'

'I see.'

'It's really quite simple,' the clerk went on, looking from Patsy to Meredith. 'If a person's name is not in one of the registers, then that person is not dead. He or she is still alive.'

Meredith gaped at the clerk.

Patsy said, 'Thank you very much for your help,' and with a slight nod she turned away. She took hold of Meredith's arm, led her down the short flight of steps and along one of the aisles.

They stood in front of the glass doors opening onto the street, staring at each other.

Meredith looked stunned and she was slightly trembling.

Patsy, who was nobody's fool, understood all of the implications inherent in this unexpected knowledge, and she murmured, 'I know what you're thinking, darling.'

'I'm sure you do,' Meredith answered, her voice so low it was almost inaudible. 'If my mother's not dead, which according to those ledgers she isn't, then she's alive. Somewhere. In England probably.' Meredith paused, took a deep breath and clutched Patsy's arm. 'Why did she send me away when I was a little girl? Why in God's name was I sent to an orphanage in *Sydney*, of all places? The other side of the world. Why? *Why*, Patsy?'

Meredith's eyes were filled with misery and her face was so bleak Patsy's heart went out to her friend. For a moment she was speechless. She swallowed hard, and replied in a gentle voice, 'I don't know, Meredith, it doesn't make any sense to me.'

*'She sent me away because she didn't want me.'* After she had said these words Meredith was so shaken she went and leaned against the wall, biting her lip. For a moment she was floundering; her senses were swimming.

Patsy took charge. 'Listen to me, if your mother's alive, which she must be since there's no death certificate, then we are going to *find* her. Whatever it takes, we're going to do it. Come on, let's go back and look for your birth certificate.'

'Why?' Meredith asked miserably. 'What for?'

'We're going to get a copy of your birth certificate. If you *were* born in this country, as you think you were, and not Australia, then your birth will be registered in one of those red books.'

'How will my birth certificate help us to find my mother?'

'There's a lot of information given on a birth certificate, Meredith. I know from my own and my children's. The name of the father, his occupation. The married name of the mother, and her maiden name.

Place of birth of the child, residence of the parents, date and year of birth, obviously. We'll have enough to start with. Besides, I would have thought you'd like to have a copy of it . . . just for yourself, your own edification. And peace of mind.'

Meredith nodded but said nothing. She was reluctant to start a search for her birth certificate. What if it wasn't there? She would feel even worse than she already did.

Patsy coaxed her a little more, drew her slowly back to the aisles of ledgers. This time they went down the one on the right-hand side, where all of the red-bound books were stored. Fifteen minutes later she discovered that she *had* been born in Great Britain. Her birth *was* registered.

'You see, I knew you'd find your name in one of those lovely red books,' Patsy exclaimed, smiling at her, wanting to cheer her up. 'Now let's order a copy of the birth certificate. Maybe they will be able to have it ready for us later today.' Patsy pulled an order form out of the lucite pocket attached to the end of the reading stand, handed it to Meredith and said, 'Fill this in, and then we'll take it over there, to one of those windows, to order the copy.'

Meredith nodded and pulled out a pen. After completing the form they went to a window. She was able to get priority service for twenty pounds. The copy of her birth certificate would be ready at the same time the following day.

On Friday afternoon, promptly at four, Meredith and Patsy returned to St Catherine's House. Within minutes she was holding a copy of her birth certificate in her hands.

The two women went out into the street, got into the waiting taxi and headed back to Claridge's Hotel.

Settling back against the seat, they pored over the certificate. Meredith saw that her mother's full name was Katharine Spence Sanderson. Her father's name was Daniel Sanderson and his occupation was listed as accountant. Was it from him that she got her head for figures? she wondered. The address given for her place of birth was Three, Green Hill Road, Armley. Her parents' residence was listed as Hawthorne Cottage, Beck Lane, Armley, Leeds. Her date of birth was shown as the ninth of May, 1951, and her birth had been registered on the nineteenth of June by her mother. Her name *was* Marigold Sanderson.

'You know quite a lot about yourself now,' Patsy said, turning to Meredith, squeezing her arm affectionately.

'More than I've ever known, Patsy.' Meredith cleared her throat, and went on, 'I never had any sense of identity when I was young. Not knowing who you are and where you come from is very frightening. It's almost like being a non-person. Since I didn't have an identity, I invented myself.'

'Getting your birth certificate must mean a great deal to you.'

'It does. It's . . . well, it's a kind of validation of who I really am.' Meredith forced a small smile. 'At least I've been celebrating my birthday on the correct date. The orphanage did get that part right.'

'What are you going to do next? Oh, stupid, stupid

question, Patsy Canton.' Patsy looked at her intently. 'You're going to Leeds, of course.'

'Tomorrow, Patsy. We were going to Ripon on Sunday anyway, so I'm going to make it a day earlier.'

'I'll drive you.'

'But – '

'No buts,' Patsy exclaimed. 'For one thing, you need my help, my expertise. I know Leeds very well, and the rest of Yorkshire, and you're going to need a guide. Besides that, I care about you, Meredith. I wouldn't let you embark on a search like this alone. The whole situation is too emotionally fraught. You're going to look for a long-lost mother, and who knows what you're going to unearth in the process. You really do need a friend with you.'

'Especially a good and dear friend like you, Patsy. Thank you. Thank you for helping me.'

'We'll set off at the crack of dawn tomorrow, and get to Leeds in about two and a half hours. Maybe three. I think our first stop should be Hawthorne Cottage in Armley.'

'Do you know this place?'

'Oddly enough, I do. I had an uncle who owned a woollen mill there, and he lived in Farnley, which is nearby. Farnley Lee House, lovely old manor it was. Well, anyway, I used to go there with my parents, and we usually drove through Upper Armley to get to Farnley. Do you have any recollection of Hawthorne Cottage?'

'Vaguely. The cottage was near a river. There was wildlife on it . . . ducks, I think.'

'The more we talk, the more you'll remember, I'm

sure of that,' Patsy said. 'Isn't this what your psychiatrist said?'

'Yes, it is.'

As they got out of the cab in front of Claridge's, Patsy linked her arm in Meredith's. 'Let's go and have a drink. Celebrate.'

'Celebrate what?'

Patsy laughed. 'I always said I'd make a Yorkshirewoman of you. Now I don't even have to try, because you actually are one by birth. I'd like to drink a toast to that.'

The phone was ringing as Meredith came into her suite at Claridge's. As she picked it up and said, 'Hello?' she heard Luc's voice saying, '*Chérie, comment vas tu?*'

'I'm fine, darling. I was just going to call you in Paris. Guess what happened today? I found out that my mother is alive.'

'*Mon Dieu.*' There was a moment's silence and then he asked, 'But how did you find out?'

She proceeded to tell him in great detail, then added, 'We're leaving for Yorkshire tomorrow instead of on Sunday as planned . . . to begin the search.'

'Do you want me to fly over and go with you?'

'No, no, that's not necessary. I'd love to see you, darling, but I've got Patsy to help me. She knows Yorkshire like the back of her hand.'

'All right, I understand. You want to concentrate. But I will be thinking about you. Call me tomorrow, *chérie*, I'll be anxious. I love you.'

# Twenty-two

They left for Yorkshire very early on Saturday morning, and arrived in Leeds in record time. Patsy circumvented the busy city centre and took Stanningley Road to Armley. After asking directions a few times, she soon found Beck Lane.

As she pointed the Aston Martin down the lane, she glanced at Meredith and asked, 'Does anything seem familiar to you?'

'Not really, not even Beck Lane. It looks so short, so ordinary. But then again, when you're a small child things always appear to be so much bigger, more impressive. And also more frightening, of course.'

'That's quite true,' Patsy agreed. 'We're almost at the bottom of the lane, and it looks to me as if it ends in a cul-de-sac.'

Meredith peered out of the car window, her eyes scanning the scenery. 'What I don't understand is why we're not seeing the river.'

'I'm sure we will in a minute. When I looked up this area on a map of Leeds last night, I noticed that the River Aire and the Leeds and Liverpool Canal are adjacent to each other, run parallel. We learned that at school but I'd forgotten. Those two waterways *are* ahead of us, Meredith, you'll see.'

Beck Lane came to an abrupt end at a partially demolished brick wall, which cut the lane off from a large field beyond. It was here that Patsy stopped, turned off the ignition and parked.

'Let's go and investigate,' she said, opening the car door, getting out.

Meredith followed suit.

The two women glanced around. They were standing in a deserted area; there were no houses, no buildings of any kind in sight. But back down the lane a few yards there was an old gate set in a ramshackle wooden fence, and Meredith suddenly noticed this.

'I didn't see that gate as we drove past,' she said, 'and it must lead somewhere.' As she was speaking she began to walk down the lane towards it.

Patsy followed her.

The gate was open, hanging off its rusted hinges; Meredith went through it and realized that there had once been a pathway here. Now it was overgrown with weeds and grass, barely visible. The partially obscured path led towards a tumble-down building, in reality several large piles of bricks, stones, wood and other rubble.

'Could *that* be Hawthorne Cottage?' Patsy asked, catching up with her.

'Possibly,' Meredith replied quietly. Suddenly, she felt deflated, sad. During the drive from London she had begun to believe that Hawthorne Cottage was still standing, that her mother still lived there. But this had been wishful thinking on her part, she accepted that now. How foolish I am, she thought, expecting things to be the way they were almost forty years ago. Everything changes.

Arriving at the demolished building, Meredith circled it several times, then she turned to face the River Aire which was visible from this vantage point. She could see it gleaming in the pale spring sunshine, and, just behind it, flowed the canal. She wondered why she had never noticed the two waterways running parallel when she was a child.

Turning to Patsy, she voiced this thought.

Patsy said, 'But you were so little, darling, only five or six. You wouldn't have paid any attention to something like that. Or maybe you've simply forgotten.'

'I guess you're right.' Meredith half smiled. 'Also, I was much shorter then, I might not have been able to see that far.'

Patsy laughed. 'True enough.'

Meredith remained standing in front of the mounds of stone and rubble, still gazing thoughtfully towards the River Aire. She was trying to move backwards in time, concentrating hard on the past, in the way Hilary Benson had told her to do.

Unexpectedly, in her mind's eye, she saw a neat little lawn and flower beds, and, beyond the garden, a white gate set in an old brick wall, rambling roses growing all over it.

Hurrying forward, she walked through the desolate garden, heading for the river, and as she approached the bank she saw, behind a clump of overgrown bushes, the wall and the remnants of the gate. The wall had been reduced to a crumbling pile of brick but the rambling rose bushes still spread themselves over it, and she supposed that in summer the roses would be in full bloom.

Her heart gave a small leap. She recognized this place, knew it well. Then she saw the rock and she stood perfectly still. A memory came rushing back, almost knocking the breath out of her with its clarity and vividness.

She saw herself as she had been as a small girl, sitting on that rock, always sitting there daydreaming. It was her favourite place, that rock high up on the river's bank. It was her view of the world.

She went and sat down on the rock; her eyes were moist as she gazed out at the water flowing past, splashing and tinkling as it fell down over the dappled stones of the river's bed. There was wildlife on this river, and she remembered how she had loved to watch the antics of the ducks, the moorhens and the other birds on the water.

Hugging her knees with her arms, she rested her head on them and closed her eyes . . . memories . . . memories . . . they were coming back.

The mother was there. The mother with the red-gold curls and very blue eyes. Eyes so supernaturally blue they were almost blinding. The mother loved the child on the rock, loved her to distraction. The child was the mother's whole world.

Then why did she send me so far away from her. *Why?*

Meredith had no answer for herself. Only Kate Sanderson could answer that question. If she and Patsy ever found her, which was most unlikely in her view.

The pain came back all of a sudden, the pain of her childhood, the constant she had lived with as a little girl. 'Mam, Mam, where are you?' she heard the small girl cry, and Meredith's heart tightened. How she had dreamed of that face, the mother's pretty face. How she had longed for her, longed for those soft arms around her, longed for the warmth of her love, the soothing voice, the comfort of her presence. Meredith's heart held the memories intact, held them inviolate . . . the pretty face, the sparkling eyes of blue, the love, the tenderness, the scent of her . . . the mother she had never stopped loving or longing for . . . *her* mother. Kate Sanderson.

Meredith squeezed the tears back and swallowed. Her throat ached.

'Are you all right?' Patsy asked softly.

Unable to speak for a moment, Meredith did not answer. She sat up straighter and flicked the tears away from her eyes with her fingertips.

'I just don't know why she did it,' she said to Patsy at last. 'A moment ago I thought we'd never find her, but now I know we *must*. Just to ask her that question. *Why?'*

Patsy was silent; she simply nodded, affected by Meredith's emotion, the pain reflected on her face.

Finally, Meredith got up and looked at her friend, met her steady gaze. 'You see, Patsy, my mother loved me very much. The way I love Cat and Jon . . . and that's why I can't fathom out why she did what she did. It's a mystery.'

Patsy put her arm around Meredith's shoulder. 'We'll find her, I promise you that.'

Together they walked back through the weed-filled garden, heading for the car. As they passed the mounds of rubble, Patsy asked, 'Do you think that is Hawthorne Cottage?'

For a moment Meredith did not answer. She stood staring at the mass of old stones, but she did not really see them. Instead she saw Hawthorne Cottage as it had been thirty-eight years ago. She saw the sparkling windows, the fresh, white lace curtains, the copper pots gleaming in the kitchen. She saw her neat little bedroom with the rose-patterned quilt. And she heard that mellifluous voice. '*A wizard sells magical things at this stall, astonishing gifts you can see if you call . . .*' The voice faded away.

'Yes,' Meredith said softly, 'that's Hawthorne Cottage. What's left of it.'

'This is number Three, Green Hill Road,' Patsy said, slowing the car, indicating the big Victorian building set behind wrought-iron gates. 'You were born there, Meredith. For years it was a maternity hospital. Now that I see it, I remember coming here with my aunt, when my cousin Jane had her first child. They used to live at Hill Top. I'll show you where on our way into town.'

Meredith stared at the building with interest, and then asked, 'You said *used* to be a maternity hospital. Isn't it any more?'

'I don't think so,' Patsy replied. 'I vaguely remember that it became a general hospital, or perhaps a home for the elderly, I'm not quite sure.' Glancing at

Meredith, she finished, 'Do you want to get out, go over there and have a closer look?'

Meredith shook her head. 'No, no, that's fine. But I can't help wondering where I was christened though.'

Turning on the ignition, driving on, Patsy said, 'Probably at Christ Church in Armley. Do you want me to take you there?'

'I don't think so, I'm sure I won't remember anything. But thanks, honey.'

'What about Leeds Market? Would you like to stop off, see whether or not it triggers any other memories? It was rebuilt in the seventies, after it burned down in a fire. But fortunately it was rebuilt in the same Victorian style it had always been. So it's the same now as it was when you were five or six.'

'I doubt I'll have any significant recollections there, Patsy. I think that we ought to go to Ripon. We've quite a lot of things to review, and to discuss with the Millers. By the way, that was good news that they're going to stay on as the managers.'

'Isn't it just,' Patsy exclaimed, a smile flashing on her face. 'I was thrilled when they first told me last week. I hope you're not angry that I didn't pass it on then, but I wanted it to be a lovely surprise for you when you arrived.'

'No, I wasn't angry, and it was a *marvellous* surprise. Now we don't have to search for a good management team or interview anyone.'

'True, but we do have to interview the various chefs. The Millers have done a lot of weeding out, as I told you, and we're down to three.'

'That's not too bad, but hiring a chef is always

a tricky business; you know that, Patsy. They usually do a lovely meal to impress, but invariably that happens only once ... disaster frequently follows.'

'The Millers have tried out these three off and on for a couple of weeks. One's a man, Lloyd Bricker. The other two are women, a Mrs Morgan and a Mrs Jones. So we'll be eating well this weekend, that's a certainty. However, I tend to agree with you: hiring a chef is dicey.'

'We should be able to open the inn in May,' Meredith remarked. 'You don't foresee any problems, do you?'

'No, I told you that when you arrived. It's just this chef business that nags at me. It's going to be fine, let's not worry.' Patsy threw her a quick glance, then focused on the road again. 'By the way, when are you planning to leave for Paris?'

'I had hoped to go next Wednesday. Now I'm not so sure. Agnes and I are supposed to visit Montfort-L'Amaury on Thursday, so that I can see the progress they've made with the remodelling. And then I was going to Talcy with Luc. For the weekend. However, now that we're looking for my mother, I don't know what to tell you.'

'Let's just take it day by day,' Patsy suggested.

That afternoon, after they had eaten a delicious lunch prepared by the chef, Lloyd Bricker, Meredith and Patsy did a tour of Skell Garth House.

Each of them made copious notes, and once they had reviewed every room in the inn they found a corner in the empty dining room and went over their punch lists together.

'There're still a lot of things missing in many of the rooms,' Patsy said. 'Claudia's only partially understood me, I think. I explained to her several times that we're upgrading the inn, creating much higher standards, both in accommodation and service. She seems to have missed the point that real comfort and luxury are absolutely mandatory.' She glanced at her pad, and added, 'I'm sure you've listed the same things as I, Meredith. Hot-water bottles in covers, oodles of towels in every room, bowls of potpourri and scented candles, hairdryers, etcetera, etcetera, etcetera.'

'Yes, I've noted all those things, Patsy, and they're easy items to add. We just have to ship them up from London.'

'They've already been shipped,' Patsy replied, making a moue with her mouth. 'Well, perhaps she just didn't put them out yet. I'll talk to her about it. What do you think about the refurbishment in general?'

'It's good, Patsy, we picked some lovely fabrics and carpets. I noticed the draperies and bedcovers have been extremely well made, and the sofas and chairs beautifully reupholstered. Thanks to you. And the wallpapering and painting is excellent. But I am going to have to rearrange all of the furniture – and in most of the rooms.'

'I knew you'd say that. When I came up two weeks ago to oversee the installation of the carpets and the draperies, I gave them your floor plans for the furniture arrangements. They seem to have ignored them completely.'

Meredith nodded. 'They certainly did.' A faint smile flickered. 'The Millers simply put everything back where it was before, and those old groupings were not the best. Or the most comfortable.'

'I hope we haven't made a mistake, keeping them on,' Patsy murmured, throwing her an apprehensive glance. 'Do you think they're too set in their ways?'

'Perhaps. But I'm sure we can overcome that. I'll have a long talk with them over the weekend. They've simply got to understand that we're raising our prices. Therefore our standards have to be higher, too. They're both bright, so I'm sure we can re-educate them, help them to operate the inn the Havens way.'

Patsy grinned. 'I'm glad you're such an optimist, Meredith. I was getting really concerned about them when we were upstairs.'

'If I hadn't been an optimist, I don't think I would have survived that orphanage in Sydney.'

'No, you wouldn't.' Patsy glanced down at her pad, and went on, 'The rest of the stuff on the hit list is all minor, to do with electrical outlets, the wattage of the light bulbs, and such; so we don't have to worry now. It can wait.'

'I don't have a lot of other things either,' Meredith said, and pushing back her chair she stood up. 'I'm going to take that walk, Patsy.'

'Are you sure you don't want me to drive you to Fountains Abbey?'

'No, thanks anyway for offering. I really do want

to walk, I need the exercise and the fresh air. See you later.'

Patsy smiled at her and nodded.

Returning the smile, Meredith left the dining room, crossed the foyer and headed out of Skell Garth House.

It was a fine afternoon, not too cold even though it was still April. The sky was clear, a soft pale blue filled with scudding white clouds. Wherever she looked, Meredith saw that spring was truly here. The trees were in bud, the grass already thick and verdant, and, here and there, patches of wild flowers grew in the hedges. She noticed primroses and irises, and then, as she came to the avenue of limes leading to Studley Church, she caught her breath. Daffodils were blooming everywhere, on the banks by the side of the road and under the limes.

As she walked past them, the Wordsworth poem Patsy had recited to her in January ran through her mind. It had seemed familiar then and now she realized that she knew the last verse: For oft when on my couch I lie/ in vacant or in pensive mood,/ they flash upon that inward eye/ which is the bliss of solitude;/ And then my heart with pleasure fills,/ and dances with the daffodils.

She knew it by heart because her mother had taught it to her all those years ago. And it had stayed in her mind, dormant perhaps, but nevertheless there.

Her mind focused on Kate Sanderson. The shock of discovering that her mother was not dead had partially receded, but she was still upset, troubled that Kate had apparently abandoned her, and so callously, when she was a little girl.

Meredith knew herself extremely well, and she had begun to realize earlier in the day, as they had driven from Leeds to Ripon, that anger and resentment were beginning to simmer deep down inside her. As she walked on, heading up to the church on the hill, she resolved yet again to find Kate, no matter what it took.

Upon reaching the top of the hill she stood looking down at Fountains Abbey, and just as it had in January, it seemed to beckon to her, pull her forward.

A magnet, she thought, it's like a magnet for me. She hurried down the steep path, almost running, and within a few minutes she was entering the ancient ruins.

On this clear bright April day she was more stunned than before by the dramatic beauty of the soaring ruined monolith.

Dark and imposing, it was silhouetted against the pale sky as if flung there by a mighty hand. But the blackened stones were softened by the greenness of the trees surrounding them. Just a few feet away from where she stood the Skell flowed towards Ripon. Yet another river, Meredith thought; no wonder I love to live near water. I grew up with it.

Seating herself on a piece of ruined wall, she cast her mind back in time, trying to envision herself visiting this place with Kate Sanderson, but no memory came to her, even though she sat there for half an hour. Her mind was totally blank. Still, again she had the strongest sense that she knew Fountains, had been here before, and that something momentous, and tragic, had happened to her here in this ancient spot. But what?

Only her mother had the answer.

Always, in the past, Meredith had used work to subjugate heartache, bring it to heel. Working hard until she dropped had enabled her to keep her mind off her troubles, to function properly.

And so for the rest of the weekend she threw herself wholeheartedly into creating a new look, her look, in most of the rooms in the hotel. It kept worry about her mother at bay.

With the help of Patsy, Bill and Claudia Miller and three handymen, she had furniture moved around until every arrangement pleased her, and each room had the look she was striving for. Beds, chairs, sofas, antique tables and chests were repositioned under her direction; once this had been accomplished, she set about rearranging lamps and accessories and rehanging pictures.

The Millers were astounded by her. As Bill put it to Patsy: 'We couldn't believe it when she took off her jacket, rolled up her sleeves and got down to it herself.'

Claudia Miller was particularly impressed with Meredith's energy, stamina and sheer doggedness. At one point, late on Sunday afternoon, a weary and exhausted Claudia said to Patsy, 'I've never seen anyone work like this before. She doesn't stop, she's a whirlwind.'

'I know. Meredith's never ceased to amaze *me*. She's a real workhorse. And also very talented,' Patsy pointed out. 'She has terrific style.'

Claudia merely nodded.

Patsy added, 'Meredith has really fine taste in decorating. She was born with it. And she has a great eye.'

'So I've noticed. The rooms do look better the way she has arranged everything. I suppose Bill and I were a bit slow on the uptake. We really should have followed the plans you gave us more precisely.' Claudia's expression was suddenly worried, as she asked, 'Are you and Meredith upset with us?'

'No, of course not. It's all right, don't worry,' Patsy reassured her. 'But do try and follow our instructions *exactly* in future, Claudia, please. It'll save a lot of heartache for everyone. Tomorrow I'll help you to unpack all of the items I shipped from London last week, and Meredith will finish the public rooms down here. She expects to be done by lunchtime.'

'You will interview the chefs tomorrow, won't you?' Claudia said. 'Monday *is* the deadline.'

'That doesn't present a problem. By the way, I enjoyed lunch today. Mrs Morgan cooked it, didn't she?'

'Yes. She's also going to make dinner tonight.'

'Not Mrs Jones?'

'I'm afraid not. She burned her hand cooking dinner for us last night and she begged off today.'

'I see. Do you have a favourite, Claudia?'

'Yes. Mrs Morgan. She's the best in my opinion, and besides, she's the most adaptable, more easy-going in a way, not quite so temperamental as Lloyd.'

'And Mrs Jones? Aren't you impressed with her?'

'She's a good cook, but I don't think she's right for

the inn . . . at least, not the way it's going to be in the future.'

'Do you mean she's not sophisticated enough?'

'No, I don't mean that, not really. You and Meredith said you wanted high-style English cooking, and country-type cooking to a certain extent. In my opinion Mrs Morgan's the winner. She's the most all-round cook of the three of them.'

Mrs Morgan turned out to be a woman in her middle fifties, with rosy cheeks, bright brown eyes and a cheerful smile.

Meredith noticed at once that she had a pleasant manner, and within moments of being in her company she felt quite at ease. The woman exuded calm self-confidence, and Meredith could tell from Patsy's expression that her partner had also taken an immediate liking to the chef.

'I understand from Claudia Miller that you are used to cooking for relatively large numbers of people, Mrs Morgan,' Meredith began.

'Oh yes, I am. Until a few months ago I was chef at a hotel in the Scottish border country. It was an old house turned into an inn like this, but a bit bigger. And we also got a lot of local trade in the restaurant. So numbers don't faze me, oh no, they don't at all, Mrs Stratton. Of course I'm used to having a couple of sous chefs.'

'Yes, I understand, Mrs Morgan. That's not a problem,' Patsy interjected.

'I gave Mrs Miller all of my references, so I expect you've seen them.' She looked from Patsy to Meredith.

'We have indeed.' Meredith smiled at her. 'And they're excellent. We also enjoyed the meals you've cooked this weekend.'

'Thank you very much, Mrs Stratton, and please call me Eunice. I prefer it. Much friendlier, isn't it?'

Meredith said, 'Yes, it is, Eunice.' She paused for a moment, shook her head, then said, 'I've only known one other person called Eunice. And that was my baby-sitter when I was a child.'

Eunice laughed. 'What a coincidence. You had a baby-sitter called Eunice in America, and I was a baby-sitter here in Yorkshire.'

Meredith stared at her. After a split second, she said, 'Where in Yorkshire?'

'Leeds. That's where I come from originally. My husband's from Ripon, and he's been nagging me to come back here for years.'

'Who did you baby-sit for?' Meredith said, continuing to stare at the chef.

'A lovely little girl. Her name was Mari.'

'What was her last name?' Meredith asked in a strangled voice.

'Sanderson,' Eunice answered, and threw Meredith a swift glance. 'Are you all right, Mrs Stratton? You look a bit odd.'

'I'm the little girl, Eunice. I'm Mari Sanderson.'

'Get away with you then, you can't be Mari!' Eunice exclaimed, her astonishment only too apparent.

'But I am.'

'Well, I'll be blowed, this is one for the books, I can tell you that.' Eunice chuckled. 'Can you imagine me, of all people, being a chef, Mari? Do you remember how I always used to burn your lunch? I drove your poor mother crazy.'

'I'd like to talk to you about my mother,' Meredith said, quietly.

# Twenty-three

'My mother and I got separated when I was little,' Meredith explained. 'I don't know how this happened, but it did.'

'She was poorly. In hospital, I do know that,' Eunice told her.

'Who was looking after me?'

Eunice brought her hand up to her mouth, frowning slightly, looking thoughtful. Finally, pursing her lips, shaking her head, she murmured, 'I don't know, to be right truthful with you. I suppose at the time I thought you'd been taken in by relatives.'

'*Relatives*,' Meredith said slowly, 'I don't ever remember relatives, Eunice. There was only my mother and me. Just the two of us.'

'Yes . . .' Eunice sat back in the chair, her face troubled. Hesitatingly, she asked in a quiet voice, 'So what exactly happened to you?'

'I don't exactly know. But I did eventually go to live abroad.'

Patsy glanced from Meredith to Eunice, and addressed the chef: 'When did you last see Mrs Sanderson? Can you remember that?'

'Let me think . . . Well, it must've been the summer she got ill. I've got to think back . . . yes . . . yes, it was then. The summer of 1956. I went to Hawthorne Cottage to baby-sit one day and there was no one there. So I went back home. We lived in the Greenocks, just off Town Street, in those days. Anyway, a few days later I ran into Constable O'Shea, he lived near us in the Greenocks. He told me Mrs Sanderson was in hospital. When I asked about Mari he said she was fine, being taken care of very well. And that was that. A few weeks after that we moved away from Armley. My mother found a house near her sister in Wortley, so off we all went.'

Meredith had listened carefully; leaning forward intently, she said to Eunice, 'The name Constable O'Shea rings a bell, but I can't quite place him in my mind.'

'Can't you? Well, he was very fond of *you*, Mari. Very fond. He was the local bobby, walking the beat in Armley. He used to be stationed at that police box on Canal Road. Are you sure you don't remember him?'

'No, I don't.'

Patsy said, 'Constable O'Shea might be able to throw some light on what happened to you.'

'Yes, that's true,' Meredith agreed and turned to Eunice again. 'Do you think he still lives in Armley?'

'Oh, I don't know, I mean I lost touch donkey's years ago. And he'll be retired. He was about thirty in those days; so he'd be sixty-eight, thereabouts, by now. Mmmm. Now who do I know who still lives in the Greenocks? Let me just think.'

Patsy stood up. 'I'll go and get the Leeds telephone directory from the office.' She hurried across the dining room and out into the small foyer.

Left alone, Meredith and Eunice looked at each other carefully without speaking. It was Eunice who finally said at last, 'You've grown up to be a wonderful-looking woman, and you've certainly made a go of it, you really have. Living in America, owning all these inns.'

Meredith half smiled, made no comment. She was looking back into the past again, trying to remember Constable O'Shea, but she was having no success at all. She couldn't even picture his face.

Eunice went on, 'Are you married then?'

'I was. I'm divorced now. I have two children. And what about you, Eunice, do you have children?'

'Two, like you. Malcolm and Dawn. They're both married, and I have five grandchildren. Are your children married?'

'My daughter's engaged. My son's still at college; he's only twenty-one.'

Patsy came back into the dining room carrying the Leeds telephone book. Placing it on the table in front of Eunice, she sat down next to her and said, 'Now let's look at all the O'Sheas who live in Armley. There can't be that many. Perhaps we'll find one living in the Greenocks. What was Constable O'Shea's first name, Eunice?'

'Peter. No, wait a minute, it wasn't Peter. It was an Irish name. Let me see . . . *Patrick*! Yes, it was Patrick O'Shea.'

Patsy was running her finger down the O'Sheas listed and she looked up and said, 'There are two living in Armley and one in Bramley with the initial

P. But none in the Greenocks. Well, I might as well go and phone all three numbers, that's the only way we'll find out anything. I'll use the phone over there.' Carrying the directory, she hurried over to the phone on the table at the entrance to the dining room.

Meredith got up and walked over to the window, stood looking out at the garden, her mind on her mother. Turning around, she asked, 'Did you ever run into my mother afterwards?'

'No, I didn't.' The chef's eyebrows drew together in a frown. 'She didn't die, then?'

'I don't think so, Eunice. We're trying to find her.'

'Oh.'

A moment later Patsy rushed across the dining room, still clutching the telephone book in her arms. She was beaming. 'I've found him! He now lives at Hill Top. That's near St Mary's Hospital, Meredith. He's out at the moment, I didn't actually speak to him in person. But I talked with his wife, and he's definitely the right Patrick O'Shea. He's a retired police sergeant, she told me, and she vaguely remembers Mari and her mother. Anyway, she said he would be home around two o'clock this afternoon. I asked if we could go and see him then, and she said we could.'

Meredith sat facing Patrick O'Shea in the sitting room of his house at Hill Top in Armley. She did not remember him at all; she realized that she had probably so blocked him out it was almost impossible to recover the memory. He was a tall man, well built, with greying dark hair and a pleasant manner.

'You were such a bonny little girl,' he said to her,

smiling. 'Marigold. I always thought it was such a lovely name for a child. Anyway, to continue, that morning you came looking for me you were so upset. Crying. You thought your mother was dead –'

'But she wasn't was she?' Meredith cut in swiftly.

'No, but she wasn't well. You'd come to the police box on Canal Road. I carried you home, it was quicker. And anyway you were weeping, so upset you were. We found your mother sitting in a chair in the kitchen. She was white, white as a sheet, and obviously very sick. At least that's what I thought. She said she'd fainted earlier that morning. I'd put in a call for an ambulance, and it came within fifteen minutes. They took her to Leeds Infirmary.'

'And what happened to me?' Meredith's eyes were riveted on Patrick O'Shea.

'The last thing she said to me, as the ambulance doors closed was, "Look after my Mari for me, Constable O'Shea." And I did. I spoke to my sergeant at the station, and we decided the best thing to do was take you to Dr Barnardo's in Leeds, the children's home, until your mother was well.'

'And what happened when my mother got better?'

'You went back to live with her at Hawthorne Cottage, as I recall. But I don't believe things were good with her, she was struggling, you know, trying to find a job.'

'What happened to . . . my father?'

'I don't rightly know. At least, I don't have a lot of details. Kate told me once that he'd left her, gone off to Canada. That's all I knew. I suppose he didn't come back.'

'I don't remember him. He must have left when I was very little.'

Patrick O'Shea nodded. 'I believe he did.'

'Do you think my mother became ill again, Mr O'Shea?'

'She did indeed. She was in the Infirmary a second time . . . oh, it must have been the following year . . . about 1957, if my memory serves me well.'

'Do you think I was put back into the children's home?'

'Possibly. Yes, that's very likely. There was no one to look after you. And I sort of lost track of your mother after that. In fact, I never really knew what happened to you both. Suddenly you'd left Hawthorne Cottage, another family was living there. I never saw you or your mother again, Mari. I mean, Mrs Stratton. A few years later I did hear she was working in Leeds.'

'Do you know where?'

'Yes, just let me think for a moment . . . it was a dress shop, I do know that. A posh one too, in Commercial Street . . . Paris Modes, that was the name of it.'

'Is it still there?'

'Oh yes, I think so.'

'As I explained, Constable O'Shea, my mother and I got separated. I was sent abroad. I thought she was dead. But I've just discovered she's probably still alive. I must find her.'

'I understand. She's not listed in the phone book then?'

'No, she's not.'

'Perhaps there's someone at Paris Modes who can help you, give you more information about her whereabouts.'

'Well, he was certainly nice enough,' Patsy said, as she and Meredith drove away from Constable O'Shea's house at Hill Top, heading for the city. 'But you don't remember him, do you?'

'Not really, Patsy. I wish I did.' Meredith sighed. 'I suppose I truly blocked everything out. If only I could recall those early days more fully, but I can't. I have flashes of memory like an amnesiac sometimes does, but that's it.'

'Try not to worry, I'm sure we'll get more information at the dress shop.'

'I'm not sure at all. Frankly, Patsy, we're on a wild-goose chase, in my opinion. All of this happened thirty-eight years ago, and my mother's not going to be *still* working at Paris Modes. And I'm certain there's no one there who will remember her.'

'You don't know that for sure, Meredith. So let's just go to the shop, ask a few questions. Somebody might remember Kate Sanderson, and give us a lead.'

'Yes, we can go, but hasn't it occurred to you that my mother might not live in Yorkshire any more? She could have moved away. Moved anywhere. There's a very big world out there.'

'I know what you're saying, darling, but I think you're wrong. I have this feeling inside, call it intuition if you like, that your mother is very close by. You'll see, we're going to find her.'

When Meredith was silent, Patsy sneaked a look at

her. Her heart sank. Meredith's face was bleak.

Patsy drove on in silence for a short while, but then she said, 'I'm not too sure about parking in Leeds. I think the best thing to do is to go to the Queens Hotel and park the car there, near the railway station. It's only a few minutes' walk to Commercial Street from City Square.'

'Whatever you say. I don't remember Commercial Street. Only Leeds Market.'

But twenty minutes later as they walked down that particular street Meredith suddenly stopped and clutched Patsy's arm. 'Marks & Spencers is somewhere near here. I remember that now. My mother liked to go there; she bought my underwear at Marks.' Meredith had an instant vision of herself walking down this street clinging to her mother's hand. She said to Patsy, 'Almost always my mother bought me an ice cream. Once I tripped and dropped my cone. I was so upset, I started to cry. And I remember how she comforted me . . . and gave me her ice cream . . .'

'You see, more and more memories are coming back,' Patsy exclaimed, looking pleased. 'And here we are at Paris Modes.'

Patsy pushed open the door and the two of them walked into the elegant dress shop. Immediately a young woman in a neat black dress came gliding forward.

'Can I help you?' she asked politely, smiling at them. 'We have some wonderful new lines in from Paris.'

'Oh, yes,' Patsy said, 'we know you have lovely clothes, very smart indeed. But we don't want to buy anything. Actually, we came to see the manager.'

'We don't have a manager,' the young woman replied. 'Mrs Cohen owns the business, and she runs it herself.'

'I see. Is she here? Can we see her?' Meredith asked.

The young woman nodded. 'I'll go and get her, she's in the office.'

A few seconds later a woman of about fifty, elegantly dressed and well put together, walked out into the shop from the office behind a Coromandel screen.

'I'm Gilda Cohen,' she said, extending her hand to Patsy.

'Pleased to meet you, Mrs Cohen. I'm Patsy Canton, and this is my friend, Mrs Stratton.'

'A pleasure, Mrs Stratton,' Gilda Cohen said, shaking her hand.

Meredith smiled at her. 'I'm looking for someone, Mrs Cohen. A woman who used to work here. But many years ago. I'm afraid it was long before your time.'

'Who are you looking for?' Gilda Cohen asked curiously.

'My mother. She worked here in the late fifties, or perhaps the early sixties. Her name was, or rather is, Kate Sanderson. We were separated when I was small and I always believed she had died when I was a child. But lately I've been given reason to believe she's still alive. I want to find my mother.'

'I'm sure you do, Mrs Stratton, that's quite understandable; and you're correct, Kate did work here, when my mother was running the shop. I inherited it from her. I was at college in those days, but I knew

Kate slightly. A lovely woman. My mother was very fond of her indeed, and sorry to see her leave.'

'When was that, Mrs Cohen?' Meredith asked.

'I think it must've been in the middle or late sixties. But don't let's stand here in the middle of the shop. Come into my office and sit down. Can I offer you a cup of tea?'

'No, but thank you anyway,' Meredith said.

Patsy also declined, and the two of them followed Gilda Cohen into her office. They sat down together on the sofa, and looked at Gilda, who had positioned herself behind her desk. 'As I said, my mother was rather fond of Kate, took her under her wing a bit, and she stayed in touch with her after she left.'

'Do you know where she went to work?'

'Yes, she returned to the town she came from, Harrogate, and took a job with Jaeger. My mother once told me Kate hadn't been happy in Leeds, and she always referred to her as "my wounded bird", although I'm not certain why. I married young and had a child, so I wasn't working in the shop in those days. I didn't know her all that well. But she certainly made an impression on my mother, and on other people, too. Everyone spoke nicely about Kate.'

Meredith sighed. 'I don't suppose she could still be working at Jaeger. What do you think, Mrs Cohen?'

'Oh I know she's not, Mrs Stratton. She didn't stay at Jaeger for longer than a couple of years, then she moved on. The last time I heard about her from my mother Kate was running Place Vendôme in Harrogate, a really fine boutique selling couture clothes.' Gilda Cohen leaned back in her chair. 'If only my mother were still alive, she would be able to tell you so much more about Kate.'

Meredith gave Mrs Cohen a sympathetic look. 'I'm sorry you lost your mother.'

'Yes, it was sad for us all. However, she had a really grand life and lived to be ninety. Never had a day's ill health as long as she lived.'

There was a small silence, and then Patsy said, 'Is Kate Sanderson working at Place Vendôme now?'

'I don't believe she is, Mrs Canton. The last I heard she had left there. She'd moved away from Harrogate, actually.'

'Another dead end,' Meredith said in a miserable voice.

Gilda Cohen said, 'I can ring Annette Alexander, the owner of the boutique. She just might have an address for Kate.'

'Oh, would you? Are you sure you don't mind?' Meredith asked. 'Otherwise, we can just drive over to Harrogate.' She glanced at her watch. 'It's only four-thirty.'

'Yes,' Patsy said. 'We can pop in to see her on our way to Ripon. We have to pass through Harrogate.'

'No, no, that's all right, I'll call her for you right away. I don't mind at all.' So saying Gilda Cohen picked up the phone and dialled the boutique.

'Hello, this is Gilda Cohen, is Mrs Alexander there?'

There was a small silence, as Mrs Cohen listened. Then she covered the mouthpiece, and explained: 'They've gone to get her, she's just saying goodbye to a client. Hello, oh there you are, Annette, how are you?'

Gilda listened once more, and then said, 'I have two ladies here who are looking for Kate Sanderson. I know she left you a few years ago, but you wouldn't happen to have an address or a telephone number for her, would you?' The next short silence was followed by an exclamation. 'Oh really!' Gilda cried. 'Just a minute, let me ask.'

Again covering the mouthpiece with her hand, Mrs Cohen said, 'According to Mrs Alexander, your mother left to marry someone. But she can't remember his name. She wants to know where she can contact you, if she does remember?'

'Skell Garth House in Ripon, Mrs Cohen,' Patsy said. 'The number is Ripon 42900.'

Gilda Cohen repeated this to Annette Alexander and after thanking her, saying goodbye, she hung up. Looking directly at Meredith, she said, 'If my mother were alive she'd be very pleased to know Kate got married finally. Mother always thought Kate was so sad, and she used to tell me Kate had had a tragic life.'

'You've been very helpful, Mrs Cohen,' Meredith murmured softly, standing up. 'Thank you so much.'

'Yes, thank you,' Patsy added, also standing.

'It's been my pleasure, I just wish I could have done more to reunite you with your mother, Mrs Stratton. Annette is very dependable, and I can guarantee she'll ring you up if she remembers who it was your mother married.'

'I hope so.'

Gilda Cohen escorted them to the door, shook their hands. As they stepped out into Commercial Street she said, 'I'd love to know if you do find Kate, Mrs Stratton, she was such a favourite of my mother's.'

'I'll be in touch,' Meredith promised.

'Why didn't we think of that,' Patsy muttered as they walked along Commercial Street. 'It's the most obvious thing. She was a young woman, and pretty, you said.'

'*Very* pretty. Beautiful really.' Meredith linked her arm in Patsy's, continued, 'We'll never find her. This is yet another dead end, you know.'

'No, it isn't!' Patsy cried. 'Quite the contrary. I'll call Valerie at the office first thing in the morning and she can go to St Catherine's House. They keep marriage certificates there. I'm quite sure they do. We'll find out who your mother married.'

Meredith instantly brightened. 'What a great idea! Let's call her now.'

'She's not in the office today. Don't you remember, she went to Milan for the weekend. She won't be back until late tonight.'

'Are you certain they keep marriage records?' Meredith asked in a quiet voice as they walked down into City Square.

'I'm positive. It's a general register office of births, deaths and marriages.' Patsy paused before adding: 'I've been thinking . . . perhaps we ought to go to Dr Barnardo's Home, make inquiries there. They may be able to throw some light on what happened to you. And to your mother.'

Meredith looked at her askance. 'No way. I know those places. They never tell you anything, they're cloaked in secrecy. I'd only go to see them as a last resort.' Her mouth settled in a grim line.

Glancing at her, Patsy decided to say no more for the moment. On the drive back to Ripon she talked about a variety of other things, wanting to take Meredith's mind off her mother. And orphanages.

Laughing suddenly, at one moment, she said, 'You know, Meredith, we're really quite awful.'

'What do you mean?'

'Once we'd discovered who Eunice Morgan was, we put her through an interrogation and then fled, raced off to find your mother. The poor woman must think we're crazy. We didn't even finish our interview with her.'

'I realized that myself a short while ago. Anyway, how do you feel about hiring Eunice?'

'I'm all for it. I think she's the best of the lot. I found Lloyd Bricker a bit of a snob and too arrogant by far, and Mrs Jones didn't really impress me that much.'

'In my opinion she's a shirker,' Meredith said. 'I agree with you about Lloyd. So let's hire Eunice, shall we? She's certainly a good chef. We've sampled her fare.' Meredith gave Patsy a small smile. 'And obviously she no longer burns the food as she did when I was a child.'

Patsy laughed, glad to see a flash of Meredith's good humour.

The telephone call came the next morning.

Meredith and Patsy were sitting in the dining room, having breakfast and going over their notes about the inn, when Claudia Miller came hurrying over to their table.

'Excuse me. You have a phone call, Meredith. It's a Mrs Alexander.'

Meredith and Patsy exchanged startled glances, and Meredith immediately got up. 'Thanks, Claudia. I'll take it over there on the phone by the door.'

'All right. I'll just go and put it through.'

A few second later Meredith was saying, 'Hello, this is Mrs Stratton.'

'Mrs Stratton, good morning. Annette Alexander here, I hope I haven't called too early.'

'No, not at all, Mrs Alexander.'

'I thought I'd better ring you immediately. I just received a bit of information that might help you. Do you know, I wracked my brains last night, trying to remember the name of the man Kate married, but to no avail. And then it occurred to me that my sister might know who he was. She used to work for me at Place Vendôme, at the same time as Kate Sanderson. In any case, I rang her up last night, but she was out. She just got my message and phoned me ten minutes ago. Apparently Kate married a man called Nigel. My sister thinks his last name was Grange or Grainger, and that he was a veterinarian. In Middleham. I know it's a trifle sketchy, but I do hope it helps.'

'It does, thank you very much Mrs Alexander. Whilst I have you on the phone, perhaps you can tell me something else. Do you recall when Kate Sanderson left Place Vendôme?'

'She left my employ in the early seventies.'

'I see. Well, thanks again, Mrs Alexander.'

'I was happy to be of help, and give Kate my best, if you find her.'

'I will. Goodbye, Mrs Alexander.' Meredith hung up and returned to the table.

Patsy looked at her questioningly, raising a brow. 'Well?'

Meredith took a deep breath, exhaled, then said, 'According to Annette Alexander, my mother married a man called Nigel, and his last name was either Grange or Grainger. He is, or was, a vet. And in the early seventies, when my mother left her employment, he was living in Middleham. Or rather, *they* were.'

'Middleham! Good heavens, Meredith, that's right next door practically. It's a small village on the moors, about half an hour from Ripon. You see, I told you I had a sense that your mother was close by.'

'We don't know that she is. We don't know what happened really. And they could have divorced, or moved away.'

'I'll soon find out if he's still around,' Patsy cried assertively and jumped to her feet. 'I'm going to look him up in the local telephone directory. He's bound to be listed if he's the vet in Middleham.'

Meredith sat back in her chair and watched Patsy walking across the floor with great determination. Whatever it took, her friend was hell-bent on finding Kate Sanderson. And what a *good* friend Patsy had turned out to be. Meredith knew that she would have been lost without her in the last few days.

Patsy was suddenly back at the table, looking pleased with herself. She sat down, glanced at the paper she was holding, and said, 'His name's Grainger, not Grange, and he lives in Middleham. At Tan Beck House. And there's the phone number.'

Meredith took the paper and glanced at it, then raised her eyes to meet Patsy's. 'Thank you,' she said, and looked down at the paper again. 'Now that I know she could only be a few miles away I feel rather strange.'

'Do you mean about seeing her?' Patsy asked, her brows furrowing.

'Yes.'

'Perhaps you're afraid.'

'Do you know, I think I am.'

'I'll go with you to Tan Beck House.'

'Thank you, but perhaps I should go alone, Patsy.'

'Shouldn't you phone her first?'

'I'm not sure. In a way I prefer to see her face to face before she knows anything about me. If I phone first I'll have to start explaining myself.'

'You're right. So do it your way.'

# Twenty-four

It was with some trepidation that Meredith walked up the path to the front door of Tan Beck House.

For the last thirty minutes she had been sitting in Patsy's Aston Martin, trying to gather her courage to go there in search of Kate Sanderson.

Since her apprehension had only seemed to increase the longer she sat, she had, in the end, turned on the ignition and driven back down the road.

As she had alighted from her car a moment ago she had seen that the lovely old stone house was substantial but not overly large, the kind of house a vet or a doctor or lawyer would live in. It was well kept, with a freshly painted white door, sparkling windows and pretty lace curtains; an array of spring flowers brought colour and life to the beds in the garden on either side of the flagged path.

Now she stood at the front door, her hand on the brass knocker. Her nerves almost failed her. Taking a deep breath she banged it hard several times and then stood back to wait.

The door was opened almost instantly by a youngish woman with dark hair, who was dressed in a grey sweater and matching slacks under a green striped pinafore.

'Yes, can I help you?' she asked.

'I'm looking for Mrs Grainger. Mrs Nigel Grainger. Is she at home?'

The young woman nodded. 'Is she expecting you?'

'No, she's not.'

'Who shall I say is calling?'

'I'm Mrs Stratton. Meredith Stratton. She doesn't know me. I'm a friend of a friend. I was hoping she could help me with something.'

'Just a minute,' the young woman said and leaving the door ajar she hurried across the highly polished floor of the small entrance foyer.

She returned within seconds, opened the door wider, and said, 'Mrs Grainger would like you to come in. She won't be a minute, she's on the phone. She told me to take you to the sitting room.'

'Thank you,' Meredith said, stepping into the foyer, following the young woman, at the same time glancing around quickly, wanting to see everything.

She noticed a handsome grandfather clock standing in a corner and a collection of blue-and-white porcelain effectively arranged on an oak console table.

Showing her into the sitting room, the young woman said, 'Make yourself at home,' and disappeared.

Meredith stood in the middle of the room, thinking how welcoming it was, struck by its warmth and charm. It was of medium size, tastefully decorated, the walls painted red, with bookshelves running floor to ceiling on two of them. The woodwork was a dark cream, handpainted to resemble *faux* marble, and there was a dark red-and-blue oriental rug in front of the stone fireplace. Between two tall windows an antique desk faced out towards the back garden and a small lawn. Beyond were rolling moors and an endless expanse of blue sky filled with scudding white clouds.

Meredith turned away from the window at the sound of footsteps. She held her breath as she waited for Mrs Nigel Grainger to open the door.

At the first sight of her Meredith's heart dropped. This was not the beautiful young mother of the red-gold curls and bright blue eyes whom she had worshipped in her childhood dreams.

Mrs Grainger was a woman in her early sixties, Meredith guessed. She wore beige corduroy trousers and a white shirt with a navy-blue blazer; she looked like a typical country matron.

The woman hesitated in the doorway, looking at Meredith questioningly. 'Mrs Stratton?'

'Yes. And hello, Mrs Grainger . . . hello. I hope you'll forgive this intrusion, but I came to see you because I'm hoping you can help me.'

'I'm not sure how, but I'll try,' Mrs Grainger said, still poised in the doorway. 'You're American, aren't you?'

Meredith nodded. 'Mrs Grainger, I'll come straight to the point. I'm looking for a woman called Kate Sanderson. Annette Alexander of Place Vendôme in Harrogate gave me reason to believe that you and she are the same person. Is that so?'

'Why yes, it is. I'm Katharine Sanderson Grainger, and I used to work at Place Vendôme, years ago, before I was married.' Kate frowned, the quizzical expression reflected in her eyes again. 'But why are you looking for me?'

Meredith was extremely nervous. She had no idea how to tell Kate who she was and, momentarily, she was at a loss for the right words. Finally, she said in a tremulous voice, 'It's about ... about ... it's about Mari.'

Kate Grainger looked as if she had been slapped in the face, and slapped hard. She recoiled, gaped at Meredith, and took hold of the door to steady herself.

Then recovering her equilibrium to some extent, she asked in a tense voice, 'What about Mari? What is it you want with me? What do you want to tell me about Mari?'

'I ... I knew her, Mrs Grainger.'

'You knew my Mari?' Kate cried eagerly, sounding breathless. She took a step forward.

Meredith could see her better now. She noted the vividness of the blue eyes, suddenly filled with tears, the reddish-gold hair, paler than it once was and shot through with silver; recognized that well-loved, familiar face, touched by time but still quite lovely. And she knew with absolute certainty that this *was* her mother. Her heart tightened imperceptibly, and she was seized by an internal shaking. She wanted to go to Kate, put her arms around her, but she did not dare. She was afraid ... of rejection ... of not being wanted.

'You knew my Mari,' Kate said again. 'Tell me about her, oh please tell me ...'

Choked up, unable to speak, Meredith simply inclined her head.

'Where? Where did you know my little Mari? Oh please, please tell me, Mrs Stratton. *Please,*' Kate pleaded.

'In Australia,' Meredith answered at last in a strangled voice.

'*Australia.*' Kate sounded outraged, and she drew back, her eyes wide.

'Sydney.' Meredith's eyes were riveted on Kate, who was shocked and also puzzled.

'She loved you so much,' Meredith said, her voice a whisper.

Kate reached out, grabbed the back of a wing chair. She gripped it tightly to support herself. 'You speak of her as if she's . . . you speak of her in the past tense. She's not . . . *dead,* is she?'

'No, she's not.'

'Oh thank God for that,' Kate exclaimed. 'I've prayed for her every day for years and years. Prayed that she was all right, that she was safe. Please, Mrs Stratton, tell me something. Did she send you to me? Send you to find me?'

'Yes.'

'Where is my Mari? Oh do please tell me.' Kate's emotions were very near the surface, her feelings visible on her strained face. Who was this woman bringing news of Mari? News of her beloved child, lost to her for so many years? She began to tremble.

Meredith took a step forward, drew closer to Kate. Kate's heartache was written on her face, and Meredith realized how distraught she was. And also how sincere.

Groping around in her mind, she sought appropriate words to explain to Kate who she was.

Stepping closer to Kate, she looked into her face, and before she could stop herself she said, 'Mam . . . it's me . . . Mari . . .'

Kate could not speak for a moment, and then she exclaimed, 'Oh my God! Oh my God, Mari, is it really you?' Kate took hold of Meredith's hand and drew her to the window. 'Let me look at you. Is it you, Mari, after all these years?' Reaching out, she touched Meredith's face tenderly, with one hand. 'Is it really you, love?'

Tears were spilling out of Kate's eyes, trickling down her face. 'Oh Mari, Mari, you've come back to me at last. My prayers have been answered.'

Meredith was also crying. And the two women, separated for almost forty years, automatically moved into each other's arms, held onto each other tightly.

Kate was sobbing as if her heart would break. 'I've waited for this day for over thirty-eight years, prayed for it, begged God for it. I'd given up hope of ever seeing you again.'

Mother and daughter stood holding one another for a long time, drawing comfort from each other as they shed their tears of sorrow and joy . . . sorrow for the past, for all those years they had missed together . . . joy that they had been reunited at last, before it was too late.

They sat together on the small sofa in the sitting room, a tray of tea and sandwiches on the coffee table in front of them. But neither of them had touched the sandwiches which the young housekeeper, Nellie, had prepared.

They held hands, kept staring at each other, searching for similarities. And there was a kind of wonderment on their faces. It was the special wonder a mother feels when she sees her newly-born child. And in a way, Mari was newly-born for Kate today.

'I never came to terms with my loss,' Kate said, her voice soft, echoing with sadness as she remembered all those grim years she had endured without her only child by her side. 'I thought of you every day, Mari, wondered about you, yearned for you, longed to hold you in my arms.'

Meredith stared deeply into those marvellous eyes. 'I know, Mam, I know. It was the same for me always, and when I was very little, especially. I was always wondering about you, wondering why you'd sent me away from you, why you didn't want me. I never did understand that.' Meredith brushed the tears away from her eyes. 'How did you . . . lose me? How did we get separated?'

'It was a terrible thing and it really started with Dr Barnardo's home . . . do you remember that day when you were five, when you found me passed out on the kitchen floor?'

'Oh yes, I went to fetch Constable O'Shea.'

'He'd arranged for an ambulance. I was put in Leeds Infirmary and he took you to the children's home. I never blamed him, he didn't know what else to do, since I didn't have any family. Anyway, I was in hospital for about six weeks. As soon as I was on my feet again, I went and got you, and we were together at

Hawthorne Cottage, the way we'd always been. But about a year later, in the spring of 1957, I became ill once more. I took you to Dr Barnardo's myself this time. I'd nowhere else to put you. Dr Robertson was worried about me, he wanted me to go into the Infirmary for some tests. It was there that they discovered I had tuberculosis. Seemingly it had been dormant for several years. Suddenly it had flared up, fanned no doubt by undernourishment, worry, stress, and a run-down condition in general. Tuberculosis is very contagious, it's air-borne, and I couldn't be near you, Mari, for your own sake. The doctors at Leeds Infirmary sent me to Seacroft Hospital, near Killingbeck, where I was treated. I was in quarantine for six months.' Kate paused, took hold of Meredith's hand, held it tightly, and looked into her eyes. 'I sent you messages all the time, Mari. Didn't you get any of them?'

'No.' Meredith returned her mother's intense look. 'Why didn't you come and get me when you were better?' she asked, a hint of resentment flaring. She pushed it down inside her.

'But I did! As soon as I was released from Seacroft Hospital. I was on the mend, no longer contagious, taking antibiotics. But you weren't there any more. The people at Dr Barnardo's told me you had been adopted. I was in shock. Distraught and angry. And heartbroken. I didn't know how to find you. I had no one to help me, no family, not much money. It was like battering my head against a brick wall. They just wouldn't tell me anything and there was no way I could get you back.'

Kate shook her head sorrowfully, found her handkerchief and wiped her streaming eyes. 'I was utterly powerless, helpless, Mari, and so frustrated. I've never really dispelled my anger, it's still there inside. It's gnawed at me for years. What happened ruined my life. I have never recovered from the loss of you, never really been happy, or had any peace of mind. I've always been haunted, worried about you. My only hope was that one day, when you were grown up, you might want to meet your biological mother, and that *you'd* try to find *me*.'

Meredith, who had again been moved to tears by Kate's words, exclaimed, 'But no one adopted me! They lied to you at Dr Barnardo's. They put me on a boat with a lot of other children and shipped us all to Australia. I was in an orphanage in Sydney.'

'An orphanage!' Kate was stunned. She stared at Meredith in horror as the terrible truth dawned on her. 'What kind of thinking is that? It was stupidity to send you from an orphanage in England to another one at the far side of the world. And why?' She closed her eyes for a moment, then snapped them open. 'They said you'd been adopted by a nice family, that you were living in another city in Britain. It was my only consolation . . . that you were growing up with people who cared about you, loved you, and were good to you. Now you're telling me you were never adopted.'

Kate was shaking.

Meredith soothed her, tried to calm her, then explained. 'Well, I was adopted, but in Sydney of course, not in England. When I was eight. But it was only for two years. The Strattons were killed in a car crash when I was ten. They weren't very nice people. His sister put me back in the orphanage.'

Stiffening on the sofa, grasping Meredith's hand tighter, Kate said in a fearful voice, 'The Strattons didn't hurt you in any way, did they? Abuse you?'

'No, they didn't. But they weren't very loving or kind.' Now staring at Kate in bafflement, Meredith went on, 'If you didn't give them permission to send me to Australia, then how could Dr Barnardo's do that? I mean, they did it without your consent.'

'Yes, they did.' Kate drew away slightly. 'All of a sudden, you sound as if you think I'm not telling you the truth. But I am, Mari. You must believe that.'

'It's not that I doubt you. I just don't understand this whole thing.'

'Neither do I. I've never been able to understand it. All these years it's been like living a nightmare.' Kate extricated her hand from Meredith's and stood up.

Slowly, she walked across to the desk, opened a drawer and took out a large envelope. Tapping it, she said, 'A few years ago in the late eighties, I read some articles in the *Observer*. And what I read truly frightened me, filled me with horror, not to mention sorrow. The articles were about child migrants being sent alone to Australia and put in homes and institutions. At the time I prayed that you hadn't been one of those children. I suppose I clung to the belief you were living somewhere in England with your adoptive family. Now my worst nightmare has come true.' Kate's voice faltered and she was close to tears again. 'You *were* one of those children, Mari.'

Fighting her tears, Kate paused, and then after a

moment she asked in a low voice, 'You are telling me the truth, aren't you, Mari? You weren't abused, were you?'

'I promise you I wasn't . . . I *wasn't*, Mam. I was in mental anguish, and I cried myself to sleep for years, missing you so much. It was such a loveless upbringing. And, of course, I had to work hard, we all did, scrubbing floors, doing mountains of washing. And we weren't very well fed. But no, I wasn't physically or sexually abused.'

'Just mentally and emotionally,' Kate said, anger surfacing again. 'Imagine, sending you and other little children 12,000 miles all the way across the world just to put you in another institution. It was wicked.'

Kate walked back to the sofa, sat down, still clutching the envelope. Finally she gave it to Meredith. 'The articles were called *Lost Children of the Empire*. I kept them. You can read them later. They'll make your hair stand on end.' She shook her head. 'No, of course they won't . . . you lived through it . . . lived what the journalist wrote about.'

'Why did you keep the articles?'

'I don't know. Later Granada Television made a documentary about the child migrants. I watched it with growing horror. It left its terrible imprint on me, I've never been free of it.'

'So Dr Barnardo's sent a lot of children to Australia. Hundreds. Is that what you're saying?'

'No, Mari, thousands. Over a hundred and fifty thousand, actually. Probably even more, but it wasn't just Dr Barnardo's. Many other worthy charities were involved in the child migration schemes.'

'Such as?' Meredith asked, staring at Kate questioningly.

'The Salvation Army, the National Children's Home, the Children's Society, the Fairbridge Society, and a variety of other social and welfare agencies operating under the aegis of the Catholic Church, the Church of England, the Presbyterian Church and the Church of Scotland.'

'Good God!' Meredith exclaimed, aghast. 'It was enormous.'

'I'm afraid so,' Kate answered. 'And a lot of those children, especially the boys, were made to work outside in the blistering sun, doing all manner of chores, bricklaying, building dormitories. And they were often horribly abused – sodomized by the priests. It was an horrendous life for them.'

'But *how* could it happen? I mean why didn't the government intervene?'

'The British Government weren't going to do that. They were part of it. What *they* did to us, to mothers and fathers and children, was unconscionable.'

'It was also illegal,' Meredith pointed out. 'Hasn't anyone thought of suing the British Government? I certainly feel like it . . . all those wasted years, all those years of grief.'

'I don't know whether anybody sued or not. There was a huge public outcry after the documentary was aired. It revealed an horrendous scandal. People were outraged. The government tried to deny their complicity, but everyone understood there had been collusion.'

'But why did the government do it?'

Kate said in a voice of scorn, 'What an easy way it was to populate the colonies, sending children to the far-flung corners of the empire. It's been going on for hundreds of years, and small children were still being shipped off as late as 1967.'

'How appalling. It's contemptible.'

Kate nodded and said, 'You'll see a clipping from the *TV Times* in the envelope, announcing the documentary. The magazine listed telephone numbers, help lines. I rang them up, Mari. I was so worried you might be one of those children. I wanted to know how a mother could find a child that had been sent as a migrant. The help-line people told me that wasn't possible, that a mother couldn't find a child. Apparently a parent and child could only be reunited if the child set out to find the long-lost mother or father.'

Kate leaned back against the sofa, closed her eyes for a moment. Then, looking at Meredith at last, she said, 'You grew up to be a beautiful woman, Mari. You look like my mother. You have her face, her eyes.'

Meredith was thrilled to hear this, and a vivid smile flooded her face with radiance. 'I don't remember having a grandmother.'

'She was already dead when you were born. She was killed in a bombing raid in the Second World War. It was my father who brought me up after he got out of the army. He died when I was seventeen.'

'What about my father? Where is he?'

'He's dead too, Mari. He left us when you were about eighteen months old. He went off to Canada with another woman, deserted us. I finally divorced him when Nigel wanted me to marry him.'

'Has he made you happy?'

'He's tried very hard, very hard indeed, Mari. But I haven't been easy to live with over the years. My grief for you has always consumed me to a certain extent ... it's so hard to lose a child, especially the way I lost you. It's not as if you died. I knew you were out there somewhere. I yearned for you ... yearned to see you, to touch you. My heart was broken. Poor Nigel, he's had a lot to contend with. But, he's patient. Long-suffering. He's a good man.'

'And you never had another child?'

'Oh no. I was thirty-eight when I married Nigel. Perhaps I should have, maybe it would have helped me, I don't know ... Nigel was a widower, his wife had been a friend of mine. Veronica. A lovely woman. She died of a brain tumour, and I helped Nigel through that very bad period in his life. Comforted him as best I could. Five years after her death he proposed. I brought up his two sons, Michael and Andrew. And it's been a good marriage in so many ways.'

'I'm glad you've had someone nice like Nigel. I've wondered ... how old were you when I was born?'

'Nineteen. I'll be sixty-three this summer, Mari.' Kate let out a deep sigh. 'All those years without you. How did you find me? Did it take you a long time?'

'No, not really, once I'd started looking. Before I tell you how I *did* locate you, I have another question for you.'

'Anything, Mari, ask me anything.'

'Did you ever take me to Fountains Abbey?'

'Yes, several times. It's a favourite spot of mine, always has been. Coming from Harrogate as I do, I've spent a lot of time in Ripon over the years. But why do you ask?'

'Did anything terrible or upsetting ever happen to me or to us at Fountains?'

'Yes. I started to feel unwell there in the spring of 1957. I'd taken you on a picnic, and I passed out for a while. I know you were very frightened because we were alone. Eventually I came around, and somehow we made it into Ripon and caught the bus back to Harrogate, then another one to Leeds. It was a Sunday. Later that week I was diagnosed as having TB, and I was packed off to Seacroft.'

'I never saw you again, did I?'

'No, you didn't.'

'That explains it.' Meredith recounted her experiences at Fountains, told her about her sense of *déjà vu*. 'No wonder I felt a tragic thing had happened there, had such a sense of loss. Anyway, what that experience did was create something called psychogenic fatigue in me. My physician sent me to a psychiatrist and she and I began to dig into my past. She was convinced I was suffering from repressed memory.'

'You mean you repressed your memories of me?'

'No, not exactly. I did remember certain things. But being torn away from you so cruelly, wrenched away from your love and care as a child was so painful to me I'd blocked everything out. Doctor Benson managed to get me on the right track, but it was my daughter Catherine who triggered the most important memory, at least so *I* think.'

'You have a daughter and you named her for me?' Kate exclaimed, her face lighting up.

'She's twenty-five and beautiful. She has your eyes. And I think your disposition. I didn't actually know I was naming her after you . . . I spelled her name with a C. But obviously I'd remembered your name was Kate . . . Katharine. It was buried in my subconscious.'

'What was the memory she triggered?'

'Just before I left for London last week I went to see her, to discuss plans for her marriage. She made tea, later brought out a dish of strawberries, and she said something to me that brought a memory rushing back. I saw your face very clearly, that face I'd loved all of my life and longed for. And I just knew it was my mother's face I was seeing in my mind.' Meredith had begun to weep; she searched for her handkerchief, blew her nose.

Kate's eyes were moist when she asked, 'What was it Catherine said?'

'Just a few simple words actually . . . "I have a treat for you, Mom. *Strawberries.*" Instantly your face was before my eyes and *you* were serving me strawberries. At that moment a variety of other memories came back to me, and I had many more on the plane coming over to London that same night.'

Meredith paused, blew her nose again, and continued, 'There's something I should explain to you. I'd always believed you were dead. That's what they told me at Dr Barnardo's. So when the memory of you had fully returned, I confided in my English partner, Patsy Canton. She took me to the General Register Office in London to look for your death certificate. You see, I wanted, *needed*, to visit your grave. I wanted closure for myself at long last. But of course there was no certificate; we knew you must be alive. It was Patsy's idea to look for my birth certificate, since we were seeking as much information as we could. My birth certificate led us to Armley and Hawthorne Cottage. Although it's now a pile of rubble, I did discover how well I knew that spot, and more lovely recollections of you surfaced.'

'I'm glad you found me before it was too late,' Kate murmured.

'So am I.'

Now Kate glanced at Meredith curiously and said softly, 'You don't wear a wedding ring. Are you divorced?'

'Yes, I am. You have a grandson, by the way. His name is Jon and he's twenty-one. He's studying at Yale. I can't wait for you to meet him and Catherine.'

'*Grandchildren,*' Kate said wonderingly. 'I have grandchildren. How wonderful.'

'I'm very proud of them. They've turned out well.'

'The one thing you haven't told me is how you got from Australia to America.'

'That's a very long story,' Meredith responded. 'I'll explain everything later. After all, we've got the rest of our lives.'

There was the sound of footsteps in the hall, and Meredith swung her head. She saw a tall, distinguished-looking man standing in the doorway observing them.

Kate had also turned around. She jumped up, exclaiming, 'Nigel, she's found me. Like I always prayed she would. My Mari's found me. She's home to me at last.'

'Thank God,' he said, walking into the sitting room to join them, a look of immense relief spreading across his face.

Meredith rose, stretched out her hand to him.

He took it. And without any kind of preamble he pulled her into his arms and embraced her. 'Now, at last, Kate will have peace of mind,' he said.

As they drew apart Meredith found herself looking into one of the kindest faces she had ever seen.

Nigel Grainger's smile was warm as he gazed at her.

'Thank you,' she said. 'Thank you for keeping my mother safe for me.'

# EPILOGUE

## *Time Future*

# Twenty-five

'Now ladies, look right at me and smile,' Jon said, picking up his camera, peering into the lens. 'Not quite right,' he muttered. 'Mom, move in closer to Grandma. And Cat, you do the same thing. I want to get a really tight shot.'

'Oh do hurry up, Jon, I want to go and find my lovely new husband!' Cat exclaimed.

After a few minor adjustments, Jon finally began to shoot the roll of film. Within minutes he was exclaiming, 'There, all finished, and it wasn't so bad, Cat, was it? Now I have a lovely set of shots for Grandma's album, and for you if you want them. *Three generations of women*. I never dreamed I'd see that day.'

Cat offered him a loving smile. 'I just know I'm going to like yours better than the professional photographer's pictures.'

Grinning, he said, 'Go on, scoot. Find that new husband of yours. In a few minutes there's going to be chaos here, once the Pearson clan start swarming all over like locusts.'

'Hey, watch what you say,' Cat cried, waving her hand at him, displaying her wedding ring. '*I* just became a Pearson, remember.' Walking over, she kissed him on the cheek and said affectionately, 'Thank you for giving me away, Jon.'

'Did I do okay, Sis?'

'You were terrific.' She laughed again and floated off on a cloud of white silk and tulle, heading towards Keith, who stood talking to his father in the entrance hall of the inn.

Jon strolled over to Kate and Meredith. He said, 'It was a great ceremony, Mom, and the old barn was really effective as a church. I guess it was the way you decorated it with all that white silk and the banks of white flowers.'

'Thanks, darling. I was pleased myself with the way it turned out.'

Kate murmured, 'I found the ceremony very moving.' She smiled at her daughter and grandson. 'I must admit, I cried.'

'Most women do cry at weddings, Grandma.' Jon squeezed her arm. 'And you're the icing on the cake. I'm so glad Mom found you.'

'Oh, so am I,' Kate answered.

'Well, I'm off to have a drink with the guys,' Jon announced, edging away.

'Guys?' Meredith repeated, raising a brow. 'Who do you mean?'

'Luc and Nigel. They just came in.'

He strolled off, leaving Meredith and Kate near the entrance to the inn's dining room.

Both women looked elegant; Kate was dressed in a dark rose-pink wool suit and Meredith in a smoky blue dress and coat; standing close together as they were, it was easy to see they were mother and daughter. They bore a strong resemblance to each other, although Meredith was taller.

It was the second Saturday in October, a lovely Indian-summer day. The sky was cerulean blue, clear and cloudless, filled with brilliant sunshine, and the foliage at Silver Lake was spectacular. The trees had just turned, were a riotous mass of reds and pinks, russets and golds.

'We couldn't have asked for a better day,' Kate said, glancing out of the window, looking down towards the lake. 'It's perfect for the wedding.'

'We've been lucky, although Connecticut usually is lovely in October.' Taking hold of Kate's arm, Meredith ushered her into the dining room, recently enlarged to accommodate the many guests attending the wedding today. 'Just come in here for a moment, Mother, I want to say something to you.'

Kate threw Meredith a concerned look. 'Is there something wrong? You sound so serious.'

Meredith shook her head. 'No, I just wanted to thank you for being here with me these past two weeks, and for doing so much to help with Cat's wedding. You've been wonderful.'

'I should be thanking you, Mari,' Kate replied and smiled. 'I'll never be able to call you anything else but Mari, you know.'

'That's all right . . . I understand.'

'I never thought this would happen,' Kate suddenly volunteered. 'That I'd be able to spend this precious time with you. You'll never know what it's meant to me.'

'Oh but I think I *do* . . .'

'You've spoilt me, Mari, and Nigel. The trips to Paris and the Loire, as well as New York. All this wonderful travelling – why we'd hardly been out of Yorkshire until you came back into my life.'

Meredith made no comment, she simply touched her mother's arm affectionately. There were moments when she couldn't quite believe that she had found her mother after all these years.

Kate glanced out of the window again, her face thoughtful when she finally turned back to Meredith. 'I'm glad you found your way here to Silver Lake those many years ago. It's such a beautiful spot, so like Yorkshire. You must have had a guardian angel watching over you.'

'Perhaps I did.'

'Yes, you were lucky to find Amelia and Jack, to have them in your life, if only for those few brief years. They made up for your earlier heartbreak, Mari, that loveless upbringing at the orphanage in Australia. You had love and kindness and caring from them, and I will be forever thankful for that. They helped to make you what you are today.'

'Who knows what I would have been like, if I hadn't met them. A terrible mess, probably.'

'Maybe not, we'll never know. But I think there's something special in *you* . . . a will to endure, to succeed, no matter what.'

Meredith leaned into Kate, kissed her on the cheek. 'I love you, Mother.'

'And I love you too, Mari.'

The two women walked back through the dining room, their arms linked. Just before they reached the door, Kate said, 'It's going to be wrenching, leaving you. I wish I didn't live so far away.'

Meredith was silent.

Kate looked at her swiftly, and added, 'I know you said I can visit any time. But I can't very well keep leaving Nigel alone. And he can't always come with me, Mari, because of his practice.'

Meredith said, 'As it turns out, I'm not going to be so far away after all.'

'*Oh.*'

Meredith peered across the entrance hall of the inn, now crowded with people. The reception was in full swing. A small smile flitted across her mouth.

Kate noticed this, followed the direction of her daughter's gaze, then looked back to Meredith.

'I'm going to marry him, Mother,' Meredith said, her gaze still resting on Luc. 'And so I'll be living in Paris. Only a couple of hours from Yorkshire.'

'Oh darling, I'm so happy for you. Congratulations!' Kate exclaimed. There was a brief pause before she said worriedly, 'But what about your business here? It means so much to you.'

'There's only Silver Lake Inn left, now that I've sold the one in Vermont. Blanche and Pete have been running this place for years, and doing such a good job of it. They'll continue. I've enough to keep me busy with the inns in England and France.'

'It's good that you've been able to work it out. Luc's such a wonderful man.'

'He's had his share of heartbreak, too. I think we both deserve a bit of happiness . . .' Meredith broke off as Luc walked over to join them.

Putting his arm around Kate, he looked down at her and said, 'Ever since we met in June I had a feeling I knew you, Kate. Suddenly, a moment ago, I realized why. You remind me of the woman who brought me up, my grandmother.'

Grandma Rose, of course, Meredith thought, recalling the painting at Talcy. They had the same colouring, the same blue eyes, the same heart-shaped face.

'How lovely,' Kate murmured. 'I understand congratulations are in order. I'm so happy the two of you are getting married.'

Luc beamed at her. 'Ah, so Meredith told you the good news.'

Kate nodded, excused herself, wanting to leave them alone. She walked across the room lightly, as if floating on air, went in search of her husband. She was so happy, so proud. Who would have thought that her little Mari would turn out to be such a remarkable woman?

Luc took hold of Meredith's hand, stared deeply into her smoky green eyes. 'You know, *chérie*, you look so very serene today. It lifts my heart to see you so happy. From the moment I met you, I wanted to erase the sadness from your eyes, dispel the pain I knew lurked deep within you. But now I don't have to . . . I believe finding your mother has done that.'

Meredith did not answer for a moment or two. She simply returned his penetrating gaze; then finally she said, 'It was finding *both* of you, Luc. You and she make me feel complete, whole.'

Luc smiled at her. 'That's because we love you.'

He tucked her arm through his, and together they moved forward into the throng of wedding guests.